Short of a soldier fighting and dying for a cause in which he truly believes, very few have ever given so much for so many and so unselfishly.

THE GREATEST
PATRIOT

Dan Sullivan

The Greatest Patriot © 2010 by Dan Sullivan.

Published in the United States by:

OLD STONE
PUBLISHING

Old Stone Publishing
4918 W. Navaho Court
Boise, ID 83714
info@oldstoneppublishing.com
First Edition
ISBN 9781451557343

Printed in the United States of America

ACKNOWLEDGEMENTS

I'd like to thank those who helped make *The Greatest Patriot* a better story, either by their direct contributions or by listening to my ramblings during the writing process. My brother Dale was instrumental in helping me cook this one up during long bike rides and over multiple post-ride pitchers of beer. My dear friend, Shannon Borchert, provided incredible enthusiasm for the project and kept me motivated. Authors Larry Wood and Brian Doke read some of the earliest drafts and provided their insights. Friends Dave Monahan, Misty Young, and Laura King added far more than their two cents, and my editor Jean Terra really made '*Patriot*' shine.

Finally, I need to thank the late Ted Sorensen, JFK's Special Counsel, speech writer, advisor and friend from 1952 to1963. Ted's personal correspondences with me provided an insider's view of the man and the era. Ted described his Kennedy years to me as "an extraordinary time period with an incredible cast of characters." In my last email from Ted, received on October 18, 2010, he congratulated me on finishing the initial draft of *The Greatest Patriot* and he said he looked forward to reading it. I sent him a copy a few days before he suffered a massive stroke. He died on October 31, 2010. I never had the privilege of meeting Ted, and for that I will always carry a great feeling of profound regret.

GREECE
Present Day

At this time of year the wind always blows from the south, up from Africa. It starts in Libya, in the Great Sand Sea, near Al Jawf, where the sun unmercifully bakes the desert floor. As the heat rises from the sand as from a furnace, the expanding air creates its own high pressure system. The winds swirl and rise, then blow north across the Cyrenaica Plains and out to the Al Akhdar Peninsula. Fueled by the heat from the rock-strewn hills they cross the Mediterranean Sea picking up speed and intensity. They focus their hot breath on the first landfall they reach, the Ionian Islands in Greece.

The brothers knew the day's catch probably wouldn't even pay for the gasoline for their little fishing boat, but they had to try. Their families needed the food and if the two had a good day at sea they certainly could use the money they would make from selling the extra catch.

Geordi, the older of the two brothers, had five growing boys at home; Kissos, younger by three years, had one boy, two girls, and his wife was pregnant with their fourth child. The brothers also supported their parents and Geordi was 'fortunate' enough to be able to provide for his wife's parents as well. This day, the two of them were fishing for sixteen people and with a little help from the Gods, they'd be able to put dinner on the evening's table.

When it was this hot, the fish swam too deep to be captured in the fishermen's shallow water net. The fish the brothers did catch at this time of year were either old or sick. Geordi's mother-in-law complained that they tasted stale.

Kissos turned off the motor as they approached a favorite spot off the point of one of their neighboring islands. Geordi cursed from the bow as the beat-up little boat slowed down in the still water. Without the motion of the boat, the hot winds made him feel as though he was standing next to a fire. For most of the year the wind had a cooling effect but during the summers, it only made the heat from sun feel more intense. To make matters worse, the temperature of the sea also rose during the summer so even swimming in the ocean wasn't refreshing.

Geordi looked up as a gray and white helicopter rose from the island, the island owned now by the billionaire's granddaughter, Athina. As he watched the Sikorski S-76 chopper banked around to the north. Geordi wondered which rich and famous passengers might be aboard.

The helicopter flew towards them as the brothers returned to the task at hand, untangling the knots in order to get their net into the water.

"Kissos!" exclaimed Geordi as the helicopter flew past their bow.

Kissos looked up to see the chopper losing altitude while turning back towards the island. The Sikorski bucked and swayed from side to side as the pilot desperately tried to control the craft before it crashed with a huge splash into the water two hundred meters off the bow of their little boat. Pieces of the rotor blades flew in all directions. The scream of twisting aluminum and the hiss of water on hot metal sounded eerily loud.

Kissos pulled the starter rope on the little motor four times before the engine caught and belched a cloud of blue smoke. He pushed the throttle to its stops as the helicopter rolled onto its side and began to sink. Within a few seconds, the brothers were at the side of the aircraft. Geordi dove over the bow with a mooring line in his hand while Kissos pulled the choke lever, killing the motor, before diving over the side as well.

Just as Geordi reached the chopper, the front door opened, then fell shut again. He climbed up and grabbed it as it was pushed open from the inside. He held the door as the pilot climbed out and slid into the water.

"Get that damn door open," yelled the pilot, pointing to the rear door. Kissos forced open the door to the passenger compartment and found it almost full of water with just the top of a man's head showing. He plunged his hands into the water, grabbed the man under the arms, and pulled as hard as he could. His back and arms straining, Kissos lifted the passenger out of the compartment just as the helicopter slid under the surface. He held the man's face out of the water and was relieved to hear him start coughing.

"The boat, Kissos, to the boat," yelled Geordi. The two fishermen had been swimming their whole lives in these waters and holding the frail old man in his arms didn't slow Kissos down. Within a few seconds, he planted his hand on the side of his boat.

Kissos waited while Geordi clambered over the opposite side of the boat and pulled the pilot aboard. He heard a loud 'thump' and a groan as the man fell to the floor. Then Geordi reached over the side of the boat and grabbed the shirt of the man Kissos was holding.

"Easy, Geordi," Kissos cautioned, "This man is hurt." Kissos heard another loud 'thump' as the old man's body was dropped onto the bottom of the boat. Kissos swam to the back of the boat and used the motor as a handhold to climb over the transom.

The two men from the helicopter lay on the floor of the boat coughing. The pilot was obviously in great pain; his right leg below the knee was twisted in an awkward position, obviously broken. Kissos stepped forward to see if he could help the men as Geordi moved past him and started the motor. Kissos was worried about the pilot's leg but he knew he could do nothing about it for the moment. The old passenger continued coughing up water but he had managed to raise his head up off the dirty floor of the boat.

"Nydri?" Geordi asked his brother. Nydri, on Lefkada Island, was farther away than their little island but it had better medical facilities than the little clinic on Meganisi.

The pilot raised his head, "No, no, no, Skorpios!" He pointed and yelled, "Take us to Skorpios, now!"

Kissos moved the pilot into what he hoped was a slightly more comfortable position as the boat picked up speed, leaping across the swells. "Slowly, Geordi," Kissos begged. He moved to the older man and carefully held his head to keep it from bouncing on the bottom of the boat. "Geordi, please, go slow!"

The old man looked up at the Greek fisherman and tried to speak but only coughed out water mixed with blood, his skin had turned an ashen gray color, he now had a look of death. "Go faster, Geordi," Kissos said.

As they rounded the west end of the island of Skorpios the old man grew paler. He muttered only a few unintelligible sounds but his eyes held warmth and appreciation. As Kissos moved his head into a more comfortable position, the old man slipped a large gold ring off his finger and pushed it into Kissos' pocket. His index finger slid over his mouth silently asking Kissos to keep the secret. A thin smile came to his lips and then it faded away.

Two security guards dressed in fatigues waited anxiously on the concrete jetty as the little fishing boat approached the island. As Geordi eased the bow close to the jetty, the larger man jumped down and kneeled at the old man's side. He tried to talk to the old man but then shook his head and gently lifted the man up to his partner. The guard on the jetty carried the old man to a waiting golf cart while his comrade in the boat lifted the pilot onto the jetty, ignoring his screams of pain.

Kissos watched the old man with growing concern, he didn't look good. His eyes were closed and his arms hung limp.

The large guard climbed out of the boat and turned back to the two fishermen to say, "Thank you for your help. You should go now. And it would be best if you did not speak of this."

BOCA RATON, FLORIDA
Present Day

Tomorrow was going to be another hot, humid, and miserable day according to the so-called meteorologist on the six o'clock news. All summer long, Hal Rumsey cursed his decision to move to Boca while all winter long, he congratulated himself for being a genius at making the move.

Hal got up slowly and painfully from his easy chair and shuffled into the kitchen for another glass of scotch as the local newscasters finished up their daily diatribe of who had shot whom, which politician had screwed the most people this week, and what former allies were now rattling their sabers at the U.S.

"The news hasn't changed in fifty years," Hal thought to himself as he dropped fresh ice cubes into his glass. The only things that had changed over the years were the names and the places.

"And finally tonight," said the anchorman, "an Ocala man recovering from a helicopter crash in a hospital in Greece is claiming that John F. Kennedy, the 35th President of the United States, died in that crash, just a few days ago. The man claims that Kennedy and others faked his 1963 assassination and that the 93-year-old President has lived on the private island belonging to Aristotle Onassis for the last forty-seven years."

The four talking heads on the television continued to fill time by bantering with each other about the pilot's mental well-being and speculating on the possibility of Elvis and Marilyn Monroe being aboard the helicopter also.

Hal set his glass down, steadied himself with both hands on the counter and dropped his head, his eyes closed tight for a few moments. Then he walked over to the phone and dialed a Virginia phone number he knew by heart. The phone rang once and was answered by two short computerized beeps. Hal entered a six digit number and waited fifteen seconds for a familiar voice to answer.

"Operations, good evening, Hal," said the voice. The Op's officer on the other end of the line sounded tired and defeated.

"Is it true?" Hal asked.

"Yeah, the chopper went down off Skorpios yesterday and the boss didn't make it. I'm sorry Hal."

"You know the pilot's talking?" asked Hal.

"Yeah, I heard," said the voice quietly. "Maybe it's time, Hal, maybe it's time."

WASHINGTON, D.C.
Present Day

The sun was just rising over Andrews Air Force Base as the Lear 45 taxied to a stop in front of a hanger on the field's southwest corner. Robert McQuade, Deputy Director of Special Projects, stepped down the air stairs feeling as if he had been run over by a truck. He had flown across six time zones for a quick meeting only to turn around and fly back to Washington arriving at 5:45 a.m. He was unshaven, tired, and his ulcer was killing him from the stress of the trip and the subject of the meeting. His cell phone rang just as he reached the bottom of the stairs; the ring tone indicated a secure call. McQuade hit the receive button and was greeted with two computerized beeps prompting him to punch in a code that connected him to the caller.

"D. D. McQuade," he said rapidly, looking around to see if he was far enough away from the ground crew to speak.

"Deputy McQuade, this is Brenda Critell at Ops. We were told to notify you immediately if the Ionian situation changed. The pilot died a few hours ago at the hospital in Patra," said the voice.

Robert McQuade dropped his head, "Cause of death?" he asked.

"Unknown at this time, sir. We'll continue to monitor the situation and contact you the moment there is any further information," said the Operations Specialist in a carefully controlled voice.

McQuade held his stomach as he walked to the Lincoln Town Car that waited to take him back to his office. Once in the back seat, he closed the divider between himself and the driver and called another secure number from his cell phone.

The phone made a series of beeps and clicks before buzzing to indicate the line was secure. "Telleria" said the man on the other end.

Jose Telleria, Robert McQuade thought to himself, what a unique individual. He pictured the short, stout Basque agent in his mind. Telleria was one of the Service's "utility men", a guy who got it done, whatever "it" was and whenever it needed to be done. He shuddered to think how ugly things could get if that man ever talked.

"McQuade here," he said in his official tone. "Ops just called and passed on the news that the pilot died."

Telleria sounded as if he was smiling when he replied, "Yeah, I heard that also. Too damn bad, isn't it."

McQuade wasn't in the least amused, "What did the pilot die from?" he asked in an irritated voice.

"I don't know, I guess they missed something in his initial diagnosis. He must have been more seriously injured than the Greeks originally thought."

McQuade was not in the mood for games; he was tired and didn't feel well. "What-did-he-die-from?" he asked again, carefully enunciating each word.

Telleria got the message. "He died from a stroke. Apparently, he had an undiagnosed concussion that must have thrown a blood clot causing a massive stroke. With his head injury, who knows what he might have been rambling on about over the last few days?"

"What about the fishermen?" McQuade asked next.

"I'm pretty sure we are clear there. I don't see any need to engage. They don't suspect anything unusual," said Telleria.

In a much more relieved tone the Deputy Director said, "Thanks, Jose. I appreciate it," and then hung up without another word. He reached into his briefcase and fished around for an aspirin bottle and a roll of Tums before closing his eyes as the Town Car turned onto the Capital Beltway. His stomach was churning.

WASHINGTON, D.C.
December 1962

The meeting had been scheduled to be thirty minutes in length. According to the clock on the wall behind the Secretary of the Interior, Stewart Udall, there were still twenty minutes left. The President would be expected to ask some intelligent questions about the state of the Alaskan ecology when Udall had finished his report. Kennedy tried to force himself to listen but his mind drifted from the problems of the decreasing seal population on the eastern ice floe to a much larger issue at hand.

The press was starting to pick up on the term "Cuban Missile Crisis" even though the issue had not been on his official agenda for about two months. Somebody in the White House or the Pentagon had leaked to the *Washington Post* truly how close the United States had really come to a nuclear showdown with the Soviets. The press worked to build a controversial story but they were less than accurate on the severity of the crisis or how close the U.S. had come to launching a multi-theater nuclear attack against the Russians. In perhaps the longest two weeks in history, the discovery of Russian missile bases being constructed in Cuba had developed from a surprising irritation to what many feared would be an imminent war.

Kennedy believed that ultimately just ten simple words may have saved the world from nuclear holocaust. In a final last ditch effort to avoid war, Kennedy had sent a telegram to Khrushchev that would never be fully documented and never publicly disclosed. It read: "I consider my letter to you of October twenty-seventh and your reply of today as firm undertakings on the part of both our governments which should be promptly carried out. We will remove all missiles from Turkey with your removal of missiles and military forces from Cuba. Failure to immediately agree with these terms will result in hostilities. Nikita, let us both stand down." Kennedy ended with ten words, "Let us do this for the children of our countries. Kennedy."

The non-coded reply came across the teletype within a half-hour, a messages reading simply: "Health and prayers to your children. Khrushchev."

Moments later, on October 28 at 9:00 a.m., a new statement from Khrushchev was broadcast on Radio Moscow. "The Soviet government, in addition to previously issued instructions on the cessation of further work at the building sites for the weapons, has issued a new order on the dismantling of the weapons which you describe as 'offensive' and their crating and return to the Soviet Union."

World War III had been averted by pulling on the heart strings of one of the world's toughest leaders.

The immediate acceptance of his simple gesture disturbed Kennedy more than it should have and added to his sleepless nights during the month of November. Something was amiss, he felt something was wrong but he couldn't put his finger on it. Either the Russians were up to something or Khrushchev was simply a man who was growing more unpredictable by the moment.

A long rambling letter to Kennedy, written in Khrushchev's own hand, arrived in late November. The letter lauded about the great friendship between the two men and referred to the new friendships about to be formed between the peoples of the Soviet Union and of the United States. Then, two paragraphs later, the letter discussed the need for the United States to provide grain exports to the U.S.S.R. or risk hostilities.

Kennedy asked psychiatrists employed by the FBI to evaluate the letter and give him their analysis of Khrushchev's state of mind. Just that morning they had submitted a report saying that it was quite possible Khrushchev was suffering from "Manic Depressive Disorder", a condition accompanied by profound mood swings and further complicated by stress. It was not a desirable mental state for the man who controlled the largest military force in the world.

Kennedy had read and re-read the report before he lifted the phone and dialed a two-digit number. "McNamara."

"Good afternoon, Bob," said the President. "I'm just stepping into a meeting with Stewart but can you come over in thirty or forty minutes? I want to talk through the report the shrinks did on Nikita's letter. And can you check with Bobby's office to see if he's available?" It was phrased as a question but it really wasn't a request at all.

"Sure, Jack, I'll be over shortly," said the Secretary of Defense. He hung up and called his wife to tell her he wouldn't be home for dinner, again.

BOCA RATON, FLORIDA
Present Day

Harold Edward Rumsey had lost close friends before and he had lost his parents at a fairly young and impressionable age. While each of those deaths was painful and hard, none of them had hit him so squarely in the gut. Jack had been his closest friend, his confidant, and his boss for forty-three years, although they had never had an employee/employer relationship, even from the first day. They had spent long days and nights in deep conversation regarding everything from politics and history to religion to philosophy, to family and friendships. Together they had talked through problems and found solutions to issues that most men would never have to face.

Hal hadn't seen Jack in several years and hadn't even talked with him for six or eight weeks yet he was profoundly hurt at the news of his death. Maybe it was the feeling that if he had been there, he could have somehow saved Jack's life, maybe he could have willed the helicopter to stay in the air or thrown his body between his friend and the ocean. He knew he probably wouldn't have been able to do anything and yet his feeling of helplessness was overwhelming.

What was really hitting Hal hard was that his hero had died. Jack Kennedy, a man he had respected more than any living person, had done more for his country than perhaps any man since Thomas Jefferson. In the forty-seven years since he had held public office, Jack Kennedy had done more to change the face of world politics than any man before him and he had accomplished it all while hiding out on a small Greek island in the Ionian Sea. Few would ever know the true story of this man or of the real history behind many of the events that had changed the world since 1963. That greatly bothered Hal.

Maybe it was time, he thought to himself, remembering the words of the Ops Director. Maybe it was time.

WASHINGTON, D.C.
December 1962

"Are there any questions I might answer?" asked Secretary Udall followed by a pause.

Shit, thought Kennedy, he knew he should have paid attention. "No, Stewart," he said with a well practiced introspective furrow of his brow. "You have given a very clear and comprehensive report. Do you have anything to add?" He thought he saw a glimpse of disappointment in the Secretary's eye.

"No, sir. If you have any follow-up questions, please feel free to call me."

Kennedy thanked him and walked him to the door, trying to come up with anything worthwhile to ask but he was drawing a blank. The two men shook hands and Stewart Udall left the office.

"Sir, the west gate called. The Secretary of Defense has just arrived," said the President's personal secretary, Evelyn Lincoln, while he was still standing at the office door. "The Attorney General will be here in about five minutes, traffic," she explained with a grimace.

Kennedy was going over the psychiatric report again when Evelyn buzzed to say the Secretary of Defense had arrived. The President asked her to show the Secretary in but because Evelyn had been with Kennedy for more than ten years, she knew to wait a few seconds before saying to the visitor, "The President will see you now".

Jack Kennedy liked to meet his appointments at the door of his office with a hearty handshake. He despised people of power who sat behind their desks when someone came to see them. He felt it showed a conceited distain for the visitor.

Jack and Bob McNamara enjoyed a long history together; they had known each other for years and had enormous respect for each other. Kennedy shook McNamara's hand and explained that Bobby had just called to say he was going to be a few minutes late. While they saw each other almost daily, the delay gave them a few rare minutes to chat about their families and catch up on what was happening with mutual acquaintances.

Five minutes later, the Attorney General, as he often did, blasted his way into the President's personal office. Jack could always tell when there was something important on Bobby's mind because he was already talking when as came through the door. It was as if he had started the meeting thirty seconds before he walked into the room.

"He's over the edge, completely irrational and, quite frankly, I'm scared to death of the man," said Bobby Kennedy as he walked into the office. The President could see the staffers in the anteroom looking after Bobby with concern.

"Bobby, would you wait until the door is closed before you start talking about things that scare you to death. You're scaring the staff to death," Jack cautioned his brother.

Ignoring the admonition, the Attorney General said, "How are we supposed to react to a man who changes his mood every few minutes? How do we keep peace with the Russians if their leader is determined to destroy you?"

Jack looked up with surprise, "Destroy me?"

"Between the FBI's psychiatric analysis and Mac's backline contacts I think it's fair to assume that Nikita is hell-bent on revenge for the Cuba situation," said the Attorney General. "I hate to say I told you so, but I still believe we should have used an initiative in October that would have allowed Khrushchev to save face with the Politburo. Now his back is up against the wall and he's placing the blame squarely on the American President."

"Wait a minute," said Jack while adjusting in his chair, "what back channel, Bob? Who are you working with?"

McNamara shot a glance towards Bobby who had began to pace back and forth in front of the President's desk, before saying, "I started receiving some messages through a number of different channels a few weeks ago. At first it was sketchy, nothing really worthwhile, but now I'm starting to think that we may be speaking with somebody of consequence."

"You have no idea who it is?" asked Jack.

"No, sir, none whatsoever, but we are receiving communiqué that seem to reflect concern regarding Khrushchev's irrational resentment of you over his loss of confidence within the Central Committee regarding Cuba."

The President looked suspicious, "What assurance do we have that the sender is authentic and not someone trying to leading us down a rabbit hole?"

"We have none, sir," said McNamara. "We are currently managing the contact as we would any new source. There has been some information passed that would seem to authenticate the contact as somebody close to Khrushchev but at this point our information is quite limited."

"So that being the case," Jack could tell that Bobby was about to explode if he didn't ask the question, "what do you have besides the FBI analysis and some unconfirmed back-channel messages to create such concern?"

Bobby continued to pace in front of Jack's desk. He was composing himself and collecting his thoughts so that when he spoke, every word would come across as well-thought-out and powerful, a technique he had learned in law school that was effective if not a little out of character. "What Mac won't say, because it's not his job to speculate in cases such as these, is that we think with a fairly high degree of confidence that the back-channel messages are coming from somebody very high in the Politburo, possibly from Leonid Brezhnev."

"What content in the messages specifically led you to think that Khrushchev might be unstable?" asked the President.

McNamara reached into his briefcase and pulled out a piece of paper then scanned down it until he found the sentence he wanted. He said, "We are specifically concerned by a message received a few weeks ago that said, 'Of great concern to both your side and ours is Castle's state of mind.' A follow-up message received the next week spoke about Castle's increasing hostility towards Pig. There are several other references I can share."

It was widely known that "Castle" was the KGB code name for Khrushchev, and after the failed invasion of Cuba at the Bay of Pigs, the KGB had started using the code name "Pig" for Kennedy.

"How do we find out, Bob, who it is you are talking to?" asked Jack.

McNamara readjusted himself in the chair and thought about the question for a few seconds. "I think the best way to find out is simply to ask."

BOCA RATON, FLORIDA
Present Day

The clock beside his bed read 4:33 a.m. The pain seemed to start low in Hal's back and radiate all the way through his body. He lay there in a pool of his own sweat, suffering through yet another sleepless night. Within his reach were his untouched prescription pain pills which would quickly dull the pain and trick his brain into a numbing unconsciousness but he ignored them.

Tonight, his mind was clear. Hal refused to acknowledge the pain of the cancer, he was too busy reliving the last 49 years of his life. Hal had been 27 years of age the day that JFK was "assassinated" in Dallas. He was in Washington, D.C. that day, working for the Secret Service, which had recruited him out of the College of William and Mary.

Everyone remembers exactly where he was and what he was doing when he heard the news. Hal was taking a shit when somebody walked into the men's room and said to someone else, "Did you hear Kennedy's been shot?" And he was standing in front of a television in the Ops Center when Walter Cronkite announced to the world that John F. Kennedy had died. Even though he worked for the very organization whose primary purpose was to protect the President's life, Hal heard about Kennedy's death in the same way and at the same time as ordinary citizens throughout the U.S. and all over the world.

Hal had seen President Kennedy up close only once during his four years with the Service. His first assignment had been in New York working on a counterfeit currency investigation team. He had come to Washington just two months earlier to work on the Vice President's detail, but found himself doing junior agent grunt work rather than actually protecting Vice President Johnson.

Chaos and complete disorganization was the only way to describe the state of the Secret Service in the days following Kennedy's death. Hal remembered thinking that anybody could have walked up and shot Johnson during his first few days as President because the entire Service was walking around like zombies in a disbelieving daze. The Vice President's team was immediately designated as the Presidential team and JFK's team was ordered to stand down for thirty days of debriefing and reassessment.

Hal recalled that he was working up the security assessment for a previously planned Vice Presidential visit to Los Angeles, a trip that now wasn't going to happen, when Section Director Chuck Thornton stuck his head into the office and barked, "Mister Rumsey, will you please follow me."

Hal followed Thornton out of the office and down a long corridor. He tried his best to think of anything he had done that might result in his being subject to disciplinary action but couldn't come up with a thing. Thornton opened the door to his office and motioned Hal inside, silently directing him to take a seat. After closing the door, Thornton moved around and sat at his desk, straightened some papers, and carefully set his pen down on his desk pad, seeming to collect his thoughts. "I don't know you very well, Mister Rumsey," he said in a fatherly tone, "I think it's time we get to know each other better. Tell me about yourself."

Hal sat in amazement; he had been concerned that he was going to be reprimanded for something and now it seemed the guy just wanted to get chummy. Hal stumbled a bit before commencing to tell Thornton about being raised in a small town in Illinois. He moved on quickly to his days at William and Mary, and then gave a quick synopsis of his four years with the Service.

"Your parents are both deceased according to your file," Thornton stated.

"Yes, sir, my father died several years ago of heart disease, my mother died a few years after," Hal answered in an unemotional tone.

"And you have no siblings?"

"No, sir, I was an only child."

Thornton paused and then lowered his voice a bit. "I don't mean to get too personal, but are you dating anybody seriously? "

Hal laughed, "No, sir, with my schedule and the time I put in here I couldn't find a date if I had to."

Thornton chuckled, "Boy, I understand that. I worked my tail off here as a new agent. If it hadn't been for my cousin Elena setting me up with her best friend, I would never have met my Marilee."

Chuck Thornton then leaned forward with his elbows on the desk and he asked seriously, "How would you like to do something really important for your country?"

"Sir, I'd do anything for my country as long as it wasn't immoral or illegal. I think the Service knows that."

"Yes, son, I think you've made that clear. The assignment I'm referring to is extremely confidential. You would be unable to talk about it, and I mean not now, not ever," said the Director.

Hal was immediately excited, but what 27-year-old wouldn't be? His government, just days following the assassination of the President, was asking him to be part of a very important top-secret mission. The request had a super-spy feel to it. Without a moment's hesitation, Hal told the Director how enthusiastic he was to take on this incredibly important mission. Then he started gushing about how patriotic he was and going on about his devotion to his country.

The Director cut him off saying, "I'm glad you are interested. Keep this conversation strictly between us, I'll get back with you shortly." Then he motioned Hal to the door.

In the hallway, Hal felt fairly certain he had just blown his big chance by being overly enthusiastic. Damn, he thought to himself, can't you learn when to keep your mouth shut?

WASHINGTON, D.C.
January 1962

The back-channel messages continued to arrive at fairly regular intervals. Some arrived by telegram, others came brazenly in the weekly diplomatic bag from the Soviet Embassy, some were routed through the U.S. Embassy and Ambassador Galbraith, and still others came through a spy ring handled by the CIA.

McNamara's inquiry to the author of the messages regarding his identity was met with the reply, "In time, my friend." The decision was made that for the time being only the Kennedy brothers, Bob McNamara and, over Bobby's objection, Special Counsel Ted Sorensen would be privy to the existence of a back-channel and the content of the messages. As the weeks dragged on into the New Year, the messages became more direct and also contained small but important pieces of intelligence concerning Afghanistan, Iraq, and China.

McNamara believed that the intel was being shared to help foster trust in the contact. The information was sent up to the CIA where nearly all of it was quickly authenticated. The CIA began snooping around McNamara's office and questioning his staff but they found only brick walls in their probing. The return messages were carefully constructed to give the Russians an equivalent amount of intel regarding movements of militaries and dispositions of governments around the world.

Information acquired by the CIA regarding the Chinese Navy using their Soviet made Golf-I submarines to sneak incredibly close to and photograph the submarine base on the Kamchatka peninsula was passed on to the back-channel contact. A week later the CIA reported that a Chinese submarine had been lost and possibly sunk by the Russian Navy in the Sea of Okhotska near Kamchatka.

While the back-channel messages gave hope to Kennedy, they also continued to report a heightened concern regarding Castle's increasing anger towards Pig. Reports coming from other channels including a CIA-sponsored spy ring in Moscow indicated that Khrushchev was rapidly losing power within his own administration and was beginning to be seen by his peers as unstable. On January 16th Khrushchev made the public statement that the Soviets had developed and possessed a 100-megaton nuclear bomb, a clear fabrication but also a fairly ominous indication of the state of mind of the disturbed leader.

Even Khrushchev's staunchest supporters began talking to the press about his poor handling of the Cuban situation and how the Motherland had been weakened by the resulting loss of face. By February of 1963 there appeared to be a growing consensus among the intelligence communities on both sides that Khrushchev was blaming Kennedy for all of his problems at home.

The Russians didn't seem to be content to let things settle; twice on March 13th, the U.S. scrambled fighters to intercept Soviet spy planes that were spotted over Alaska. Kennedy sent a wire to the Kremlin stating in no uncertain terms would further incursions into U.S. airspace would not be tolerated. He ordered the military to shoot down the next Russian aircraft that crossed into any American airspace.

After a two-week gap in communication, a back-channel message was delivered to McNamara on March 27th stating, "Advise caution. Believe Castle will stop at nothing to exact revenge for current state of affairs. Do not allow minor confrontations to escalate from your side. Working to find solution here; may need to enhance communication on this issue. Roman."

For the first time ever, McNamara uncharacteristically burst into Kennedy's office and called the President by his nickname, "Jack! We just received a back-channel signed 'Roman'!"

Kennedy looked up surprised from his desk, "God almighty, could it really be Brezhnev himself?" Kennedy read the message from beginning to end twice before looking up, "By 'enhancing communication' does that mean he is ready to talk?"

"I think so," said McNamara. "With your permission I'm going to invite him to meet with me."

"As long as the usual security elements are in place, I think it is time to go face to face with this person," said Kennedy.

The concern regarding Khrushchev's stability apparently had become so elevated that somebody or some group high in the Russian government had taken the unusual and unprecedented risk of communicating that concern to McNamara using the normal diplomatic mail.

McNamara carefully composed his response to Roman. "Understand risk, will make appropriate adjustments to rules of engagement in all theaters immediately. Propose we meet, top secret, neutral site, perhaps Sarajevo mid-April." The previous rules of engagement, including the order to shoot down any Russian aircraft encroaching on U.S. airspace were repealed.

A week went by without a reply which only increased the tension among the Washington insiders. The next diplomatic bag would not arrive in Washington until April 11th.

Then on April 10, 1963 the stakes were raised dramatically when the *USS Thresher* (SSN 593), a nuclear submarine, sank 220 miles off Cape Cod killing all 129 aboard her. Publicly it was announced that she was undergoing deep sea trials and had imploded after the failure of a weld in the saltwater piping system.

The real story was far more disturbing.

BOCA RATON, FLORIDA
Present Day

Hal's body suffered from the great pain brought on by his disease but his mind chose to ignore the discomfort; he was in another time and another place.

There are days in everybody's lives that evoke great change but seldom are the changes as dramatic as those cast into motion on December 2, 1963.

Shortly after Hal had arrived at work, Thornton again called him into his office and offered him a temporary assignment. Unknown to either of them, this "temporary assignment" would last forty-three years. Thornton emphasized once again that the assignment was top secret. Hal could not talk about it now or ever. If he accepted the assignment, he would be leaving Washington that day for an undisclosed location and for an undetermined period of time. Hal accepted.

The story allowed to circulate within the Service and amongst his peers was that he was fired for an undisclosed malfeasance. He was quickly whisked away by two men in dark suits who told him, when he asked, that their names weren't important. Based on their attitudes, Hal couldn't care less if he ever knew their names. They first took him by car to his apartment where, with their help, he packed the contents into ten boxes and two suitcases. The suitcases were to go with him, the boxes were to be put into storage. He was then taken to a downtown office building where he signed several legal documents including his will. He was told that he would be leaving the country and all of his legal and financial matters needed to be put in order. Arrangements were made to pay off his few outstanding bills and to close out his utility accounts.

Hal and his two nameless "suits" munched on sandwiches as they drove to National Airport where they boarded a C-56 Lodestar, a twin-engine propeller-driven aircraft fitted for corporate use. Hal fell asleep during the second half of the two-hour flight and awoke just before they landed at a remote airstrip somewhere in the mountains. He guessed they were in the Poconos but he wasn't sure. The aircraft taxied to the end of the grass strip where a single man was waiting. Hal stepped off the aircraft into a cold December wind that blew down the valley.

"Harold, I'm Walt McCullough," yelled the man who had been waiting at the end of the strip. He appeared to be in his early sixties, with a friendly face and a warm handshake. Dressed in a tweed hunting jacket and a felt hat, he seemed to blend into the mountain scenery as though he belonged there as much as the trees.

"I understand you've had quite a day," he said. "Let's get on up to the house and get you a good stiff drink and then something to eat. After that, we'll tell you more about your new job."

Hal turned around to see his two companions re-boarding the plane as the pilot started the engines.

Walt helped Hal load the two suitcases into the back of an aging Chevy pickup and motioned him to the passenger's side. As they bounced up a rutted dirt road, Hal had a chance to look around. They had landed in a beautiful small valley; the airstrip was cut across a natural meadow that was also being used as a pasture for several grazing horses and a dozen or so cattle. At the edge of the meadow were several out-buildings and a large barn. On the hillside above the meadow tucked back in the trees was a magnificent lodge constructed of hand-hew logs. Lights glowed from most of the windows. The "house" as Walt called it appeared to be a hunting lodge complete with rocking chairs on the large front porch and an old coon dog sleeping near the front steps. The sun had just dropped below the mountains and the light was beginning to dim as Walt pulled up to the back of the lodge.

"Just leave your suitcases where they are," he told Hal. "I'll move them up to your room in a bit."

They walked through the back door of the lodge into the kitchen. Hal was struck by the warmth of the room and the medley of wonderful smells emanating from the oven and stove. Walt took Hal by the arm and turned to the cook, a woman about Walt's age, "Jo, I want you to meet Harold. He's our special guest. Harold this is my wife Jo."

Jo set her spoon down on the counter next to the stove and wiped her hand on her apron. "Hello Harold, it's a pleasure to meet you," she said. She had the kindly look of a grandmother and the soft voice that reminded Hal of the type of woman one might expect to find in a Sunday school class.

"Please call me Hal," he said to the both of them. "Something sure smells wonderful, ma'am," said Hal with a smile and a sudden reappearance of his western Illinois accent.

"I'll have dinner out in twenty or thirty minutes," Jo said then she shot Walt an annoyed look and said, "Well, don't just stand there, Walt, get this boy a drink and introduce him to the rest of the boys."

Walt laughed, "Follow me, Hal. What's your pleasure?"

As they walked from the kitchen to the dining room, Hal said, "Oh, um, bourbon or scotch on the rocks if you have it."

Walt stopped almost as if he was shocked by the request, "You'll do just fine on this assignment," he said with a chuckle.

From the dining room Hal followed Walt into the large great room of the lodge. It was a fantastic room with a massive stone fireplace at one end; couches and chairs were arranged to handle a fairly large group of people. Along the wall separating the dining room from great room was a very well-stocked bar. Deer heads and mounted fish hung from the walls along with a Navajo blanket and a bear skin. A group of six men sat around the fireplace obviously enjoying some high-spirited conversation and laughter. It was clearly happy hour at the lodge. Walt stepped behind the bar and poured a good measure of scotch into two crystal tumblers. He handed one to Hal and kept the other for himself.

"Come on over, I'll introduce you to the boys," said Walt with a grin. They walked across the room and in a booming voice Walt interrupted somebody's joke midstream, "Gentlemen, I'd like to introduce you to Hal Rumsey."

They all stood up and Hal quickly scanned their faces. He recognized them as Bobby Kennedy, Bob McNamara, and Chuck Thornton. Two men he didn't recognize but the sixth man was the 'late' John Fitzgerald Kennedy.

ATLANTIC OCEAN, ABOARD *USS THRESHER*
April 9 1963

"Conn, sonar contact bearing one two five and fifteen thousand, submerged!" said the sonar technician in an excited voice. It was the first time he had ever picked up a real submarine outside of exercises and training. "Designate contact sierra-six," he sounded as if he was completely out of breath.

Lieutenant Commander John Wesley Harvey was standing just outside the sonar "shack" when the contact was made. He was taking his nightly walk around the boat before heading off to bed.

"Settle down, son, tell us who it is," said the Commander in a calm voice.

The *Thresher* was in the middle of sea trials and while it was uncommon, it was not impossible that the navy had sent another sub into their area to check *Thresher's* noise output. Above and a few miles behind them, the *USS Skylark*, a Penguin-class submarine support vessel cruised on the surface.

On the *Thresher*, the tech clamped his hands over his headset to help drown out the background noise and listened to the "whump, whump, whump" being generated by the contact a little more than eight miles off their port side.

"Sir, she's not one of ours," he said in a slightly calmer voice. He listened a bit longer before reaching under the console and pulling out a notebook. He quickly paged through the notebook until he found what he was looking for, set it back down and clamped his hands over his headset again. "Sir, I believe Sierra-six could be a Golf, definitely not one of ours."

Commander Harvey's hair began to stand up on the back of his neck. A Soviet sub just over two hundred miles off the U.S. eastern seaboard? That wasn't good. Harvey turned to the Officer of the Deck and said, "Maneuver to intercept; let's make sure this guy knows that we know he's here."

"Helm, come left to one two five, make turns for twenty knots," said the young officer at the OD station.

"Left one two five, twenty knots," returned the Chief sitting between the two helmsmen.

Commander Harvey looked at the clock, it was just after 11:00 p.m. A few minutes earlier he had been dead tired and heading for his bunk but now his adrenaline was pumping and there was no way he could go to sleep. In the short span of ten minutes he had gone from the drudgery of reviewing personnel reports to possibly chasing a Russian sub out of his country's back yard. Damn, he thought elatedly, this is why I signed up for the Navy in the first place.

"Give me the target's course and speed when you have it, son," said Harvey in a quiet and slow voice. He wanted to convince the "kids" in the control room that he was calm and collected but he was so excited that he found himself badly in need of a trip to the head.

"Sir, target aspect is changing. He's turning almost directly away from us to course one eight zero. Sounds like he making turns for about twelve knots."

Perfect, thought the CO. If he turns away from us he'll never hear us coming up from behind him. Sonar was blind directly behind a submarine because of the noise of its propeller.

BOCA RATON, FLORIDA
Present Day

As the first signs of light began to show under the blinds in his bedroom, Hal decided to give up on sleep and get out of bed. He moved gingerly to the easy chair in the living room where he instinctively reached for the remote control to turn on the TV set. After thinking about it for a moment he decided the news would be the same as last night and set the remote back down. Who the hell cared about that shit, he thought.

As he sat there in the waning darkness, a melancholy mood came over him as he recalled the evening he had met Jack Kennedy, forty-nine years earlier. What do you say when a dead President suddenly reaches out to shake your hand? As he took the man's hand, Hal said, "Good evening, Mister President. I'm happy to see that you are feeling better."

Even now, the events of that day and that evening were crystal clear in Hal's mind. He could remember every word spoken, the taste of every bite of food he had eaten. He remembered the smell of the cigars, the expressions on the faces of the other men and even the bite of the scotch. Hal recalled the promises he had made and the documents he had signed. He had promised he would never talk about his assignment, what he did, what he heard, or what he saw and to this day, he had never mentioned to a single soul outside "the circle" a single detail of the last forty-three years of his career.

He remembered the first days of his assignment and he thought about the last few days and especially the day he had left the island and the parting words of his good friend, his best friend. He was reminded of the bitter feelings he had towards the Service for kicking him off the island, moving him out of his home, taking him away from his friend, and forcing him to retire just because he had reached some magical age at which the Service deemed him too old to adequately perform his duties.

Now, just four years later, he was living in southern Florida, his body was quickly rotting away with cancer, and his best friend was dead. He could imagine the relief the Service must be feeling; with Kennedy dead they no longer had to run the Skorpios operation and more importantly, the chances that the secrets of Skorpios ever being discovered diminished daily.

Hal ached to have one more conversation with Jack, to have one more chance to bounce his thoughts and feelings off the most intelligent man he had ever met, but that couldn't and wouldn't happen. "What would Jack say?" Hal asked himself.

He closed his eyes and tried to will away the pain he felt welling up from his abdomen. Then he tried to imagine how the conversation with Jack would go.

"When you're dead, Jack," Hal could imagine himself saying, "they are going to cremate you and bury everything they can to make sure nobody ever finds out about any of this."

He could hear the soft, melodious, and reassuring voice of his aging friend, "Hal, that's okay. I died a long time ago. I chose to die for my country and live out my years here. It was my choice, and I firmly believe it was the right choice for my country."

Yeah, thought Hal as he slowly opened his eyes, that's just about what Jack would say. It was the right choice for his country but how could it have ever been the right choice for the man or for his family?

Jack Kennedy chose to 'die' for his country and spend the remainder of his life on a remote little island in the middle of nowhere, continuing to work for his country and thereby changing history, Hal thought. The man was a great American, a great statesman. Hal knew that when his cancer finally killed him, a huge piece of American history would die with him.

For most of the forty-three years Hal had spent on the island he had been the sounding board for his friend. He listened and acted as the devil's advocate as Jack worked through solutions to world problems, master-minding coups, and offering advice that had started, ended, and prevented wars, including the Cold War. And he did it all behind a thick veil of secrecy on a little patch of land in the Ionian Sea.

Who would know that one of the greatest men to ever live unselfishly gave up the American Presidency, sacrificed his future, and did it without once complaining that it was unfair or unjust? Who would know how much Jack Kennedy did to mold world history from the mid-sixties through the millennium? How many lives had been saved, how many wars had been prevented?

The sound of the newspaper, thrown by the paperboy, hitting the front door startled Hal. It was like a slap to the face, a glass of cold water tossed on him; it was the shock he needed, the wakeup he was looking for. It was clear now what he had to do.

Once he had made up his mind about what he was going to do, the question was how was he going to accomplish it. He glanced towards the front door and saw the box sitting there, addressed and ready for him to take down to the Post Office, a task he had continued to put off. The content of the box was his proof of Jack's existence. It was addressed to:

John F. Kennedy Presidential Library and Museum
Columbia Point
Boston, MA 02125

Hal fished in the basket next to his chair and pulled out a two-week-old copy of *The Washington Post*.

"Mike Mahoney," Jack would often say while reading the *Post*, "now there's a guy who gets it. There's a guy who thinks before he writes. You know, he went to college with my Caroline? She never said so but I think he liked her."

The Washington Post was among the four or five papers that arrived to the island at least a week late along with the regular delivery of food and supplies. Kennedy read each paper with a pen in one hand, marking the articles with circles, underlines and other symbols. It was his method of emphasizing points in the articles with which he agreed, disagreed, or found inaccurate. After Hal retired, he found it hard to read a newspaper free of Jack's pen markings.

Hal thumbed through his paper until he found the contact number for the *Post*. He jotted it down on the pad of paper he kept on the table next to his chair and then carefully leaned back in his recliner to see if he could catch a few more minutes of sleep. Maybe later in the afternoon, he would take his pain medication and drift off for ten or fifteen hours, but not now.

Hal awoke with a start and saw the clock above the TV showed it was after 9:00 a.m. He was surprised but happy he had been able to get a couple hours of sleep. After a quick run to the bathroom, he returned to his chair and looked at the number scratched on the pad; he looked at the box near the front door, picked up the phone and started to dial the number on the pad. Then, a thought flashed through his mind. He looked at the phone as though he was holding a poisonous snake and slammed the receiver back down. What if they had tapped his phone. That made him pause to wonder just who "they" might be and if they really took Hal Rumsey seriously enough, then or now, to concern themselves with what he might be saying on the phone. He decided not to take the chance.

Hal pulled on a shirt and pants over the tee-shirt and shorts he had slept in and walked across the street to the community center where he could use the pay phone. An automated voice asked him to deposit one dollar and seventy-five cents. Hal pulled some coins out of his pocket and started dropping quarters into the slot. When his seventh quarter fell, the phone began to make clicks and soon started ringing. After the second ring, an appropriately pleasant female voice answered the phone, *"Washington Post*, how may I direct your call?"

"Mike Mahoney, please," said Hal, while wondering if he would get another gatekeeper or go directly to Mahoney's voicemail.

"One moment please, I'll transfer you right up," said the lady.

The phone rang four times; Hal was thinking through the carefully worded message he would leave when the phone picked up and he heard, "Mike Mahoney".

Hal was momentarily shocked; he had never even considered that the reporter would actually answer his call. He cleared his throat, "Mister Mahoney, my name is Hal Rumsey. I was a Special Agent for the United States Secret Service from 1961 until I retired seven years ago. I'm dying of cancer and I have a story to tell you."

ATLANTIC OCEAN, ABOARD *USS THRESHER*
April 10, 1963

"Conn, Sonar. Sierra-six target aspect is changing," said the sonar technician which brought everybody in the small and confined control room to full alert. The *Thresher* had been following the sub for five hours, they had closed to three thousand yards or a little over a mile and a half. The sub had been moving at twelve knots to the south and had only changed course or speed once since they acquired her. Twice *Thresher* had gone to periscope depth to send and receive messages from COMSUBLANT. The last message received had instructed them to follow the sub, remain undetected at all costs, and ordered them to not engage.

"So much for scaring her out of the area," said Captain Harvey after reading the last set of orders. This was the biggest event of his career and he was ordered to "do nothing."

"Where in the hell is she going?" asked Harvey.

His question was met with silence as the tech listened and turned dials at his console. Finally, he said, "Turning to the west, maybe coming around."

"All stop, quiet on the boat." said Harvey. The *Thresher's* propeller came to a stop and the long skinny boat glided silently forward, three hundred feet underwater. After another minute of silence, Harvey asked, "Sonar, what's she doing?"

"Sir, aspect is still changing, she's now closing on us, at our ten o'clock, course 110 degrees, 12 knots," said the tech. "I believe she's doing a one eighty and should pass us about a thousand yards off our starboard," he continued.

Suddenly, every speaker and headset aboard *Thresher* started emitting a loud squealing sound then went dead. The sonar screens flashed a brilliant flash of light before they went black and a split second later the lights on *Thresher* went out. There was nothing but darkness and the sounds of men scrambling to find flashlights and battle lamps. Some resourceful men used their cigarette lighters to illuminate their areas.

In a matter of seconds, every electrical system aboard *Thresher* had gone completely dead. Shipboard communications weren't working; in fact, the entire electrical system aboard *Thresher* was inoperative. The smell of burning wires soon permeated the submarine.

With no communication system, Commander Harvey sent a runner to the engine room to order "ahead full". With propulsion, there was a chance to gain a nose-up attitude but what Harvey didn't know was that there was no power feeding into the electrical motors that drove the main shaft.

In the reactor compartment there was nearly chaos. Without power from the batteries, the engineers couldn't control the reactor. The safety systems recognized the situation as a failure of the reactor and automatically opened the seawater system which immediately cooled what little steam they had to drive the electrical generators. *Thresher* began to sink towards the bottom of the ocean.

The last line of defense, the last tool available to Harvey to save his boat was a pair of handles located in the control room called, the "chicken handles" that controlled the valves that would fill the ballast tanks with pressurized air and send the submarine on an uncontrolled, rapid ascent to the surface.

Harvey ordered the emergency blow but nothing happened. Strainer screens installed two months earlier, designed to prevent debris from entering the moving valves of the blow system, quickly clogged with ice created by the rapidly expanding compressed air, defeating the emergency blow.

The brave men of the *USS Thresher* would battle to restart the reactor. In limited light they would try to diagnose the failed emergency blow, and they would pray as their ship slid backwards into the depths of the ocean.

Aboard the Soviet submarine *B-36*, Captain Aleksei Dubivko picked up an extra set of headphones and listened to the American boat implode as it passed its crush depth. He said a quick and silent prayer for the families of the American crewmen and gave the command to turn to the northeast and make the best possible speed.

BOCA RATON, FLORIDA
Present Day

Mike Mahoney had been with the *Post* for sixteen years. He had listened to crackpots ramble on numerous times; it was the cost of having your name and phone number listed in the daily newspaper. But he had also learned that for every fifty or sixty crackpots, there was occasionally one who had a legitimate story to tell. Several of Mike's biggest stories, the ones that had earned him a respected name and several awards, started with this type of phone call. The minute any of the callers started talking about conspiracies though, he usually branded them a nut and quickly ended the conversation.

"I'm sorry to hear you're ill, Mister Rumsey. I love hearing old stories from the men who were there," said Mahoney politely, assuming that Rumsey wanted to tell a story about his own past. "What story did you want to tell me?"

Hal paused a moment before saying, "I want to tell you about the last forty-seven years of John F. Kennedy's life."

Mahoney silently groaned, another JFK story, he thought. "Quite a bit has been written on the President's life, what can you add Mister Rumsey?" he asked.

"Quite a lot has been written about Kennedy's first forty-six years, Mister Mahoney. But nothing has been written about his last forty-seven years, from 1963 to just a few days ago," answered Hal. "I want to tell you about the greatest American who ever lived, a man who sacrificed more than any other American I personally have known."

Mahoney remembered a snippet he had caught in the paper the day before, a story regarding a pilot in Greece who was claiming JFK had recently died in a helicopter crash. He assumed he was now talking to a very sick and delusional man who had read the same article.

"Mister Rumsey, I would love to hear more about this but I am really very busy today. Perhaps we can speak another time."

Hal was prepared for the blowoff. "Fine, Mister Mahoney, I'll take my story to someone else. You're a smart man, that's what Jack Kennedy always said about you while reading your articles in the *Post* Caroline said nice things about you also. Before you write me off as a lunatic, have somebody over at the Kennedy Library check the coconut. It's a replica; I have the real one right here in my home. If you want to talk more, you can find me in Boca Raton, Florida." Then Hal hung up and returned to his home.

"What the fuck was that all about?" Mike Mahoney asked himself. "Check the coconut?" Was that what the old man said? Was that some sort of code? Mahoney dismissed his caller as a poor confused soul and went back to work.

"I've done all I can today," Hal said to himself walking back to his house. He took two of his pain pills and washed them down with a half-glass of scotch. Then he went to bed where the drugs dulled the pain and muddled his mind. He dreamed strange dreams. He and Jack were on a warm beach with John Wayne and Willie Nelson. As Willie played his guitar, Jack and John sang along while sitting around a smokeless fire. The old coon dog from the lodge in the mountains lay at their feet. The hours drifted by as Hal lay there motionless in his drug-induced haze.

WASHINGTON, D.C.
Present Day

"Boy the crazies are out in force this week," said Mike Mahoney to the group of people assembled around his table at the Post Pub for a few after-work drinks. Since his last divorce from wife number three, he had become a regular at the pub. Mahoney was always happy to have a few drinks with his co-workers before he went home to his little apartment.

"Have you heard the latest, that JFK actually died in a helicopter crash in Greece a few days ago?" he said, which drew laughter from around the table. "Today, I had a guy call me who said he could tell me all about the forty-seven years of JFK's life since his assassination."

Dayna Teutsch, sitting next to him, laughed saying, "That sounds like a boring story, he probably just laid around Arlington

Cemetery all day. I had a guy call me a few years ago saying he was one of the survivors of PT-109 and wanted to tell me the entire story about the alien abduction of the crew." Everybody laughed and others around the table started recalling stories of calls from nuts.

Mahoney was not laughing. "Check the coconut," the old man had said. That had made no sense at all to him until Dayna had made the PT-109 reference. And, "Caroline said nice things about you." How the hell did this wacko know about his history with Caroline?

He looked across the table and said, "Hey, what was the deal with the coconut and PT-109?"

Jim Poston looked up from his gin and tonic and said, "You remember, Kennedy carved a message into a coconut and gave it to a native to take to the navy. The message on the coconut saved them because the natives didn't speak English."

Holy shit, thought Mahoney. "Did Kennedy save the coconut?" he asked the group.

"Yeah, it's at the Kennedy Library up in Boston," said Tim Davis, the youngest of the group. "It's encased in a plastic dome; pretty amazing that it didn't get lost back then."

"Do any of you know anybody who works at the Kennedy Library?" Mahoney asked the group. Everybody shrugged their shoulders and somebody changed direction of the conversation.

ATLANTIC OCEAN, ABOARD *USS SKYLARK*
April 10, 1963

"Sir, besides the sonar, all systems seem to be back to normal," reported the Officer of the Deck to the Captain of the *Skylark*.

Captain Joe Bristol frowned; he didn't like the fact that his ship had lost all electrical power and he especially didn't like the fact that he had lost sonar when they were tracking a Russian sub. "Any word from *Thresher*?" he asked the OD.

"No, sir," answered the OD nervously.

"Make sure they keep trying," said Bristol as the Executive Officer, Mac Redford, walked onto the bridge leafing through the pages of a magazine.

"Cap, I think we may have been hit by an E.M.P.," Redford answered without taking his eyes off the magazine article he had found.

The Captain said, "We got hit by a what?"

"Sorry, sir. I believe we may have been hit by an electro-magnetic pulse," said the XO. "I remembered an article in *Scientific American* from a year or so ago and I dug it out. According to the article, we have been messing around with electro-magnetic pulse technology for several years. There is no reason to believe the Russians couldn't be using it now."

"What's this E.B.D. do, how does it work?" asked the Captain.

"E.M.P., sir. According to the article, it is a very high power and high frequency signal, not unlike radar. When fired, it has the ability to disrupt or destroy electrical fields in its path. It's Buck Rogers type of stuff but if the Russians have perfected it, and are using it, that would be a plausible reason for us simultaneously losing electrical power to multiple and unrelated systems at the same time."

"We were ten to twelve miles behind *Thresher* and the Russian when we lost power," said the Captain, carefully reconstructing the sequence of events. "If we lost power at that distance, what would happen to *Thresher*? She was within a mile of the Russian last time we had a fix on her?"

"It wouldn't be good, sir," said Redford with a concerned look on his face.

WASHINGTON, D.C.
Present Day

Mike Mahoney was at his desk early the following morning. He searched for the Kennedy Coconut on Google and found that the actual coconut shell that was inscribed by Kennedy after the sinking of PT-109 was in fact later encased in plastic by Kennedy and now on display at his Presidential Museum in Boston. His research on Harold Rumsey showed that an employee by that name had worked for the Secret Service from 1961 to December of 1963 but beyond that he couldn't find any record of Rumsey with the government. He searched Boca Raton, Florida, and found one Harold Rumsey listed there.

When Mahoney put the facts together, he had a man who may have worked for the Secret Service forty-seven years ago, a coconut on display at a museum, and a phone number for a man in Florida, not very compelling. He turned the page on his yellow pad and went back to work.

Shortly after 10:00 a.m. Mahoney came out of the men's room and passed two junior staffers in the hallway. He nodded in their direction and continued to walk away but as he did, he overheard one of them say, "I'm just saying I think it's weird. A day after he says JFK died in his helicopter crash, he dies?"

Mahoney turned on his heel, "I'm sorry, were you guys talking about the nut who said that JFK died in a helicopter crash a few days ago in Greece?"

The staffers were caught off guard, "Yes, sir," said the early twenties, pimple-faced kid. He pointed to his buddy, "Chad thinks there's a conspiracy behind every story. Some pilot cracked up his chopper and made some wild claims before he died, I think that's all there is to it," said the kid.

Mahoney turned to the other staffer who was equally as green, "And what do you think?"

The kid looked down at the ground, "I just think it's funny that after the guy claims Kennedy died in his helicopter, he suddenly dies."

Mahoney smiled, "Well, I'll tell you right now, you're both right and you're both wrong. Reporters need to be careful to not jump to conclusions. Where did you hear the pilot died?"

"It came across the AP wire a few hours ago," said the pimple-faced kid.

"Can you email me the link?" Mahoney asked. It was as if the King of England asked a pauper to shine his shoes. They both welled up with pride and rushed off to see who could email Mahoney the information faster.

Kids, Mike thought as he walked back to his office. He remembered having the same arguments in the hallway with his buddies. Back then, when you believed something you believed it with all your heart and you would argue your point even after somebody proved you wrong. That's what he was missing now, the passion to believe in something with such zeal. The newspaper business could do that to a person. Years of reporting on the world's crime and corruption steals a person's youthful passion for the truth, he thought as he walked back to his desk.

BOCA RATON, FLORIDA
Present Day

Hal woke from the best night's sleep he had experienced in months. The pain had crept back as the medications wore off but he had awoken both rested and hungry. He decided that after some breakfast he would go for a walk before his doctor's appointment.

He had just finished his eggs and bacon when the phone rang. "Hello?" he answered.

"Mister Rumsey, this is Mike Mahoney at *The Washington Post*. Do you have a few minutes to chat?"

Hal remembered his concern about the phone tap and said, "May I call you back in a few minutes, Mister Mahoney?"

"Certainly, and please call me Mike."

Well, thought Hal, we're on a first name basis now. "I'll call you in about ten minutes, Mike. And please call me Hal."

Ten minutes later Hal was standing at the pay phone in the community center with the quarter collection from his old poker-playing days that he kept in a Pringles Potato Chip can. Mahoney fired off the first salvo, "First of all, Hal, I want you to know up-front, because I think it's important, I don't believe that you have anything of great value to share with me."

Hal liked the fact that he was talking with a straightforward and up-front type of man. He had learned the value of that from Mr. Onassis back in the late sixties. "Well, I appreciate your skepticism, that's an important quality in your business. Here's my story, Mike. Former President John F. Kennedy died a few days ago in a helicopter crash off the island of Skorpios in the Ionian Sea. He faked his assassination in 1963 to throw off Khrushchev who was going to stop at nothing to kill him and then he lived out his life on an island owned by Aristotle Onassis."

Hal glanced around nervously. He had just let go of a secret that he had promised to take with him to his grave. He half expected men in suits and dark glasses to suddenly appear to arrest him but nothing happened, the phone didn't blow up, and his heart didn't suddenly quit beating.

Mahoney was surprised by the lucidity the nut on the other end of the line. The man spoke as though he believed every word of what he was saying. "That's quite a story, Hal. Do you have anything to back it up?"

"Yes," said Hal thinking of the box by his front door. "It just so happens that I do have something. And here's how you're going to find out if it's real."

A few minutes later Mahoney walked out into the "bullpen", a collection of desks where *Post* staffers, researchers, runners, and others were busily engaged in their work. "Who the hell knows *anybody* who works at the Kennedy Library in Boston?" Mahoney yelled across the room, startling nearly everybody within earshot.

WASHINGTON, D.C.
May 12, 1963

Bobby was furious when he read the report. "They sank the *Thresher*?" he shouted across the room. "We need to respond by sinking every god-damn Russian warship we can find! Those bastards need to be taught a lesson once and for all!"

"Let's think about this for a moment, Bobby," said the President. "That report is all based on speculation from the Navy and the CIA. Why would the Russians sink the *Thresher*?"

Bobby took a deep breath and stared at his brother for a moment before saying, "Because, Jack, they thought you were on board."

"Where in the hell would they get that idea?" Kennedy asked

"Teddy Kennedy, not Jack Kennedy, was scheduled to be aboard *Thresher* last month. He was invited by the SECNAV to go out for an overnight cruise during her sea trials," said Bobby.

John Kennedy stepped toward his brother, "First, who knew Teddy was scheduled to be aboard and secondly, how would the Russians find out and confuse a Senator for the President?"

Bobby brushed the hair out of his face, "Hell, Jack, everybody knew he was going to be on the *Thresher*. It wasn't in the media but my entire office knew, his entire office knew, and with Teddy's mouth everybody on the Senate floor knew it along with everybody from the SECNAV to the lowest man on *Thresher's* totem pole. As far as how the Russians knew, there would have been communications going back and forth, probably un-coded since they didn't refer to the President, that contained references to "Kennedy and *Thresher*". We've got so damn many Russian spies around here anymore that I'm surprised Moscow didn't hear he canceled."

"Son of a bitch," said the President. Kennedy turned and walked towards the office windows with his head hanging down, it was his thinking posture. He turned to face the two men, "Bobby, there's more," he said quietly. He nodded towards McNamara.

McNamara paused before saying, "The FBI arrested a man by the name of Adrik Fedorov last week. He's a former KGB agent who now does freelance work for the highest bidder. Somebody had hired him to make a hit and he was here in D.C. to do that job."

"Who was he here to kill and who hired him?" asked Bobby.

McNamara looked at the President who was still staring at the floor. Kennedy looked up and said, "According to the FBI, he was hired by somebody high in the Russian government to assassinate me."

Now Bobby really hit the ceiling. "What in the hell, how are we going to respond to these bastards in a way they will understand? We need to. . ."

The President cut him off, "We need to figure out how to stop Khrushchev without starting World War Three. And I am wide open to suggestions."

The room was silent for several moments before McNamara cleared his throat to speak, "Sir, according to the back-channel, Khrushchev will stop at nothing, he's determined to exact revenge for Cuba."

"He sunk our sub and killed all those men aboard her, how much revenge does he plan to take?" asked Bobby.

The President, still standing in front of the window in the sunlight, turned and faced the other two men, "Bobby, I don't think he is going to stop until he kills me. I believe, based on the reports from the CIA and our back-channel contact, that Khrushchev is so crazy with revenge for the spanking I gave him in Cuba that he won't stop until he gets back at me. He is personally blaming me for all of the problems he's having at home."

"So how the hell do we respond to that?" asked Bobby.

"I don't know," said the President. "I don't know."

WASHINGTON, D.C.
Present Day

It turned out to be a fairly easy thing for Mike Mahoney to confirm. First, he called his old college friend, Caroline Kennedy, and was surprised when she answered her cell phone on the third ring. "Hi, Caroline, it's Mike."

Mahoney thought she sounded down, depressed, not her usual perky self. He asked her if everything was all right and she assured him it was. After a few minutes of catching up Mike said, "I have a funny question to ask you. I heard a rumor that you scratched your initials in the wooden base of your father's coconut, the one he kept on his desk? The PT-109 coconut."

Caroline was silent for a moment, "I haven't thought about that in years! Why do you ask?"

Mahoney ducked the question, "I'm just doing some research for the paper, sort of a history's mysteries piece. Not a lot of people know the PT-109 coconut is still in existence. Do you remember scratching your initials into it?"

Caroline didn't buy it, "Mike Mahoney is doing research? Okay, whatever. Yes, I scratched 'C.K.' into the side of the base with a letter opener a few weeks before Dad died. I remember Mom being really mad but Dad said it added something extra special to something that was already very special to him."

Caroline's voice trailed off and she excused herself for a moment; Mike could hear her blowing her nose. When she came back on the line, Mahoney quickly changed the subject and chatted for a while longer. They promised to have lunch soon but both knew that wouldn't happen, and then they said goodbye and hung up.

The call to the Kennedy library wasn't much more difficult. Jenny Perry, a research assistant with the *Post* had a friend whose aunt, Margaret Spencer, was the assistant curator at the Kennedy Library and Museum. He left a message for her on her voice mail and busied himself in researching Skorpios Island, the marriage of Onassis and Jackie Kennedy, and other information that might fit into Hal Rumsey's impossible story.

An hour later Mahoney's private line rang, "Mike Mahoney," he answered.

"Hello Mister Mahoney, this is Margaret Spencer with the Kennedy Library in Boston returning your call. How may I help you?"

Mahoney smiled, "Miss Spencer, I am doing some research for the *Post* regarding some of history's more intriguing stories. One of our readers asked the location of the coconut shell that President Kennedy used to save the crew of PT-109."

"Well, Mister Mahoney," said the assistant curator, "you certainly called the right place. The coconut is on display here in the museum. While he was a Senator, I believe, JFK had it encased in a plastic dome and used it as a paperweight. In fact, you can find a picture of it on our website."

Mahoney faked his exuberance, "Fantastic, I'll go look at it right now! While I have you on the phone, perhaps you can answer one other question from another reader concerning the coconut."

"Certainly, Mister Mahoney, I'll try," said Margaret. "What's the question?

Mahoney readjusted the phone, "The reader heard that Caroline Kennedy, when she was about six years old, scratched her initials into the wooden base of the coconut's display case. Do you know if that's true?"

"That's something I have never heard before," said Margaret. "I'll have to go take a look and see if I can see any initials carved into the base. The coconut is in a display, our replica of the Oval Office just down the way from my office. May I call you back in a half hour or so, dear?"

"That would be fine, and thank you so much for doing this for me," said Mahoney.

"It's not a problem. In fact, now I'm curious too!"

Mahoney got up and walked down the hall to get another cup of coffee. When he returned after only five minutes he noticed there was a message on his phone. It was from Margaret Spencer saying that she had looked over the entire piece and there were no initials carved in the wooden base. Mahoney felt a shiver going up his spine. He picked up the phone and called his Editor, Bob Blurton.

"Bob, Mike here. I need to go to Florida and I need to go this afternoon!"

SARAJEVO, YUGOSLAVIA
April 25, 1963

Bob McNamara arrived at the small but comfortable Hotel Belvedere in the heart of Sarajevo after two days of travel to find the inn looking closed. Scaffolding and tarps covered the front of the building and a few workers lingered about eating lunch. McNamara got out of the car and stood there for a moment wondering if the hotel was even open before the driver said, in a heavy accent, "Come, we go in."

Despite the outward appearance, the inside of the hotel was in impeccable condition and quite active. The staff stood ready when the Manager started barking orders. McNamara was immediately escorted to his room and as the bellhop carried his bag, a stuffy Concierge told him in excellent English about the history of the area and of the hotel. Before leaving him alone in his room, the Concierge said, "Mr. Brezhnev will meet you on the veranda in thirty minute's time. If you will come to the front desk, somebody will escort you there."

The hotel was obviously vacant of other guests; the few that seemed to be around were probably staff or security for Chairman Brezhnev. Despite the President's insistence of proper security, McNamara had decided to travel to Sarajevo alone.

As he walked down the corridor to the lobby, he realized he was nervous. He had met with world leaders many times before but this was the first time that so much was riding on the outcome of the meeting. The staff and the Concierge stood at attention as McNamara walked into the lobby area. The Concierge made a big deal out of the fact that he himself would walk the Secretary to the veranda. Two imposing men stood guard at the door and for a moment McNamara wondered if they were going to search him for weapons but they made no moves or requests. One of the large guards opened the door for McNamara and, once he was through, shut it behind him.

The room was really more of a hall than the porch McNamara was expecting. It was probably a deck or veranda that had been covered and walled-in sometime after the original construction. The wood floors were shining with a fresh coat of wax, comfortable couches and chairs were arranged here and there for both privacy and small groups. Plants were placed throughout the area which, combined with the rugs and rustic décor, made the area seem very inviting.

A stern looking man with combed-back grey hair and thick eyebrows stood as McNamara entered the room. A thin smile appeared on Brezhnev's face as he held out his hand. He spoke in broken English with a heavy Slavic accent, "Secretary McNamara, it is my honor to meet you."

Bob McNamara was surprised by the Chairman's use of English. He took the man's hand and said, "Chairman Brezhnev, it is indeed an honor to meet you. I appreciate your meeting with me."

"Please," said Brezhnev, "join for tea," motioning to a pair of chairs arranged around a table holding a silver tea set.

After the appropriate amount of casual conversation regarding the weather in Sarajevo, Brezhnev sat forward in his chair, set down his teacup, and got right to the point. "Secretary McNamara, our countries have problem, we must work together for find solution."

"I appreciate your candor in this matter, Mister Chairman. And I appreciate the risks you have taken in contacting me over the past several months," McNamara responded.

"I, too, appreciate that you treat this meeting and the discussions with much discretion," the Chairman said.

"Of course, Mister Chairman," answered McNamara.

Brezhnev sat back in the high-backed wing chair, rubbed his temples as though he had a headache and said, "As you know, Secretary Khrushchev is not well."

McNamara didn't respond but instead showed a look of concern as though this was the first he had heard of the issue.

"In past several months, the Secretary's actions have become great concerning to much of us," Brezhnev continued. "We are concerned his mental health is not good and affects his leadership of Republic."

"How can I help?" asked McNamara with the correct level of compassion in his voice.

Brezhnev shifted uncomfortably, "At this moment, I need American leadership to understand problem."

"Certainly," said McNamara, "perhaps you can explain it to me in your own words so I can explain it to our President."

"You understand, Mister McNamara, this is most delicate matter. I only talk to you about this because of concerns for both countries."

"Of course," said McNamara, "I understand."

Brezhnev crossed one leg over the other and folded his hands in his lap, "The Cuba matter was not good idea. Many of us in Party advised against buildup in Cuba but Secretary Khrushchev pushed for it as answer to your missiles in Turkey."

McNamara nodded but said nothing.

"We forced President Kennedy into corner, his only response was to put nuclear missile to Secretary Khrushchev's head and threaten to pull trigger if missiles in Cuba not removed. Secretary Khrushchev had no option but to comply. Many in party believe his actions did great damage to reputation of Soviet Union around world. Khrushchev has tried to correct situation and rebuild respect with members of Politburo but is not working. His reputation is . . ." Brezhnev shook his head, "not good now."

McNamara wanted the Chairman to get to the point as quickly as possible, "How does this affect the United States?"

"I speak for me only, yes?" said Brezhnev. "I believe my friend Nikita will do whatever it takes to make better himself in eyes of world. He believes to do that is to have revenge on President Kennedy. We are fearful he will continue in attempts to assassinate your President, even if means open act of war against your country."

There it was, out on the table, McNamara thought to himself. "I assume," McNamara paused for effect, "that there is an effort within the Politburo to remove Khrushchev from power before he creates any major issues?"

"There is not," said Brezhnev in a very direct tone. "You must understand that Secretary Khrushchev controls great Soviet military. Until we find change, a move against the Secretary would be suicide."

McNamara rubbed his forehead, "So you are saying that the leader of your country is crazy and hell bent on killing the leader of my country and there is nothing we can do about it?"

"There is old saying that comes to mind," said Brezhnev. "The Englishman, Sir Francis Bacon said, 'Knowledge is power'. By knowledge you have of what is in my country, you now have some power for control destiny of your nation."

"I'm sorry, Chairman Brezhnev, but I have come a long way to see you and I was hoping you would have answers and not riddles."

Brezhnev smiled, "But I have given you answers. Secretary Khrushchev's hatred of President Kennedy grows every day. Until we find way to remove Secretary from power, he will continue to look for way to kill your President, as long as they are both alive."

BOCA RATON, FLORIDA
Present Day

Hal was feeling the need for a nap and he thought he felt good enough that he could probably sleep without the pain pills. He got up from his chair and shuffled into the kitchen to pour himself a glass of scotch when the phone rang.

"Hello?" he answered.

"Mister Rumsey? It's Mike Mahoney."

Hal chuckled to himself. He knew that if this guy did his homework he would be calling with this sense of urgency in his voice. "Call me Hal," he said in a teasing voice.

"Do you have time to see me this evening," Mahoney asked. "I'd like to see the coconut and hear what you have to say."

"I've got nothing but time for the next few months, I'd be happy to chat with you. Do you need my address?"

Mahoney smiled, "No, Hal. I have your address. I'm on my way to the airport now. I'll be at your home around six this evening if that's all right?"

"That's just fine, Mike. I'll see you then," he said and then hung up the phone. Hal suddenly felt excited and reenergized. It was almost as if his life now had a purpose. He no longer felt the need for a nap and he decided to go for a walk instead.

At a little before seven that evening, Mahoney's cab pulled into the retirement community and found Hal's small home among the many pastel-painted homes with well kept yards and flower boxes. Mahoney paid the driver and eagerly walked to the door and knocked. Mahoney was a little taken aback by the appearance of the man who greeted him on the other side of the screen door. He was so thin that his clothes seemed to hang on his skinny frame. He looked much more like a tired and frail old man of ninety than a retired Secret Service agent of seventy-four.

Hal opened the screen door and thrust his hand forward, "Mister Mahoney, I assume? I'm Hal Rumsey. Please come in."

"It's a pleasure to meet you, Hal," said Mahoney as he stepped through the door and into a small and meticulously clean home.

Hal motioned Mahoney towards the kitchen, "I assume you'd like to see some proof before we spend a bunch of time talking?" said Hal. "I didn't open the box but you're welcome to. You can see that I was about to ship it to the museum in Boston. That's where it really belongs."

Mahoney walked to the kitchen table that held a medium-sized box. The mailing label address was that of the Kennedy Library and he noticed there wasn't a return address. The only other item on the table was a box knife. Mahoney turned to Hal and asked, "May I?" pointing to the box.

"Of course you can, that's why you came here," said Hal.

Taking the knife in hand, Mahoney carefully cut the tape on the top of the box in such a way that it could be easily re-taped after his inspection. He lifted the flaps and found a handwritten letter on top that read:

Dear Sirs,

Please find enclosed the real coconut from the PT-109 incident. This was entrusted to me by President John F. Kennedy many years ago and now deserves to replace the replica you have in your museum. You can authenticate this with a call to Caroline Kennedy to verify her initials carved into the base.

Regards

The letter was unsigned.

Mahoney carefully reached into the mass of Styrofoam peanuts until his hands found an item wrapped in newspaper. Some peanuts fell onto the table as he pulled the wrapped parcel from the box. As he set the item on the table next to the box he noticed the newspaper Hal had used was the *Washington Post* and he gave a quick chuckle. He carefully unwrapped the piece and found himself looking at an exact replica of the plastic-domed coconut he had seen on the internet. It was smaller than he had imagined, about the size of a large grapefruit.

Encased in the plastic dome was a piece of coconut shell that had writing carved on it. The writing was hard to read through the scratched and clouded plastic but with a little effort he could see that it said:

"11 alive native knows postit & reef Nauru Island Kennedy"

Mahoney slowly turned the globe in his hands and on the side of the wooden base he saw what appeared to be the scratched initials of a six-year-old, *"C.K."*.

He was about to set it down but turned it over and found a handwritten note was taped to the bottom that read:

"To Hal on your retirement,
Thanks for all of your years of friendship, Jack"

All Mahoney could say at first was, "Wow!" He finally composed himself and realized he was getting his dirty hands all over an important historical artifact and he carefully set it down. "Kennedy gave this to you?" he asked.

Hal moved forward and looked at the paperweight sitting on the table, "Yeah, it was one of the few items he took with him when he left the White House. He knew I admired it so on my last night on the island he gave it to me. I was obviously going to get it to the museum before I go. I'm just having a hard time letting it go. It's the last piece of Jack that I have."

Mahoney suddenly felt bad, he had been so focused on figuring out if the man before him was a nut that he had forgotten his manners, "I'm sorry to hear you're ill. How are you doing, Hal?"

Hal didn't want to talk about his condition. Pointing to his head he said, "I'm doing just fine where it counts. I'm a tough customer, Mister Mahoney. Can I get you something to drink? I have water, milk, and scotch,"

"I'll have a scotch if you don't mind," said Mahoney as he continued to inspecting the coconut without touching it.

Hal poured two glasses of scotch and said, "Let's sit in the living room, it's more comfortable."

After a few minutes of talking about Mahoney's flight and the weather in Boca, Hal said, "You didn't come down here to talk about the humidity."

Mahoney smiled, he liked the older man very much. "You're right, Hal. I came down here to listen to whatever is on your mind?"

Hal took a sip of scotch and looked at the ceiling; he could feel his eyes starting to well up with tears but he fought them back, "Jack Kennedy was my friend. He was a man who gave his entire life to the service of his country and now he's dead and nobody will ever know how much he sacrificed for the United States."

Mahoney reached into his briefcase and found his digital mini-recorder; he set it on the coffee table and pushed the 'record' button. "You told me on the phone that John F. Kennedy died a few days ago in a helicopter crash in Greece, that he faked his assassination in Dallas in 1963, and that he lived on an island owned by the Onassis family until his death."

Hal squirmed uncomfortably in his easy chair; he was finding it harder to talk about in person than it had been when he blurted out that statement on the phone. He reminded himself that Jack gave up so much and that he had already come so far, he needed to simply summon up the courage to go all the way. "Yes sir. That is a completely true statement."

Mahoney knew the story was implausible yet he had come to Florida to hear it because there was something believable about it. He couldn't put his finger on the reason but something about the old man's story seemed possible to him. He glanced across the room at an artifact that matched Caroline Kennedy's description.

"Why don't we start from the beginning, Hal? How did you get involved in all of this?"

Hal sat back in his chair trying to ignore his pain. He closed his eyes, calling to memory the hunting lodge and said, "I met Jack Kennedy ten days after the assassination in Dallas, how much tape do you have in that machine?"

"Plenty," smiled Mahoney.

"I was a young, dumb, pimple-faced agent with the Secret Service when they picked me for the assignment," said Hal. "I was single, I had no family, no attachments, so they thought they could use me for a few years. You see, they had another couple of guys handpicked well before the assassination but they didn't tell them exactly what the assignment would be until after Dallas and almost every single one of them asked for re-assignment when they found out the real duty. I guess they took a new tack when they chose me. I didn't know what the assignment was until I found myself shaking Kennedy's hand."

"Where did you first meet?" asked Mahoney.

"They flew me up to a hunting lodge in the Alleghany Mountains. My boss, Chuck Thornton, was there, Jack and Bobby Kennedy were both there, Bob McNamara was there, and that was where I first met Ari Onassis."

"You actually met Onassis?" asked Mahoney.

"Well, of course. After all, I lived on his island for forty-three years. I met lots of people."

Mahoney was cautious. "Who else did you meet over those years?" he asked.

"Well, let see, I met Leonid Brezhnev. We eventually took that two-faced skunk down, by damn," said Hal proudly.

A hundred questions were passing through Mahoney's mind but he knew better than to get off track. He rummaged through his briefcase to find a pad to write down questions as the occurred to him. "Okay, let's get back to that, so tell me about your first meeting with Kennedy and Onassis."

"Well," said Hal, "it was quite a shock to see the President standing there, relaxed and enjoying himself with a drink in his hand. Ten days earlier he had been killed in Dallas. I had talked to some of the fellas who had been there. Clint Hill had so much blood on his jacket that he threw it away. He hadn't slept a wink and was walking around the office like a zombie the last time I saw him. There were others like Paul Landis who saw the whole thing. Some of these guys were messed up for the rest of their lives. I had no doubt in my mind the President was dead right up until I came face to face with him and shook his hand. Even then I wasn't sure that they hadn't made up his brother Teddy to look like Jack for some reason."

Hal shifted a little to relieve the pain in his back and continued, "The meeting at the lodge with Ari Onassis was held to finalize the details of Kennedy's move to Skorpios."

"Okay, wait a minute," Mahoney said, "I have about a hundred thousand questions about the assassination, and even more about why Kennedy would go to these lengths in the first place?"

Hal sat silent for a moment before looking up, "I had the unique opportunity to spend more than four decades sitting on a little island with Jack Kennedy. We had lots of time to chat about all of that so give me a few minutes to lay it out for you as best I can."

Hal labored out of his chair and retrieved the scotch bottle from the kitchen counter. After refilling their glasses he set the bottle down on the table between them and started telling the story.

"I guess first of all, you need to remember all the things that were happening in late 1962 and early 1963. The President had all sorts of problems on his hands. George Wallace was elected as Governor of Alabama with his "pro-segregation" stance and that was a blow to the Kennedy boys. It was pretty clear that the battle against racism was about to come to a head. The conflict in Vietnam was taking more and more "military advisors" every day and the writing was on the wall that the situation in that little Asian country was about to become a full-scale war. And the situation with the Russians in Cuba, while it seemed to be solved, was building into a major scrap. Then add to all of that, the leader of the world's other major power was a crazed lunatic who wanted to kill Jack Kennedy out of revenge, and you had some reasons to lay awake at night."

Hal turned in his chair to look straight into Mahoney's eyes, "That's what caused the whole thing. Did you know that Khrushchev was completely off his rocker?"

"What do you mean?" asked Mahoney with his eyebrows raised.

"After the Cuban Missile Crisis," said Hal after a pause, "Khrushchev lost every bit of respect he had within the Politburo and the Central Committee; he rightfully feared for his position within the communist party. He apparently cooked up in his own mind the idea that if he took revenge on Kennedy, he would regain the respect he had lost."

Hal rubbed his chin and looked down to the floor, "Things started to happen in early 1963. First, the Russians flew several recon flights over Alaska, just to see how upset we would get. Then the FBI arrested a known assassin with ties to the Russkies, a guy who it seems, was in the States to take out Jack and or Jackie. Then there was the *Thresher* incident and . . .."

"Wait a minute," interrupted Mahoney, "What about the *Thresher*, the submarine?"

"The Russians sank her. You've heard that before, haven't you?"

Mahoney uncrossed his legs; he was growing more and more uncomfortable. He was starting to feel as though he was back in Los Angeles during the Northridge earthquake in 1994. Mike Mahoney, like many Americans, had always believed that two constants in life were that the earth didn't move and history didn't change.

"I've never heard about any Russian involvement in the *Thresher* accident," said Mahoney. "Do you have any way of proving they had anything to do with it?"

Hal shot him a look, "Accident, my ass. The Russians hit the *Thresher* with some sort of electrical pulse or something and we lost 129 good men. Khrushchev had heard, mistakenly, that Kennedy was going to be aboard her during some of her sea trials. He ordered one of their subs to find the *Thresher* and hit her with an experimental weapon, an electro-something or other pulse that screwed up the electrical system and caused her to sink. Even though Kennedy was not on board, Khrushchev figured that the attack would get us to engage with the Soviet submarine and sink it so he could escalate the entire incident into a full scale war. Luckily," Hal paused a moment as a warm smile broke across his face, "luckily Jack Kennedy was too damn smart to allow himself to be suckered in by Khrushchev. I guess I should give some credit to Brezhnev for tipping us off that Khrushchev was crazy and alerting us not to get suckered into something."

"Wait a minute, time out," said Mahoney. "Brezhnev told you guys that Khrushchev was crazy and not to get involved in a war?"

"No," said Hal, "I misspoke there. I wasn't involved with Jack and his bunch during the initial conversations with Brezhnev. Those all took place before the assassination. And to answer your question, no, I cannot prove the Russians sank the *Thresher* but I know they did. Jack told the Navy to cover it up to keep us out of a war with the Russians. And yes, Brezhnev started sending messages to Kennedy through Bob McNamara sometime in late 1962. It was probably those messages that kept us out of World War Three."

Mahoney stood up and walked silently to the other side of the room then turned and looked at the frail old man sitting in the easy chair. It was obvious that Hal was feeling discomfort from the pain of his disease but Mahoney detected something else in his voice, something about the tone of his voice or the pattern of his speech. The story the old man told was so unlikely, so unbelievable that only another nut would continue to listen, yet Mahoney found himself believing the guy. Hal Rumsey reminded Mahoney of somebody he had met before but he just couldn't put his finger on it.

"If Brezhnev and the Politburo knew Khrushchev was crazy, why didn't they simply remove him from power?" asked Mahoney.

"At the time, Khrushchev held the power of the military. To try to remove him would have been unsuccessful because he held all the chips and would have simply beaten down any coup. Brezhnev and his supporters in the Politburo felt they had to do what they could to keep the U.S. from engaging Khrushchev. They opened a line of communication and warned us to keep from getting involved in a war until they could put the pieces in place, gain the support they needed within the military and the Politburo, and then remove Khrushchev from power without starting a civil war."

"There it was," thought Mahoney. It had suddenly come to him. The tone, the feeling, the tenor of the conversation was just like the Albert Gandy confession! A few years ago Mahoney had had the opportunity to interview another elderly man who was confessing to killing his wife thirty years earlier. For thirty years, Gandy had held a secret and when he finally started talking he couldn't stop. It was like removing a weight that had sat on his chest for thirty years. Hal was regurgitating secrets he had held inside for forty-seven years.

Mahoney reminded himself of interview techniques he had learned as a cub reporter; Keep your mouth shut, ask only relevant questions, don't, for even a second act as if you don't believe the source. And most of all, listen.

"Hal, you said you met Brezhnev. Can you tell me about that?"

Hal put his hand up, "I met him, but that was later, out on the island. We'll get to that."

"Fair enough," Mahoney nodded, "So Brezhnev was secretly talking with McNamara?"

"Yeah, it started as some notes and cables being passed secretly between McNamara and some unnamed source in Moscow. I think as the two of them grew more confident with each other they passed more information and then, finally, McNamara and Brezhnev met face to face. That was before the assassination and, if I remember right, I think they met somewhere in Europe, Venice or Sarajevo or someplace like that." Hal chuckled, "I heard it was hard to get reservations at some of the upscale hotels in Europe in those days because of all the clandestine meetings taking place."

"I didn't know we were all that friendly with Brezhnev," said Mahoney. "Was his motive to keep us out of a war simply to save lives?"

"I don't think that asshole ever worried much about human lives. I think he worried that the Soviets couldn't afford a war with the U.S. His driving motivation was to position himself as the next leader of the USSR and to take that position while the country was still economically viable."

Mahoney was shocked. "You just called him an 'asshole' and earlier you said he was 'two-faced'. Didn't he save our bacon?"

"Sure, he helped keep us out of a war with the Russians in 1963 and prevented a war with China in 1967. I'm getting ahead of myself in calling him names, I guess." Hal looked into Mahoney's eyes, "We have a lot of history to cover, Mike. Do you think I'm a crazy old man yet?"

Mahoney laughed and took a sip of his scotch. "Yeah, Hal, I think you're a crazy old man. The crap coming out of your mouth is the most unbelievable slew of shit I have heard in a long time, but I gotta tell you, I'm intrigued. Are you doing okay or would you like to take a break?"

"I'm fine, where were we?"

Mahoney moved back to sit in his chair near Hal. "1963, Brezhnev is talking with McNamara."

"Right, so McNamara came back from his meeting in Europe with Brezhnev. Based on the firsthand knowledge Mac acquired in that meeting it was apparent to the Kennedy's that something drastic had to happen. You see, while publicly he was making all the right moves, agreeing to the nuclear test ban treaty and setting up a direct hotline between Moscow and Washington, Khrushchev was carefully planning and plotting ways to kill the man he saw as the devil himself, Jack Kennedy."

He took another quick sip of his scotch and continued, "The way that Jack and Bobby figured it, the only way to stop Khrushchev was to kill him or dethrone him. They couldn't figure out a way to get him thrown out of office and they couldn't figure a way to kill him without the possibility of starting a war, so they cooked up the plan to publicly assassinate Jack himself. I think when they originally came up with the plan they thought they could bring Jack back to life in six or eight months after Brezhnev had put all the pieces in place to remove Khrushchev."

Hal paused for a moment, then said, "I think they came to the realization that the American public and the world in general would be outraged at something like that. If they were going to do it, they had to be all in, with the exception of the actual death of the President."

Mahoney jotted down a note on his pad before asking, "Were they really a hundred percent sure there was no other way to stop Khrushchev?"

Hal rubbed the back of his neck, "By November of '63, it was pretty clear that they had run out of options. Something had to give."

Mahoney sat forward on the edge of his chair, "Who all knew about the plan?"

"I don't really know. I know there were a few Secret Service agents involved, and obviously my boss, Chuck Thornton. There was Bobby Kennedy, Secretary McNamara, Governor Connally and his wife, Nellie, and of course Jackie. And there were a few well-placed people at the hospital, but Johnson didn't know."

Mahoney's head shook involuntarily, "President Johnson didn't know that Kennedy faked his own assassination?"

"No, sir, and to the best of my knowledge he never found out. Jack made it clear that Johnson couldn't be told and could never find out. He knew it was important not to undermine Johnson's public credibility or the office of the President if the public ever found out."

"What about the other Presidents, Nixon, Ford, Carter and the rest?" asked Mahoney?

"I'm a hundred percent certain that Nixon didn't know but I also know for sure that Ford did. Hell, Ford was on the Warren Commission. They were supposed to give the final report that would convince everybody that Oswald did it and that he acted alone. The Warren Commission's only task was to get people to stop looking under rocks. They obviously failed."

"Good God," said Mahoney, "how deep does this thing run?"

"We haven't even scratched the surface, Mike."

WASHINGTON, D.C.
May 1, 1963

"He said that?" asked Bobby. "He actually used the words, 'as long as they are both alive?'"

McNamara turned towards the President and addressed him directly, "I believe he was suggesting that Khrushchev is going to continue to do whatever it takes to try to kill you, sir. I am convinced that Brezhnev wanted me to understand that he will try to do it with a single bullet or even a single missile if that's what it takes.

Kennedy turned towards the window, his right hand covered his mouth, his left arm crossed his body to help support his right elbow. It was the classic Jack Kennedy pose. "Can we reason with him?" asked Jack.

"Brezhnev made it clear that Khrushchev wasn't in any state of mind to negotiate. Our experiences in the past with him may lead us to believe differently but it is pretty clear that his mental condition is deteriorating as fast as his power base."

"Are we talking to and believing the right people?" asked Bobby. "What if Brezhnev is trying to talk us into believing Nikita is crazy to prompt us to make a move that will benefit him? What is his motivation? Does he hope to take over after Khrushchev is gone? According to the CIA, Brezhnev isn't the most likely successor to Khrushchev at this point in time."

McNamara took a sip of coffee hoping that somebody else would take that question but he noticed that both Jack and Bobby were looking directly at him, waiting for a response. "We have the letter from Khrushchev, we have reports from several different sources, and the general speculation is that he is suffering from stress, depression, syphilis, or something. We know he has lost face both in Moscow and across the world. We also know that right now Brezhnev wouldn't likely take over in the event of his death or resignation."

McNamara paused for a moment to think. Then he said, "It is quite possible that we are right on both fronts. Khrushchev is losing his marbles and Brezhnev sees it as an opportunity. If Brezhnev was seen as the man who prevented a war with the U.S., he could possibly leapfrog his way to the top position in the Soviet Union."

"Do you think that Brezhnev's communications with us is a power play on his part?" asked Bobby.

McNamara shook his head, "I'm only guessing."

The President was clearly frustrated, "We cannot operate on guesses and speculation. We need to know what in the hell is going on before we are forced into a war with the Russians. Let's set up a meeting with Nikita when I'm in Berlin in June. I don't care if it's disclosed or is a secret meeting but I want to look that bastard in the face so I can tell for sure whom we are dealing with."

BOCA RATON, FLORIDA
Present Day

"So how did they do it?" asked Mahoney.

"The actual assassination? Hell, the way Jack told it, it was pretty easy. Peter Lawford put Bobby in touch with some Hollywood special effects genius. They put together a plan and bamboozled the public for forty-seven years."

"Do you know the details of how they actually pulled it off?" asked Mahoney.

"Oh hell, yeah," said Hal with a small grin. "Jack told me the whole thing. It was simple yet brilliant. They devised a plan that allowed for both a very public event and also for an easy cover-up. The reason most cover-ups don't work is because they aren't planned. If you shoot somebody and then try to cover it up, you run into all sorts of problems. If you plan to shoot somebody and also plan to cover it up from the beginning, you have a much higher chance of success."

Hal let that sink in for a moment before continuing, "So first they needed a convincing patsy, somebody who was willing to go down for the worst crime of the century. After a little searching they found Oswald who was part of a special CIA program."

"Wait a minute," said Mahoney. "This is getting a little wild. Now you're saying that Lee Harvey Oswald was a CIA Operative?"

"I'm just telling you what Jack told me. If you'd rather I only stick to the popular story, Kennedy died in '63 and you wasted a trip down here."

Mahoney felt embarrassed; he put up his hands and said contritely, "Geez, Hal, I'm sorry but you're changing history that has been set in my brain for damn near fifty years."

Hal smiled, "Do you wonder why nobody's ever talked before? It's because they'd be labeled a nut and then put away, maybe even silenced."

Mahoney nodded in agreement and tried quickly to get the conversation back on track. "So what do you know about Oswald?"

"Oswald was recruited by the CIA almost the same day he joined the Marines in the mid-1950s. He was a poor kid who was raised by his mother. He was a loser, probably the kind of kid who got beat up a lot for being weird. He was exactly the type of young kid the CIA wanted to find for some of their more questionable operations. He was intelligent, came from a broken home, and he was so odd that his cover story was easy to make up. The agency built him a background of abuse and scattered trouble with the law. They sent him to Russia and laid the background story that he had been studying Communism for years which made it believable that he defected."

"Was he ever involved in anything with the CIA?" asked Mahoney.

Hal crossed one leg over the other before saying, "The CIA used him for a variety of small ops here and there while they continued to build his back-story as a real weirdo. After he returned to the U.S., they had him supporting the Pro-Castro Cubans and even got him interviewed by a TV station while he was handing out leaflets in New Orleans. Everything was pretty well scripted for some future operation. Rumor was that in those days, the CIA maintained quite a large crop of both men and women that they cultivated for future assignments, assignments that didn't even exist yet. Some of these people were eventually used and some simply faded away. And some may have even gone off the reservation, acted out on their own and created potentially embarrassing situations for the CIA. Every time a new serial killer, another presidential assassin, or some other crackpot showed up in America I would wonder if they were part of the same program in which Oswald had been enrolled."

Hal shook his head, "Anyway, Bob McNamara found Oswald after some discreet inquiries and he was assigned to the Department of Defense for a special operation."

"Isn't that type of information traceable? Wouldn't somebody have discovered that he was a CIA Operative who was assigned to the DOD?" asked Mahoney.

"Apparently, it isn't," answered Hal. "I got the feeling that the government had the ability to do a lot of record changing. Hell, look at me. I worked for the Service for forty-five years. The last forty-three of them don't show up on anybody's records, anywhere. Yet a direct deposit appears in my checking account every month."

"Did Oswald agree to be the patsy?" asked Mahoney.

"Sure he did. He had a pretty nice offer," Hal said while again adjusting painfully in his chair. "For participating, he was offered a nice chunk of money. After the trial of the century, in which all doubts would be removed that he was lone assassin based on his eventual confession, he would be executed in the electric chair. After his execution, he would receive radical plastic surgery and spend the rest of his life somewhere in South America."

"So how did Ruby figure in?" asked Mahoney.

"Hell, Mike, Ruby wasn't any part of the plan," Hal said with a chuckle. "Ruby strolled into the middle of the perfect crime and killed the perfect criminal. That opened the door to every damn conspiracy theory that has cropped up over the last forty years."

"Holy shit, you mean Ruby was a complete outsider?" asked Mahoney.

"Yeah, Ruby was just what he appeared to be, a local bar owner who really thought he would be hailed as a hero for killing the man who had killed the president. Nobody outside of Dallas had ever heard of Jack Ruby before he shot Oswald."

Mahoney looked up at the ceiling and laughed, "Damn, that must have come as a surprise to Kennedy!"

"It was a game-changer," said Hal.

WEST BERLIN, GERMANY
June 25, 1963

Evelyn Lincoln was a slight, soft-spoken woman who dedicated her life to the service of John Fitzgerald Kennedy. She was the consummate professional assistant that every politician and corporate CEO searched for but seldom found. Lincoln and Kennedy had a special working relationship based on trust and respect. At times, they would become engaged in long conversations that ranged from affairs of state to the challenges of raising children. Kennedy had learned to admire Evelyn's opinions and in several matters, even to solicit her opinion and advice. Despite their close relationship, or maybe because of it, Evelyn hated to be the bearer of bad news.

On the morning of June 25, she walked from her adjoining hotel suite into Kennedy's sitting room and waited quietly until a break in the conversation allowed her to speak. Kennedy understood her body language, arms folded in front of her and steno pad tightly grasped in her hands indicated his assistant had something important to say to him.

"Yes, Evelyn?" asked Kennedy.

"Sir, a message from the Kremlin, Secretary Khrushchev sends his regrets but he will not be able to meet with you this afternoon."

Kennedy leaned forward in his chair, his back was aching from the long flight. "Damn it," he said under his breath. He sat up straight and looked to Evelyn, "Did the Kremlin give an excuse for Secretary Khrushchev's last minute cancellation?"

"They only indicated the situation was unavoidable, sir."

Kennedy looked to the ceiling, considering his next move. Then he said very calmly, "Evelyn, will you please cable both Bobby and Mac to let them know Mister Khrushchev has canceled our meeting?"

"Of course, sir," said Lincoln before walking rapidly out of the room. She breathed a long sigh of relief. That was over!

BOCA RATON, FLORIDA
Present Day

Mahoney noticed that Hal was wincing in pain as he shifted in his chair. "That's enough for tonight, Hal. Let me borrow your phone book and I'll call a cab."

"Where are you staying?" asked Hal. He wasn't going to argue if his visitor wanted to leave. His pain was starting to wear him down.

"Just down the road about two miles on the freeway, at the Hampton Inn."

Hal struggled to his feet, "Do you mind doing me a favor, Mike?"

Mahoney jumped to his feet, "Sure, anything."

"My old car could use a little workout. I haven't been driving it much and I'd sure appreciate it if you would take her for the night, charge up the battery, warm up the oil and all."

Mahoney looked a little shocked, "Well, I certainly appreciate that but I'm just fine calling a cab."

"Please take my car, Mike. She needs to get out of the garage, seriously."

Mahoney was pretty certain that he wasn't going to win the argument without a long debate so he agreed to take the old man's car. What the heck, he thought,, it will save me from having to wait for a cab.

They walked together to the kitchen door where Hal motioned Mahoney to go ahead of him. Hal turned off the lights in the living room and as they continued through the kitchen he turned off the light in that room as well before they walked out to the single-car garage. Hal flipped on the garage light illuminating his immaculate 1962 Oldsmobile StarFire Convertible.

"Damn, Hal, that's a beautiful car!" said Mahoney.

"Thanks. I was saving my money to buy a used car when I accepted the assignment in 1963. I never had the need for a car again until I retired. When I got back to the States I decided to buy the car I had wanted back in 1963. I found this little gem in St. Louis; she had been completely restored and ran like a dream. Drive her easy until you get her warmed up then go ahead and put your foot into her a little. That big Olds 394 will surprise you," Hal said with a proud smile.

Mahoney was surprised by the car's perfect leather interior. Hal pointed out the air conditioning controls and the headlight switch and then he asked Mahoney to keep the top up. The big Oldsmobile fired up on the first try and Mahoney carefully backed her out of the garage. He waved goodbye as Hal pushed to button to lower the garage door.

Once the door closed, Hal hurried back into the living room, careful not to trip over the furniture, and watched his car go around the corner and out of sight. He looked up and down the street from behind the curtains in his dark living room but couldn't see any movement, nobody walking, no cars moving. Then he saw it.

About half a block down the street a white sedan was moving towards his home with its lights off. Just as it drew close to the front of his home, the driver turned on the lights and picked up speed. Hal ducked out of the way even though he knew it would have been nearly impossible for the driver to see him in the darkened window.

Hal watched the Ford Sedan until it rounded the corner on the heels of his Oldsmobile. "Damn it," he said to himself softly. "Damn!"

WASHINGTON, D.C.
July 25, 1963

The messages from Brezhnev continued to arrive on a regular basis, each containing a more ominous description than the last of Khrushchev's state of mind. Even while agreeing to sign the Nuclear Test Ban Treaty and to install a hotline between Washington, D.C., and the Kremlin, two events that would lead the people and press of both nations to believe the world was about to enter a new era of peace, Khrushchev appeared by many accounts to be losing all touch with reality.

Bob McNamara arrived in Bobby's office with the latest message. Bobby read it quickly before turning to McNamara, he started to speak but stopped himself and read the message again. "What are we going to do Bob? What the hell are we going to do?"

BOCA RATON, FLORIDA
Present Day

Following a fairly restless night, Hal was awake, dressed and sipping a cup of tea when his phone rang. "Good morning, Hal," said the voice. "It's Mike Mahoney. How was your night?"

"Oh, just fine, Mike. Any problems finding your hotel?"

"Not at all, drove right to it and you're right, that is one fine automobile. I could have kept right on driving all night."

You probably are going to wish you had of, Hal thought to himself. "Are you ready to chat some more this morning?" he asked instead.

"That was my next question. I'm ready if you are, Hal."

"I'll be ready by the time you get here," said Hal in his most convincing voice.

"Great, see you in half an hour."

CREAKAN UPPER, IRELAND
July 25, 1963

Devon Clancy was starting to put two and two together. He had never granted the law any real respect and in his twenty-three years often had found himself in the poor graces of the local Gardai. But a day after his mysterious guests had arrived at his farm, he was worried and suspicious that whatever they might be planning would lay far outside even his concept of lawlessness.

Devon had been contacted a few weeks earlier by a man he knew from Dublin. Kevin Doyle was known to traffic in women, drugs, and illegal whiskey throughout the country and he seemed to do it without any interference from the local authorities which made him somewhat of a celebrity in Devon's mind. When he was asked by Doyle if he could board three men for a few days he was happy to lend a hand. He couldn't wait to see the looks on faces of the local ruffians when he would brag to them later that he had worked side-by-side with the great Kevin Doyle. He was even happier with the promise of a hundred pounds that would be forthcoming for his troubles; it was more money than he had expected to see all year.

When Doyle and his three compatriots arrived they quickly moved into the main house. Devon had promised to keep out of their way and had moved into the small shed that sat several yards away from the farmhouse. He watched as the men, who certainly were not Irish, moved several heavy boxes and half a dozen duffel bags into the house. As he was loading the coal box near an open window, Devon heard them speaking and it was no language he had ever heard before.

It was when Devon went into town to get the supplies Doyle had requested that he first heard that the American President, John F. Kennedy himself, would be coming to County Wexford, to his family's ancestral home in just two days time. Doyle, the strange foreigners, and their heavy boxes and bags started to add up. These men were planning something for Kennedy, Devon concluded.

As much as Devon relished the idea of becoming a part of Doyle's band of miscreants, there was no way he could allow them to harm a man whose family was from County Wexford, and who was the first Irish President of the United States to boot.

Walking back to his home with the groceries, Devon considered his options. He could go to the local authorities but he had pretty much emptied his bank account of trust and favors with them. And there was the added problem that he himself was harboring the assassins. He could try to handle the situation himself or with the help of some of his local friends but he was pretty sure that the group was heavily armed and well trained. Or he could try to find the American security people and alert them to the threat.

The people in town had told him that Kennedy would arrive in Wexford, give a speech in New Ross and then visit his ancestral home in Duganstown. "That was the place to start," Devon told himself.

Doyle was sitting outside when Devon walked up the path to his home. "Devon," he laughed, "let me help you with those bags. My god man, did you carry these from town all by yourself?"

"Thank you, Mister Doyle, but they weren't heavy at all. I found everything on your list."

Doyle grabbed for the bag slung over his back saying, "That's a good lad. Did you learn anything in town?" he asked.

"I did, in fact," Devon lied. "My poor aunt in Whitechurch is not doing well, not well at all. If you'll not be needing anything else from me this afternoon I would like to go see her, to see if there are any jobs that need to be done around her home."

Doyle took the other bags of food from him at the door and said, "I'm sorry to hear that, Devon. We are fine here. You go and take good care of your Auntie. Did you say Whitechurch? Is that far? Can I take you there in the car?"

"God Bless you, Mister Doyle. I won't put you out. Whitechurch isn't far, not far at all, really just down the road a bit. I'll catch a ride down on the main road and I should be back later this evening."

Devon thought he saw a look of suspicion in Doyle's eye but the man simply said, "You're a good lad, Devon. God go with you."

BOCA RATON, FLORIDA
Present Day

Hal rose from his chair when he heard his Oldsmobile's high compression engine as Mike Mahoney turn into his driveway. He walked to the window and scanned the street in both directions for any strange cars, a white Ford in particular, but he saw none. Mahoney parked the car in the drive and start towards the front door. Hal had it open before Mahoney had a chance to ring the bell.

"Please come in, Mike," said Hal as he scanned the street again.

"How are you this morning, Hal?" asked Mahoney.

"I'm fine, Mike. But I think I had better take you to the airport so you can get back to Washington."

Mahoney was shocked, "Why would I go back to Washington now?"

Hal walked to the front windows again and looked out. "Last night, after you pulled out, I'm pretty sure you were followed. Somebody was watching the house."

"Who do you think would have been watching?" Mahoney asked.

Hal turned back towards him and looked him in the eyes. "I don't know who but I can't think of a single agency in the United States government that would welcome the idea of a massive cover-up being exposed. Can you imagine the Congressional hearings that will take place, the backlash in the media that will result, and all the suspicion that the government will face when this story breaks?"

"Hal, have you thought through the mess this will cause?" asked Mahoney.

Hal responded, a mild anger evident in his voice, "Oh, I've thought it through. I've been thinking about it for 47 years from the day I met Jack Kennedy and realized what he was sacrificing for his country."

Hal put out his hand, "Give me the keys, we'll go for a drive this morning and then you can decide if you want to stay or go."

Mahoney handed over the car keys. "Oh I'm staying. I'm dying to hear the rest of this story and drink more of your scotch," he said good-naturedly.

Hal lowered the top on the Oldsmobile and eased her out of the subdivision. As he turned onto Yamato Road he punched the gas on the big Starfire and felt a satisfying tail-wag when the automatic transmission shifted from first to second. He looked down and saw that in just a hundred yards, they had accelerated to over sixty miles an hour. He took his foot off the gas and smiled.

Mahoney thought there was something new, something different about Hal this morning. He seemed a little quicker to show anger but he was also a new and energized man. The old, cancer-ridden retiree Mike had met last night was now burning rubber in his vintage muscle car; he seemed to sit a little straighter and his voice was much stronger.

"Where did we leave off last night?" asked Hal.

"You were telling me that Oswald was a patsy and Ruby was just a loose cannon who wasn't part of the plan."

"Right," said Hal, changing lanes. "So according to the plan, Oswald would fire three blank shots from the Book Depository window. Then he would . . .."

"Wait a minute," Mahoney interrupted. I just read last night that the first shot missed everything and hit the curb taking a small chunk out of the concrete. How did a blank do that?"

"I asked that same question after reading a book about the assassination. According to Jack, the chip in the curb was placed there by an agent the day before. He walked along the street with a piece of rebar and smacked the curb in about the right place."

Mahoney brushed the hair out of his eyes as they came to a stoplight at St. Andrews Boulevard. Realizing he hadn't started his recorder, he took it out of his pocket and pressed the red button. "Okay, so Oswald was to fire the three blanks, then what?"

"He was to stash the rifle, which was easily tied to him, on the sixth floor where it could be later," said Hal. Then he was to go to the theater and wait to be arrested by the Dallas Police who got a tip he was there."

"What about the Dallas cop he killed?" asked Mahoney.

"Officer Tibbit? That one is still a big mystery," said Hal as the traffic light turned green. "Oswald had no reason to kill Officer Tibbit. He could have surrendered to him and been arrested right there on the street, it wouldn't have messed up the plan at all. Oswald never got the chance to talk to any of the Secret Service boys who helped pull this off so Jack never knew for certain if he was involved in Tibbit's death or not. Jack did his best, however, to make sure that his widow and his children were reasonably well taken care of. He couldn't do much without somebody asking questions but he did a good share."

Traffic slowed in the right lane. Hal checked his rearview mirror before shifting over to the faster moving left lane. That's when he saw it, a white Ford sedan a few cars behind them. Don't get loopy, he told himself, there had to be a thousand white Ford sedans within a few miles of his home.

"Hal?" said Mahoney, "I still don't understand why Kennedy felt that faking an assassination was his only way to deal with Khrushchev. Was he sure that a serious attempt on his life was imminent?"

"I think after Ireland he was pretty well convinced," said Hal.

"What the hell happened in Ireland?"

DUGANSTOWN, IRELAND
July 25, 1963

Devon Clancy stepped down from the lorry and thanked the driver for the ride. He had a few pounds, change from the money Doyle had given him for groceries, in his pocket. The local pub, Delany's, was right across the way. "Coincidence?" he asked himself. "I think not."

Duganstown wasn't what most people would call much of a town at all. It was really a crossroad with a collection of homes, a small store, one church, and two pubs. As Devon walked across the street to Delany's he noticed a number of activities that were taking place. The local shopkeeper was washing his windows while a woman swept the walk in front of the store. Across the way another woman pulled weeds while her husband whitewashed the small fence in front of their home. Two men who appeared to be of some official status stood in the middle of the street pointing at the power poles as if discussing where to hang a banner. The only other pub in town was flying an American flag. It was clear that Duganstown was getting ready for the big visit.

Devon stepped from the bright and sunny day into the dark, smoky pub, stopping just inside the door for a moment to let his eyes adjust. It was mid-afternoon so the only patrons were a few of the village's most dedicated drinkers, every one of them a stranger to Devon. He ordered a pint and sat between two older gentlemen whom he acknowledged with a nod. He had spent more than his fair share of time sitting in a pub and he knew the little dance that was necessary for a stranger to go through.

He sat silently until the man behind the bar set a pint of Guinness in front of him. He waited another minute for the beer to settle and then lifted it, turned slightly to the man to his right and the man to his left and said just loud enough for them to barely hear, "To your health." The man to his right grunted which translated as, "And to your health, as well. Welcome to our little pub." The man to his left didn't make a sound.

Devon took a few sips and set his beer back on the bar as the door behind him opened, flooding the interior of the pub with light. Two more men entered and stood there a moment waiting for their eyes to adjust.

"Quite the weather we've been having," Devon said to the man on his right.

"Brilliant weather," the man replied. "It's good to warm up me old bones after the wet spring we've had."

Devon looked straight ahead rather than at the man himself, "I hope we get a few more days of it for the Americans."

The man sat up a little straighter on his barstool, "Can you believe it? John Fitzgerald Kennedy himself right here in Duganstown? Why it's the biggest thing to happen since I don't know when."

"It is, in fact, a huge happening," Devon agreed. "Have you seen any of the Americans around town yet?" he asked.

"Oh, they've been snooping around here all day. In fact those two blokes over in the corner there eating lunch are part of it all," said the man.

Devon wheeled around and saw two men, dressed in suits too fine to be from this part of Ireland, sitting at a table eating stew. He hadn't noticed them when he first entered. "Well," he said, "I believe I should make them feel welcome here in our fair county. Excuse me for a moment."

Devon picked up his pint and walked over to the two men.

"Hello," one of the men greeted him as he approached their table.

"Good day to you both," Devon said. "A lad at the bar said you might be here with President Kennedy, is that true?"

The agent sitting in the corner slowly slipped his right hand off the table and reached inside his jacket to his right hip. "That's right," he said cautiously.

"There's no need to get your dander up," said Devon. "My name is Clancy. I live on my family's broken-down place up the road a bit here. A group of men just paid me to put them up for a few days but now I'm a little worried about their intentions."

The older of the two agents sized up the man standing before them before saying, "Sit down, Mister Clancy. Tell us more."

Devon pulled a chair from the next table and sat down. "I don't want to offend you, but would you mind showing me some identification?"

The older man reached into the inside pocket of his jacket and pulled out a small wallet which he flipped open showing a Secret Service identification card with his photo on it; the younger man did the same. "I'm Agent Lawson, this is Agent Johnson," said the older of the two. "So what can you tell us about these men and what do you think they are up to?"

"About a week ago, this bloke I know from Dublin shows up at my farm. He promises to pay me a hundred pounds for the use of my home for a few nights, he does. He says to me, he will pay me but I'm to ask no questions and never speak of it, not a word. I figured they were going to move some booze or drugs, maybe even drop a bank or something, and needed a place to hole up for a while."

Agent Lawson listened skeptically while Agent Johonson took out a small notebook and made a few notes. As part of the advance team, it was their job to check out any possible threats. Agent Lawson asked, "What's the name of the man who came to your house?"

Devon looked around the pub to see if anybody was paying them any attention, "The man's name is Kevin Doyle. He is what you Yanks would call a mobster. I know he's been dealing in women and booze in Dublin. I thought it would be exciting to help him out, to have a real mobster staying at my home."

Agent Johnson jumped in, "Why do you think Doyle is up to something?"

"Yesterday, just like he said, he shows up to my farm with three other men. Together, they carried in enough bags and boxes to feed a family for a year. It looked to me as though they figured to stay more than just a few days. Today, they asked me to go to town to get food for them so I knew those boxes weren't full of food. When I get to town, all the talk is about President Kennedy himself coming right here to little County Wexford. I might be a bit of a scamp myself but I'm not going to let these lads harm a hair on the man's fair head, if that's what they're up to."

"Tell us about the other three men," said Lawson.

"They're not Irish, I'll tell you that much for sure. I overheard them talking and they didn't use any type of speech that these ears have ever heard before," said Devon.

Lawson looked at Devon with a more interest. He slowly said, *"mnEn Uzhena PrackickovAt'sa v Russkam."*

Both Devon and Johnson were surprised, "Bloody hell! That sounds just like the men at my house."

Johnson leaned forward, "What the hell did you just say?"

Lawson frowned as his mouth tightened, "I said, 'I need to practice my Russian'."

"Why are you coming to us with this?" asked Agent Johnson, still somewhat suspicious. "You are harboring criminals in your home."

"The way I figure it, Mister Johnson, if they are really going to make a play on Kennedy then they aren't going to want anybody around to talk about it afterwards," said Devon. He looked down at the table, "I'm a dead man either way. It doesn't matter any longer who takes my life but maybe I still have a chance to save Mister Kennedy's."

"Damn fool," Kevin Doyle said to himself when he saw Devon Clancy walk out of the pub with the two men in suits. His suspicions about Devon making up the story about his sick auntie had been right. He ducked around the corner and hurried back to his car then drove back to the Clancy Farm.

Doyle was barely out of the car when the older Russian walked out of the farmhouse. "We need to move, Vlas," said Doyle to the man, Vlas Kalmakoff, who had hired him. "The bloody fokin' farm boy has ratted us out, he has."

Kalmakoff looked at the ground, obviously irritated by the Irishman's lack of diligence. "I was afraid of this, Mister Doyle. Do you have a backup plan?"

"I do," Doyle lied. "If you'll get everything to the car, I'll watch the front road."

Kalmakoff said something in Russian to his two men who immediately jumped into action. "Mister Doyle, we cannot have the farm boy talking anymore."

"I'll take care of it," said Doyle. He had feared from the beginning that he was going to be the one who would have to kill the boy.

Agent Lawson had to think fast. The threat could be real but he felt he needed more information before he alerted the Irish Gardia. While he did some background checks on Doyle he would send Devon back to his home to keep an eye on the men at his farm. He instructed Devon to try to get into the house to see what he could see in the way of weapons and such and then report to him as soon as possible in the small village of Lower Southknock, about a mile north of the Clancy farm.

Devon caught a ride back to his farm from a passing friend. As he walked down his lane, he could feel his knees shaking, his mouth was dry, and if felt as though there was a rat gnawing at the inside of his belly.

As he walked quickly past the house and directly towards the shed, Doyle opened the side door and yelled, "Devon, how is your poor aunt?"

"She's doing fine," he yelled out over his shoulder, "I'll be with you in just a minute's time, Kevin," and continued walking quickly to the shed.

"No time like the present," Doyle said to himself. His plan was simple, walk into the shed and fire before saying a word. There was no reason to let the boy get himself worked up or have a chance to beg for his life. And quite frankly, Doyle wasn't sure he could do it any other way. He wouldn't want his current employers to know but despite his reputation, he had never actually taken another human life.

The door to the shed was closed but unlatched. Doyle pulled a Browning 9mm pistol from his waistband and pulled back the hammer. He kicked the door open with his foot and stepped into the dark shed with the gun leveled and his finger on the trigger. Doyle never saw or heard the blast from the ancient double-barrel shotgun.

Devon was so surprised when Doyle burst through the door with a gun in his hand that he aimed at the man's chest and pulled both triggers as hard as he could. The jerk from his finger on the triggers lifted the barrel and when both blasts hit Doyle in the face, the effect was gruesome. Devon dropped the shotgun and grabbed the nearly decapitated body by the feet and pulled it fully inside the shed. He picked up Doyle's pistol, sat down on his cot and nervously loaded two more shells into the shotgun.

Inside the house, Kalmakoff heard what sounded like a single gunshot. He turned to his two men and said in Russian, "Go make sure it is done and finish Mister Doyle. Then we will go."

Devon saw the two goons emerge from his house with the Walther pistols that Doyle had supplied at the ready. "Doyle?" one of the men yelled. He couldn't speak English but knew the man's name.

"I've got him, come help," yelled Devon.

The two men seemed to become more at ease hearing a friendly Irish voice coming from the shed. They dropped their weapons to their sides and casually walked towards the shed.

The taller of the two walked through the door first. He saw a body on the floor and a man standing over it in the shadows just before he saw the double-barrel pointed at his chest. He dove to the right half a second before the barrels flashed. The second man never stood a chance; he took both barrels solidly in the chest and fell backwards.

Devon realized he had made two fatal errors. Once again he had shot both barrels at once. He also realized he had left Doyle's Browning on his cot. He dove to the cot as the man on the floor fired, the shot just missed him. The Russian fired again at the noise in the corner as Devon recovered the Browning pistol and fired three shots wildly. The first hit the man in the right shoulder, the next two missed. As the wounded man shifted the gun to his left hand Devon took careful aim and squeezed the trigger.

Kalmakoff watched from the window as his two men walked into the shed. He heard the shotgun blast and saw Yosef fall backwards out of the shed. Several shots followed in rapid succession followed by silence. When Nicol didn't reappear, Kalmakoff knew he must be dead. Either the farm boy or Doyle, perhaps both, had just killed two very experienced and two very good men. He had obviously underestimated one or both of the Irishmen. It was clearly time for Kalmakoff to leave this place.

Devon glanced out the door and saw Kalmakoff running towards the car. The Russian fired two cover shots towards the shed. Devon dove out the back window and ran thirty feet to a rock wall built by his great-grandfather. He flung himself over the fence and ran crouched down along it towards the lane. His only thought, his only hope, was to get to the safety of the Americans and the others in the village.

Devon heard the car start and the engine race. He peeked over the top of the wall as Kalmakoff backed wildly out of the farmyard and onto the lane. The driver excitedly ground the gears but found first gear and gunned the engine, spinning the tires in the soft mud. Devon thought about shooting at the driver through the back window as the car accelerated down the lane but decided against it. If the man wanted to leave, Devon was more than willing to let him go. Crouched behind the wall, he watched the car to the end of the lane and then took off in a full run across the field towards town.

Agent Lawson hung up the phone and turned to Johnson. "We need to seriously check out the boy's story. This Doyle fellow is just a low-level hood but he has ties to some of the bigger fish in the Dublin underworld."

Johnson was just about to suggest they make a call to MI-6 in London when they saw Devon running up the street. Johnson stepped outside the small store and yelled, "Over here, Mister Clancy." Just as he yelled, he noticed the boy's blood-soaked coat, "What the hell happened?"

Devon was out of breath. Sweat, mud, and blood streaked across his face. "They tried to kill me. Doyle first, and then the other men."

"Where are they now?" asked Agent Johnson.

Devon fought to control himself, "I shot Doyle and the other two bastards. The older man, he made it away in the car."

Johnson grabbed Devon and pulled him into the store as the shop owner looked on with a shocked expression. "Quiet!" the agent said. "No reason to start a panic here. Settle down and tell me what in the hell happened."

Devon's eyes were wild with panic, "When I got back to me farm, they all came after me, like they knew we'd been talking." He labored to catch his breath, "First, Doyle came at me in the shed but I had me father's shotgun waiting. As soon as I got him, the other two bastards came out and yelled for Doyle. I answered and they thought I was Doyle. I got the first with the shotgun, the second I got with Doyle's gun." He looked into the agent's eyes. "Ya got to believe me, I never wanted to kill anybody. I never did!"

"And the other man?" asked Agent Lawson.

"He drove away in Doyle's car," said Devon. "I don't know where he went, I was just happy to see him go."

Lawson looked at Johnson, "Let's get the locals involved and go out there to see what we can find!"

BOCA RATON, FLORIDA
Present Day

"Can I buy you a cup of coffee, Mike?" said Hal as they wheeled down Camino Real Boulevard towards the ocean.

"Sure, sounds good," said Mahoney just as they turned into the front gate of a posh resort with a long palm-lined drive leading back from the guard shack.

The guard at the gatehouse stepped out and said, "Hello, Hal. How the hell have you been?"

"Hi, Ed. I'm doing okay. How's Fran?" he responded.

"She's doing a little better, thanks for asking. Go right on up," the guard said with a sloppy salute.

Hal waved and started to pull forward then stopped, "Hey, Ed, if a white Ford sedan comes through your gate in the next ten or fifteen minutes, somebody who isn't a guest here, can you get the guy's driver's license and copy down the name for me? Can't tell you why, you understand."

Ed stood up straight and gave a very smart salute, "Yes, sir, official business?"

Hal laughed and said, "I'm just curious about the driver."

"Old friend of yours?" asked Mahoney as Hal let the car idle down the long drive.

"Oh, we used to play a little poker together up until a few years ago," said Hal. "He thinks I'm still a CIA spook. I told him once that I was with the government and mentioned to him another time that I lived in Greece for a lot of years."

"Do you still think you're being watched?" asked Mahoney as he looked over his shoulder.

"Just a little precaution," smiled Hal

As they drove up to the grand old resort, Mahoney changed the subject. "So did the attempt in Ireland ever leak out to the press?"

"Both attempts were hushed up. In recent years there has been talk about some death threats but I don't think anybody knew how serious either of them were," said Hal as he eased the Olds up to the front door. A valet ran to the driver's side of the car and opened the door for Hal.

Hal wasn't usually the type of guy who liked to have much done for him but he loved the opulent feeling that he associated with arriving at the Grand Boca Resort and having his car valet-parked before enjoying lunch or a cocktail.

They walked into the grand old hotel and Mahoney said, "You love dropping little bombs into our conversations. You didn't mention two attempts in Ireland."

Hal laughed, "One if by land, two if by sea."

"What?" asked Mahoney.

ABOARD THE *USS KEARSARGE*
Off the Southern Coast of Ireland
July 27, 1963

After steaming at flank speed from her station in the Far East, the '*Mighty Kay*' now stood watch off the southern coast of Ireland while President Kennedy visited his ancestral homeland. Commander Rod Mills stood behind the bank of sonar and radar technicians in the Combat Information Center (CIC) where he had been since the last report, three hours earlier. For the last five hours they had been receiving sporadic reports of a submerged contact, not confirmed reports, just little hits here and there, only a possible contact but enough to cause Commander Mills to worry. At his disposal were three destroyers, a light cruiser, and his own SH-3A Sea King helicopters equipped with anti-submarine-warfare sonar and torpedoes.

Now cruising an area about 100 miles south of Kinsale, Ireland, and 125 miles due west of Plymouth, England, they had been chasing the phantom contact most of the night. In a few hours, the President of the United States was scheduled to speak at New Ross, a town less than 150 miles to the north. If there was a Soviet sub out here, there wouldn't be time to evacuate the President from New Ross should it launch a missile. Commander Mills had no reason to believe the Russians wanted to launch a missile at Ireland but at the same time he had to question the submarine's intentions and its location, if in fact it was a submarine they were hearing.

As Mills stood leaning against the frame of the empty plotting board, Captain Snodgrass came through the door and silently motioned for Mills to follow him. Once in the corridor Snodgrass held up a piece of paper and said in a hushed tone, "Rod, you're not going to believe this."

Mills waited until a passing seaman walked beyond them, "What is it?"

"I have an order direct from SECNAV. If we encounter and identify a Soviet sub out here before 15:00 Zulu, we are ordered to sink it without provocation," said Snodgrass.

"Jesus H. Christ!" said Mills. "That's in writing?" he asked.

"In writing and verified," answered Snodgrass.

Mills whistled, "Sounds like the Mighty Kay is about to start a war."

"God, I hope not, said Snodgrass. "Keep this on the QT, Rod. It's top secret unless we fire."

Mills nodded and turned back towards CIC. "Damn, what in the hell is going on?" he muttered under his breath.

For the next forty-five minutes, there wasn't much activity in CIC. Mills eyed the clock showing Greenwich Mean Time or "zulu" as it was known in the military. The damn thing wasn't moving very fast towards 15:00. Oddly enough, as much as "zulu" was used as a reference of time in his everyday life, Mills had only been in the "zulu" time zone a few times. He instinctively wanted to add or subtract hours from zulu to convert it to local time but here off the coasts of England and Ireland, no conversion was needed.

Suddenly the speakers above the console panel cracked, "Bishop, this is Vision Two, sonar contact. Fifteen thousand yards, bearing one nine zero, making turns for five knots, submerged." One of the Sea King helicopters had a confirmed contact.

An Ensign standing behind the sonar console answered, "Vision Two, designate contact as Sierra one-six. Close and identify."

Mills picked up the phone on the command console and rang the captain. "Sir, Vision Two has a positive contact, Sierra one-six about 45 miles east-southeast. We are waiting for them to close and identify now."

Petty Officer Second Class Norman Jensen sat at his console aboard Vision Two, a huge twin-engine Sea King helicopter listening to the sounds from his headphones and staring at the scope in front of him. He adjusted the system to pinpoint the exact location of the contact as they flew closer by the moment.

For practice, every contact was considered a target and a firing solution was worked up just in case the Navy ever found the need to fire on a luxury yacht or cruise ship. Before they launched today, however, it was made rather clear that any submerged contact was probably an enemy and would be treated as hostile.

Jensen directed the pilot closer to the contact and with each mile they closed, the sub in the shallow water became an easier prey. When Jensen was sure, when he was 99 percent certain, he hit the button on his console and said, "Bishop, this is Vision Two. Sierra one-six is a Whiskey Class, about two hundred feet at five knots, course one nine zero."

Back on the *Kearsarge*, Mills picked up the phone and waited for the skipper to answer up on the bridge. "Sir, Vision Two confirms Sierra one-six is a Soviet Whiskey Class, moving to the south.

"Son of a bitch," replied Captain Snodgrass. He recomposed himself and said, "We have our order, Commander". "Order the Sea King to fire on target. Bring the ship to General Quarters."

Norman Jensen had been part of the crew on Vision Two for just over six months. He felt he was part of a special team and that he and his fellow sonar tech, Steve Wilkens, who was sitting next to him, were two of the best "sub chasers" in the Navy. Never, or at least rarely, did their foe get away when they were on the chase and now they had found the Whiskey Class before anybody else.

Petty Officer Jensen's feelings of his team's excellence were dampened by the next sound he heard in his headphones, "Vision Two, you are authorized weapons free, mark-four, mark-four."

"Oh shit!" he heard Wilkens say into the intercom, they had just been ordered to drop both of their Mark 44 torpedoes on the Whiskey.

Jensen's brain performed as it had been trained. He began plotting a firing solution to the enemy submarine.

"Bishop, verify weapons free, Sierra one-six, for Vision Two" said Wilkens into his boom mike.

The answer was immediate and unmistakable and even delivered with that certain tone of command that Navy personnel knew better than to question, "Vision Two, you are authorized weapons free, Sierra one-six, mark-four, mark-four."

Jensen keyed the intercom, "Final solution set; Chappy, bring us to one three zero and launch altitude."

The chopper banked around to the left and dove before settling at a course and altitude; the pilot's voice sounded as calm as if this was simply another training exercise, "One three zero, two hundred feet and stable."

Jensen looked over at Wilkens who glanced at him and shrugged his shoulders in a look of helplessness. Wilkens pressed a button on his console and the helicopter bounced as the 342 pound weight of the Mark 44 torpedo fell from the underbelly. "Mark one is away," he said over the radio. He counted to ten and pushed a second button which caused a similar bounce, "Mark two is away."

WASHINGTON, D.C.
July 29, 1963

Evelyn Lincoln poked her head into the President's office, "Sir, the Attorney General just called; he and the Secretary of Defense are on their way over and would like a few minutes of your time."

Kennedy looked up and verbally groaned, he knew they wanted to talk about Khrushchev. "How is my schedule, Evelyn?"

"You have a meeting with Terrence Bond at ten. It's his first time here so I can have a staffer give him a quick tour and buy you a half-hour."

"Excellent. Thank you, Evelyn."

Ten minutes later the intercom on the President's desk buzzed at the same time that Bobby came though his office door with Bob McNamara on his heels. Kennedy saw the serious looks on their faces but hoped he could throw them off track. "Hello Bob, Bobby. Evelyn found some fresh bagels and cream cheese. Care for one with a cup of coffee?"

Bobby didn't hear a word, "Jack, they tried for you twice in Ireland."

"I'll get Maurice to run them down and toast the bagels if you like," said the President.

"What?" asked Bobby.

"Your bagel," Jack continued with a straight face. "Would you like your bagel toasted or not?"

McNamara couldn't help but smile at the president's humor, "Nothing for me, Mister President."

"Damn it, Jack," said Bobby. "They tried to kill you twice in Ireland. He's going to keep trying until he's successful and now it doesn't appear that he cares how many others he kills along with you."

The President got up from his desk chair and walked over to the window. "What happened in Ireland?"

McNamara pulled a piece of paper from a folder, "First of all, sir, we believe that there was a hit squad planning something around New Ross. It appears to have been a poorly-planned, ill-conceived attempt at best. Three men, probably Russians but unconfirmed, hired a local mobster to help them. They rented a home from a local farmer who actually tipped off our guys. Then the farmer got into a shootout with them and killed two of the Russians and the Irish mobster, a third man got away. We found a variety of weapons including a sniper's rifle and a U.S.-made bazooka." McNamara winced, "There are still a bunch of those lying around Europe from the war, sir."

"That is one handy Irish sod farmer," commented Kennedy with a slight laugh.

"Devon Clancy, sir," said McNamara. "Early twenties, he's had several brushes with the locals himself but told our guys he couldn't let the Russians harm you."

The President turned away from the window to face the men, "Can we send him a nice bottle of something? I'll write a personal note to go along with it. And perhaps we should give his name to the CIA. That is either one very lucky farmer, or a young fellow who is very good."

McNamara took out his pen, "I'll take care of both, sir."

Bobby had stayed uncharacteristically quiet but now ended his silence, "Jack, it's the second attempt that I am far more worried about."

Kennedy laughed, "I'm glad that one attempt on my life has you more worried than another. I lay awake at night worried about them all."

Bobby didn't laugh and seemed again to ignore the President's attempt at levity. "A Sea King off the *Kearsarge* dropped two torpedoes on a Russian Whiskey Class that was sitting off the southern coast of Ireland."

President Kennedy's head snapped around, "Damn it! When?"

"On the morning of the 27th, Sir," said McNamara.

The President was instantly and obviously angry, "Why am I first hearing about this two days later?"

Bobby stepped forward, "We think the Russian got away. One of the torpedoes failed on launch, the other exploded but there is no evidence that we sank the Whiskey. We were unable to reacquire her after the initial attack."

Bobby's explanation didn't quell the President's anger. "Bobby, Mac? Why am I first hearing about an attack on a Russia submarine 48 hours after the incident?"

"We don't know for sure that it was a Russian, sir," said McNamara.

"You just said it was a Whiskey Class."

McNamara let out an audible sigh, "Yes, sir. The *Kearsarge* identified it as a Whiskey Class but according to our sources at Soviet Fleet, there were no Whiskey Class subs deployed, no subs are currently missing, and there have been no reports of hostile activities at any level of the Soviet Command."

"So, was it misidentified? A Chinese sub, or somebody else?" asked the President.

"Perhaps," said Bobby. "There is one other possible explanation. In January of 1961, the Soviets lost a Whiskey Class with all hands in the Barents Sea. They have never located the wreckage of their sub," he glanced down at his notes, "the *S-80*. We have have received sporadic reports that the Russians have at least one sub that nobody can explain."

"I don't understand, what would be the purpose of such a submarine?" asked the President.

"If you wanted to have a sub, and a crew for very black missions," answered Bobby, "missions that you may later want to deny such as sinking the *Thresher* or launching a missile at the U.S. President while he is giving a speech in Ireland, you may want to keep a sub around that nobody knows about. That way you could prove the locations of all of your other subs and deflect any blame to another direction."

"That sounds like you're reaching," said the President.

"I hope so, Jack," his brother answered.

ABOARD THE SOVIET SUBMARINE, *S-80*
NORTH ATLANTIC SEA
July 29, 1963

Captain Naryshkin headed aft to survey the repairs himself. The nearby explosion from the American torpedo had shaken his submarine as if it was a toy in the mouth of a dog. He first thought there had been only minor damage but the housing of the snorkel valve continued to leak from a growing and worrisome crack. After the attack, they had been able to lie silently on the bottom for six hours until the American Fleet moved to the south. Then they crept farther out into the Atlantic where they were able to get the crippled *S-80* to the surface just before her batteries lost all power. As they cruised to the north on their diesel engines, the pumps were just able to keep up with the flooding but only because the cracked housing remained mostly above the waterline. If the *S-80* had to dive to avoid detection, or if the weather worsened and caused more swells to wash across the growing crack, the pumps might not be enough.

His welder, a novice but the only qualified man on board, had tried his best but the crack was in a difficult, hard to access location. It would be a tricky repair even by an expert welder once they made it back to the shipyard at Gremikha, which was still 2500 miles away.

Everything was difficult when it came to the *S-80*, the Captain thought. His crew begged to have their lives back. His command was virtually a one-ship navy with no support from other ships or his own countrymen. The mission of S-80 was to avoid detection by all governments. Even in Gremikha, the submarine was hidden away and Naryshkin and his crew were sequestered in special quarters under guard. They sailed only under the protection of darkness and were not allowed to use their radios for anything other than listening to orders.

The S-80 had reportedly been sunk with all hands, lost in a remote area of the Atlantic Ocean where the wreckage would never be found. More than once it had occurred to Naryshkin that when his government was done with him and his boat, he and his crew couldn't simply resurface from the dead. He quelled those thoughts. He was a man true to his party. His mission was for the good of his motherland and not his or his crew's to question.

BOCA RATON, FLORIDA
Present Day

The Grand Boca Resort main dining room was magnificent. Built in the opulent style of the 1920s, remodeled in the '50s, and brought back to its original splendor just a few years earlier, the Grand Boca was fitted with granite tile floors and massive columns rising to the high ceiling. Palms and other plants were used to soften the look of the hard floors and massive columns but it was impossible to hide the grandeur of the room's original design.

A young and pretty waitress brought two cups of coffee and a cinnamon roll for Mahoney while the two men chatted about the history of the resort. Once the waitress had moved beyond earshot, Mahoney glanced around and then leaned forward, "Okay, what happened in Ireland?"

Hal took a sip of his coffee, "They do make damn good coffee here, Mike." He leaned back in his chair. "There were two attempts. The first was a kill squad of three or four men, probably Russians. It was a simple plan; they were either going to take JFK out by sniper or take his helicopter down with an RPG. Sometimes the simplest plans are the easiest ones to pull off. This one failed because some Irish farm boy figured it out and killed several of them with his grandfather's old scattergun."

"What was the other attempt?" asked Mahoney.

"The Soviets tried to get a submarine close enough to launch a missile, close enough that there wouldn't be enough warning to get Jack out."

"What happened?" asked Mahoney.

"We found the sub. We chased it around with a couple of torpedoes but the Navy didn't think they got it and the Russians never reported anything missing so it must have gotten away," said Hal.

Mahoney looked at the table while thinking. "Were the Kennedy brothers convinced that it was the Russians behind all of this?"

"They must have been certain to some degree. Certain enough to justify the biggest cover-up in history," said Hal

"Can you prove any of this, either of the attempts in Ireland?" asked Mahoney.

"Nope, I can only tell you what Jack told me."

WASHINGTON, D.C.
August 1, 1963

President John Kennedy walked back from recording his speech that would be broadcast in a few hours across the nation's radio waves with a feeling of disgust. He had just spent twenty-two minutes talking about the newly installed hot line that provided direct access between the Kremlin and the White House. He had talked about the new era of peace, a new level of understanding and the anticipation of great change in the relationship between these two countries . . . and he didn't believe a single word of it.

The hot line, known as the Red Telephone, was a full-time duplex wire telegraph circuit, based on the idea that spontaneous and immediate communications could prevent miscommunications and misperceptions. The circuit was routed Washington-London-Copenhagen-Stockholm-Helsinki-Moscow with the Washington-London link carried over the new transatlantic submarine telephone cable.

While the new direct link would help prevent the type of time delays that had nearly caused a war during the Cuban Missile Crisis, Kennedy was under no illusion that it would ease the current tense issues with the Soviet leadership, Khrushchev in particular.

Bob McNamara was waiting outside the President's private office and he had that look on his face.

"Hi, Bob, come on in," said Kennedy, maintaining an upbeat tone of voice.

Kennedy opened his office door and motioned for McNamara to walk in ahead of him. He followed and closed the door behind them. "What's up, Bob?"

"I have another dispatch from Roman," he replied.

Kennedy found it amusing that McNamara was still using the man's codename when it was well known among the inner circle that Roman was Brezhnev. "And what does Roman have to say today?"

McNamara reached into his briefcase and pulled out a piece of paper. "I brought you a copy. He is mainly passing along additional information regarding Khrushchev's diminishing mental state, but he also warns of the potential of submarine-launched missile attacks against Pig."

Kennedy laughed, "He's a few days late with that warning."

"Or perhaps a few days early?" commented McNamara.

"Do you think they might try again?" asked Kennedy, while glancing at a wall map of the United States. The short distance between the Atlantic Ocean and Washington, D.C., seemed to shrink as he was looking at the map.

McNamara looked at the copy of the dispatch, "You will notice that the word 'attacks' is plural."

Kennedy's mind immediately went to Jackie, Caroline, and John, Jr., who were all upstairs in the residence at that very moment. Perhaps it was time for them to take a little secret trip to somewhere in the middle of the country. "Any suggestions?"

"I think we should seriously consider Bobby's idea," said McNamara. "We have done some initial planning and I think we can pull it off in the next few months."

"We cannot be seriously considering that as a real alternative, can we?" asked the President.

"Unless we can come up with something else, some way to keep that nut from dropping a missile in your cornflakes, sir, I think we have to consider it."

"I cannot believe we would really consider such a thing. Have we assessed the political and economic impacts?" asked Kennedy.

"We're working on all the likely scenarios now, sir," answered McNamara.

Jack looked at the floor, "Damn."

ABOARD THE SOVIET SUBMARINE, *S-80*
NORTH ATLANTIC SEA
August 2, 1963

Captain Naryshkin had been warm under the covers in his bunk when his Executive Officer woke him. He had been dreaming of being at home with his wife and daughters enjoying a gentle conversation with laughter in the cozy kitchen of his small home. In seconds he went from those warm thoughts to the cold reality that the aft pump had failed and the water in the engine room was rapidly rising. Naryshkin could feel *S-80* wallowing in the worsening seas, a sure sign that she was heavy and flooding.

He hurried through the control room where the radio operator asked if he should contact fleet for help. There was officially no *S-80* and, therefore no possibility of asking for help. "Nyet" was the Captain's short reply to the frightened seaman.

As the Captain and the XO rushed to the engine room, they encountered water on the deck. Just before stepping through the open watertight door there was a brilliant flash of blue light and a loud pop. Naryshkin felt an electrical charge hit his feet and climb his legs in the brief moment before all the lights went out. He felt along the wall for an emergency lantern and flipped it on before removing it from its mount. The acrid smell of ozone and burnt flesh hit him as he stepped through the door. Two bodies lay in the water near the relay circuit for the aft pump. They were both dead from electrocution, one he recognized as his chief electrician.

The designers of the *S-80* submarine had anticipated the possibility a pump failing and had designed a system that allowed the next pump forward, at mid-ship to take up the slack. What the designers had failed to plan for was a massive amount of flooding in the engine room and only a two inch pipe to move great amounts of water forward. They also didn't think through the problem that if you diverted the pumping ability of one pump to another area, there would be no pump to cover flooding in that particular section.

As the weather worsened the *S-80* continued to flounder. The water coming through the crack in the snorkel valve housing was increasing by the minute despite the crew's attempt to plug the leak with anything they could get to it, including their own clothes. The diesel engine was submerged and failed just before 4:30 a.m. The backup electric motors failed just fifteen minutes later. Captain Naryshkin ordered his crew to abandon ship but it was too late. Water poured through the open escape hatches and only eleven men were able to scramble out the hatch at the top of the sail but they had no raft and no life jackets. In the North Atlantic, they would survive in the cold water for less than fifteen minutes. With no propulsion and too much water aft, *S-80* slid backwards beneath the swells. She wouldn't be found for five years.

WASHINGTON, D.C.
August 11, 1963

It was the first time that many of the twelve men seated around the conference table in the White House Situation room had ever actually been in that room. Most of them had no idea why the meeting had been called or why they were told to keep even their summons to the White House under wraps.

Secretary McNamara entered the room first. "Good morning, gentlemen," he said as he opened his briefcase on the large conference table. He proceeded in a rapid but professional tone, "Most of you know each other so I will dispense with introductions. You have each been asked here to discuss a matter of the highest security. The future of our country depends on the actions of this group," he said as he started passing forms around to each man at the table.

"The form before you that you will be asked to sign is a strict confidentiality agreement. Should you agree to the terms, you will be entering into a contract that will prohibit you from ever speaking of the contents of this meeting along with future meetings and correspondences associated with this mission. Breach of this contract will be grounds for prosecution under the provisions of the U.S. Treason Act. If you are unwilling or unable to agree to the terms of the agreement now in your hands, I would ask that you walk out of this meeting now and never speak of your involvement with this group again."

A few of the twelve men at the table looked at each other but none of them made a move to leave. After reading through the form in their hands, each of them signed, dated it, and passed it back to McNamara.

McNamara looked over each form to confirm that it had indeed been signed and when he checked all twelve forms, he placed them carefully into his briefcase and began. "Gentlemen, we have a very serious situation with the Soviets."

"Approximately ten months ago we began receiving back-channel communications from an unidentified source within the Soviet government. Based on the type and validity of the information received, we quickly determined that the contact was not only valid but somebody well placed in Moscow, possibly even a member of, or somebody close to a member of the Politburo."

McNamara paced back and forth at the head of the table, "The contact, known only to us as 'Roman,' wanted the American President to be aware that many within the Soviet leadership were greatly concerned about the declining mental health of Secretary Khrushchev. Of even greater concern to us was the information provided regarding Khrushchev's growing anger towards President Kennedy. Apparently, the Secretary blames our President for his loss of face in the Cuban Missile Crisis and also blames him for the subsequent damage to his own political standing within the Politburo."

McNamara paused for a moment, then he reached into his briefcase and retrieved a manila folder which he opened on the table and from which he pulled out a single document. "Normally, we would consider such information to be hearsay and investigate it through the normal channels. This threat, however, has become all too real."

"In the past several months," he continued, looking at the document in his hand, "there have been multiple threats against both the President and our nation." He reached into the manila folder and pulled out a small pack of papers and passed half down each side of the table. "The most serious of these are summarized on the document in your hands. They include the Washington,

D.C., arrest of a former KGB agent who is a known assassin and evidence that the Russian Navy may have been involved in the sinking of the *USS Thresher*. Two incidents that occurred during the president's visit to Europe last month may have ties to the Soviets. The first was the identification and neutralization of a hit squad in Ireland and the other was the detection of a submarine only a hundred miles off the south coast of Ireland while Kennedy was making a visit to New Ross. Please be clear that neither of the Irish events has been confirmed as having direct ties to the USSR at this time."

McNamara spent the next eight minutes outlining the information they had received from Roman, never using Brezhnev's name or identifing Roman as anything but a "very qualified source high in the Soviet leadership.

When he was finished he looked up from his outline and saw in the twelve faces what he was hoping to see, fear and hopelessness.

"As bad as it sounds," he stated, "we have a plan. The plan is not legal. The plan involves a huge deception of the American public and the world in general. And the only way to make the proposed plan work is with the full cooperation of the men in this room. Each of you will be risking your reputations and your political future by even acknowledging the existence of the proposal we will be placing in your trust. But I assure you it is for the good of our nation."

McNamara made eye contact with each man at the table without saying a word. After a long pause he continued. "Again, if you would like to leave you may do so now, but this is your last and final chance." Not a man moved.

McNamara picked up the phone on the table in front of him, dialed a two-digit number and said, "Please tell the President we are ready for him." The men glanced nervously around the table, each wondering what the next few hours held for him.

A few moments later, when the President of the United States and his brother, the Attorney General, walked into the room, every man seated at the conference table jumped to his feet.

"Sit down gentlemen," said the President as he walked over to his chair at the head of the conference table and stood behind it as the other men took their seats. He spoke directly and precisely. "I assume Mac has briefed each of you on the situation with Secretary Khrushchev. It is our belief that he will make another attempt on my life again in the next few months. If he does, even if he is unsuccessful, it would likely start a war. Any attempt by us to assassinate the Secretary or organize a coup to remove him, probably will have the same results. We are short on options. You have each been hand-chosen to serve on this committee and it will be your responsibility to maintain world peace at all costs."

Kennedy looked directly at each of the men around the table, "I assume you have also been briefed on my proposed plan, at least as it now stands?"

McNamara turned, "Actually, sir, they have not yet been briefed. I didn't expect you to be so expedient when I called."

Kennedy looked surprised, "Then, if I may, I'll share with these men how we intend to keep world order despite the intentions of the lunatic leader at the helm of the USSR."

McNamara gave a slight bow saying, "By all means, sir."

Kennedy took a deep breath and looked at the floor for a moment while he gathered his thoughts. "Gentlemen, we have been going over options for the last six months. By the way, if anybody can come up with a better idea than the plan were about to present, I'll buy you the best bottle of Scotch available."

Each man around the table chucked quietly before the President continued. "The mental state of Secretary Khrushchev seems to be worsening by the day. He sees me as Satan and is convinced that the only way to restore his power within the party is to eliminate Satan. Based on recent events and on information received from informants inside Moscow, both from the Soviets and from our own assets, we believe that Khrushchev may go to any extreme to achieve his goal. Therefore, the Secretary of Defense, the Attorney General, and I have come to the conclusion that I should remove myself from office in a very dramatic and very public manner."

Uncomfortable talking about the details, Kennedy motioned to McNamara. "Bob will fill you in on how this plan will work."

Robert McNamara stood again, "Gentlemen, our plan is to fake an assassination of the President of the United States." The room went from completely silent to a hushed murmur of whispers and quiet comments.

Jim Rowley, Director of the Secret Service, was the first to speak up. "With all due respect, have you lost your minds?"

Kennedy turned, "We probably have, Jim. However, my offer to buy a bottle for the man who comes up with a better idea still stands." Kennedy waited a moment then continued, "You, Jim, even more than the other men in this room, know of the heightened level of threat and the possible methods in which the Soviets may try to carry this out."

Rowley pushed his chair back from the table, as if he was pushing himself away from the group and the plan. "Sir, you cannot actually believe that you can pull off a fake assassination in such a convincing manner that the public will not question it?"

"I believe we can, Jim," said the President.

The room now erupted into a tense argument among the men who were present. Kennedy stood silent and allowed the men around the table to voice their opinions for about thirty seconds before he again took control of the meeting by simply raising his hand. Silence was immediately restored.

"What I'm hearing," said Kennedy in a calm voice, "is that you don't like the book in front of you but not one of you has yet opened the book. If you will give us a few minutes, we would like to explain the plan to you. Then we would be greatly interested in hearing your opinions." Kennedy slowly pulled out his chair and sat down. "Bob, will you give us an outline of the proposal?"

"Yes, sir," said McNamara. He reached into his briefcase and pulled out another document. The piece of paper in his hand only held a few lines of text but the Secretary was convinced that a leader looked more believable if he was referring to a document in discussions such as these.

"Gentlemen," he paused, "in the next two or three months, the President of the United States will be assassinated by a sniper's bullet in a public venue. The assassin will be arrested, and in the subsequent trial, it will become apparent to all that he shot the President purely for reasons of establishing his own notoriety. The person we have tapped for the plan is a young man who will appear simply to be craving fame, not unlike the motives of many of history's assassins."

McNamara paused and glanced at the nearly blank document in his hand before continuing, "After the assassination, the President will be secretly transported to a remote location where he will live until we determine how to explain our actions to the American public in such a manner as not to undermine their trust in the government . . . if possible."

Kennedy leaned forward, his elbows on the table. "We have spent months going over options. It is only through pure luck and some fortunate intelligence that the Soviets have not yet been able to launch a missile at this very building." The men around the table shot each other concerned glances.

"Khrushchev has tried his best to goad us into a war. He has made attempts on my life both here in Washington and in Ireland. Now there is growing concern that out of frustration he may use any means, even nuclear options, to achieve his goal."

Kennedy paused for effect; his hands were on the table and he twisted his wedding ring around his finger several times before continuing. "I cannot, I will not allow innocent people to die when a simple solution exists. I will step down from the presidency and go into hiding for the remainder of my life, if necessary, if it will save the life of one American."

Chuck Thornton, a mid-level section director with the Secret Service raised his hand tentatively.

"Yes, Mr. Thornton?" asked the President.

"Assuming you can stage a convincing assassination, where in this day and age do you hide the President of the United States for months or even years?"

"That's a very good question, Mr. Thornton," said the President, "but one that we do not intend to answer here. This entire plan is compartmentalized. Very few people will know all the details. Each of you is now aware of the general plan because each of you is an integral part of it. Some of you will be briefed on specifics, some of you will not. Some of you will be told where I am living but many of you will not. If this fails, each of you will only be held accountable for a small part of the overall scheme."

The President rose slowly from his chair. It was evident that his back was aching. "Vice President Johnson, for instance, will know nothing of this plot. If we are found out, it is very important that his hands are clean. We need to make sure the American public can continue to trust their President. We need to make sure that the public maintains a belief in their government in the days after the cover-up is discovered. Are there any other questions?" Kennedy asked.

"Gentlemen," said the President after a long pause, "this is clearly an act of desperation. It is not how I envisioned my presidency would end. It is not the legacy I hoped to leave in the history books but it is the hand that God has dealt us and the hand we must now play as best we can. The future of our country, both throughout the next few months and for the next hundred years rests heavily on the actions of the men around this table. I want each of you to know how much I appreciate the risks you are taking. If we fail, if the plan is discovered, I hope history eventually will be kind to the few present here in our attempt to protect the many."

President John Kennedy stood and walked out of the room alone.

"When you mentioned this to me a few months ago," said Ted Sorensen, "I probably didn't voice my opinion strongly enough because it was such an outlandish plan. I never thought it would become anything more than a crazy idea that would die after five minutes of consideration," he continued as he paced the floor of the Oval Office in front of Kennedy's desk.

Ted Sorensen, Kennedy's speech writer and one of his top advisors, was a stark contrast to Kennedy in nearly every way. He had been born to a middle-class family in Nebraska; his political, religious, and moral views were often completely different than Kennedy's. He wore horned rim glasses and off-the-rack suits with plain ties and was probably as liberal as liberals came in the early sixties. Ted Sorensen was one of the assets that made Kennedy the politician that he was. He often took on the roll of the devil's advocate in conversations with the President.

"Ted, if you can come up with a better idea I'm happy to hear it," said the President.

"Damn it, Mister President, Jack," said Sorensen out of frustration, he hadn't called Kennedy by his first name since the inauguration. "I don't have a better idea but this one certainly cannot work. And when it tumbles down, you will undermine the Presidency, the government, and your family's reputation. The backlash from this will last for decades."

Kennedy respected Sorensen; he always had and always would. But his back was against the wall and he said, "That's why it's up to you and the men around that table to make this work. We are out of choices, Ted."

Kennedy reached into his desk drawer and pulled out a file clearly marked "Eyes Only," a top secret designation, and laid the file on his desk. "I just learned that Khrushchev is backing the North Vietnamese. He knows we'll do just about anything to stop the spread of communism in Asia, and now he's in there promoting it. The man is doing everything he can to goad us into war, we cannot let that happen. Give me another option, Ted. Give me something or get on board with what we've got."

Sorensen looked at his friend. Even in the darkest days of the campaign, in the late hours of the Cuban Crisis, and even after the death of his newborn baby, Ted Sorensen thought, his friend had never looked so tired and so defeated.

WASHINGTON, D.C.
November 21, 1963

President Kennedy was up earlier than usual and surprised several members of the White House staff as he walked around the historic building and grounds. Later many of them would comment that the President seemed contemplative and maybe even melancholy that morning, perhaps taking a last look at the trappings of his Presidency as though he somehow knew he wouldn't returning to Washington.

Kennedy knew that it was important he act as normal as possible that morning in light of the following day's plans but he rose early after a sleepless night. He dressed and strolled the halls, looking at the paintings of past presidents, Washington, Lincoln, Truman, Roosevelt, and others. He wondered if, based on the same circumstances, they would have made the same decision as he had made. He stopped to talk with the housekeeper dusting in the East

Room, taking the opportunity to compliment her and the staff in general. He asked the guard at the South Doorway what time he came to work; he had seen the man there nearly every morning for as long as he had been President but had never said more than "Good morning" to him before today. He made his way back to the residential quarters where he had breakfast with his family. He didn't know how the events of the following day would turn out, he didn't know if this was the last time he would enjoy such a breakfast for many months, as was the plan, or even if this might be the last time he would ever have this opportunity.

After breakfast, the president made a brief stop in his office to finish a draft of a message asking Congress for an additional $95 million in supplemental appropriations for fiscal year 1964. As he and Jackie walked down the path towards Marine One, the presidential helicopter, he heard footsteps rapidly approaching and turned to find Ted Sorensen running after him with some additional notes he would need for his comments at the evening's dinner honoring Representative Albert Thomas in Houston.

Kennedy had the urge to hug his counselor, speech writer and confidant of more than ten years but he simply took the notes and said, "See you on the other side, buddy."

Sorensen stood for a few moments longer and watched the helicopter lift off and fly over the trees before returning to his office. Staff members who also witnessed his actions noted that it was out of character for the Special Counsel to stand in the cold to watch the president's departure. They would later wonder if perhaps he had also felt in his heart a sense of foreboding.

ABOARD *AIR FORCE ONE*
November 21. 1963

Kennedy took a few moments to freshen up before they landed in Houston. As he splashed water on his face, he looked at his reflection in the mirror and, not for the first time, asked himself if he was really going to go through with the plan he and his team had worked out. For months, he and Bobby, Bob McNamara, Ted Sorensen, Ken Galbraith and several others had gone over the possible reactions to both the successful outcome of the plan or of its catastrophic failure. They had taken into account the economic factors, the reaction from the Soviets, the reaction from the U.S. allies, the impact on the American public's faith and trust in their government, and a hundred other factors that had been identified. And then, as any good plan required, they analyzed potential outcomes if they chose to do nothing. Time and time again, the Dallas plan came out as the best option, even above taking no action and simply praying for the best possible outcome with the Russians.

The great unknown factor in the plan was how long would it take for the USSR to peacefully remove Khrushchev from power. Back-channel information still led Kennedy to believe the situation was not improving in Moscow but to his knowledge there hadn't been any more attempts on his life since Ireland.

He looked into the mirror as he dried his face with an *Air Force One* monogrammed towel and silently asked himself one more time, "Are you really going to do this?"

BOCA RATON, FLORIDA
Present Day

Hal finished his coffee as Mahoney feverishly wrote down the high points of their conversation in his notebook. Scanning the room, Hal saw only the regular clientele he would expect to see there. He might be imagining that he was being tailed but the coincidences were piling up too fast for him to ignore them.

"So how did they actually pull it off?" asked Mahoney. "How did they convince so many people the assassination was real?"

Hal leaned back, "Hollywood theatrics," he said with a grin. "They rigged a tank of compressed air into the trunk of the limo and ran an air hose to a rig under the President's coat. He was wearing a tube taped to his back filled with his own blood and pieces of skull and brain fragments from a cadaver.

The first shot was designated as a miss. It was Jack's signal to get ready. The second shot was the shot to his neck. He reached for his throat where the release valve was and when he heard the third shot, he turned the valve and the compressed air blew the contents of the tube out of the nozzle taped to the collar of his jacket. Then all he had to do was fall over into Jackie's lap and stay there for the ride to the hospital."

Even though Mahoney's digital recorder was running he continued to write feverishly, mostly noting follow-up questions. "So every bit of it was staged and rehearsed?" he asked.

"Well, they rehearsed it a couple of times but never with the gunfire and the blood. It almost didn't come off and it's pretty amazing it still hasn't ever been detected as a hoax."

Mahoney leaned forward, "How so?"

"Well, first of all, Jackie was completely unprepared for the blood and gore. She was supposed to have stayed in her seat but she panicked; she thought it was real even though she knew what was going to happen and when and where. Clint Hill, the agent who climbed onto the back of the car and pushed Jackie back into the limo, almost missed the car all together. He reacted a couple of seconds too late and then nearly fell off because the driver accelerated a few seconds early. His job was to shield the President's head from view on the trip to the hospital and to have it covered with his jacket when they got there."

Hal looked around him to double- check there was nobody paying attention to them or standing close enough to hear. He leaned forward, "Secondly, and perhaps more amazing, is that nobody has ever checked the bone and brain fragments from the street and the car against the President's DNA."

"Why not?" asked Mahoney.

"I don't know," said Hal. "In 1963, nobody had heard of DNA. They were careful to get brain and skull fragments from a cadaver with the same blood type as Jack but that's as far as science went in those days. If somebody got hold of that evidence today, it would scream of a cover-up," said Hal.

Mahoney wrote for a few more seconds then looked up, "If the samples didn't match the President's DNA, you would have to conclude that either somebody had switched the evidence samples sometime during the last fifty years - and wonder why anybody would do that - or the evidence would support everything you are telling me."

"That's right. It gets even better. There's one other interesting piece of evidence nobody has ever really looked into," said Hal with a devilish smile.

"What's that?"

"Have you seen the Zepruder film?" Hal asked.

"Yeah, a couple of hundred times," answered Mahoney, a note of renewed interest in his voice.

"There's too much blood," said Hal.

"What do you mean?"

Hal glanced around the room once again, "In the frame that shows the impact of the bullet to Jack's head, there's too much blood, skull, and brain matter flying around. The guys from Hollywood who helped build the rig were always trying to make things look dramatic for films. Remember the movies where a small car explodes as though the gas tank held a hundred gallons of fuel, or when a 200 pound man gets shot with a .38 caliber pistol and is blown ten feet across the room? They wanted this to be convincing but they grossly miscalculated the amount of blood and tissue needed, they had more than two pints loaded in the tube on Jack's back. There was enough shit flying around for ten headshots," laughed Hal.

"And nobody has ever noticed that before?" asked Mahoney.

"A few experts have brought it up from time to time. It was even brought up in the Warren Commission hearings but it didn't appear in the final report. Nobody has that much blood in their head, not even Jack Kennedy," Hal chuckled.

"Unbelievable," said Mahoney, making a few more notes before asking, "Okay, so the President appears to be shot, the limo is racing to the hospital, what about Governor Connolly? He was wounded also, wasn't he?"

Hal smiled, "Another great American. Connolly spent a month in the hospital. He actually had some plastic surgery done to look like scars from bullet wounds, and then he lied his ass off to everybody from the Dallas police to the Warren Commission."

"What was his motivation for doing all that?" asked Mahoney.

"His motivation?" Hal asked. "He was asked to serve his country at a critical time. As I recall, either Bobby or Bob McNamara flew down to Texas and told him what was going on and what they needed from him. He and his wife volunteered. She was even willing to take a fake bullet for her country, according to Jack. He always spoke very highly of the two of them."

Mahoney rocked back in his chair as he took it all in. "Un-fucking-believable," he said before catching himself. "Oh, excuse me Hal."

"Oh, don't worry about it, Mike. I cussed a lot myself in those first couple of months after Dallas," said Hal.

Mahoney laughed, "I'll bet you did."

The waitress showed up with the check which Mahoney grabbed before Hal could get his hands on it. As he slipped a couple of bills into the vinyl-covered folder he said, "I've got a thousand follow-up questions Hal, but I don't want to overdo it. How are you feeling?"

Hal put his hand to his stomach and said, "I actually feel pretty good right now, but let's get out of here. How about we take a walk along the beach before it gets too damn hot?"

Mahoney pushed his chair back, "Sounds perfect!"

The humidity was already creeping up into the uncomfortable range and the sun was beating down on them. Both men were sweating as they pulled up to the security gate. "Any sign of our friend, Ed?" Hal asked.

Ed said, grinning from ear to ear, "He drove by here a couple of times, a middle-aged guy in a white Ford sedan. He was eyeballing the place and me real good, Hal. All I could get is a partial license number but I called the police and told them it looked like a drug deal was going down," Ed was laughing. "The locals probably have him pulled over somewhere and are asking him a bunch of questions."

Hal smiled, "Thanks, Ed, you have great instincts. If we were both fifty years younger, I'd recommend you for service." As they drove away, Ed beamed; the compliment had made him feel that he was fifty years younger.

After driving a few miles, Hal pulled into a large parking lot next to the beach with plenty of empty spaces. He handed the attendant at the gate eight dollars and took a spot close to the sidewalk that bordered the beach. He pushed the switch that raised the top before getting out. "Don't bother locking the door, Mike.

I've found that if somebody wants to get into a convertible down here, it's better to just let them in rather than give them a reason to cut the top."

They walked south along the winding concrete sidewalk at a comfortable pace. A slight breeze blew in off the ocean which helped alleviate the rising heat and humidity. "What can you tell me about the hospital, Hal?" asked Mahoney.

"Well, I know how they pulled it off there, if that's what you're asking," said Hal after a brief pause.

"That's exactly what I'm wondering. It seems like that would be the place where the whole plan could have fallen apart."

"I wish I had been there," Hal chuckled. "Jack broke out laughing every time he talked about it or watched the films."

Mahoney studied the old man for a moment, "That seems like an odd reaction to watching a film of your own death."

"I guess you're right but in Jack's view it was all pretty damn funny. He told me that from the moment he flipped the valve that released the blood, he couldn't stop laughing. All he could do is fall over in the car seat but Jackie flipped out and tried to crawl over the trunk of the car. He said he was laughing uncontrollably while yelling at Jackie to get back in the car. He said he laughed all the way to Parkland because the amount of blood and gore and the reaction of Jackie, the Connollys, and the three agents in the car.

Can you imagine that scene? Jackie was furious at Jack, Connolly was trying hard to make himself look convincingly injured, Jack couldn't stop laughing, and Clint Hill was trying to get everybody focused on their appropriate roles before they got to Parkland. Apparently, it was a wild four-mile mile ride to the hospital."

An elderly couple stood on the edge of the sidewalk looking out towards the ocean as Mahoney and Hal walked past. Mahoney held his next question until they were safely past them and out of earshot. "Do you know how they made everything look convincing at the hospital?"

Hal stopped walking as they reached the shade of a small group of palms, "It was a lot of planning and a bunch of luck, according to Jack." Hal pulled a handkerchief out of his back pocket and wiped his brow. "The Service created a communications glitch so the hospital wasn't notified that the motorcade was heading their way with the injured President. There would have been forty or fifty people waiting if they had received the message correctly but it was garbled. Just a few people actually saw Jack's limp body lifted out of the car and onto a gurney, and his head was wrapped with Clint Hill's jacket. They rushed him inside and into an emergency room where it seemed like pandemonium but was actually very controlled. Only people who were 'in the know' were allowed inside the room. The doctors and nurses in the room had been handpicked in advance." Hal paused for a moment and looked at the ground. "You know, there's been a lot of controversy about the hospital over the years, I guess it's all real now that I think about it."

"What do you mean?" asked Mahoney.

"Some people have said that there seemed to be a bunch of Secret Service agents there at the time the limo showed up. The conspiracy theorists seemed to think the Service knew he was going to be arriving there, as if they knew he was going to be shot. I've never thought much about it but I guess those accusations are true," said Hal.

"Well, that brings up several questions, Hal," said Mahoney. "There has always been a lot of controversy about Dealey Plaza. Conspiracy theorists have always talked about the second shooter on the grassy knoll or the men on the railroad trestle. I guess none of those hold any weight anymore."

"Actually," said Hal with that twinkle in his eye, "they all have some truth to them."

"Really?" asked Mahoney.

"Sure. There *was* a shooter on the grassy knoll. It was a Secret Service agent with a camera in his hand, not a gun. The three bums on the railroad trestle were another camera crew. Somebody else saw a man in the window adjacent to the Book Depository; it was another agent with a camera. The service wanted to make certain they had plenty of film of the event."

"What happened to those films," asked Mahoney.

"Most of them were destroyed after they got a look at the Zapruder film. He captured such a clean and close shot of the assassination that there wasn't any need to provide the other films and try to explain where they came from."

Mahoney looked out towards the ocean and thought about Hal's statement for a moment before asking, "Was Mister Zapruder part of the service?"

"No, he was just a guy who came out with his secretary to watch the President and his wife drive by."

A couple of teenagers sitting on a bench in the shade of a shave ice stand fifteen yards away stood up to leave. Hal motioned to the bench, "Let's have a seat and I'll see what else I can remember about the hospital."

Mahoney watched the old man wince as he eased himself down on the bench. "Would you like to go home?" he asked.

Hal managed a thin smile, "Not just yet. My body may be tired but my mind hasn't had such an invigorating workout in years."

Fifty yards down the beach a man dressed in slacks and a tropical shirt stared at the photo that had just come across his phone. "I'm certain it's him," he said to the person at the other end of the connection. "What do you want me to do?"

"Just continue to watch them at this point," said Deputy Director McQuade from his Washington, D.C., office. "Keep me up to date," he said before he hung up.

McQuade's stomach started to turn again. He looked at Hal Rumsey's dossier one more time. Had he missed anything? There was really only one topic that the old man would be discussing with the *Washington Post's* top reporter. There was nothing else of interest that he had done in his entire life. He had to be telling the *Washington Post* about his years protecting Kennedy. The timing of Kennedy's death and the appearance of a reporter at a former agent's home could not be coincidental.

"According to Jack," said Hal from the comfort of the bench in the shade, "he was finally able to compose himself by the time they made it to the hospital. They carried him into Trauma Room One where the only people allowed in were those who previously cleared. While the doctors worked to "save" the cadaver that was already in the room, others helped Kennedy clean himself up. Then he changed into hospital scrubs, pulled on a surgical mask and cap, and walked right out the door of the room past the police, fifty or sixty hospital staff, and a few reporters who were in the hallway. Somebody handed him a jacket and he walked out the back door of the hospital to a waiting car that drove him to Love Field where a private plane was waiting to fly him back to the east coast."

Mahoney laughed, "It couldn't really have been that easy, could it? What about the body in the hospital?"

Hal shifted on the bench, "According to Jack, it *was* just that easy. It was a magician's sleight of hand. Everybody was paying attention to the right hand, or the cadaver in Trauma One, while the left hand, the President, dressed in doctor scrubs, was ignored. Everybody in the hallway was trying to get a look into the room whenever the door opened. Nobody was looking at the faces of those coming and going."

Hal gave Mahoney a moment to write more notes in his little pad. "The plan almost failed after the announcement was made that the president had died," said Hal. "The Dallas Police and the Secret Service nearly got into a fist fight over the Service's snatching of the body. The body clearly should have been under the control of the Dallas Police since the murder had taken place in their jurisdiction, but the Secret Service forcibly took the body back to Washington, in effect illegally removing evidence from the crime scene."

"Damn," said Mahoney, "that's right." He made another note before asking, "So what about the doctors and nurses in the emergency room, or the special effect guys from Hollywood? How is it that not one of them has spoken a word of this in the last fifty years?"

"Most of them kept quiet. You might remember that there were a few who tried to say something. They were discredited as crackpots, they were probably threatened. A few of them died in questionable accidents." Mahoney looked up in astonishment as Hal quickly added, "I'm not saying anything, but it has been suggested that some key witnesses died under questionable circumstances."

Mahoney thought for a moment, "Should I be frightened?"

Hal laughed as he glanced down the beach, "See that guy over there, the one in the tropical shirt? He's been standing there in the sun too long. I'll bet he moves right after we do."

Mahoney glanced down the beach. There was a man, he looked like a tourist standing on the walk looking out towards the sea. "What should we do?"

Hal rubbed his hand across his stomach, "I think I should probably go home. I need a little rest, I don't want to overdo it," he said as he struggled to his feet. Mahoney stood and followed Hal as he shuffled along the walk towards the car and the man in the flowered shirt who remained standing in the sun.

Hal and Mike didn't say a word to each other as they approached the man. He was leaning against a railing and looking out towards the ocean, not seeming to notice their approach. Mahoney was starting to wonder if the old Secret Service agent was simply seeing ghosts. Maybe the man was just enjoying a little 'alone' time on a nice day.

When they were about twenty yards from the man, Hal turned to Mahoney and said quietly, "Look at the poor bastard sweat." Mahoney noticed the man's head was drenched in sweat, his forehead showed the pink beginning of a nasty sunburn. Hal continued to walk along at the same pace directly towards the man. When they reached him, Hal suddenly said to the man, "Damn hot day out, isn't it?"

The man turned towards them with a slightly surprised look, "Certainly is."

"Well," said Hal to the man, "we're done out here for now. You really need to get out of the sun." The man's face twisted just a little; either he was surprised that Hal knew who he was or he was just a tourist who couldn't figure out why the old man was expressing concern for him.

"I'll do that," he said quietly and started walking away from them in the opposite direction.

Mahoney glanced over his shoulder to watch the man walking away, "Jesus, Hal. You should have just invited him to come along with us to save him the trouble of figuring out where we were going!"

Hal chuckled, "He's just some poor Service stiff who is doing his job. There's no reason he should bake his brains any more than necessary on my account."

Agent Jose Telleria stopped and sat in the relative coolness of the same bench that his two marks had just been using. After wiping his forehead several times he pulled his cell phone out of his pocket and called McQuade on his direct line.

"I think they're onto me," he said when McQuade answered. "Rumsey made it pretty clear that he knew I had been watching them."

McQuade leaned back in his office chair. "Well, shit, let me see if I can kill the story from this end. Keep an eye on them," McQuade said the abruptly hung up.

"Prick," said Telleria to himself. Rumsey was probably going home, Telleria thought to himself. He could think of no reason not to head back to his hotel for a shower and a nap.

When Hal and Mahoney reached the car, Hal reached into his pocket and fished out the car keys. "Mister Mahoney, would you mind driving?"

Mahoney looked at the tired old man and said, "I'd be happy to!"

After dropping Hal at his home, and briefly resisting Hal's insistence that he use the car to get back to his hotel, Mahoney pulled away from Hal's home and reached for his cell phone.

"Blurton," said the man who answered the phone at the Washington number Mahoney had dialed.

"Hi, Bob, it's Mike."

"Hi Mike," said the Associate Editor at the *Washington Post*. "I was just about to call you. Are you alone?"

"I am, what's up?"

"I just received a call from a guy by the name of McQuade, a deputy director of something over at the Secret Service," said Bob Blurton.

Mahoney felt the hair rise on the back of his neck. "Interesting, what did Mister McQuade have to say?"

"He said we're being duped by an attention-seeking lunatic if we're talking to a Mister Harold Rumsey," said Blurton. "He said that every few years this poor old guy tries to get somebody to believe his stories about Kennedy being alive on an island in Greece."

"Interesting," said Mahoney. "He mentioned Hal Rumsey by name?"

"Yeah. Apparently, the guy worked for the Secret Service for a few years back in '63, almost completely administrative stuff. He got canned shortly after Kennedy's assassination and over the years has cooked up a story about spending the rest of his life protecting Kennedy out on some island," said Blurton. "Is that the story you're getting from him?"

Mahoney thought for a moment before saying, "Almost verbatim," he paused, "but I think I believe him."

Blurton chuckled. "This McQuade said he was very convincing. He's been working on this fantasy for damn near fifty years. I did a quick run on him; the guy worked for the Secret Service until December of '63 and then spent the rest of his career working for the Social Security Administration as an anonymous cubical dweller," said Blurton sarcastically.

Mahoney was surprised. "Wait, Bob, you checked the Government Edge system against the guy's name?" asked Mahoney, referring to a background system the *Post* could access.

"Yeah, did you happen to check it before you flew to Florida on my dime?" asked Blurton.

"I sure as hell did. There was nothing about Social Security the other day. I have the print-out here with me."

Blurton ran his hand through his hair while he thought. "What makes you think this guy isn't just trying to get his name in the news?" he asked. "Do you really believe that Kennedy just died in Greece?"

Talking with somebody other than Hal brought Mahoney back to reality. It caused him to step back from the old man and his story and look at things rationally for a moment. "I got to level with you Bob, I'm not sure I believe him. But I think my disbelief comes from the fact that to believe him, you have to believe that the most fantastic news story ever to hit the streets is true. And," he continued after a pause, "I have a couple of pieces of evidence that we cannot simply discount. This guy is in possession of the authentic coconut that Kennedy used to save his crew in the war. I was holding the Kennedy coconut in my hand last night, and I confirmed with Caroline that when she was six she carved her initials in the base of the coconut paperweight on JFK's desk. The one on display at the Kennedy Library doesn't have her initials carved in it; the one I held did. And there's another thing."

Blurton was feeling the urgent need for a strong drink, "What else?" he asked.

"When I talked with Caroline the other day to verify that she had carved the initials, she sounded really down. I didn't think much of it at the time, but I have known her for almost thirty years and the two times she sounded that depressed was when I called her a few days after her mother's death and on the day after her brother's. It's not much to go on, but now I have to wonder if she was upset over the death of her father?"

"A coconut?" asked Blurton. "A depressed Kennedy? It's pretty damn thin, Mike."

"I pretty sure we're being followed," said Mahoney. It was a weak attempt to convince his friend of twenty years that he wasn't being led down a false path.

Blurton leaned back in his chair and looked up at the ceiling, "Never once in all the years we've worked together have you given me reason to question you, so I'm going to give you a little room on this one but, damn it, don't embarrass me, Mike."

Mahoney smiled, "What did you tell the Secret Service?"

"I went with plausible deniability," said Blurton, "I told him that I have no idea where you are and, that if you were in fact in Florida, it was probably a personal trip."

"Nice! That will keep them guessing," laughed Mahoney.

"You get your ducks lined up and get your ass back up here, Mike. And if you really think you are being followed, you be damn careful."

Mike looked at his note pad and digital recorder sitting on the car seat next to him, "I'm heading back for my hotel, when I get there I'm going to email you my digital file and type up my notes.

If there is any truth to this thing, they have kept it quiet for fifty years. They aren't going to let it leak out now."

Blurton suddenly found himself considering the validity of the story for the first time, "You be damn careful, Mike."

"Sure thing, boss," Mahoney said before disconnecting.

Hal shuffled to his chair and sat down, enjoying the comfort of his cool and darkened home. He debated between taking his pain pills or having a couple glasses of scotch. The pills would knock him out good but he wasn't sure he wanted to be out that long. The scotch would help him rest but probably wouldn't help him sleep soundly. There was so much more to tell about his friend Jack. He decided on the scotch so he could meet Mahoney again later. He was struggling back to his feet when the phone rang.

"Hello," said Hal after shuffling to the phone and picking it up after the fifth ring. He really needed to get one of those cordless phones to keep next to his easy chair.

"Hello, Hal," said the hollow voice on the other end, "this is Robert McQuade."

Hal felt the walls of his home suddenly close in on him, his skin tingled but he kept calm. "Hello, Robby, how are you." Hal had no respect for the 'kid' they had assigned as the Deputy Director of Special Projects several years ago and he had never tried to hide his feelings. Hal also detested the fact that the Director insisted on being called 'Robert' rather than Rob or Bob.

"I hear you're not feeling well, Hal," said McQuade in a fake tone of concern.

"Are you kidding, I don't know who you've been talking to but I feel like a teenager again. I'm just getting back from a jog on the beach with one of your spooks," said Hal. "You really need to get that guy into shape, he looked like a heart attack waiting to happen. Are things so bad that you can't afford a little sunscreen for your agents now?"

McQuade smiled, the gloves were off. There was no reason to dance around the issue anymore. "Hal, what are you doing talking with a *Post* reporter?"

"Do your homework, asshole. Mike is my nephew. He's down here doing a story on all of us government retirees who flock to

Florida. I'm showing him around; we're chasing some skirt and considering going parasailing tomorrow. What the hell did you think we were talking about?"

"I hear you're dying. I think you heard Kennedy died and now you're making an early deathbed confession," said McQuade.

Hal laughed. He had to give the 'kid' credit for his direct tactic. He hated to admit it but his estimation of McQuade had just gone up a notch. "Well, you're wrong," Hal lied.

"I certainly hope I am," said McQuade. "You are still bound by the oath you took. If I find out you even mentioned Kennedy's name or the word 'Skorpios', I'll make sure you spend the rest of your life so locked away you'll never have to worry about sunscreen again."

Hal felt a rare feeling of anger swelling up inside of him, "Listen to me, you pimple-faced son-of-a-bitch, I was protecting Jack before you were born. You are threatening the wrong guy, Robby."

McQuade repeated himself, "I certainly hope I am," and hung up the phone.

Hal slammed the phone down. "Damn it!" he said to himself.

McQuade was right. Hal had taken an oath and had sworen to keep the secrets of Skorpios to, and beyond his death. He had clearly violated that oath, he had in fact shattered it and deserved to spend the rest of his life in federal detention. He had also put Mahoney at risk. The Service had in its power the ability to discredit Mahoney and ruin his career. They had the ability to lock him away for some trumped-up charge, Hal was pretty sure people had died in the past for threatening to tell what they knew, maybe even as recently as the last few days. Hal wondered about the helicopter pilot

He had two options as he saw it. He either needed to change his story and start discrediting himself to Mahoney, perhaps start rambling on about conspiracy theories and such, or he could continue telling the real story. He weighed the value of his 'oath' against the significance of the real Kennedy story.

Hal poured himself a tall glass of scotch and moved back to his easy chair to relax for a few hours. He knew the answers would be much clearer after he had rested for a while. Suddenly he felt tired, drained, and very alone. He kicked off his shoes and walked to his bedroom leaving the glass of scotch untouched on the table beside his recliner.

Robert McQuade also was considering his options. He flipped opened Rumsey's dossier again to see if anything in the thin file would offer him a solution to the problem. Two items suddenly glared at him, Rumsey was an only child and he had never married. Hal had just told McQuade that Mahoney was his nephew. "Nephew, my ass," McQuade said to himself. He shut the file, pushed himself back from his desk and walked quickly out of his office.

Mike Mahoney arrived back to his hotel room and opened the blinds to let the sun shine into the room. He retrieved his laptop from its case and hit the bathroom while it powered up. He was excited to get some of his notes down in an outline form.

First he downloaded the hours of conversation from his digital recorder to his laptop and emailed them to his own email address at the *Post* and to his home email address, and then copied them to Bob Blurton as well. Then with the recorder sitting on the right side of his computer and his notepad sitting on the left, he began typing. The burger and Coke he had bought at a fast food drive-thru on his trip from Hal's sat forgotten on top of the TV. Mahoney was working on the first story that had really excited him in years.

The phone call from the Secret Service to Blurton only convinced him more that Hal Rumsey was telling the truth. "Why," he asked himself, "would the Service bother to call a newspaper to warn them that they were interviewing a nutcase?" Government agents rarely went out of their way to keep the media from inadvertently making fools of themselves. Why would they do so now?

It was a little after six in the evening when Hal woke. He was hungry, a sensation he seldom felt lately. He made his way out to the kitchen and scrambled a couple of eggs which he enjoyed with the glass of milk. When he was done he washed the dishes and then pulled Mahoney's business card out of his pocket and dialed his cell number.

"Mahoney," came the answer on the second ring.

"Hello, Mister Mahoney, how was your afternoon?"

Mahoney was happy to hear Hal's voice sounding refreshed and upbeat. "I had an interesting afternoon. I'm looking forward to telling you about it."

"Well, I had a nap and a bite to eat. If you are up for it, I'd like to chat for a few more hours this evening," said Hal.

"I'll finish up here and be over in a half hour if that works for you."

"Great," said Hal, "see you then."

Mahoney finished typing the outline he was working on before emailing the notes to the three email addresses he had used before. Then he grabbed the car keys, his warm Coke and cold burger and hurried out the door.

The garage door was open when Mahoney arrived so he carefully pulled the car in to where Hal had hung a tennis ball at the height of the windshield to indicate the long car was in far enough to close the door. Mahoney laughed; his father had employed the same system to park his Buick in his garage in Waukee, Iowa.

Hal opened the door between the garage and his home as Mahoney crawled out of the car, "Hello, Hal," Mahoney said. "Boy, I sure love that car!"

Hal laughed, "She's a runner. I wish we had time to get her out of town, somewhere where I could really show you how well she runs when she has some room. Come on in, Mike."

Mahoney followed Hal into the living room where he had taken the liberty of pouring two glasses of scotch. Hal motioned for Mahoney to sit and then looked at him sternly and said, "They are on to us, Mister Mahoney."

"Do you mean the Secret Service, Hal?"

"Yeah, I got a call from the Director of Special Projects, the squirrel in charge of the Skorpios project. He knew I was talking to you. I gave him a fake excuse but he's not going to buy it for long."

Mahoney leaned forward, "My editor got a call today, probably from the same guy. He told my boss that I was talking with a nutcase. He said you worked for the Service for a few years back in the early sixties and spent the rest of your career working for the Social Security Administration. Are you a nutcase, Hal?"

"Do I appear to be crazy?" asked Hal. "Do I appear to be trying to profit from this? Have I asked you for any money? I'm not looking for fame. I don't want to be on the Oprah Show, I'm not going to live that long anyway. Maybe I'm just a lonely old man who wants a few hours of company so I dreamed this whole thing up in order to get you to fly all the way from Washington just to drink my scotch. What do you think, Mister Mahoney?"

Mahoney glanced at the box, still on the table, that contained the coconut. "I think you have a pretty compelling story, Hal. I'm still here."

With both of them airing their feelings, the mood in the room seemed to lighten. Hal lifted his glass of scotch saying, "To my friend, Jack."

Mahoney lifted his glass and toasted Kennedy as well then took a sip before reaching into his pocket to retrieve his digital recorder which he turned on and set on the table between them.

"Hal, you said last night that once you accepted the assignment, you were flown to a lodge in the Catskill Mountains where you met President Kennedy, Bobby Kennedy, Onassis and some others. After you met them, how long was it before you flew to Greece?" asked Mahoney.

"We flew from there to Montreal the next day and spent the night at a private home there. We left the next morning on a private jet to Shannon, Ireland, where we refueled and then flew on to Patra, Greece," said Hal. From there, we drove up north to a small port where we took a boat out to Skorpios."

Mahoney looked at the growing list of questions he had about Hal's story until one popped out at him, one he had thought of the night before. "Hal, one thing I don't understand; why would a successful man like Aristotle Onassis risk his reputation and possibly his business empire to hide what the public would perceive as a lying, cheating ex-president if the plot ever failed?

Hal smiled, "It's what the Greeks refer to as '*epistrevo tin kalosenesou'*. It's something that most Americans probably can't fully understand. Do you understand the gist of reciprocity, Mister Mahoney?"

"Of course," said Mahoney. "If I do something nice for you, you will do something nice for me in return."

"Exactly, but Greek businessmen take reciprocity to a level we can't even begin to comprehend here in the States. It is so much a part of their business culture that they actually go out of their way to do favors for each other, just so they will have a favor to call in when they need it."

Mahoney's eyes opened a little wider, "So what did JFK do for Onassis that was so valuable that he would allow him to spend the rest of his life hiding out on Skorpios?"

Hal grinned and pointed his finger at his guest, "Not the President. It was his father, the Ambassador." Hal waited silently; he wanted Mahoney to ask the question.

"Okay, Hal," Mahoney played along, "what did Joe Kennedy do for Onassis that would cause him to owe the Kennedy family that big a debt?"

Hal smiled, "Joe helped Ari become filthy, filthy rich."

WASHINGTON, D.C.
Present Day

Lori Harris was cleaning up the glob of mayonnaise that had dropped out of her sandwich and onto her keyboard when the alert popped up on her computer screen. Earlier that morning, she had received a request at her office at the National Security Agency, to monitor several email addresses for messages that contained particular words. Her office received a hundred requests a day from different government agencies but this one had caught her eye. It was a request from the Secret Service to attempt to intercept emails to or from two addresses at the *Washington Post* that contained references to Kennedy, JFK, Jack, Skorpios, and Rumsey.

The process was actually fairly easy, especially when either the sending or receiving email address was a known server such as 'washingtonpost.com' as in this case. The NSA had learned over the years how to hack into virtually any server and insert what was essentially a worm. When directed, they had the ability to order the worm to watch for certain data. When the prescribed data was detected, the worm would forward that data to the NSA requester. Very few of the requests were accompanied by a legal warrant.

It wasn't unusual to receive such a request from the Secret Service but they usually contained much more current references. Lori found this request 'interesting' and she wondered why the Service would be asking for NSA to intercept emails with historic references and also why the *Post* would be sending or receiving such emails. She had entered the information and then quickly forgot the request, certain that if such an email ever did surface it probably wouldn't happen on her shift. She was surprised when an email was sent to one of the target addresses within hours of the Service's request.

She resisted the temptation to read the email, logged it in the system, saved it to the NSA system, and then forwarded it to the email address of the requester. Before she returned to her sandwich, however, Lori jotted down the location of the email on a sticky note, just in case she decided to look at it later.

BOCA RATON, FLORIDA
Present Day

Mahoney thought to himself that if Hal was in fact a lunatic, he was at the very least a brilliant lunatic. He was amazed at the twists and turns the story seemed to take, "I don't know too much about Onassis," Mahoney admitted, "but how and why did Joe Kennedy make him wealthy?"

"Wealthier," said Hal. "Ari was already a fairly successful man. Joe Kennedy probably never heard the Greek term, '*epistrevo tin kalosenesou*' but he certainly taught his boys to invest in their future by creating markers to be collected later. Joe didn't have enough of his own money to get his boy elected as President but he had enough markers, he had enough people who owed him favors that he simply called those favors due and 'presto', an American President."

Mahoney nodded in understanding, "So what favor did Joe do for Onassis?"

"Ari owned a successful but relatively small shipping company that operated mainly in the Mediterranean Sea. To make big money, you had to play on the big lake, the Atlantic Ocean, and in order to play on the big lake, Ari needed big ships and the money to buy them," said Hal. "The United States Navy had a fleet of cheap war-surplus ships and U.S. banks had cheap money. Ari was a smart man but he couldn't figure out how to get the Navy and the banks to give him what he needed. Joe Kennedy helped him figure it out."

Mahoney asked, "So how did it work?"

Hal smiled and continued, "One of the stipulations to acquiring these surplus ships was that they had to be sold to an American citizen. The Ambassador helped Ari set up an American company, United States Petroleum Carriers, with American shareholders, most of whom were Joe Kennedy's close friends. The corporation's first purchase, which Joe helped negotiate, was sixteen surplus Liberty Ships. The price was half a million dollars each of which the company had to put 25 percent down and then with a request from the Naval Commission, a U.S bank would finance the rest at three percent interest for seven years."

"Three percent interest on $375,000?" Mahoney commented. "That seems like a sweetheart of a deal."

"That was just another good ol' boy deal back in those days," said Hal. "Kennedy made it clear to his friends on the Naval Commission that the ships were going to some of his buddies. You see, Kennedy and the men sitting on the Commission all understood the concept of reciprocity, not as well as the Greeks but they knew that if you took care of Joe Kennedy and his buddies, they would always take care of you."

Mahoney took a drink of scotch and asked, "Did Onassis have enough money to make the down payment on the ships?"

Hal smiled, "Remind me to tell you more about Ari in a bit. No, he didn't have the money so he approached the U.S. banks for it, with introductions from Joe Kennedy. The banks turned him down for lack of collateral so he went out and contracted coal shipments back and forth across the Atlantic, from South America to France,

Germany, and other countries on ships he didn't yet own. With the contracts as guarantee, the banks loaned him the money to use as the down payment to buy the ships."

"Brilliant," said Mahoney.

"There's a reason why men like Ari Onassis and Joe Kennedy were filthy rich and people like us will never be. My mind just doesn't work that way." Hal resumed his story, "Once he had the Liberty Ships working, then Ari could go for the big deal he was after. In just a few trips across the Atlantic, the coal ships had paid for themselves so Ari set his sights on a group of surplus T2 oil tankers for which Joe Kennedy helped negotiate an even better financing deal. The day after the sale of the tankers was complete, Ari swooped in and took control of the shares of the phantom American company and within a few months established himself as one of the dominant shipping companies in his corner of the world."

"Jesus, Hal. Is all that true?" asked Mahoney.

"History, Mister Mahoney. I'm sure you can find out all about it with a little searching," said Hal as he took a sip of his scotch and leaned back in his chair. "It's all in the history books."

Mahoney took a moment to jot down a few notes before asking, "So what was the deal with Jackie's marriage to Onassis?"

"That, I'm afraid to say," Hal chuckled as he lifted his glass of scotch, "was my idea after a few too many drinks."

"Okay, this should be good," said Mahoney as he leaned forward in his chair.

"In the first couple of years after the 'assassination' Jackie's life was pretty miserable. She was constantly hounded by the press, having to live as a single mother, and not liking any of it much. She wanted to just fade away but it was clear that the public wasn't going to let that happen so it was very difficult for her and the kids to sneak away to see Jack on Skorpios.

One night after dinner, and after the kids were tucked in bed, Jack, Ari, Jackie and I were sitting around having a few drinks and Jackie was venting her frustrations. She wasn't really complaining but she was clearly upset about her situation. I said something like, 'Well, Jackie, if you were to marry Ari here, you could spend all the time you wanted on the island.' Everybody laughed at the time," said Hal.

"So there was never anything romantic between them?" asked Mahoney.

"Oh, hell no, Mister Mahoney, it was a marriage of convenience. The more the three of them discussed the idea, the more it began to make sense. It was Jackie's ticket out of the U.S. until such time as her fame faded, which as you know never really happened. It also made Skorpios a place where she and the kids could be seen without anybody being suspicious."

"This story gets a little crazier every time we talk, Hal."

"They say fact can be stranger than fiction," said Hal, "and this is certainly one of those cases."

"Okay," said Mahoney while taking a down a few notes, "you and Kennedy arrive on the island of Skorpios. Take me through the first couple of days on the island and then perhaps a brief history of the years you spent with Kennedy. Then I think we are about done."

Hal's face twisted slightly, looking like he had just been slapped in the face, "On the contrary, Mister Mahoney. If you are really here to learn about Jack Kennedy's life, this is where I believe the story begins."

SKORPIOS ISLAND
December 6, 1963

"Jesus, Jack," Kennedy said to himself as he followed Special Agent Paul Walker up the wooded path through the thick brush and black pine. "How in the hell did you get yourself into this?"

It had been a little less than two weeks since the "assassination." Although the clandestine component of the plan appeared to be secure for the moment, the whole event hadn't gone as neatly as designed. Lee Oswald was dead. A Dallas bar owner, some wannabe hero named Jack Ruby who apparently had some loose ties to the underworld, was in jail for killing him. The media was already starting to talk about a conspiracy, something that Oswald's confession and trial would have squashed.

Planning for the shooting to take place in Dealey Plaza had

seemed like a good idea at the time but the tightly-grouped buildings in the plaza caused the report from Oswald's rifle to echo and that had misled witnesses. People had heard gunfire coming from multiple directions and the investigators were involved in numerous goose chases. It didn't help that during the press conference at Parkland Hospital after the President's 'death,' several reporters misunderstood Dr. Perry to say that the wound to the front of the throat may have been an entry wound.

Finally, assuming that the Dallas Police were simply going to let the Secret Service bundle up the President's body and remove it from their jurisdiction without objection was a mistake. With all of the great minds and all the attorneys involved in the planning, including Jack himself, nobody stopped to think about the consequences of a murder committed within the jurisdiction of the Dallas Police. A shoving match broke out at the hospital when the local police tried to assume control of the "President's" body. The plan nearly failed even before it was two hours old and Jack was amazed that it hadn't yet been exposed.

As the former president of the United States hid in a luxurious hunting lodge, flew around the world on private jets, and now stepped ashore to his new home, his countrymen and much of the world was mourning his death. In Detroit, a woman threw herself to the ground in tears; in Memphis, a church group held a round-the-clock service; and in Washington, D.C., mourners lined up for hours and hours to pay their last respects as the coffin lay in state in the Capitol Rotunda.

In the hours after the assassination much of the county's phone system had failed due to the massive volume of calls being attempted. Panic-stricken families huddled in their living rooms with blinds drawn and guns loaded, fearing the President's death was part of a larger communist plot. The government had lapsed into utter chaos but Lyndon Johnson, in Kennedy's opinion, appeared to be doing a far better than expected job at picking up the pieces and putting his shattered administration together and the country back to work. Jack never thought he would say it of even think it, but he was proud of LBJ's efforts in the days following his sudden succession to the Presidency.

Kennedy walked up the trail through the trees with two Secret

Service agents ahead of him following Demetrius, the island's caretaker, and two agents behind him. The four agents assigned to him consisted of three rookies who had spent most of their short careers with the Service assigned to field offices and Paul Walker, a well-respected agent with over forty years of experiance.

As they reached a clearing above the old boat dock, Agent Walker stopped and wiped his brow. Then with a sweeping motion of his arm said, "Well here you go, Mister President, the Ritz."

It certainly wasn't the Ritz, it was two shacks and a tarpaulin-covered shade structure that appeared to be the kitchen and dining area yet also served as dry storage for construction supplies and food stores. Beyond these shacks a group of ten men were busy working on a large concrete block structure that was to be the island's main house.

"How in the hell did you get yourself into this?" Kennedy again asked himself and chuckled.

Demetrius, a short, round, little man with large eyes and a tremulous smile, nervously showed the new arrivals where they would be sleeping in the larger of the two shacks. The interior was barren with the exception of two wooden chairs and three cots pushed against the walls. A curtain separated the back area of the old shack and Demetrius proudly pulled it back to expose a small area with a single cot, a small desk, and a little table holding a lantern, the Presidential Suite. Each of the Americans looked around their new quarters but failed to see anything that resembled a sink or a toilet.

After they had dropped their bags Demetrius led a quick tour of the area. The first stop was at what would become the large deck of the main house. In his heavily accented English, he excitedly pointed out future improvements and explained the plans. The workers continued to mix mortar and stack cinder blocks, occasionally stealing glances at the newcomers. They had been told the guests were important men from America but beyond that they wouldn't have known John F. Kennedy from Benjamin Franklin.

Each man and woman on the island, whether part of the construction crew, the security detail, or the staff, was handpicked by Ari Onassis himself. They were good solid Greeks from good but simple families who could be trusted to see and hear nothing. To make certain that nothing left the island, they were well paid and sufficiently threatened. Each employee understood very well that under no circumstances did you ever want to displease, cheat, or steal from Aristotle Onassis, and the consequences would be even more severe for talking about what you saw or heard on the island.

After a brief stop at the main house, Demetrius hurried down a trail calling to his guests to follow. After about thirty yards they entered another small clearing where a small block building stood. The Greek host pointed proudly to the tarpaulin door which Kennedy pulled back, took a quick look inside, and then turned to his men and said, "There's the shitter and shower, boys!"

As the newcomers were taking turns looking behind the canvas door, another man came up the trail from below. Demetrius sprang to a poorly executed military stance of attention and announced, "My guests, may I present the director of Skorpios security, Captain Gusof Papadopoulos, retired."

Captain Papadopoulos was a tall and imposing figure of a man with a barrel chest and muscular arms. He stood with perfect posture. His hair was thinning but he had the look of a sixty-year-old who could out-wrestle men who were half his years. He was dressed in a field jacket, pressed khaki slacks and perfectly shined military boots. Before he said a word he looked carefully at each of the Americans, seemingly size them up as one might an opponent. When he spoke it was loud, commanding, and completely in Greek, as though he were addressing new military recruits on their first day.

"Captain Papadopoulos welcomes you to Skorpios and would like to review the security rules," said Demetrius.

The Captain shot the caretaker a sharp look and barked something at him. Demetrius motioned towards the men and shook his head indicating "no". The Captain rolled his eyes.

Agent Walker turned to Kennedy, "I'm not sure the General here likes the fact that we don't speak his language."

Kennedy took a step towards the Captain, extended his hand and said "*Me lene'm Jack Kennedy. Signomi, then katalaveno. Milate anglika?*" or "My name is Jack Kennedy. Sorry, I don't understand. Do you speak English?"

The Captain's mood seemed to lighten somewhat as he looked directly into Kennedy's eyes. He took his extended hand and shook it while glancing at Demetrius and saying something in Greek. He continued to hold Kennedy's hand while Demetrius interpreted, "The Captain is honored to meet you, Mister Kennedy. He apologizes for not being able to address you in your foreign language."

"Tell the Captain," Jack said to Demetrius without taking his eyes away from the Captain's, "that I also am honored to meet a distinguished war hero and that we appreciate the wonderful hospitality of all the Greeks here on the island."

Demetrius passed along the message to the Captain who then released Kennedy's hand and gave him a slight bow of respect.

Kennedy's four-man security detail looked at him in shock. "Sir, I didn't know you spoke any Greek," said Agent Walker.

"I don't," answered Kennedy. "But while you guys were playing poker without me on the flight over here," the slight barb was noticeable, "I did manage to read a little of the phrase book we were all given. I never go to a foreign country without at least being able to say 'hello', 'good-bye', 'thank you', and 'where is the toilet'" he said with a smile.

After a brief exchange between the two Greeks, Demetrius turned back to Kennedy and said, "The Captain would like to first offer his security rules and then determine the best way both teams can work together to provide for your needs."

Kennedy smiled at them both, "Thank you, Captain. May I present the head of my team, Special Agent in Charge, Paul Walker." Demetrius translated to the Captain who quickly stepped forward and shook hands with Walker.

Agent Walker took his cue, "I'd like to introduce my team, Agent Stennfeld, Agent Haycock, and Agent Rumsey. We are at your disposal," he said diplomatically while hoping he hadn't just created a situation he wouldn't be able to live with over the coming months.

The Captain cleared his throat and seemed to collect his thoughts before speaking. "The rules are simple," Demetrius carefully concentrated to interpret every word the Captain said correctly. "My men will guard the island, your men will guard the President."

Papadopoulos paced in front of the men as though he were addressing his troops. He was annoyed because the Secret Service agents were not standing at attention rank but he didn't show his irritation. His voice was loud and commanding and certainly would have been impressive had any of the Americans understood a single word that he was saying. Demetrius the interpreter, on the other hand, had the voice of an elf and the demeanor of a mouse. The Captain's words may have been interpreted correctly but much of their significance was lost by his interpreter's delicate voice.

"At no time will any American be allowed to be seen from passing boats or aircraft, which means you cannot go to the beach, the dock, or other areas where you might be seen by telescopic devices."

"Great," said Agent Stennfeld. "We'll just hide under the trees for the next six or eight months."

The Captain shot the agent a sharp look. While he didn't understand the words, the sarcastic tone was undeniable. Kennedy's reaction was immediate as well. He turned towards his men and in a low but clear voice said, "Gentlemen, let's not forget that we are guests on this island. We will adhere to the rules of our host. Is that understood?" Then with his back still to the Greeks he winked at the men sending a message that said, we'll adhere to the rules . . . for now.

Kennedy turned back to the Captain and said, "Forgive our rudeness, please continue."

After a brief exchange between the two Greeks, the Captain began speaking again. Demetrius said, "The Captain will make you as comfortable as possible but he wants you to know that his instructions come from Mr. Onassis himself. You are to be welcomed here but it is absolutely imperative that you not be detected. The simplest way to keep you safe is to keep you invisible. If rumors start that there are Americans on Skorpios, we will no longer be able to guarantee your safety. Over the next few days we will establish methods of communication between my men and yours. We will establish plans of contingency and safe zones should the island be breached by intruders."

The Captain turned to Kennedy and said something directly to him. Demetrius sheepishly interpreted, "The Captain doesn't want your men shooting his in a midnight fire fight."

"Indeed," replied Kennedy. The Captain was certainly making it clear that he found the Americans to be unintelligent and incompetent. Kennedy really wanted to remind the Captain that the Americans had performed admirably in the last couple of wars but held his tongue.

The Captain barked an order to Demetrius who produced a map from his satchel and spread it over a small rickety table. The map showed an island that was a very rough equivalent of an hourglass shape, about a mile long and three quarters of a mile wide at its widest spot, and perhaps a few hundred yards across at the narrowest. The Captain pointed out the beaches that were of note because they were both off-limits but also the most probable place to land a small force should anybody decide to come after the President. He mentioned the existence of security personnel above the beaches but, when asked by Agent Walker, refused to disclose how many men he had on the island or how well they were armed. Then, with his finger, Papadopoulos drew a line across the neck of the hour glass shape and made it clear that the Americans were to remain on the northeastern section of the island, the southwestern end of the island being strictly off-limits.

When he was finished with the map, the Captain asked to see their weapons. He seemed put-off that the Americans had sent their President to a remote island to be guarded by four men, each armed with only a service pistol and the standard issue Uzi machine gun. "Do you think an attacking force is going to be repelled by these toys?" he asked incredulously. The Captain stomped off in disgust; it was obvious that if the President needed saving, he and his men were going to have to do it themselves.

BOCA RATON, FLORIDA
Present Day

"What more can you add other than your day-to-day experiences of living with a former President on a Greek isle owned by a very rich man?" asked Mahoney.

Hal smiled, "We haven't even started to talk about Jack's second career."

"You guys lived on a remote island, what was he, a fisherman?" asked Mahoney with a slight tone of cynicism.

Hal's smile faded away, "Jack became his own one-man CIA. He helped facilitate both the rise and the fall of world leaders and their countries. He stopped and started wars, and shaped the world in which you live."

"I don't understand, Hal. How could Kennedy wield any power once he was effectively dead and hiding on a little island in the middle of nowhere?"

Hal tapped his index finger to his temple, "Jack, probably had one of the greatest minds of our time, when he had nothing to do but think, he could look at any situation and visualize multiple sides of the equation. Given the appropriate information, he was able to sort out the positives and negatives of any issue. He could find the strengths and weaknesses of world leaders and figure out how to use other people or even other countries to help mold or destroy that leader. Jack did far to define the world we live in today and had a hand in more events in the last fifty years than you can even begin to imagine. That, Mister Mahoney, is the story I called you to talk about."

Mahoney settled back in his chair and started to wonder how any of this would play out in the media, assuming it were true. "Which events specifically did Kennedy have his fingers into, Hal?

Hal looked thoughtfully into Mahoney's eyes for a moment, "To clearly understand the last fifty years, I should go back to the early years on Skorpios."

Hal noticed that Mahoney had laid his pen down on his notepad and saw him sneak a peek at his watch. His interest was fading but Hal was determined and pushed forward, "We arrived on Skorpios in early December of '63. There wasn't much out there in the beginning, Onassis had only purchased the island a few months earlier. I never asked, but I always assumed he bought the island for this particular reason after Jack had contacted him for help."

Mahoney picked up his pen and made a note, "Check date Onassis bought Skorpios."

"When we arrived, there was just Jack, myself, and three others from the Service. Onassis had handpicked his own security team to guard the island and he had a construction crew there building the main house. They were instructed to not speak with us, in fact not to even see us," Hal chuckled. "That lasted for about a day."

"What changed?" asked Mahoney in an attempt to act interested.

"Jack got bored," said Hal. "There was nothing to do on the island so the first moment turned our backs, Jack went out and started helping the men who were building the main house. We were so busy getting prepared for the Russians, the Cubans, the Mob, or somebody to storm the island that the man we were there to protect slipped away from us to build a house," laughed Hal. "Hell, by the end of the first week he had the four of us up there helping as well. And to make sure we would really be of help, every time Greeks stopped for a break, Jack made them teach us Greek words. I learned to say 'brick', 'mortar', and 'level' before I could say 'hello' in Greek."

"I thought Kennedy had a bad back?" asked Mahoney. "How much could he do?"

"I'm glad you brought that up, I had forgotten all about that," said Hal with a warm grin. "For the first few weeks he was very careful, he only did minimal tasks that didn't require heavy lifting. One day a huge construction worker, through a series of hand gestures and broken English, asked Jack why he was such a pansy. Jack indicated that he had an injured back and showed him the brace he wore. That Greek construction worker had been a world-class body builder when he was younger and with more hand gestures, some broken English, and a few demonstrations showed Jack several exercises he could do to strengthen his back. And then he made certain that Jack did them daily."

"And the exercises helped?" asked Mahoney.

"Yeah. Remember that in the early sixties, doctors knew very little about physical therapy. If a man had a bad back, you fused bones together. Doctors would cut and paste and then give a man a back brace and tell him not to strain his back again. They didn't know anything about trying to strengthen the muscles to relieve the pain and prevent future injuries. That huge Greek construction worker-damn, I wish I could remember his name-that guy did more for Jack's back than all the doctors, the surgeries, and the drugs had since he had first injured it in college. Hell, by the end of our third month on the island, Jack was pushing wheelbarrows full of dirt and before the main house was finished, he was toting bags of concrete on his shoulder." Hal noticed Mahoney making additional notes.

"So there were four of you assigned to the president?" asked Mahoney.

"Originally," said Hal. "As time went on it became apparent that nobody was looking for Jack in the Greek islands so one by one the detail dropped from four down to three, then to two and finally just to me."

"And how was it that you were the one picked to stay on the island?" asked Mahoney.

"I volunteered," said Hal. "I had really come to enjoy Skorpios and Ari's people on the island, and over time Jack and I had become friends, or at least two guys who enjoyed spending a lot of time talking with each other."

"What did you talk about?" asked Mahoney.

"Oh, geez, any number of things," replied Hal. "At first we talked a lot about history, he was quite the historian. Then Jack started reading a collection of classic books he had brought with him, the works of Blackstone, Swift, Karl Marx, Plato, and others that he had never had the time to read before. When he had finished with whatever book he was reading, he would want to discuss it with somebody so he encouraged me to read each book as well." Hal chuckled, "I guess we had our own little book club of two, right there on the island."

"Is that how the conversations between you began, with the books?" asked Mahoney.

"No," said Hal, "it was insomnia."

SKORPIOS ISLAND
December 20, 1963

Hal Rumsey sat at his post outside the building they now referred to as the sleep shack. In the two weeks they had been on the island they had settled into somewhat of a routine. Hal had drawn the swing shift, 4:00 p.m. to midnight which suited him just fine, he was more of a night owl than an early riser. He sat in the bunker, a pile of sandbags and bricks stacked up to provide some level of protection for the guard on duty, and stared out into the brush watching for any movement and listening for the attack that Agent Walker had warned could come at any time. The Greek Captain had considered arming the Secret Service agents with the Russian AK-47s his own men used but decided against it because his men were the ones out there in the brush and the last thing he needed was to have the Americans accidently shooting at his men with 'real' weapons.

If an attack ever did become a real threat, the Americans probably would be warned about it long before the assault force got close to the middle of the island. Captain Papadopoulos, for all his pompous antics had taken the few men he had available to him and built a system of overlapping kill zones around all the potential landing sites. His men guarded the island from invisible bunkers day and night as if they were guarding Onassis himself. When Agent Walker approached the Captain to propose integrating the two defensive groups into one cohesive force, he scoffed. Walker recognized the dangers of two separate forces on a small island but the Captain looked with great distain at Walker's college-educated agents who tiptoed around the island worried about getting their shoes dirty, armed with nothing more than pea shooters.

At around 11:00 p.m., Hal heard a rustle behind him. He turned and in the moonlight he was able to see that it was Kennedy coming out of the sleep shack.

"Good evening sir," said Hal.

"Good evening Hal," said the President as he walked to the bunker.

If somebody was out in the brush with a rifle, Hal thought, Kennedy certainly would be an easy target on a moonlit night. He made it even easier when he lit a cigarette; the lighter illuminated his face, making it clear for a great distance. Agent Walker, had he been present, would have instructed Hal to move the President to a secure location but Hal knew Kennedy would have told Walker to 'shove it'. Hal chose to remain on guard without making any demands.

"Mind if I sit out here with you for a bit, Hal?" asked Kennedy. "I'm having a hard time sleeping."

"I'd appreciate the company, sir," answered Hal.

"It's a beautiful night," said Kennedy

"A bit cool for me, sir. I'll bet it will be a wonderful day tomorrow though."

Kennedy sort of grunted in agreement and sat on the sandbags that made up the top of the bunker. After a few puffs on his cigarette he turned towards Hal, "Who did you piss off to get this assignment?"

Hal laughed while his eyes continued to peer out into the blackness of the brush, "I volunteered, sir. Everybody's always told me never to volunteer for anything, everybody except for my father who had a pretty amazing military career because he volunteered for everything."

"Well, I hope someday you look back on this assignment as exciting. What kind of adventures did your father find himself in by volunteering for everything that came along?"

"He was hijacked by Claire Chennault in China," Hal replied.

"You're kidding," said Kennedy, "how did that happen?"

Hal looked up at the stars, pausing for a moment while trying to remember the details, "If I remember the story correctly, he was a seaman aboard a Navy supply ship in 1940. The U.S. Navy was actually purchasing supplies from the Japanese and then shipping them to a small port in China. From there they trucked them up to Chennault's group who were using their P-40s to attack the Jap forces. They had American planes and bullets but the pilots' bellies and their fuel tanks were filled with food and gas from Tokyo."

"You're kidding," said Kennedy. "The Japanese were supplying Chennault's group with the food and fuel they needed to attack their own forces?"

"Oh, yeah," said Hal. "The Japanese sold supplies to the U.S. right up to Pearl Harbor and the civilian suppliers probably would have sold to the Americans after that if they had the opportunity. Back in China they were looking for a few volunteers to go along on a truck convoy. Dad put his hand up and became an instant trucker. On the way up into the mountains the convoy was stopped by rebels who took the trucks and all the supplies but allowed my dad and the others to walk away unharmed. The next day, after walking all night, they finally got to Chennault's base camp. While my Dad was waiting for a ride back to the port he got talking to the aircraft mechanics who found out he had worked on planes before the war. Chennault told him he couldn't go back to the navy, he needed another mechanic. It was nearly three months before my Dad was able to sneak back to his ship. Luckily, his skipper believed his story and didn't bust him for being AWOL."

Kennedy laughed, "There are probably hundreds of stories like that from the war. And using your enemy's own supplies to attack them is fantastic. I believe I've changed my perspective of the world over the last few weeks. I think a nation could get a lot more done by using the bullets and food of other countries rather than exporting their own."

"What do you mean, sir?"

Kennedy took a drag on his cigarette then dropped it and crushed it under the toe of his shoe. "Imagine if instead of sending our men, planes, ships, tanks, and other resources to Europe and Asia during the war, we instead had remained neutral but helped the allied nations produce enough supplies to fight the battles and ultimately win the war."

Hal thought about that statement for a moment, "Could we have stayed neutral in World War II?"

"I don't think so," answered Kennedy, "but imagine if we could find a way to stay out of quagmires like Korea or this Vietnam mess. He rubbed the back of his neck and looked at the ground, "There has got to be a way we can use our brains rather than our brawn and keep American boys from dying. There has got to be a way to use other countries to fight our battles."

"Do you really think so, sir? Do you really think there is a way to keep our men out of the mud?"

Kennedy looked at Hal thoughtfully, "Maybe not, Hal, but maybe there is a way to prevent future wars by manipulating the political temperament of other countries."

Suddenly, Hal realized he was sitting with a President of the United States and talking one to one about ways to positively change the world's future. He wondered silently about the events that had transpired in his life to get him to this place at this time. How did the kid who was cut from his high school's freshman baseball team and who hadn't particularly distinguished himself in any way end up on an unknown island in the middle of nowhere strategizing with the President? Okay, Hal thought to himself, maybe he wasn't really strategizing with the man, and maybe the guy wasn't the President any longer, but wouldn't it be great if his freshman baseball coach could see him now?

"I have contacts all over the world," said Kennedy. "If I could get the information I needed from one contact, I might be able to pass that information to another in such a way as to influence that individual to act a certain way that would seem be more beneficial. It's not unlike the way we influence Congress and the Senate back home," he said as his voice that trailed off.

Hal remained quiet and continued to stare out into the brush, searching and listening for movement.

Kennedy stood and looked at his watch, "Almost midnight, Hal."

"Yes, sir," responded Hal.

"Think about how we can use political wrangling rather than guns to move the world the direction we want, Hal," said Kennedy. "Let's talk more about that tomorrow night".

"I will, sir, it's an interesting idea," said Hal.

"And one more thing," said the President as he turned towards the door of the shack. "I know you live in a world of protocol and regulations but when it's just you and me, cut the 'sir', just call me Jack."

Hal struggled for something to say, "I'll try, sir, but that's a tall order."

Kennedy laughed, "But it is an order and one you'll have to learn to obey. Good night, Hal."

"Good night, Jack." He sounded like a six-year-old calling his father by his first name.

BOCA RATON, FLORIDA
Present Day

Mahoney stretched his back and took a few minutes to check his notes. "You mentioned that Kennedy helped mold world politics over the years. Was that a topic of conversation between the two of you as well?"

"Yeah, especially early on we probably talked more about current events and theorized on how to change them than any other topic, Mister Mahoney," said Hal. "Jack told me he once read about a chess game that had been played for several years between two pen pals. One player was in Oklahoma, the other player lived in Peru. They notified each other of their moves by mail, which could take weeks to arrive, with each letter reporting only one move, Bishop to Knight's seven for instance. Jack saw himself as a long-distance and invisible chess player, his board-the world, the stakes-enormous. We spent hours and hours talking about the changes that needed to take place and how Jack, with his limited resources and lack of a communications network could invisibly introduce these changes, or make his next move. Then we would spend hours doing a post mortem, discussing how well Jack's techniques had worked and what he could have done better or how he could have influenced the desired results more effectively."

Mahoney was regaining interest, "That's a little heavier conversation than discussing the weather or fishing."

Hal smiled warmly, "I miss those conversations. I learned far more about the world while sitting on a sailboat in the Ionian Sea than I did when I worked in the White House."

"So effectively you were Kennedy's sounding board during those years," Mahoney commented.

"I believe so, or at least his live sounding board. He also spent at least an hour each day, sometimes more, writing in his journal. He would note down his thoughts and then later, the next day or the next week, go back and read his notes which would help him organize, understand, clarify, and rationalize the situation at hand."

Mahoney sat straight up in his chair, "Kennedy wrote a journal?" he asked excitedly. "Where in the hell is that?"

Hal shook his head, "I already thought of that. As much as he wrote, he would have had a hundred notebooks. I never saw him with any more than one at a time. I don't know where he kept the old ones or even if he did keep them. And if they were lying around after he died, you know sure as hell that the Secret Service went in and sanitized the island. They would have destroyed every trace of Jack Kennedy they could find. They couldn't have a journal in his handwriting, discussing current events, pop up somewhere."

"My god," said Mahoney, "if this were all true could you imagine the world history in those journals?"

Hal heard but chose to ignore Mahoney's, "if this were all true," comment.

"Would there be any other documentation regarding Kennedy's time on Skorpios?" asked Mahoney.

"Probably not," said Hal. "Cameras were not allowed on the island, we never recorded Jack's voice, and other than his journals, which he wasn't supposed to be keeping, we were careful to destroy all records. The only piece of handwriting I know of that survives past November '63 is the note he made to me on the bottom of the coconut. I don't know if there's some scientific way to determine if he wrote that before or after his assassination or if a handwriting expert could tie that note back to his hand after forty some years. Surely his handwriting would have changed over the years."

Mahoney made another note to check into both before he asked, "What specific events in history did Kennedy have a hand in? Tell me more about that."

Hal stood and stretched while he thought for a moment, "There is so much to tell. I'm not exactly sure where to begin other than at the beginning. How about another scotch?"

"Sure," said Mahoney. "So let's start at the beginning then. What was Kennedy's first order of business?"

Hal poured two more glasses of scotch while he thought about the question. "I don't think Jack had an 'order of business' when we arrived on Skorpios. I think he had resigned himself to the idea that he was going to live out his life bored to tears, self-banished to a little island in the middle of nowhere, thousands of miles from his children. Until he started to help build the main house I don't think he had any idea what his new life was going to be."

Hal settled gingerly back into his chair before continuing. "He was fairly depressed when we arrived on the island but his attitude changed greatly when he started working with his hands, and it got even better when he jumped head first into learning to speak Greek. I'm not sure, but I think Jack may have beaten the world record for becoming fluent in Greek. He absolutely gobbled up that language and then he attacked Russian."

"So take me through a 'day in the life' of Kennedy, if you would, Hal," said Mahoney.

Hal sat back in his chair and took a drink of scotch as a thin, warm smile spread across his face. Then he looked up towards the ceiling for a moment before saying, "Take you through a day in the life of Jack Kennedy in the early years. Well, Jack always woke up early, around daylight and did his exercise routine. In the early years, I didn't work out with him but he finally goaded me into it when I was in my mid-thirties and I realized he could outdo me in just about anything physical. By the time Jack had finished his exercises, the cook would have a small breakfast ready and after that it was time to go to work. In the forty-some years I was out on the island we never stopped building, rebuilding, refinishing, or remodeling something. Jack was born with a silver spoon but once he discovered life with a rusty shovel he never turned back. The man loved to work with his hands, to build and create. He had his hands on everything from building houses and boats to working in the garden. In the early afternoon we would knock off and catch a small bite to eat before retiring for a mid-day nap."

Hal was quiet for a moment then said, "Something interesting occurred every day about this time. When Jack came out of his room around mid-afternoon, he was cleaned up, wearing a good shirt and either a clean pair of trousers or shorts, and he was ready to really get to work. During *oress keeneese esee heeas*, that's Greek for siesta, he changed from a laborer to an intellectual. It was then that he worked on financial dealings or other matters. It was then that he wanted to discuss politics, economics, world leaders, and current events."

"And he discussed those topics with you? What about the others?" asked Mahoney.

"I was interested in those subjects, those topics. I was the only American on the island that had a degree in political science. The other three agents had all come to the service through the military. Not one of them seemed to have even the vaguest interest in the subjects that Jack wanted to discuss. Now, compared to Jack, I was a neophyte in nearly every subject but as he shared his knowledge I learned. Then he encouraged me to read books that were both in agreement with and contrary to his way of thinking. He loved it when I took the opposite side of an argument. Because of Jack's schedule, I volunteered for the second shift, four in the afternoon to midnight. That's when Jack wanted to 'work things out,' as he called it."

Mahoney was trying to be tolerant with the old man but his patience to hear details about JFK's activities was growing thin. "So what did Kennedy actually do?" he asked again.

"His first order of business," said Hal who recognized his guest's growing edginess, "was to get Khrushchev out of power in the USSR."

SKORPIOS ISLAND
December 21, 1963

"What keeps you awake at night, sir?" asked Hal. Kennedy sat on the edge of the bunker silently smoking a cigarette in the dark.

"Are you kidding?" Kennedy replied with a laugh. "I'm sitting out here on a little island with no real future. If I try to change that, my deception will be uncovered and my own reputation along with our family name will be destroyed. Jackie, my now single wife, is getting ready to celebrate Christmas with my two children who believe that their Daddy is dead. Those three didn't sign up for the life they are being forced to live."

Hal searched for something to say to comfort the man, "Didn't you do this for your children, sir?"

Kennedy watched the smoke from his cigarette rise in the light from the half moon. "I did this to prevent World War Three . . .," he stopped in mid-sentence. "Yes, I guess when I think about it I did do this for my family and my country. I need to remember that."

Kennedy threw his cigarette out towards the middle of the clearing. "Two things, Hal, you've got to talk me into giving up these damn cigarettes and two, quit calling me 'sir.'"

"The first one is easy, I can't stand the smell of those things," said Hal. "The second request might take a bit of time."

Kennedy dropped his head and looked at the ground near his feet. In a dejected tone he said quietly, "I've got a feeling we have plenty of time. We've got nothing but time, Hal."

Hal looked at the man with concern as Kennedy sat on a sandbag on the edge of the bunker with his head hanging. He was trying to think up something to say when Kennedy suddenly looked up.

"Here's what we're going to do," said Kennedy. His voice had changed from depressed and withdrawn to authoritative and decisive, a unique trait that Hal would eventually become accustomed. "My two most pressing concerns for our country at the moment are NASA and Khrushchev."

"Sir?" Hal responded.

Kennedy shifted to face Hal directly, "Don't call me 'sir'." Without skipping a beat he continued, "I'm concerned that Johnson doesn't have the same level of urgency about getting to the moon that I do. If the President isn't pushing that initiative it will die and we can't let that happen."

Hal hadn't missed the fact that Kennedy had used the term "we" several times in the last few moments. He didn't ask who "we" included.

"Our first task is to figure out how to continue our efforts to reach the moon," Kennedy continued. "I think we can get Bobby,

Ted, and others to push Congress to continue funding NASA as a tribute to the poor, dead President. It's my legacy," he said.

Hal wasn't completely sure if Kennedy was addressing him or just talking out loud.

"I'll draft an outline to Bobby, Ted, and Mac with some ideas regarding who we need to get in our corner in Congress. I also think we need to push for public support of NASA; we can pull on their heartstrings if we can get the press to talk about the moon landing as a tribute to me. God, that sounds arrogant when I say it," he commented. "Once I draft the plan, Hal, I want you to go over it for me and poke holes in it."

Hal was surprised, "Me, sir? I don't know anything about the level of politics you're playing in."

"Bullshit, Hal. We haven't had much of a chance to chat but I can tell that you're as level-headed and intelligent as anybody else on this island. You're here to protect and serve me, right?"

"Yes, sir, that's my duty."

"Then quit calling me 'sir' when we are alone and start serving me by listening to and reading my proposals and ideas and finding the holes in them. I don't have Bobby and Ted Sorensen here with me so you're going to have to fill that role," said Kennedy. "We have a lot to accomplish and you're the guy who can help me do it, do you have an issue with that?"

Hal welled up with pride, "No, sir. I mean, no, Jack. I'll help you any way I can."

"Excellent. Our second task is even more pressing than the first. We avoided a major war by pulling off this scheme but Khrushchev is still in control of a nation with biggest army in the world, and he's still crazy. We need to figure out how to remove him from power without causing a civil war in Russia. Any ideas?"

Geez, Hal thought to himself, he had never spent a single moment of his life thinking about how to dethrone a world leader. How was he going to get it across to Kennedy that these conversations were way out of his league? He tossed out the first question that came to him, "Is there anybody in Russia you can trust?"

"Brezhnev," said Jack. "He must suspect that the assassination was a fraud."

"Who's Brezhnev?" asked Hal.

"Leonid Brezhnev, he's the President of the Presidium for the Soviets and the guy who started the back-channel communications with us that helped us avoid a confrontation." Kennedy gazed up towards the top of the trees and out to the stars beyond while he thought for a moment. "I don't need to mention to you that the content of these conversations are top secret?" he said.

Hal chuckled, "Hell, sir, my entire life is top secret now."

"Good point," said Jack with a laugh. "We need to figure out how to open a line of communications with Brezhnev. I get the feeling that he wants to be the next Party Secretary. If we can find a way to help him toss Nikita out and take over his position without dividing the party and the country, we'll have a friend for life and we will have helped put a more rational leader in place." Jack was quiet for a few moments before continuing, "If we accomplished that, could we ever go public with all this? Could I ever return to the States without landing in prison and destroying the reputation of the presidency and the trust in the government?"

Hal wanted to be positive, "I think the public would understand if they knew the whole story."

Jack ran his hand through his hair, "I don't know, Hal. I just don't know."

BOCA RATON, FLORIDA
Present Day

"How could Kennedy dethrone Khrushchev from where he sat?" asked Mahoney.

"Logistically, it was pretty easy," said Hal. "Remember, he and Brezhnev were very close allies at that point."

"So you are asking me to believe that Kennedy orchestrated the fall of Khrushchev?"

Hal's tone surprised Mahoney with its edge, "I'm not asking you to believe anything, Mister Mahoney. I'm simply telling you what I know about certain events."

After a moment, Hal asked, "Shall I continue?"

Mahoney cautioned himself to mind his manners, "I'm sorry, Hal, but you have to agree that this piece of history takes a bit of getting comfortable with. Yes, please continue. How exactly did Kennedy orchestrate, if that's the right word, the removal of Khrushchev?"

Hal took a sip of his scotch, "I'm sorry, Mike. I'm trying to tell you about the life of a friend who recently died. It can be difficult at times."

"Please continue," said Mahoney in a humble tone.

Hal cleared his throat, "The only time I met Leonid Brezhnev was when he came to the island in the spring of the first year . . .."

Mahoney interrupted, "He actually came to Skorpios?"

"Yes, he was there for a couple of days. It was just him, two or three security people, and his personal secretary, as I recall."

"Were you involved in any of those conversations?" asked Mahoney.

"No," said Hal. "We spent most of our time watching Brezhnev's security staff watch us while Kennedy and Brezhnev talked." Hal chuckled. "The two security details were so busy trying to prove who had the bigger dicks that the two of them could have been killed by the cook and we wouldn't have known it. Looking back, we were pretty pathetic."

"Do you know what was discussed?" asked Mahoney.

"Only from a third party point of view; Jack was eager to recount their conversations with me later but I have no way of knowing if he told me everything they discussed. Basically, they were trying to figure out how to remove Khrushchev without creating a civil war in Russia. Now, according to Jack, the biggest benefit that came from those hours of discussions was the understanding he gained of the structure of the Soviet government. It was probably the best understanding of the USSR power structure that any American had ever developed."

"Do you know if they formulated a plan then to remove Khrushchev and what it was?" asked Mahoney.

"Yes, Brezhnev walked away with a plan. Kennedy wasn't a hundred percent sure that Brezhnev had the brains and brawn to pull it off, but he had a plan. And as you would expect, it was taken from Kennedy's own playbook. Build support from the top down, one player at a time. They decided that Brezhnev needed to gain support from the central committee. To do that, he had to go over a lot of heads and get right to the upper echelons of the party and convince them that Khrushchev was unstable."

Hal continued, "Brezhnev began building a conspiracy one person at a time, convincing each person that Khrushchev's behavior was leading to his downfall and eventually would lead to the downfall of the Party. The party bosses were pretty easy to convince, given Nikita's erratic policies and his cantankerous behavior. It was easy to paint the man as an embarrassment in the light of his handling of China, the Cuban crisis, and the Soviet economy. At the same time, Brezhnev was convincing each of them that Khrushchev needed to be ousted, he also was demonstrating to them that he was the right man to take over the job."

"And obviously," said Mahoney, "he was successful."

Hal shifted slightly in his chair, "Yes, it was a brilliant combination of good old American politics combined with Russian paranoia. Once Brezhnev had convinced the power players that leaving Khrushchev in place would be the end of the USSR, he was able to get those players to enlist the support of the Army and the KGB. In October of 1964, while Khrushchev was on vacation, they put the plan into action. Brezhnev, Shelepin, and the chief of the KGB-geez, what was his name?" Hal closed his eyes and tapped on his forehead.

"Semichastny, Vladimir Semichastny," Hal said, opening his eyes wide. "Those three took a huge chance; they made themselves look as if they were leading the charge and had Khrushchev escorted back to Moscow. When he arrived, a special meeting of the Presidium of the Central Committee was called and they voted to have him removed from his position. Of course, the votes were already tallied before the meeting started. It was a railroad job from the very beginning. With no support behind him, all that Khrushchev could do was resign as Premier, leaving Brezhnev in the driver's seat, or so they thought at the time."

Mahoney was again taking notes rapidly. He looked up and said, "What do you mean. Wasn't Brezhnev the next leader of the USSR?"

Hal leaned forward, "Remember, Jack and Brezhnev had tried to use American political plays in Russia. The way things are done in the U.S. are dramatically different than how they were done in the Soviet Union. In the USSR, everything was done in a very precise manner of hierarchy and party positioning. If Khrushchev had died before all of this occurred, Brezhnev would not have been the successor. He was only able to gain the position because he was the guy with the plan and also the guy who was making promises to the players. In the U.S., you basically sell your soul to each player. If you make enough promises to enough people, you get elected to the position you are after. But then to remain in that position, you need to pay off on those promises. Brezhnev made promises to key committee members that he had to eventually make good."

Mahoney lifted his head from his notebook and turned to Hal, "So Brezhnev sold his soul to the central committee and didn't really have any power as the new Premier?"

"Exactly," said Hal. "He turned out to be a puppet. His strings were pulled by so many different players that he didn't have, and couldn't gain, any power."

"So the plan backfired?" asked Mahoney.

"It only failed in the sense of Brezhnev's actual authority as Premier. Remember, the number one goal was to remove Khrushchev from power before he started World War Three. They achieved goal number one and, after a few years, they figured out how to make Brezhnev the undisputed leader of the USSR."

"And how did they do that?" asked Mahoney.

Hal stared at Mahoney for a few seconds while he thought about it, "They simply waited for the Soviet power players to do something stupid, then they cleaned house."

Mahoney stood and stretched his legs. He walked over and stared out the front window at an elderly couple who were slowly riding their bicycles past, "So how did Kennedy stay involved in the world's political scene while he was out on the island. Was there a phone line to Skorpios?"

"No," said Hal. "We didn't really have any real communications on the island until about 1967 when we were able to link into the military's TACSAT systems."

"How did you keep up with current events?" asked Mahoney.

"We had a Hallicrafter shortwave set that we used to listen to the BBC. And we had a secure military radio but it was only as secure as a radio could be. We were directed to use it only in case of an emergency, something medical or an attack on the island."

Hal explained, "Communication to and from Skorpios in the early days was mainly telegrams sent in simple coded English and delivered by boat from Nydri, the little town about two miles west of us on Lefkada Island. If there was something of great importance going on, one of us would spend the day hanging out at this little café across the street from the telegraph office."

"Interesting," said Mahoney as he turned towards Hal. "But how did Kennedy stay in the loop, politically speaking, while he was out on an island?"

"Jack had quite a network at his disposal. Besides his brothers, Bobby and Teddy, he had a pretty impressive group of people with their ears to the ground in Washington and around the world. Just to name a few, he had the former Ambassador to India, Ken Galbraith, in his court; he corresponded regularly with Bob McNamara and with Ted Sorensen who had John McCone, the Director of the CIA, as an ally. There wasn't much of consequence that happened in Washington, including inside the FBI building, that Jack didn't hear about or couldn't find out about."

"I still don't understand the communications. The former president of the United States is on an island in the middle of nowhere, an island owned by one of the wealthiest men in the world, and your only means of communication is an emergency radio and a shortwave receiver?"

Hal laughed, "Remember, Mister Mahoney, nobody including Onassis wanted the world to know that Jack was alive. Everybody wanted him to go out to Skorpios and live out the remainder of his life under a rock. They didn't want him communicating with anybody and they didn't ask for or want his opinion on anything. If he was found, a lot of people were going to go to jail for a very long time. Even Onassis feared that his reputation would be damaged for harboring a fugitive."

"I hadn't thought about it like that," said Mahoney. "So they really thought this guy would, or even could just hang out on an island and enjoy the sun for the next forty or fifty years?"

"Yeah, I think it's important to remember that there was a lot of planning around making the assassination seem plausible, and quite a bit of planning around where to stash the president and how to keep him hidden, but virtually no forethought about what to do with him after he was safely on the island," said Hal.

"Unbelievable," said Mahoney.

"That's not the half of it. In the beginning he was a pariah, nobody including his friends wanted much to do with him during those first couple of months. After the smoke cleared a little, he started hearing from them again and then he was able to start working his way back into the loop. Two real breaks came, one when we found out there was a Greek spook on the island and the second when Ari figured out that he could use Jack to gain all sorts of information about his clients and his competitors."

Mahoney looked surprised, "Jack helped Onassis engage in corporate espionage?"

Hal took on a stern look, "Two things, Mister Mahoney. First of all you didn't know the man, please don't refer to him as 'Jack'. Secondly, no, Jack never helped Onassis engage in any sort of espionage. He was, however, able to provide certain pieces of information that helped with bids or he could arrange introductions that helped Ari obtain shipping contracts. But I don't believe it was anything illegal."

Mahoney smiled, "Sorry, I didn't mean to call the President by his nickname."

Hal brushed it off with a wave of his hand and continued. "In exchange, when Ari saw the benefits that Jack could offer, he helped him to set up rings of information around the world. Today we might call those spy rings," Hal chuckled. "Hell, back then we might have called them spy rings, too, but 'information ring' has a much more respectable sound to it."

"Who was the Greek spook?" asked Mahoney.

"There was a man on Ari's security staff who was placed there by Greek intelligence to keep an eye on Onassis. He made contact with us very early, we worked with him on one side and Ari on the other," answered Hal.

"So Kennedy and Onassis operated independent, privately-funded spy rings and at the same time, Kennedy was working with Greek intelligence?" asked Mahoney incredulously.

"Jack and Ari set up a series of small, simple rings, but yes, they had people who sold them information. Some were government insiders, some worked for various militaries or intelligence agencies around the world, and some were just janitors who sifted through the trash of high-ranking officials at night."

"And what part of buying stolen documents from janitors isn't illegal?" asked Mahoney.

"The part that prevented wars," answered Hal. "The part that saved lives and kept the world from launching missiles at each other, and the part that helped preserve certain freedoms in this country, like the freedom of the press."

Mahoney stood near the window looking at Hal without commenting. Hal paused for a moment before adding, "I'm not saying everything we did in those days was completely on the up and up. But you need to keep in mind that the cold war, was swinging into full gear, the world was crazy. Hell, Mike, sometimes half the population of Washington, D.C., was foreign spies. There were times when we knew more about what was going on in Vietnam or even the White House than Johnson did. We passed information to the CIA, the FBI, and even directly to the Johnson Administration. It was a completely different environment than what we live in today."

Mahoney got the message, no more questions about the legality or the morality of what he was learning, focus on the historical facts. "So Onassis and Kennedy had their information rings and Kennedy's buddies were starting to talk with him again, where did all that lead?"

"At first, his contacts in Washington just wanted to bounce things off him. Relations with the Soviets were cooling under Johnson, the Vietnam War was heating up but nobody completely understood how closely the two were related. In the U.S., the Civil Rights issue was starting to boil. Certain people wanted to know what President Kennedy thought about this or that and they started asking his opinion. Often his opinions on a certain matter were shaped by information he had received from his information rings. For instance, when asked once if he thought the Soviets would retaliate over a border skirmish with the Chinese. He responded, 'They will only retaliate on a battlefield level, not a full blown war with the Chinese because they simply can't afford to go to war.' Jack knew that because he and I had been pouring over economic data that had been smuggled out of Moscow."

"That had to be exciting," said Mahoney, "to be working with that kind of information next to that man at that time in history."

Hal rocked back, "It was more than exciting, Mike. During the Kennedy administration there was such a sense of hope, of change in America. We had these young and progressive politicians who were making sweeping transformations of stodgy old political patterns. Kennedy wanted to change the world so he sent kids out into it to help underprivileged people live better lives. He established the Peace Corp to help end poverty and hunger but his real goal was to make the world a smaller place by getting the youth of this country to understand that, no matter where they lived, other people were just like us."

"Kennedy wanted to revolutionize the way we thought about our earth so he pushed us into space," Hal said. "He pushed the country to support NASA. That's a move, Mister Mahoney, for which we may never fully understand the benefits. In order to send a man into space we had to develop technologies that propelled us past the Russians in every arena. We dominated the computer, aerospace, and medical industries in the 1980s and 90s because of the technology we began developing in the 1960s." Hal stared blankly at the wall for a few moments before continuing, "In November of '63, all of that hope, all that optimism was snuffed out in a flash. The news of Jack's death had far more of an impact than Jack or any of the group who planned the 'assassination' could have imagined. It was as if all the air had suddenly been sucked out of the atmosphere. I remember watching Johnson address the country that night or the next day, I don't remember which. He looked and talked like a stodgy old politician, he reinforced the desperation and sense of loss we were all feeling. We all stood around gasping, grasping for something. I have never felt such a feeling of loss, a feeling of defeat, almost a feeling of desperation."

Mahoney was taken by the emotion welling up from the old man and wisely remained quiet and let Hal continue when he was ready.

"Exciting?" asked Hal rhetorically. "It was so much more than exciting. To go from the feeling of indescribable loss at the time of his death to being one of the few people on the planet who knew the man was alive was overwhelming. To go from that desperate time to a time just a few months later when he and I would sit under the stars and theorize on how we might try to change and affect the condition of our world, that was beyond exciting, beyond amazing."

Hal closed his eyes for a few moments before opening them and looking straight at Mahoney. The two men stared at each other for a moment before Mahoney asked, "Was it a sense of a new beginning, of renewed hope?"

Hal thought about that before answering, "For me, it was more of a return to a time of hope that I felt had been taken from me, from the world. And it was better than that because I went from being a cheerleader on the sidelines to a lineman, the guy blocking for and protecting the quarterback. And then before long, the quarterback was asking for and respecting my opinions on the next play he was about to call. Never in my life have I felt as important as I did during the years on the island when we were handling all that information, when we played chess on a board the size of the world."

"You mentioned you passed information back to the United States; how did you do that in such a way that they didn't find out that the information was coming from Kennedy?" asked Mahoney

Hal pulled a handkerchief from his pocket and wiped his eyes before answering. "I was a spy," he chuckled. "At least the CIA and the FBI thought I was a spy. Not Hal Rumsey in particular, but they knew they had somebody in the region who was passing information to them. To create a level of cushion between the information and Jack, I was the one who passed the details to the appropriate people. Later, and this is spooky, we found out that the CIA gave me, or my spy alter ego, the code name 'Harvard'. They were somehow able to determine from the diction we used that the spy was born and educated on the east coast of the United States. They knew the information was coming from Yugoslavia or Greece but we didn't believe they ever tracked us any closer than that."

Mahoney interrupted, "How did you pass the information from Skorpios to the U.S.?"

"We used a variety of methods over the years," said Hal, "from the old dead drop to more progressive methods; more recently, we just sent plain old emails knowing they would be lost in the billions of emails sent each day."

"What was the dead drop?" asked Mahoney.

"That's the old method you've seen in movies. First, you indicate to your intended courier that there is something to be picked up. We used a light on the side of a warehouse down by the dock originally. If that light was on, there would be something for us at a certain location, in a crevice behind the statue in the park or behind a loose brick in a building down the alley," Hal explained. "It worked both ways; if we left the light on, they knew to pick up something and if we saw it on, we knew there was something for us."

"And who were 'they'?" asked Mahoney.

"Initially, we passed information through a group of men who were loyal to Onassis. As we built the different rings, we needed to move the information through different paths or people, and sometimes perhaps too many people. At one time in the late sixties, the Chief of Police in Nydri commented in the local paper about the number of suspicious characters who loitered about his town. We were probably responsible for most of those people," chuckled Hal.

SKORPIOS ISLAND
December 25, 1963

The construction crew and Aristotle's tiny staff including Demetrius were granted a few days off for Christmas reducing the island's population to just the five Americans and Ari's unseen security force.

The cook had prepared two large turkeys, a couple of pots of soup, and a large batch of melomacarona cookies, a traditional Greek Christmas cookie soaked in honey. The small Greek staff had done their best to give the area a bit of Christmas flair with plenty of food and a few decorations but morale among the Americans was low. Besides their families, they missed the western-style Christmas decorations and the other cheerful holiday trappings that weren't common in the Mediterranean.

Kennedy awoke early and decided he could either spend the day mired in depression and probably become more depressed watching his security detail mope around, or they could all make the best of a bad situation, bury themselves in work and then enjoy a big dinner together. He chose the latter.

Agent Mark Stennfeld was not at his post in the bunker when Kennedy stepped outside; he had heard Kennedy moving around and was now in the cook's shack brewing up another pot of coffee. Kennedy walked into the small shack they had recently walled in at the cook's request. The propane stove had been lit for a couple of hours so the room was warm and smelled of coffee and a medley of food aromas mixed with the scent of propane.

"Good morning, sir. Merry Christmas," said Stennfeld.

"Merry *Kourabiedes* to you," replied Kennedy. "Cool out this morning."

"Yes, sir. I was freezing my tail off so I decided to make a pot of coffee a couple of hours ago to help keep me warm. I'm afraid I drank the whole pot but I'll have a fresh one ready soon."

"Thanks, Mark. I appreciate that," said Kennedy. "I was poking around in here last night. I found flour, eggs, and a small tin of what I think is baking powder. We just might have all the materials for a big batch of pancakes. We'll have to substitute honey for maple syrup but I think I can put together a Christmas breakfast if you'd like."

"Sounds great," said Stennfeld. "How can I help?"

"Just give me a little room now and you can help me clean up later so we don't get in trouble with Kallisto," said Kennedy referring to the cook. Kallisto was a thin and frail older woman who scared the hell out of the big, brave Americans. "After a big breakfast, what do you say we rally the troops and finish that east wall? I'd rather work than sit around feeling sorry that I'm not at home with my family."

"I think that's an excellent idea, sir. I'll get the men up," said Stennfeld.

"Let them sleep, Mark," he said while searching for a large bowl. "I'm not a good cook or a fast one, this could take a while," he chuckled.

Stennfeld laughed as he walked towards the door then stopped and turned, "Sir, should we invite the Phantoms to dinner?"

The Greek security force was seldom seen or heard and because Captain Papadopoulos had made it clear to both his men and the Kennedy's that they were not to associate with each other, the Americans had started referring to them as the Phantom Force. They had no idea how many men Onassis had on the island and had only a vague idea of where they were camped. They spent their days and nights sitting in hidden bunkers in the brush waiting for the bad guys to attack. Word had recently gotten out that the island was now owned by Onassis so occasionally a sailboat or yacht would drop anchor off the island and some unsuspecting tourist would come ashore to see what there was to see. They were always met at the beach by a very large Greek with an automatic weapon and they always left quickly.

"That's a great idea, Mark," said Kennedy. "After breakfast let's walk over to that side of the island and see if we can convince them to dine with the infidels," he laughed.

Breakfast that Christmas morning consisted of a batch of odd tasting fried dough that resembled pancakes only in appearance, and a big bowl full of scrambled eggs. Despite the less than perfect food, the Americans were upbeat and enjoyed sitting down together for the meal. They joked and laughed and for the first time since arriving on the island, took the time to get to know each other a little better.

While Kennedy and Stennfeld cleaned up the kitchen, the other men got to work on the east wall. They were eager to surprise the Greek construction crew with their progress when they returned to the island. They worked shoulder to shoulder and quickly found a harmony that molded them into a perfect team. Bricks were placed and mortar was mixed, each man knew his job and performed it well. The men worked until mid-afternoon when they finished the east wall of the big house. Kennedy hadn't really expected that they would actually finish the wall that day or even the next but they had developed such an efficient system that they were done in record time.

The day had turned warm and the winter sun felt good as the five Americans stood back and looked at their achievement with the pride of a job well done. Kennedy looked at Agent Stennfeld who had been awake since midnight. "Stennfeld, go get some sleep. We'll wake you before dinner."

"No arguments here, sir. Don't have any fun without me," he said while turning away. He walked off towards the sleep shack with his shoulders slumped, obviously tired.

"I'm going to walk over to the other side of the island and invite the Greeks to come have dinner with us," said Kennedy.

Agent Walker furrowed his brow, "You're not walking over there by yourself, sir. And I'm not so sure you should go to that side of the island at all."

Kennedy shook his head, "It will be fine, Paul. Those men are here to protect me. I doubt they are going to shoot first in broad daylight."

"That's not a chance I'm willing to take," said Walker. "I'll go extend your invitation to them myself."

Kennedy was about to say "Bullshit," when it occurred to him that he had been somewhat circumventing Walker's authority ever since they had arrived on the island. It was Walker's command but Kennedy had been calling many of the shots over the past weeks. Even in just the past few hours he had directed the men to build a wall, ordered a man to get some rest, and decided who would attend dinner and who would go to invite the guests.

"Please don't accept 'no' for an answer," said Kennedy with a smile.

Walker was visibly surprised that there wasn't an argument. He composed himself for a moment and said, "I will make it clear to them that the President of the United States of America extends his personal invitation to dinner."

Walker decided to take Agent Rumsey along with him while Kennedy and Haycock prepared for dinner. Walker left standing a little taller and walked with a little more purpose than he had during his brief time on the island.

After Walker and Rumsey left, Kennedy and Haycock scrambled to put together a large table in anticipation of the Greeks accepting the invitation. They built a makeshift table on the veranda of the main house using the local version of sawhorses and some long planking to extend it. Then Haycock found a stack of five gallon metal buckets and some more planks they could use to make sturdy, if unstable benches for both sides of the table. They pulled a couple of oil lanterns out of the construction shed and hung them from rope they strung between the newly constructed rafters. Haycock gathered the few Christmas decorations that were scattered around and brought them to the veranda while Kennedy folded an old paint drop cloth to fit as a tablecloth. When they were done the two men stood back and looked at the veranda which overlooked the Ionian Sea. It looked like a weak attempt to disguise a bunch of construction material in the middle of a project but they both agreed that with the addition of food, wine, and a large group of men, the table it would look just like a large Christmas dinner at any home back in the States . . . sort of.

"Let's get the food ready," said Kennedy to Haycock. There was a tone of excitement in the President's voice that Haycock hadn't heard since taking this assignment. He secretly hoped that Walker and Rumsey would be successful.

From a vantage point just beyond the narrow neck of the island Paul Walker hoped he would be able to spot where the Greeks might be camped but all they could see was unbroken scrub brush and black oak trees all the way to the water. They couldn't see any buildings, tents, or clearings on that side of the island but they knew the Greeks were camped there, somewhere below and slightly north of where they stood.

Just as Walker took his first step down the trail, Rumsey pointed and said, "There!" A tiny puff of smoke rose above the brush about halfway between where they stood and the edge of the island.

"All right," said Walker. "Let's go make some friends."

They walked along a fairly well-used trail for about ten minutes before they rounded a bend to find a very large, very well-armed, and very imposing Greek man standing before them in the middle of the trail. He was dressed in dark fatigues, a tight-fitting black shirt, and leather laced boots. He held an AK-47 at the ready and also sported a sidearm and a very large knife which hung off the ammo belt he wore bandolier style across his massive chest.

The sight stopped the Americans in their tracks. For just a moment the three men simply stared at each other; then, without a word, the Greek man motioned for the Americans to follow him. He turned and led them along the trail.

Walker and Haycock followed the Greek for about two hundred yards before entering a clearing where the security force was encamped. It was exactly what Walker would have expected from Captain Papadopoulos, a very military camp. The small clearing contained a dozen small tents set up in two perfect lines leaving a space for a lane between them. At the end of the short lane was a larger tent, obviously command and communications center and behind that was a slightly larger tent that Walker guessed was the mess tent. From behind the mess tent, a thin line of smoke rose that Walker guessed was producing the wonderful smell of cooking meat that drifted through the camp. It was likely the smoke they had seen from the trail.

As the big Greek led them through the camp, the two Americans couldn't help but notice that there wasn't a speck of trash, a twig, a leaf, or a single blade of grass that seemed out of order. Some of the tents had their flaps closed, others were open and inside of those they could see perfectly made cots with everything in faultless order.

At what they had guessed to be the command tent, the big Greek stopped and stepped back to the left in a very military fashion. He pulled back the tent flap and motioned the Americans to enter. They had guessed correctly. Inside the tent, the walls held several maps, two of Skorpios and another of the islands around Skorpios. Each was marked with a series of differently colored symbols and lines that meant nothing to the Americans without a legend. The tent smelled of canvas, sweat, and cigarette smoke. Towards the back, a table held a rather large radio set; directly in front of them was a smaller table that served as a desk, it was completely clear of any paperwork or clutter. Seated behind the table was a man that Walker judged to be only a few years younger than himself.

The man behind the table looked up as they entered. Walker, uncertain if he should offer a handshake to the man or a salute, did neither. "Is Captain Papadopoulos here?" he asked.

The man stood, "No, no. Captain Papadopoulos, Athens," he said.

"Do you speak English?" Walker asked.

"No," the man answered.

He pointed out to the camp in a sweeping motion, "Do your men speak English?"

"No English," the man said in a bit of a biting tone.

Walker turned to Rumsey, "This is going to be difficult," he said.

"Let me try, sir," said Rumsey. Walker gave him a curt nod of approval.

Hal took a half of a step forward towards the man behind the table. "Merry Christmas," he said slowly. The Greek gave him a nod of understanding. "We would like you to come eat with us," he made a gesture of eating with his hands, "and drink with us," he gestured drinking. The Greek gave a look of confused interest. Rumsey tried again. "Come with us, to large house," he pointed in the general direction of the other side of the island. "Eat, drink wine, Ouzo, Merry Christmas." The man's expression changed to one of understanding and he even smiled a bit. Rumsey turned and motioned across the camp, "Everybody come."

The man pulled a piece of paper out of his shirt pocket and reviewed it, seemingly counting for a moment then smiled at the Americans. He pointed at the men, "You go, we come." He held up his hands, five fingers on one hand and one on the other, indicating either that they would come at 6:00 p.m. or there would be six of them. Neither American pressed the question, they were just happy they could report back to Kennedy that some of the Greeks were coming at some time. They both nodded in acceptance and left the tent. Their huge guard was waiting. He seemed to have a little less imposing look on his face, maybe even a hint of a smile. As he led them out of the camp, the man who had been behind the desk stepped out and barked out what sounded like orders to the men who came out of their tents and stood at attention.

Agent Walker looked over his shoulder as he and Rumsey walked out of camp and laughed, "They look like they are either getting ready to march over for Christmas dinner or they completely misunderstood and they are organizing an attack."

"Let's hope it's dinner," said Rumsey.

The big Greek led them to the top of the rise where the trail branched out in many directions; he pointed them towards the correct one and then smiled and shook each by the hand.

"Well, I'll be damned," said Walker. "I think the big lug likes us."

Kennedy was coming out of the cook's shack when Walker and Rumsey walked back into the compound. "How did it go?" asked Kennedy anxiously.

"I think they are coming over," answered Walker. "The Captain is apparently in Athens but the man who was in charge seemed excited."

"Excellent. How many are coming?" asked Kennedy.

"We're not exactly sure. Language was a bit of a barrier. The man indicated six but we're not sure if that means six men or if they were coming at six o'clock."

"How many men do they have over there?" asked the President out of curiosity.

"We saw seven in the camp including the commander and the guard who escorted us in," Rumsey answered. "We counted twelve two-man tents. They all looked like they were being used."

"Well, no matter how many show up, great job, guys. We have some work to get done and a meal to prepare," said Kennedy. "Paul, can you help Haycock up on the veranda? Hal why don't you help me in the kitchen," Kennedy had resumed his commander role.

About an hour before sundown, the five Americans gathered on the Veranda of main house. They were each proud of their accomplishments; the 'dining area' had been cleared of construction materials and now looked somewhat festive. The cooks had boiled and mashed the potatoes, deboned two turkeys, and Hal had remembered how to make gravy, lumpy and runny but gravy by anybody's definition.

"How long should we wait before we break into the wine and start eating without our guests?" asked Walker.

Before anybody could answer Hal said, "Here they come!"

Seven men, each armed with an AK-47, and a sidearm, and each carrying some food or a bottle walked into the clearing. Two of the men carried a slab of meat on a spit. Walker hoped it was the meat they had smelled cooking in their camp.

Not one of the American security personnel cared for the fact that the men came to dinner armed and, as they had been trained to do, saw them as a potential threat but Kennedy grinned ear to ear and greeted them at the front steps.

"Kalosorisma Filos! Welcome, friends," he said in a big booming voice. *"Empros, empros,"* he said inviting the Greeks in.

They each handed the President what they were carrying, wine, ouzo, bread, and dishes of various food. Kennedy passed each man's offering to one of the agents then shook their hands saying *"Kalosorisma"* to each man individually.

When the men had presented their offerings and had shaken the President's hand, they stepped back into rank. There was a moment of awkward silence before the older man, the one Walker and Rumsey had spoken with at the camp, barked an order. Each man un-shouldered his weapon and leaned it against the wall behind them and then they unstrapped their sidearms and laid them on the floor next to their rifles.

With that, the Secret Service agents relaxed. Agent Walker looked at his men and barked, "Don't stand there, get these men a glass of wine!"

The older Greek stepped forward and offered his hand to Walker who shook it. "Me Boulos, you?"

"My name is Walker."

While he still held Walker's hand he said "No wine, my friend Walker. New friend, ouzo!"

Walker laughed then turned to his men and said, "I hereby order you to drink ouzo with our new Greek friends."

Kennedy motioned the men towards the veranda while one man picked up two bottles of Ouzo Veto from the cache they had brought.

As they filed out towards the veranda Hal Rumsey said to Walker, "Sir, I go on duty in about an hour. If it's okay with you I'll pass on the drinks and pull an all-nighter so the rest of you can enjoy yourselves."

"That's a good idea, Rumsey. I appreciate that," said Walker.

Out on the veranda Kennedy passed out glasses to each man. They had just enough glasses for each man to have one but each would have to serve as a water, wine, and ouzo glass. Kennedy was fairly certain it wouldn't matter to anybody tonight.

One of the Greeks followed the president around filling each man's glass with two fingers of the clear liqueur. Standing in a loose circle, the men all facing each other, Boulos raised his glass and said *"Stini Yamas,"* before downing his drink in one gulp. The others followed his lead. The Greeks slapped their American friends on the back in a sign of comradeship.

Most of the Americans had never tasted the anise flavored spirit and the strong licorice flavor surprised them. Before they had a chance to comment, the Greek with the bottle was refilling glasses.

When the man with the ouzo came to Rumsey and saw that the American had no glass, he turned and picked one off the table. Hal tried to politely say, "No" to the man but the other Greeks noticed that an American was not drinking with them and Hal suddenly became the focus of the party. Hal said in a contrite tone, "No ouzo." He pointed to his chest, "Me guard tonight," while fashioning his fingers like guns and beading his eyes as though he was peering out into the night.

The Greeks laughed. While they would never say it, they considered the American security around the President to be a thin and worthless veil. Boulos approached Hal and put his hand on the American's shoulder in a fatherly fashion. He looked out towards the brush. "Greek there, there, there," he said while pointing his finger to different spots on the island below them. "Greek make okay, you drink ouzo."

Kennedy laughed, "That's pretty solid logic, Hal. The Greeks are on guard duty tonight, we are on what I call 'diplomatic duty'. Please drink with us. It's important to our relationship with our new friends."

With that, Hal accepted the glass from the Greek who filled it. Hal said "Salute," before gulping the drink to the cheers of the men around the table.

The language barrier seemed to fade as the drinks flowed. The Americans couldn't help but like their good spirited hosts. Before they all drank too much, the Americans started bringing food out from the kitchen. The Greeks added their lamb, marinated for 24 hours before being hand-turned on a spit for 12 hours, a dish that resembled a vegetable casserole, and an abundance of wine to the table. They ate plenty and laughed heartily. When dinner was finished, the Greeks brought out dessert, something they called *Galaktobouriko,* an egg custard baked in filo. After dessert, Agent Walker opened more wine while Kennedy passed out cigars to all the men.

Under the glow of the lanterns, the twelve men forgot for a while that they weren't home with their families. They communicated with hand gestures, facial expressions, and sometimes whole-body movements and they laughed at the men who took turns telling animated stories. During a quieter moment, a Greek man at the end of the table broke into song, a traditional Greek tune, while the Americans listened. When the Greek singer was finished Agent Haycock started broke into "Jingle Bells" and everybody joined in. To the Phantom guards out in the brush, it must have sounded like a wild fraternity party with the drunken voices of men laughing and singing loudly and out of tune.

After more wine they sang the songs of Bing Crosby and Frank Sinatra. Then Agent Haycock did a surprising rendition of an Ella Fitzgerald number. The men laughed and sang until early in the morning. Nobody was sure what time the party broke up except for the Greeks back in their camp who were awakened when their seven comrades stumbled back into their tents still singing.

BOCA RATON, FLORIDA
Present Day

Jose Telleria sat at the edge of the bed in his hotel room. He rubbed his eyes and stretched his back before getting up to splash water on his face. He had been awakened from a long nap by a call from Deputy McQuade who was short and curt. He simply said, "We have confirmation that Rumsey is talking. Please handle that situation and report back to me."

Over his lengthy career with the Secret Service, Telleria had been ordered to "take care of" many different situations. They usually involved protecting a sitting President from some embarrassment. He had made payoffs of large amounts of cash to people to ensure their silence and he had made both direct and indirect threats to others to keep their mouths shut. Once he had kidnapped a certain Senator's young son just to show that Senator that speaking out could have consequences. After Jose and the Senator's son had spent a pleasant afternoon at the Washington Zoo, the agent received a call telling him that the message had been received and he could drop the boy off near his home.

Jose had no misconceptions about this assignment. He knew that "Please handle that situation" wouldn't involve buying Rumsey an ice cream cone at the zoo. He had been trained that his job was that of a soldier and he was called into duty when the United States was under attack. He performed his job with the same attitude as that of a soldier in battle; he had to incapacitate the enemy before that enemy had the opportunity to harm him, attack his country, or injure his President.

This assignment was different, however. Jose had actually spoken to and looked into the eyes of the frail old man he had been ordered to 'silence'. Hal Rumsey was a man who had faithfully served his country and his President, much like Agent Telleria. He was an old and dying man whose only crime was failing to keep his mouth shut, a fact that actually angered Jose. If the old man and the helicopter pilot in Greece had simply kept their silence, which was clearly part of their duty, Jose wouldn't now have to do his duty. Growing angry with Hal Rumsey made the impending task easier in Telleria's mind, it didn't occur to him that his training was taking over.

After washing his face, Jose finished the last few sips of a flat and warm Diet Coke that had been sitting on the desk in his hotel room for hours. He picked his cell phone up off the bed and searched the directory for Dr. David Sheehan at Bethesda Naval

Hospital. He needed some information that he knew Commander Sheehan could quickly provide.

SKORPIOS ISLAND
December 27, 1963

In the days after Christmas the 'Phantom Force' became much more visible. A couple of the men who had been at the Christmas dinner stopped by to offer help on the construction of the main house and a few of the men who had not been present walked through the compound on their way to or from their posts, probably out of curiosity after hearing about the infamous dinner.

It was early afternoon two days after Christmas when Boulos, the older Greek man, who appeared to be in charge of the Phantom Force in the Captain's absence, walked into the compound. Kennedy and Agent Walker were looking over a masonry saw they had just broken, trying to figure out how to fix it before the construction crew returned.

"Kalosorisma, Boulos," Kennedy welcomed the man. They shook hands warmly then Boulos looked at the saw with a questioning expression.

"Kaput," said Kennedy.

The Greek stepped forward for a closer look at the broken blade. He pointed to it and said, "New this, and okay."

Kennedy laughed, "I hope so."

Boulos looked at Kennedy and inclined his head asking, "You come this way, one minute? We talk."

Walker was suspicious of the old Greek and uncertain of his motivations. "Please stay within my sight, sir," he said to Kennedy.

Kennedy followed the Boulos to the other side of the compound, out of earshot of his men, but Agents Walker and Haycock stood where they could see them.

"Mr. Kennedy," said Boulos, "please do not tell your men I speak English good or tell them who I am. I am Major with *Ethnki Ypiresia Plioforion* or Greek Central Intelligence Service, C.I.S., I believe your government calls it."

Kennedy was shocked to learn of the man's real occupation and also by his command of English. He had sat next to Boulos for several hours just two nights earlier and communicated by broken English and hand gestures. "May I ask why a Major in the C.I.S. is on guard duty on a little island in the Ionian Sea?"

Boulos smiled, "May I ask of you, why is American President hiding on little island in Ionian Sea?"

"What can I do for you, Mister Boulos?" asked Kennedy directly, hoping to avoid answering the Major's question.

"I am very interested in President Kennedy who is now living in our country. We might be able to help each other with mission?" asked Boulos.

"I don't have a mission, Mister Boulos. I am here as a guest of Mr. Onassis while we try to settle some problems in the United States," said Kennedy.

Boulos smiled and looked at the ground while kicking a small rock with his feet. "Boulos think you are here because Khrushchev try to kill you. Only way for no kill Kennedy and no war is no Kennedy."

"Boulos is a very smart man," said Kennedy. "Where did Boulos and the C.I.S. get their information and how many Greeks know I am here on Skorpios?"

"C.I.S. does not know Kennedy is here. Captain Papadopoulos and Mr. Onassis do not know I am C.I.S. I keep you secret, you keep my secret?"

"Yes," said Kennedy with no other real options. He shot a glance at Walker and Haycock who were being very attentive and curious of the conversation. "Mister Boulos, can you meet with me tonight about ten o'clock to talk more?"

"Yes," answered Boulos.

"I'll meet you behind the main house. I will have one man with me, a good man who can be trusted," said Kennedy.

Boulos nodded, offered a slight bow and then turned and left the compound.

Kennedy returned to the agents and the broken saw. "What did Mr. Boulos want?" asked Walker.

"I'm not a hundred percent sure," lied Kennedy. "I think he was hoping that I had some connections to help get his daughter into the

States. I assured him that all of my connections thought I was dead."

BOCA RATON, FLORIDA
Present Day

Mahoney was growing fatigued and the scotch wasn't helping but if any of the information he was recording was even remotely true, he was working on the biggest story of his career and probably the biggest news story in the history of the media. He looked at Hal who also seemed to be growing weary, "How are you holding up, Hal?"

As Hal shifted again in his chair, he winced in obvious pain. "Don't worry about me, Mr. Mahoney. I'll be the first to tell you when I've had enough."

Mahoney laughed, "Fair enough, Hal. You mentioned there was a Greek Intelligence agent on the island to watch Onassis. Why were the Greeks concerned about him?"

"Well, remember, in the years prior to our arrival, Ari had been able to purchase ships from the Americans, the French, and the Brazilians. His net worth was almost the same as the entire country of Greece and he appeared to be in bed with a variety of foreign governments. When he purchased an island and started hiring his own security force, Greek Intelligence sat up and took notice. They started embedding agents into his organization including his Skorpios security force. Our old buddy Boulos thought his assignment was to report what Onassis was up to on the island when all the sudden the recently assassinated President of the United States appeared on his doorstep," laughed Hal.

"So, Greek Intelligence knew Kennedy was alive?" asked Mahoney.

"No," said Hal with a smile. "I'm not sure they ever knew."

"Wait, why wouldn't Boulos tell his superiors that the leader of the free world, who had just been publicly assassinated, was on the island and that was really what Onassis was up to?"

"Boulos was a very intelligent guy," answered Hal. "He had been with Greek intelligence since the war. As much as he loved his country he was frustrated with the bureaucracy of his organization. He was convinced of a couple of things, one that he was the only C.I.S. agent on the island. He also was certain that if the C.I. S. knew of Jack's existence on the island, they would screw it up, they would try to use him, to extort him. Boulos believed he could better manage the relationship with Jack if he kept it close to his vest. He believed he could build a relationship with Jack and find ways that they could accomplish great things together. And finally, he believed that his mission was to gather information on Onassis. In his mind, the best way to gather intel Onassis and his organization was to build relationships with the staff and the guests on the island. He saw the bigger picture and figured out how to optimize the situation, initially for the C.I.S. and later for Boulos."

SKORPIOS ISLAND
December 27, 1963

Because of the shifts the Secret Service maintained, and because there wasn't anything to do on the island after dark, the off-duty Americans often went to bed very early. On this night, Kennedy lay on his cot in his 'Presidential Suite' writing in the glow of a candle until 9:45 p.m. when he stood up, slipped on his shoes and a light jacket and quietly walked out of the shack past the sleeping men.

The skies had cleared but a stiff wind blew in from the west which dropped the temperatures and made it seem much cooler than it actually was. A half-moon was low near the horizon but the stars seemed unusually bright and took the moon's place to provide some ambient light.

Rumsey turned in the bunker to see who was exiting the shack but before he could say anything Kennedy put his index finger to his lips silently telling Rumsey to be quiet. Then Kennedy gestured for Rumsey to follow him away from the shack.

"Evening, sir," said Hal when he caught up to Kennedy. "What's up?"

"Good evening, Hal. Do you remember my new best friend, Boulos, from dinner the other night?" asked Jack.

"The older guy who sat next to you?" Hal asked.

"Yeah, he came to see me this afternoon and he's coming to see you and me in a few minutes. It turns out that he speaks pretty damn good English. He also claims to be a Major with Greek Intelligence."

"Oh, shit, sir. Is our cover blown?" asked Hal.

"I don't think so, not yet anyway," said Jack, zipping up his jacket. "Boulos told me he had infiltrated the security team in order to help Greek Intelligence keep an eye on Onassis. I don't think he had any idea that we were going to show up out here."

Hal eyed the brush around the clearing; with the wind blowing as it was he would never be able to hear anybody approaching and he worried that standing where they were, they were too exposed. He motioned for Jack to walk with him closer to the shadows of the main house. "He's got to report your presence to his organization. It's too big to ignore."

"We'll see," said Jack. "He said that if I keep his secret and not tell Onassis and Papadopoulos who he is, he would keep my secret. He also said we might be able to help each other out with our 'missions' but I let him know that I didn't have a mission."

Hal stood silent for a moment thinking about the older Greek man. He tried to imagine his thought process and his motivations before saying, "Damn it, Jack. I think we have to snuff this guy out." As he said it, he realized the ramifications of his statement. He didn't want to 'snuff anybody out' but still thought it was the right course of action.

Jack looked at him with surprise. "Look," Hal continued, "if this guy is with Greek Intel, it's his job to report what's going on out here on this island. He thought he was going to catch Onassis getting in bed with the Turks or something but now he's got the biggest story of the decade sitting on his little island. He's got to run to his superiors with this."

"I'm not a hundred percent convinced of that," said Jack. "If Boulos was going to turn me in to his superiors, he would already have done it. He's had three weeks or more to decide on his moves, accepting our invitation to dinner was his opportunity to connect with us.

Jack pulled a pack of cigarettes out of his jacket pocket and flicked one out but then decided against it. He really was trying to smoke less. "I think Boulos is going to try to exploit the situation. As long as I help him gather intel and gain access to lines of communication in the U.S., I'm pretty certain he will keep our presence here his little secret."

"Which is exactly why we need to end this right now," said Hal very uncharacteristically. "We'll just tell Papadopoulos who he really is, they can drop him in the ocean and tell the Greek government that they don't know what happened to him. He just disappeared one night."

Jack flipped the pack of cigarettes around in his hand while thinking for a moment. "You might be right, Hal. But let's see what Boulos has to say to us tonight before we turn him over to Papadopoulos. His intentions might be far more innocent than what we think."

"When are we meeting with him?" asked Hal.

Jack held his watch up to get a better look in the star light, "In a few minutes on the other side of the house."

They quietly made their way around to the back of the house through the stacks of construction materials and piles of rubble. Standing under the veranda, they couldn't see anybody in the low light but a moment later both men were startled when the flame of a cigarette lighter glowed just fifteen feet away from them at the base of a tree. In the light of the flame, they could easily make out Boulos' face.

"Good evening, President Kennedy," said Boulos as he stepped forward.

"*Kalispera,*" replied Jack. "Good evening. Boulos, I'm not sure if you met my friend, Agent Hal Rumsey, the other night.

Boulos gave a slight nod of his head saying, "Yes, is good to see you, Agent Rumsey."

"And it's very good to meet you, Mister Boulos," said Hal. "Thank you for your continued hospitality to us in your country."

Jack glanced at Hal thinking, He's going to make a fine diplomat someday. Then he turned to Boulos, saying, "Thank you, Mister Boulos, for coming to this side of the island on such a cold night."

Boulos nodded slightly again, "Is my pleasure."

"How can we help you, Mister Boulos?" asked Jack.

"I like you get to point, Mister President," said Boulos. He took a long drag off his cigarette and blew the smoke into the wind as though he was carefully considering his next move. "Before, I tell you I am here to find out what Onassis is doing with island and large security team and this is true. Then I find he is hiding American President and Boulos ask why? Onassis must owe big favor to Americans for something, I do not know what. Or he provide island for President Kennedy to hide and wants big favor from Americans. Am I right?"

"You are correct," said Jack. "Onassis owes my family a big favor."

Boulos smiled, "So you are here and I am here. How do we make best of situation? I tell Greek C.I.S. you are here? Or I keep secret and you help me get information for C.I.S. and I no tell them where I get it."

Kennedy wasn't opposed to the proposition. A working relationship with a Greek intelligence agent could help him with the plans he was formulating but he wasn't about to be held hostage. "Mister Boulos, I think you and I can work very well together but I will not be a victim of extortion."

"Please excuse my not good English, what is this 'extortion'?" asked Boulos.

"It means, if I don't work with you, you will tell Greek C.I.S. I am here. It means I am forced to provide you with information to keep my presence here a secret," said Kennedy.

The Major's face twisted slightly, "No, no, no. You not understand. Boulos, no extortion to President Kennedy. Boulos and Kennedy and Agent Rumsey work together." He put his hands together, "We work as team, no extortion. Boulos no tell secrets to C.I.S., Kennedy no tell secrets to Onassis or Captain Papadopoulos."

Jack held out his hand, "Agreed."

Boulos wanted to make sure the Americans clearly understood him, "You tell Captain Papadopoulos, Boulos is C.I.S, and," he made a motion of a knife cutting across his throat, "in my sleep."

"We understand," said Kennedy. "It is our secret." Jack didn't feel like he needed to review with Boulos the ramifications of the world finding out that he was on the island.

"How can Boulos help Kennedy and Agent Rumsey?" he offered.

"I need to get a personal message to Chairman Brezhnev. Do you know how to do that?" asked Jack.

Boulos smiled, he knew Kennedy was up to something. "I have people who know right people. What is message?"

"Jack looked up at the stars for a moment while thinking, "Get a message to Brezhnev that 'Pig is on ice and needs to talk'. He will understand'."

BOCA RATON, FLORIDA
Present Day

"So you had this guy, Boulos, on the island. What were you able to do for each other?" asked Mahoney.

"First of all, he was able to put us in contact with Brezhnev. Jack sent a message to Brezhnev through Boulos, another risky move since we didn't really know Boulos very well at the time and we also didn't know Brezhnev very well either."

"What was the message?" asked Mahoney.

"If I remember correctly, all it said was something like, 'Pig is ready to talk'," said Hal.

"And that worked?"

Hal smiled, "I was surprised myself, but it took just 48 hours to get a reply back. We knew that King Constantine was again flirting with the Soviet Communists but we had no idea how close the Greeks were to the Russians in those days. Our missiles in Turkey had been clearly aimed at the USSR but the Greeks feared them as well. They had re-opened talks with the Russians about possible affiliations before we even had the Turkish missiles fully installed."

"What did the return message from Brezhnev say?" asked Mahoney, making a note to check out the relationship between the Greeks and the Soviets in the early sixties.

"I don't remember word for word, but the message conveyed a tone of relief and also a bit of humor. It said something like, 'Roman is pleased the pig is cool but not cold, would like to see pig as soon as possible'."

"That is funny," commented Mahoney. "And did you guys set up a meeting with Brezhnev right away?"

"We did," said Hal. "Jack wanted to set up something in a neutral location so the Russians would never know where he was but Boulos reasoned that if Brezhnev really wanted to figure out where he was hiding, it wouldn't take him very long to find out. So Boulos set up a meeting on Skorpios in February of '64. Jack told everybody that Jackie was 'probably' coming to the island in early February. That really spurred Demetrius to kick the construction crew into high gear to finish the main house. With our help and 'volunteers' sent to us by Papadopoulos and Boulos we were able to get the house almost finished."

"And that was the meeting you mentioned in which Kennedy and Brezhnev came up with a plan to remove Khrushchev from power," Mahoney clarified.

"Yeah, the two main goals of that meeting were to build a working relationship with Brezhnev and to find a way to get him into power and Nikita out of power without starting a civil war."

"And Jack was successful on both points?"

Hal rubbed the whiskers on his chin and stared at a small painting hanging on the wall of his living room across from him. Then he struggled to his feet, wincing in pain and shuffled across the room to straighten the framed piece. He pointed to the piece, obviously a water color painted by a child. It was the type of painting that any grandparent might have hanging by a magnet on the refrigerator door or framed and hanging like this as a keepsake in the living room, "John John painted this for me on his first trip to the island. It was his view of the ocean through the trees. We didn't have any blue paint so he painted the ocean orange instead."

Mahoney stood and walked across the room for a better look at the very abstract blotches of color. "John Jr. painted this? That's amazing."

"We knew back then he wasn't going to be an artist," Hal laughed. "I'm sorry, Mike," Hal continued. "The meeting with Brezhnev was in February of '64, Jack felt it was very successful at the time but as I said earlier they tried to employ American political moves in Russia. So they were successful in getting Khrushchev out and Brezhnev in his place without a single bullet being fired but

Brezhnev was then just a puppet leader, his strings were pulled by so many different people that he was incredibly ineffective as Secretary. He and Jack kept an open line of communications and they met again in '65 and '67 to try to find a solution since the plan had not gone as they had hoped it would."

"So if I understand you, John F. Kennedy was an advisor to Secretary Leonid Brezhnev, the leader of the Communist Party?" asked Mahoney.

Hal turned and faced Mahoney, "I guess that's true in that he offered advice to Brezhnev, but I'd like you to hear the whole story before you run off and report completely out of context that Jack was a Communist sympathizer and an advisor to the General Secretary."

"Fair enough," said Mahoney. "I don't plan to print a word until I understand everything. Let's get back to Brezhnev's first visit to Skorpios. You said he and Jack talked mostly in private while you and the Russian security men spent all your time facing off with each other," said Mahoney, thumbing through his notes.

"Yeah, those two spent most of their time inside because it rained the entire time they were on the island. We had finished construction on the main house but not much of the finish work, the tile and woodwork. Ari had sent a container of furniture and other supplies that arrived just a few days ahead of the Russians so, under the direction of Demetrius, we had the house looking fairly decent. Brezhnev and his men arrived just after dark; I never did hear how they traveled from Moscow to Greece but they arrived by boat in the dark so nobody passing by would see them."

Hal chuckled, "Looking back, we were such idiots. It was the first time I had ever seen a real honest to goodness Russian. There was a Russian family living in my neighborhood when I was growing up but these guys were real Russkies, right from Moscow. Both security forces were ordered to not show any weapons but we were packing every gun we could carry and they were too.

Agent Walker blew a cork when Jack told him on the afternoon before Brezhnev arrival that he was hosting the General Secretary. And Papadopoulos absolutely went through the roof when he found out that his American guests were hosting Brezhnev on "his" island. Luckily, we didn't have secure communications on the island so neither was able to report Brezhnev's presence to their superiors for a day or so. But talk about the shit hitting the fan on both sides of the Atlantic!" laughed Hal.

"What was the reaction from Onassis and the Americans?" asked Mahoney.

"Within a day of Brezhnev's departure, Onassis came to the island for the first time since he had purchased it. Then we had Bobby, McNamara, Ted Sorensen, and Jim Rowley, the Director of the Secret Service. They were all pretty sure that Jack had gone stir crazy in the two months he had been on the island. They were convinced he had just pulled the biggest bonehead move of all time and that when the Russians told the world where Kennedy was, they would all end up in prison or at least in political purgatory."

"But obviously, Brezhnev and his men never told anybody that Kennedy was alive."

"Yeah," said Hal, "I think Brezhnev tucked that little piece of information away until such time as he might need it. And I think we were damn lucky that he never used it as a bargaining chip."

"So you didn't have a chance to discuss the meeting with Kennedy until after Brezhnev left the island?" asked Mahoney.

"Right, we discussed it in length then but I cannot tell you that what Jack and I discussed was the entire sum of the meeting or that he divulged to me everything that he and Brezhnev discussed. I wouldn't want you to believe that what I am telling you is the complete history of the event because I don't know that I have the whole story," said Hal.

"I appreciate that," Mahoney said, making a note of it. "So, as far as you know, the first meeting on the island was all about coming up with a way to get Khrushchev out of power and Brezhnev into his seat without it appearing to be a coup?"

"It was that, and also Jack was trying to build an ongoing working relationship with the new General Secretary. He really wanted to end the Cold War and find a way to get the U.S. and the Soviet Union to start working together to solve other world problems. He thought, probably naively, that he could make that happen if he could just sit down face to face with Brezhnev. To both of their credit, when Brezhnev left the island after that first meeting with Kennedy, they both thought they had made great strides in making the world a better, more peaceful place."

"What happened to that plan?" asked Mahoney.

Hal rubbed the back of his neck; his fatigue was really starting to show. "It was thwarted by a power greater than the United States and the Soviet Union together, human nature. The quest for power is far greater than the desire for peace."

Mahoney had at least ten follow-up questions but decided to make a note of them rather than asking right then. "Hal, it's really late and I've got to get some sleep. I'm flying back to D.C. tomorrow afternoon but I'd love to chat some more in the morning if you have more to tell me."

"There's so much more, Mike. I'll keep talking as long as you're willing to listen."

"I'm absolutely fascinated so far. Let's get some sleep and take up where we left off in the morning," said Mahoney.

Hal tapped his forehead with his index finger. "Damn, I almost forgot that I have an appointment at the clinic tomorrow morning. They're going to shoot me full of more of that damn juice to try to get another few weeks out of this old bag of bones and several thousand dollars more out of my insurance company. If you can be here by eight or so, you can drive me to the clinic and then we can talk while I have my infusion."

"I won't be in the way?" asked Mahoney.

"No, they encourage you to bring a friend or family member to keep you company," said Hal with a bit of a smile.

"Great, I'll be here at eight tomorrow morning," said Mahoney.

SKORPIOS ISLAND
February 12, 1964

Brezhnev and his men departed the island by boat just after dark on an evening that was blowing up a strong wind. The two-mile ride back to Nydri wouldn't be pleasant. Their boat was no more than a hundred yards off the island when Captain Papadopoulos and his right hand man, Boulos, came storming into the compound with Demetrius in tow. Papadopoulos barked an order to

Demetrius in Greek but then didn't wait for him to interpret the demand. "Kennedy, now!" he said in an angry tone.

Hal sat calmly on the edge of the bunker and said, "I'm sorry. Mr. Kennedy has retired for the evening. He is quite exhausted and won't be able to see you until morning."

The Captain's face twisted in reaction to the American's peaceful reply to his order. He was not used to insubordination by any man and especially not by these inferior American college boys. Demetrius nervously interpreted Hal's response to the Captain who turned and started walking towards the sleep shack. Hal stood up from his seat on the edge of the bunker which placed him directly between the Captain and the door, his .38 caliber service revolver clearly hanging in his right hand. Papadopoulos stopped and simply yelled, "Kennedy, now!"

Hal smiled, "I'm sorry, you'll have to see Mr. Kennedy in the morning. Good night."

Demetrius nervously pleaded, "Agent Rumsey, please, you will ask Mr. Kennedy to come out and talk with Captain Papadopoulos?"

"Hal's smile faded and his hands crossed bringing the revolver to his waist level when Papadopoulos took a step forward, "When he wakes, I'll let the President know you came to see him. Have a good evening."

"What's all the yelling about?" came Kennedy's voice from the trail that led to the clearing from the dock.

Captain Papadopoulos turned to see Kennedy coming up the trail with Agent Walker. He turned back to Hal, his eyes held a burning contempt for the infidel who had tried to make a fool of the Captain. His mouth started to open as if to say something but he stopped himself and turned and advanced towards Kennedy.

The Captain said something to Demetrius in Greek to be translated to English but before he had a chance to do so, Kennedy calmly said, "I'd be happy to meet with you right now. Shall we sit in the main house where it is warmer?"

The five men, Kennedy, Papadopoulos, Boulos, Walker, and Demetrius turned towards the main house. Hal eased his .38 back into its holster while Agent Mark Stennfeld who had been watching from the corner of the sleep shack stepped out of the shadows and holstered his service pistol as well. "What the hell were you thinking, Hal?" asked Stennfeld.

"We are here to guard the President," said Hal. "I'm not about to be pushed around by some Greek Army has-been. No second-rate security guard is going to come blasting in here trying to tell my President when and where to meet."

Stennfeld shook his head, "Jesus, Hal. A little diplomacy goes a long ways. These guys are our hosts."

By the time the men had made it to the living room in the main house Papadopoulos had composed himself. He walked over to the unfinished fireplace then turned and said to Demetrius in Greek, "Please tell Mr. Kennedy that he is not allowed to have visitors to Skorpios without the permission of myself and in many cases also the permission of Mr. Onassis."

Kennedy didn't wait for the translation. He had caught most of the message. "Captain Papadopoulos," he said with a slight bow of the head. He continued in broken Greek, "My work may be secret. My guest may be secret. My work may be very important to world. I cannot always ask permission for guest."

The Captain was both impressed and irritated by Kennedy's newfound use of his language. "Permission must be received for any guest to the island, clear?"

"No good," said Kennedy without emotion.

Demetrius tried to intervene in English, "Please, Mr. Kennedy. In order to maintain security on the island the Captain must know who is to come and go. Please, in future advise the Captain in advance of who you bring to Skorpios as guest, yes?"

"Please tell the Captain," replied Kennedy in English, "that my guests in the future may be here under very top secret circumstances and I will not ask for his permission. If he doesn't like it, we can take it up with Mr. Onassis."

Just then one of the Captain's men walked in and handed a note to Boulos who read it before saying, "Mr. Onassis here tomorrow."

"Excellent," said Kennedy. "I have nothing more to discuss with you gentlemen. Good night." Kennedy stood and walked out of the room.

An hour later when the Greeks had left and things had calmed down Kennedy came out of the sleep shack and sat on the edge of the bunker. "Good evening, sir," said Hal.

Kennedy looked over at the dark windows of the main house. "First Brezhnev, now Onassis. We may never get to move into that house," said Jack.

"I can't sleep on those damn Greek Army surplus cots forever," said Hal with a chuckle.

"Greek cots, hell," said Jack. "I checked underneath mine the other day, these are German Army cots."

"Well that explains the excruciating pain I feel every morning," laughed Hal. "How did your meeting with Brezhnev go?"

"It went very well," relied Jack. "Our two main goals were one, to come up with a plan that would remove Khrushchev from office while maintaining stability in the USSR and two, to establish a working relationship between the two of us so we can began working towards common goals. I think we came up with a plan for the first and made huge strides towards the second. Can you imagine this world if the two superpowers worked together? Christ, Hal, we talked about everything from sharing resources in space rather than duplicating efforts to joining forces to stabilize the Arab region. There's so much that we could accomplish if we would simply agree to disagree on capitalism and communism and spend our money on research and technology rather than submarines and missiles."

"But they seem hellbent on taking over the world, Jack. How do we work with them when they want to take over Southeast Asia, Turkey, Greece, and hell, Europe if they can get it?"

Jack answered, "Brezhnev seems to be much less interested in globalization than Stalin or Khrushchev."

"If he gets into power, will he be able to convince the other members of the Central Committee and the Politburo that the globalization of communism isn't as important as the human condition of their citizens?" asked Hal.

Kennedy turned and studied the younger man for a few moments. It was clear that he understood the political landscape and the issues at hand better than he let on."

BOCA RATON, FLORIDA
Present Day

Hal was sitting in the shade in a cheap aluminum green-webbed lawn chair when Mahoney came around the corner in the vintage Oldsmobile. Hal stood slowly, folded the lawn chair and placed it on a hook inside the single car garage while Mahoney parked in the driveway.

"Beautiful morning!" commented Mahoney.

Hal had a large smile on his face, "It certainly is. I was up and ready early so I decided to wait out here and enjoy it. Do you mind driving, Mike?"

"Not at all," said Mahoney with a grin. He was really growing fond of the powerful classic car.

At Hal's request they put the top down so they could enjoy even more of the wonderful morning before it changed into the hot and humid day that the forecasters predicted.

"How did you sleep, Mike?" asked Hal.

"I slept great once I finally went to bed. I was up doing research, checking facts, and organizing my notes for several hours after I got back to my room."

"Did all my stories check out?" asked Hal.

"Of course they did," said Mahoney with a smile. "When we ended last night you were telling me about Brezhnev's visit."

"I think we covered Brezhnev's first trip to the island pretty well. Did I mention the aftermath?" asked Hal.

"You mentioned it but not in detail. What happened afterwards?"

"Turn left at the next light," Hal pointed. "All hell broke loose after he left the island. The very next day Onassis came to Skorpios and raised hell with Jack."

Mahoney turned in surprise, "He was angry because Kennedy was trying to build a working relationship between the Americans and the USSR?"

"No," said Hal. "Ari was angry for two reasons. First, that Jack Kennedy, his secret guest, was telling people that he was alive and even inviting world leaders to come see him. Onassis was concerned about his reputation in the business world if it became public knowledge that he was hiding Kennedy. He also worried about his staff and investments on the island in the event somebody decided to take out Kennedy. A lot of good people could be hurt if the island was invaded."

Hal paused for a moment before he said, "Secondly and more importantly, Onassis was concerned about the communist insurgency that he felt was brewing in his country. King Constantine and his group of merry men had been flirting with the Russians for quite awhile. Ari loved two things, Greece and money. Money came from capitalism. His shipping business could not operate from a country that was communist so if Greece was to fall in that direction, he would have to move every ship, every dollar - I mean every drachma, everything from his homeland in order to keep his business alive."

Mahoney changed lanes and gave the Olds a kick in the pants to get around a city bus that was slowing, preparing to stop and pick up a group of passengers. "Didn't Onassis see the benefit of Kennedy opening a working dialog with Brezhnev? Did he know that Kennedy was trying to get Khrushchev out and Brezhnev in?"

"All he saw at that time," said Hal, "was a guest on his island who had promised to live there quietly and who was not only telling the world he was alive, he was also inviting the world to come see him. And to make matters worse, he had invited the damn wolf into the hen house."

"Did Kennedy and Onassis agree on anything during that visit?" asked Mahoney.

"Yeah, they agreed that the next time Jack made direct contact with, or invited anybody to the island without Ari's personal approval, we could find a different place to live," said Hal.

"And how did that work out?" asked Mahoney.

"Fine for two days, until Bobby, Bob McNamara, Ted Sorensen, and Jim Rowley showed up," said Hal with a chuckle. "But technically Jack didn't invite them, they just showed up to read Jack the riot act after Agent Walker sent a message that Jack was running his own little intelligence agency."

"Did it make Kennedy mad that Walker was snitching on him?" asked Mahoney.

"I don't think so," answered Hal. "I think Jack expected Walker to do his job and reporting what was happening on the island was part of his job."

"And how did that meeting go?"

"About like you might expect," said Hal.

After they had maneuvered into a parking spot at the clinic, Hal asked Mahoney to raise the convertible top. The heat and the humidity were both rising by the minute and the shade and air conditioning would be welcome by the time Hal was finished with his treatment.

The nurse behind the desk saw Hal walk in and said, "Good morning Mr. Rumsey. Please have a seat. We'll be right with you."

Hal shrugged his shoulders and shuffled over to a chair in the waiting room, Mahoney followed.

After a few minutes a nurse with a kind face and a warm smile approached them. "Good morning, Hal, how are you today?"

"I'm just short of fantastic," he answered in a sarcastic tone.

"We're just getting set up, I'll be out to get you in a few minutes," said the nurse.

"Thank you, Nancy," said Hal after stealing a glance at her nametag.

"I'm getting too old for this shit," Jose Telleria said out loud from his rental car across the street. In his younger days, he would have found this assignment easy but the older he got, the less he liked 'defending the country' in this manner. He watched Hal Rumsey and Mike Mahoney walk into the clinic, right on time. He would wait for the C.I.A. nurse to come out and give the heads-up signal then he would head back to the hotel and make a report to McQuade.

With the right request, a nurse working for the C.I.A. had been dispatched to Boca Raton and through the 'magic' of the Service's computer hackers, was quickly assigned to the clinic as a 'temp' nurse. There was a little confusion upon her arrival but the clinic manager brushed it off as a fortunate mistake, she was happy to have the extra help.

SKORPIOS ISLAND
February 15, 1964

It had never occurred to Robert Kennedy that getting to a little island in Greece could be so difficult. He and his team flew aboard an Air Force jet to Athens then transferred to a smaller propeller-driven plane for a short but bouncy flight to Prevezai. Once there they donned their disguises, hats and sunglasses, and took a two-hour car ride to Nydri where they were to meet a man who would take them out to the island on his boat. They couldn't find the man or his boat so they started asking the local fishermen if they would take them to Skorpios.

The locals were immediately suspicious of four Americans, dressed in hats and sunglasses who were pushing American dollars at them to take them to the island owned by Onassis. They had all heard the stories of the large security force now on the island, big men with big guns.

Bobby thought he might have to buy a boat to make it out to the island when Ted Sorensen, his brother's former Special Counsel, came running down the pier, "I found a guy, come on."

For five American dollars, Ted had talked a young man into taking the four of them out to Skorpios on his uncle's boat as long as they could leave right then so the young man could be back before his uncle returned from the taverna. The four Americans were traveling light; they quickly followed Sorensen down the dock to where the young man named Neo was waiting next to a squalid little fishing boat.

"Jesus, Ted, do you think it will make it?" asked Bobby.

Ted laughed, "I figure it will make it half way at least. That only leaves us half the swim we're currently facing."

The young Greek fisherman fired up the motor as Ted untied the bow line and Jim Rowley released the aft line. A dozen fishermen lined the pier as Neo motored out in his uncle's boat towards Skorpios. They all agreed that if the Onassis security force didn't kill the youngster, his uncle surely would when he returned.

Jack Kennedy and Agent Walker were working with the construction crew to finish up the tile flooring in the main house just before knocking off for the day when they saw three armed guards run through the compound and down the trail leading to the dock. Kennedy walked out onto the veranda to look down towards the dock and could see a small fishing boat that was coming into the mooring with at least five men aboard. Out of curiosity he picked up a set of surplus field glasses that one of his agents had brought along. He found the boat in his field of vision and after struggling with the focus looked down at a boat carrying his brother, Ted, Mac, and Jim.

"Son of a bitch," he said loudly.

"What is it, sir?" asked Walker.

"Bobby and the others are on that boat," he replied.

"Are you sure?" Walker asked before replying, "That's where the Phantoms were heading so fast. We better get our butts down there right now!"

The two men sprinted down the trail picking up Rumsey along the way. When they reached the dock they found a chaotic scene. A small fishing boat was standing just off the dock with the Director of the Secret Service and a young Greek standing on the bow trying to reason with the Phantom guards who held their AK-47s level at the boat, yelling for them to go away.

Jack recognized one of the men from the Christmas dinner and approached him pointing to the boat, "My *adelfos*, my *adelfos*," he pleaded, explaining that this was his brother arriving.

The man barked a command to the other guards who lowered their guns. The big Greek waved the fishing boat in to the dock.

"Son of a bitch, Jack. Is that how you greet all your guests?" yelled Bobby as Neo maneuvered the small boat towards the dock.

"Only those guests who come uninvited," Jack yelled back with a big smile.

Before the boat was tied to the dock, Papadopoulos arrived followed by a very winded Demetrius. Captain Papadopoulos was yelling, Demetrius was trying to interpret but he couldn't catch his breath. The Captain barked an order to his men and they again raised their weapons towards the boat.

In his broken Greek, Kennedy said, "Captain, this, my brother from United States. Did Ari not tell you he would come?"

Papadopoulos looked at Kennedy with great suspicion. He replied in Greek, "Mr. Onassis did not say this to me. I will notify him. If you are lying you are off this island." Then he ordered his men to again lower their weapons and he motioned the visitors off the boat.

Jack gave the Captain a smile and a slap on the back saying, "You good man," as he walked to the edge of the dock and embraced his brother.

"Jesus, Jack," said Bobby. "I guess I don't need to worry much about security."

Jack laughed as he shook hands with Mac, Ted and Jim. "No, Captain Papadopoulos runs one hell of a tight ship."

"Well he comes from a very qualified family," said McNamara. "Got anything to drink around here?" he added before Jack could ask him about the comment.

"Hell, yes, we do. Let's get you up to the house and then you can tell me what brought such a motley crew all the way out here," said Jack with a smile. While he suspected the group was here to raise hell over his visit with Brezhnev, he was thrilled to see his brother and his friends. As far as he was concerned they could yell all they wanted as long as they stayed for a few days.

Jack led the group to the main house where he instructed them to drop their bags near the door and find chairs out on the veranda. He then politely asked Demetrius to get drinks for the men. He knew by heart what they would want; Bobby would like a glass of bourbon with ice, Mac and Jim Rowley would be ready for a beer, and Ted would ask for a club soda with a twist of lemon. Demetrius was happy to oblige. He hurried off to get the drinks and alerted the cook that they would have four more for dinner.

The four new arrivals on the terrace looked tired. "Christ, you guys look like hell," said Jack with a big smile.

"This easy island living certainly seems to be working out for you, Jack," said Sorensen.

"It is," replied Jack. "I'll suggest it to anybody. I exercise every day and I have a job in construction," he waved his arm as though he was presenting the house. "And I don't have to deal with political bullshit from people like you," he said, continuing to smile.

"Then why are you still playing politics, Jack?" asked Bobby.

"Are you talking about my little visit with Brezhnev the other day?"

"You know that's exactly what I'm talking about," said Bobby in a tone that was almost angry.

"I wish I had known you were coming," said Jack. "I've almost completed my report on his visit. I picked up more information about the inner workings of the Soviet bureaucracy in twenty-four hours than a hundred analysts could get in years. Between the two of us we came up with a plan to get Khrushchev out of office and put Brezhnev in without risking a civil war. And to top it off, I think we've developed a long-term working plan, once Brezhnev is in office, to get our countries to really work together to solve issues like southeast Asia."

Bobby leaned forward in his chair, now obviously angry, "Jack, you just gave the USSR a piece of information that they can use to tear apart our entire political system. Imagine if they broke the story that our top leaders defrauded the country and faked your assassination; that, in and of itself, could break the back of the U.S. political system. And if Johnson was able to hold the country together after such a revelation, the five of us along with twenty or thirty more good people would face public and political persecution. Hell, Jack, they would probably throw our butts in prison for the rest of our lives while they came up with laws to justify it. What is going to keep Brezhnev from using this little piece of information as a bargaining chip with us for the remainder of his political career?"

Jack didn't want to discuss that right now, he wanted to have a drink with his brother and friends but they all had traveled a long way to hear his answer. "I asked Leonid not to disclose my presence or to try to extort us in any way with the information. In return, I promised not to disclose his plot to overthrow the Soviet political structure."

While Bobby was dwelling on his brother's answer Bob McNamara stood up and walked to the railing. "Why here, Jack? he asked.

"We were almost finished with the main house, we needed somebody to try out the guest bedroom," Jack laughed.

"Damn it, Jack, I'm serious," said Mac.

Ted Sorensen, Kennedy's longtime friend and advisor, tried to calm the waters by explaining the issue in an analytical tone, "Here's the picture as we see it, Jack. The Greeks under Prime Minister Papandreou and King Constantine are considering some sort of affiliation with the Soviet Union. The resistance to that is coming from the left which includes Onassis and his very close friend, Major Georgios Papadopoulos, who happens to be the younger brother of your retired Captain Papadopoulos."

Demetrius arrived with a tray full of drinks and set them on the small table in the center of the group. "Thank you, Demetrius," said Jack as he passed the drinks around. Without a word, the small Greek gave a quick nod and left.

"What did Onassis have to say about Brezhnev's visit?" asked Bobby.

"He had the same concerns as you," answered Jack. "He was worried both about his reputation and a possible communist insurgency in this country. He was quite angry until I mentioned that I might be able to get him some contracts to ship oil for the Russians. Then his temper lightened up considerably and he asked me to let him know in advance if I was going to have visitors on the island. Look, fellas, we can sort all this out a little later, I'm just glad you're here. Let's have a drink and then I'll show you around my little world. How long are you staying?"

Each one of the visitors felt the same. It was great to see Jack looking more fit and relaxed than he had in years. "We need to leave tomorrow," said Jim Rowley.

Bobby sat back, enjoying the sun on his face and savoring the moment before saying, "Look, Jack, we can find you some way to keep your fingers in the mix and we could all use your opinion from time to time but you cannot let anybody else know you are alive. This is a secret that could topple a 190-year-old government if it became public. We can't take that chance."

Jack sipped his drink and stared at the ground in front of his chair. In an uncharacteristically repentant tone he said, "I know, I understand." And then, with hardly a breath, he raised his head, smiled, and asked "So what's new around Washington?"

BOCA RATON, FLORIDA
Present Day

Nurse Nancy returned and led Hal and Mahoney back to the treatment area, a room with half a dozen reclining easy chairs separated by curtains hung from the ceiling to give a bit of privacy to the patients. The room was dimly lit, the sound of soothing elevator-type jazz emanated from the ceiling speakers. After checking Hal's blood pressure and taking his temperature, Nurse Nancy brought in an I.V. bag and in less than a minute had a clear fluid dripping into Hal's vein. She helped recline him back in his chair, covered him with a soft blanket, and then told him she would be back to check on him in a few minutes.

"How often do you get this soft treatment?" asked Mahoney.

"Twice a week," Hal responded. "I came for the drugs but I return for the service."

Mahoney fished in his bag for his recorder and his notes. He flipped through his notebook for a moment before saying, "Geez, I have so many questions, Hal."

"I happen to have a little free time. What can I tell you?"

Mahoney flipped to another page, "Tell me about Aristotle Onassis? What was your opinion of him?"

Hal eyes seemed to focus on something out in the corridor while a look of deep thoughtfulness came across his face. "Ari . . . Ari is a tough guy to put a finger on. I found him to be one of the most black and white people I ever met; there was very little, if any, gray area in Ari's world, he saw everything as right or wrong. For instance, if you and Ari were walking around the island and came to a fork in the path, and neither of you had ever been down either one, he would decide which one was the right one based on his own unique form of logic. You didn't question his decision because, in his mind, he was correct. I imagine it was that type of decision-making that made him such a successful business man."

"Did you like him?" asked Mahoney.

"I respected him. I enjoyed the conversations we had over the years but I don't know that I would have ever called him a friend. Once you were in his camp, or in our case on his island, he treated you like family. He was incredibly generous and very concerned about the well-being of his staff and his friends."

"It must have been amazing to sit in on a conversation between Kennedy and Onassis," commented Mahoney.

"It sure was," replied Hal. "Jack liked to think out loud. He sometimes voiced things that he didn't exactly believe or yet embrace, almost to see how they sounded when he said them out loud. If something came out of Ari's mouth, it was already gospel, it was the truth, or what he believed was the truth. That led to some amazing discussions and debates. I wish I had had your little tape recorder there!"

SKORPIOS ISLAND
February 17, 1964

Jack stood on the dock with Agent Walker as they watched the launch carrying Bobby, Ted Sorensen, Jim Rowley, and Bob McNamara motor away. He waved one more time then turned to find Captain Papadopoulos standing in the shadows of the trees behind them.

"Captain, may we talk?" Jack asked in his rudimentary Greek.

The Captain nodded and pointed up the path making it clear that he wanted to walk and talk. Agent Walker followed at a distance far enough back that he couldn't hear the conversation but could easily see them both.

"Captain Papadopoulos, for Brezhnev I am sorry. I was wrong for bringing Brezhnev without talking to you."

The apology took the Captain off guard. In his culture, especially in the Greek military structure, an apology was either a confession of weakness or a symbol of great respect to a superior. The former President of the United States was apologizing to him; he wasn't sure how to react. "Mr. Kennedy, Brezhnev and his government are bad people. They do not belong in Greece. Had I known exactly who Brezhnev was while he was here, I would have killed him myself."

It took Jack a moment to process the words in his mind and while he didn't get them all he certainly understood the gist of the statement. "Captain, Soviets are bad but not all Soviets. I'm on Skorpios because Khrushchev is bad man. Brezhnev here because we have plan to get Khrushchev out and Brezhnev in to make Soviets better. For this, I need you to help. I understand you want no communist in Greece. You understand I want no communist in Greece."

The Captain's expression seemed to lighten, "How can I help?" he asked.

Kennedy stumbled over the words but got the message across, "We need meeting, you, me, and Major Papadopoulos, on Skorpios soon, yes?"

The Captain smiled. So Kennedy knew who his brother was and perhaps he also understood how important the Papadopoulos family was in this country. Kennedy was smart, maybe smarter than he had originally thought. "Perhaps," said the Captain.

Later that evening Jack came out to sit with Hal. It was their first real chance to talk in days. "That was an interesting couple of days," he commented.

"To say the least," said Hal. "After Brezhnev, Onassis, the Attorney General, McNamara, Sorensen and Mr. Rowley, I'm sort of waiting for Jesus Christ to show up next. Who else is there?" he laughed.

Jack smiled and shook his head, "I don't know if we have room for anybody else on the island. It turns out that Captain Papadopoulos is the older brother of Major Papadopoulos, the head of the Army and a major player in the left-wing faction. Then we have Boulos who is with Greek intelligence and apparently close to the Russians based on the speed of his communications with Brezhnev, and we're sitting in the middle trying to figure out how to keep our own tails out of trouble."

"Do we know that Boulos is supporting the right?" asked Hal. "I get the feeling that Boulos is supporting Boulos."

Jack turned in surprise, "I'd never considered that, Hal. You might be right."

"In either case we need to figure out how to manage both Papadopoulos and Boulos, get the most out of each that we can without tipping the other that we are working them both," said Hal.

"Son of a bitch, Hal," said Jack. "I think you have found your niche in life!"

BOCA RATON, FLORIDA
Present Day

A tall pretty nurse that Hal had never seen at the clinic before walked around the corner as Mahoney was getting ready to ask another question, "How are you doing, Hal," she asked as she pumped up the blood pressure cuff again.

"Where's your name tag?" asked Hal.

The nurse smiled, "I left it at home. I got called in to cover at the last moment so I was a little disorganized. I'm Charlene," she said while smiling at Hal.

"My arm feels like it's on fire. Did you guys screw up and put turpentine in my bag today?" he asked sarcastically.

She glanced at his arm, "You do seem to be having a bit of a reaction to the meds today. Have you had that in the past?" she said while looking at the notes in his chart.

"No," said Hal.

"I have something to help with that," she said, pulling a syringe from her pocket and adding the contents to the I.V. The nurse glanced at the redness in his arm again, "Let's keep an eye on it; if it gets too uncomfortable I'll have the doctor come take a look."

"Health care professionals," Hal said with an eyeroll after the nurse had left.

Mahoney changed the subject, "Tell me about Jackie, when did she first come to the island?"

Hal smiled, "About a month after Bobby's first visit."

"And how did that visit go?" asked Mahoney.

"That was a big event on the island," said Hal. "Jack cleared the visit with Ari and, of course, Ari rolled out the red carpet. His yacht, the *Christina,* where Ari usually spent the nights showed up in the harbor a few days before Jackie's arrival and Ari arrived one day before. He had poor little Demetrius and his small staff running their tails off to get things ready."

"And how did the President and former First Lady get along?" asked Mahoney.

"Jackie was on the island for about five days on that first visit and we didn't see too much of either of them. I know things weren't perfect; I was standing guard one evening and I could hear them arguing, not yelling but certainly disagreeing about something but I can imagine they had a lot to discuss. The only time I spent with them during that first visit was the night we had a big dinner hosted by Ari with Jack, Jackie, Papadopolous, and the four of us Service agents. They seemed very at ease with each other that night, very much as if they loved and missed each other."

"Did you get a chance to talk with Jackie?" asked Mahoney.

"I didn't say much to her other than to exchange small talk in passing on that first trip. On later visits I had the chance to have long conversations with her," Hal said, pulling the blanket up over his chest. "They keep it so damn cold in here," he said.

"So tell me about Jackie. There's been a lot written about her, and Caroline has told me a little about her, but I'd like to know your opinion of the lady?"

A warm smile came across Hal's face, "Please don't print this, but I've only loved one woman in my life and that was my best friend's wife. Jackie was the most beautiful and classy lady I have ever met. She treated me like I was Jack's good friend, not his watchdog. What I found most interesting was that in the public eye she was always perfect, she stood tall, spoke eloquently, and dressed perfectly. On her visits to the island she was away from the cameras and could dress down, occasionally let a curse word fly, and walk around with a floppy hat or her hair a little messed up rather than having to look perfect. The woman was as beautiful without her makeup and her hair styled as she was after spending hours perfecting her look."

Mahoney smiled, the old man was actually blushing. "Did you see much of Jackie on the island?"

"I saw quite a bit of her once but I didn't know she was showering outside," Hal said with a laugh. "Don't print that either." He took a moment to gather his thoughts before saying, "We didn't see her much for the first two years or so but we started seeing more of her once the press quit hounding her so much. And in late '66 or early '67 she brought the kids to the island for the first time."

"Wow," said Mahoney. "Did they know their father was alive?"

"No, Jackie was always afraid to tell them because they were so young and she didn't want them to say anything to anyone."

Mahoney leaned forward in his chair, "How did that first trip to the island go?"

"Not really well. John John was so young at the time of the assassination that he didn't really comprehend the whole thing, other than he knew his daddy had gone to heaven. Now at age five or six, the little guy was taken to a strange island where he met a strange man who wanted to hug him and be his friend. It was a bit much for him. Caroline on the other hand was almost six at the time of Jack's death and nine or ten when she found out her father was alive. She had a hard time understanding why he would leave them and go live on an island. I remember her going from being really happy to see him to being afraid that he might really die, then to feeling anger and finally becoming withdrawn and wanting to cling to her mother. It was hard for everybody."

"You called him 'John John'. I read somewhere the family never called him John John," Mahoney commented.

Hal smiled, "John Junior was known as John John from the day he was born until he reached his early teens. Then Jackie made a big deal out of getting the press to quit calling him by that name because it was a child's name. She told a group of reporters that the family had never called him John John. I certainly don't want Jackie to rise up out of her grave over this, but that's not true."

"Did the children spend much time on the island over the years?" asked Mahoney.

"We saw quite a bit of them during the years, 1968 to about 1975, when Jackie and Ari were supposedly married but we almost never saw them after that. When they were in their teens, neither of them liked coming to the island much. I don't blame them, they had friends back home and there wasn't anything for a teenager to do on Skorpios."

Mahoney shifted in the hard hospital chair, "And how about when they became adults?"

"By the time both John and Caroline reached their early twenties, they better understood the reasons their father made the decisions he had. We still didn't see much of them but the quality of their time with Jack improved greatly as they matured. I think they both learned to appreciate and love their father and I know he treasured every moment he spent with them."

"On the drive over here you were telling me about the backlash from Onassis and Bobby after Brezhnev's visit. What became of all that?" asked Mahoney.

"Almost nothing," Hal said with a smile. "Jack listened to them, agreed with them in principle, promised nothing, and went right on doing things his own way. In my opinion, one of Jack Kennedy's greatest strengths was also one of his most profound weaknesses; he thought he could get away with anything. And, if you look at his record, he was right. He lost a boat in the war and survived. He was misled by the CIA in the Bay of Pigs but he survived that politically. He had a win-loss record that any football team would be proud of."

"But even after the warnings from everybody he continued to play super-spy?"

"Even after all the warnings," said Hal. "It was certainly a boost to his ego that the Khrushchev Coup went exactly as he and Brezhnev had planned, at least in the beginning. In mid-October of 1964 Khrushchev was forced into 'voluntary retirement'. Once he was out of office and Brezhnev was firmly seated, Jack started plotting his own return to public life or as he liked to call it, his return from the dead."

Mahoney looked up from his notepad, "And why was it that John Kennedy never returned from the dead?"

"I said that he believed he could get away anything but we couldn't figure out how to get away with this one. We spent probably a thousand hours going over scenarios, press releases, speeches, anything we could come up with to bring him back to the States. Jack always believed we could just tell the truth, that he faked the assassination to prevent World War III and now that Khrushchev is out of office, here I am! But he was smart enough to get other's opinions on the public's perception of such an announcement.

We had Ted Sorensen come back and sit with us for several days; we consulted with Bobby and Teddy but we could never come up with a way that Jack could return to 'life' without creating a massive distrust of the U.S. political system and ruining any chances for Bobby and Teddy to succeed. You see, Mike, the one thing Jack hadn't counted on was the general public's incredible emotional reaction to his death. Everybody remembers where they were when they heard about his death. People cried for days and some for weeks. During the year or so following his assassination, Jack Kennedy became bigger than life. He became bigger in some people's eyes than George Washington or Abe Lincoln. There was no conceivable way he could suddenly reappear.

Jack became pretty solitary and he fell into a fairly deep depression. He had always believed that his time on Skorpios was short-term; now he was starting to see things in a different light. He was starting to understand what his future might be."

Mahoney made a quick note, "What brought him out of his depression?"

Hal looked up at the ceiling, "A pretty unlikely source, Captain Papadopoulos. By November or December of '64, I was pretty worried about Jack. I had gotten word to Jackie that he probably needed a Christmas visit and heard back that she was trying to make that happen. The construction crew was hard at work on both a guest house and a staff house and I eventually goaded Jack to get off his ass and get back to work.

But what really seemed to bring him out of his depression was when the Captain approached him and asked for his advice. The Captain's brother, Major Papadopoulos, was very concerned that the current regime in Greece was about to turn to communism and crawl into bed with the Soviets. Neither Jack nor Ari would have been able to live or operate in a communist country. He agreed to help in any way he could and his mood changed immediately."

"What did they cook up?" asked Mahoney.

"By the time Major Georgios Papadopoulos made his first visit to the island in January of '65, Jack had learned everything he could about the Greek political system, the military power structure, and the culture. We were getting word back from Brezhnev that in his takeover he had given up too many markers and was struggling to gain power and respect. Jack felt that he had personally screwed up by not having a clearer understanding the Soviet political culture and climate and he wasn't going to make the same mistakes in Greece that Brezhnev had made in Russia."

"How do you learn about the Greek political system, the military structure and culture while sitting on a remote island thirty years before the internet?" asked Mahoney.

Hal gave him a smile, "You ask Boulos to explain it to you. By this time, we had figured out that Boulos, the island's resident spy, was really in business for himself. While he worked for Greek Intelligence and was on the island to report on Onassis, he had quickly realized that if he snuggled up to Jack, he could profit by buying and selling bits of information that passed through Skorpios.

In early '65, I don't remember exactly when, Agent Haycock was injured in a car accident while he was back in the States for his father's funeral. He never did return to the island and they never replaced him so my guard shift was extended from six in the evening until six a.m. Jack, Boulos, and I met nearly every night for several months to discuss the political and military structure of Greece. Boulos knew his shit and it certainly paid off. Jack impressed the Papadopoulos brothers with his unique understanding of their country."

"And how did they fend off the communists?" asked Mahoney.

"At first they tried to influence King Constantine and Prime Minister Papandreou," said Hal. "They worked to get inside both of their camps and in some cases both of their heads. Jack felt that if Onassis and Major Papadopoulos could get close to the men advising Constantine and Papandreou, they might be able to sway them back to the center and away from the Soviet influence. That might have worked but by the middle of 1965, Papandreou was forced to resign and Constantine put a new Prime Minister in place. He wasn't there long and I don't remember his name, there were a couple of years when the PM changed every few months. Papandreou wasn't finished; he made a play for control of the army by getting the new Prime Minister to appoint him as Defense

Minister but King Constantine refused to honor the appointment. The whole government was pretty much a mess from early '65 until April of '67."

"What changed?" asked Mahoney.

"With the Greek government in a constant state of turmoil, they were ripe for a communist insurgency. Our old buddy Brezhnev saw Greece becoming communist as a way to strengthen his standing in the party; it was the chink in NATO's armor that he needed. By late 1966, Jack and the Papadopoulos brothers were down to two options. One, structure a coup by the military to overthrow Constantine and his current Prime Minister or two, find some way to get NATO to invade and take over the government. We were pretty sure that a takeover wouldn't work because Greeks, at any level of society, hate to be told what to do. The Romans, the Turks and the Germans each figured that out when they had tried to occupy Greece. The only thing left on the table was a takeover by the Greek Army, secretly supported by the U.S., Onassis, and Jack."

"And that was the coup of 1967?" asked Mahoney.

"You've been doing some homework," answered Hal with a surprised tone.

"I read a little about it last night," said Mahoney. "But I didn't read about any connection between Papadopoulos and the United States."

Hal threw his blanket off to the side, he looked flush and feverish. "Damn it's hot in here. There's a lot of history that you won't find in the history books or on the internet. Not that it couldn't or shouldn't be told after all these years, but when it happened it wasn't documented and by now all of the players are dead. If I wasn't suggesting a connection between the U.S. and Papadopoulos to you now, that piece of history might simply fade away after I die."

"I'd never thought of it that way. I wonder what percentage of significant history has simply died off with the only people who possessed knowledge of it." said Mahoney. He made a note to remind himself to look into that as the subject of a potential future column. "What roles did Kennedy, Onassis, and the U.S. play in the coup of 1967?"

Hal stared at Mahoney for a moment while he tried to replay the sequence of events in his mind. "Jack had Bobby convince his contacts in the C.I.A. to provide covert intelligence and communications to Papadopoulos and then he talked Onassis into pledging a few million dollars for bribe and blood money. Jack then called on McNamara to bring in some of his top military advisors to meet with Papadopoulos and his men. They planned the whole thing out, step by step and minute by minute. Finally, to make sure we didn't end up with another Bay of Pigs, Kennedy convinced Mac to put a carrier group in the Mediterranean, just in case."

"And it appears that the coup was executed almost flawlessly," said Mahoney.

"I don't know if flawless is the right word but it generally followed the plan. The conspirators were able to quickly gain control of Athens by sweeping through the city with surprise and confusion. Once they controlled the major buildings and intersections, they began wholesale arrests of anybody who might be tied to the left-wing and even suspected left-wing sympathizers. They arrested so many people that they filled a stadium in the first day. King Constantine quickly figured out that he had lost control of his military and decided it was best to cooperate with Papadopoulos and his men, probably as a way to stay out of prison until he could figure out how to organize a counter-coup. So with the exception of a few hundred people who were brutally murdered by the new regime, you could say the coup was fairly flawless."

"It kept Greece from falling to the communists, right?" asked Mahoney.

Hal shifted in his recliner, "It did that, but the promise made to Jack by Major Georgios Papadopoulos, to put a democratic government in place, was suddenly forgotten. He first declared martial law, which was part of the plan and fully expected in a military takeover. But then he and his buddies either changed their minds or it was part of their plan all along, to rule by dictatorship rather than by democracy. It was a twist that we hadn't expected and now Jack and I were living in a country ruled by dictators, and by a dictator who knew Jack Kennedy's secret. Absolute power corrupts absolutely."

Mahoney was about to ask a follow up question when Nurse Charlene came in to check on Hal again. "Let's have a look at that arm," she said.

Hal looked at his arm as she touched the area around the IV drip, "The redness seems to be going away but there's a burning sensation all the way up to my shoulder now," he said.

"If the discoloration is going away, I'm sure the burning sensation will too as soon as your treatment is finished," Charlene said. She took Hal's blood pressure one more time and then turned and left without another word.

"My arm could fall off and she wouldn't give a shit," said Hal.

"Do you want me to go find a doctor and drag him in here?" asked Mahoney.

"I'm sure I'll be fine, or at least that nurse is sure I'll be fine. Where were we?" said Hal.

"You were talking about Georgios Papadopoulos. Did you have any contact with him after the coup?"

"Once he declared that he was the head of state and the supreme power, Jack sent him a letter that requested, and damn near demanded, a meeting. There was never a response," said Hal.

"And what about Captain Papadopoulos?" asked Mahoney.

"The Captain returned to the island about a month after the coup. He seemed tired and deflated. I think it was his dream to end up with a big important job in the new government but he disagreed with his brother about the direction they were taking the country and the important position he had been promised never materialized," said Hal.

"What about Onassis, what did he think of the new dictatorship in his country?" asked Mahoney.

"For Ari, it was all about the money. Georgios Papadopoulos had asked for and received support from Onassis and, in turn, according to the Greek rule of reciprocity or *epistrevo tin kalosenesou*, Onassis was free to operate his company without any government intervention."

Mahoney's head came up quickly from his notes, "Including the watchful eyes of your Mister Boulos?"

Hal smiled, "Boulos lost his job with Greek C.I.S. when the new regime under now, General Papadopoulos shut it down, but Boulos was still employed with Onassis security and his cover remained intact on Skorpios. Boulos clearly understood the value of staying on the island close to Jack and Onassis. In 1967 there was more money in trading information than in trading diamonds, gold, and oil combined."

Mahoney stood up and stretched. He looked at the gray metal-framed chair with green vinyl padding he had been sitting on and wondered if every hospital in the world was required to have the same uncomfortable chairs. He was certain that it was the same brand of chair he had sat on for hours and hours when his mother had been in the hospital a few years earlier. "Hal, tell me your thoughts on the three years, 1967 to '69. From your perspective has there ever been a more significant or historically charged time period in history?" asked Mahoney.

Hal looked at his arm and then stared at the floor in front of his recliner for a long time. "That's an interesting question, Mike. There was so much that happened in those three years, so much pain . . .," his voice drifted off for a moment. Hal continued to stare at the tile floor but his voice came back strong, "We turned on the shortwave and tuned it to the BBC in April of '67 to listen to news reports coming out of Athens about the coup. That radio was on 24 hours a day, every day, every night until at least 1970. The only time that thing wasn't squawking was when I was replacing the vacuum tubes that would burn out from the extended use. Jack and I and the others, while they were still there, would sit up sometimes all night long listening for new reports of whatever was going on.

"The radio," Hal continued after collecting his thoughts for a moment, "was in a small room in the guest house. We didn't have a chalk board or any large sheets of paper so to keep track of what was going on we would write with black markers on the smooth white walls of the room. During the coup in '67 we covered most of the four walls with notes like, '7:53 a.m. tanks reported in the streets of Athens' and '8:15 p.m.Prime Minister arrested'. We always started in the same corner and worked clockwise around the room with new information as it came in. When it became time to erase the 'board', we'd simply paint the walls white again. Boy, if those walls could talk."

"I made some notes last night," said Mahoney. "Maybe you can walk me through some of the major events of those years. I'd be interested to hear your perspective of them."

"I'll try, Mike. I don't know if I can be unbiased about all of those events but I'll give it a try," said Hal. He knew that some of the events the reporter would bring up, he didn't want to talk about. But he had initiated this series of interviews so he felt he had to try.

Mahoney flipped his notebook back a few pages and took a moment to find his notes. "Hal, in 1967 the buildup of U.S. troops in Vietnam was enormous. You said earlier that Kennedy had realized before Dallas that we shouldn't even be in Vietnam. What were his thoughts on the half-a-million men we put in Vietnam?"

"Let's get to that, but first let me give you a little background. We haven't talked much about the years 1964 to 1967," said Hal. "During those years, Jack typed hundreds of letters, memos, and notes to his Washington insiders urging them to both promote NASA and to try to build a groundswell of support against the Vietnam War. Jack wrote letters to the editors of newspapers across the country under assumed names to try to sway public opinion on both matters. We had many meetings with Bob McNamara, with Bobby and Teddy and others to try and get them to see the big picture from Jack's perspective but they, like everybody else, were so frightened of the communists taking over the world, one little country after another, that they couldn't see the forest for the trees. I'm convinced the only reasons NASA continued to receive funding was that it had been Kennedy's baby and it was the only game that we thought we had a chance in hell at beating the Russians."

Hal closed his eyes for a moment as a wave of pain and nausea clutched at his stomach. Recognizing that Hal was feeling very uncomfortable, Mahoney remained silent. Hal opened his eyes after a minute. "What did Jack think of all those boys in Vietnam?" he repeated the earlier question. "He was mad as hell at himself, McNamara, and Johnson for allowing the escalation of troops to go that far."

"He was mad at himself?" asked Mahoney with surprise.

"He wished he had made his thoughts on Vietnam clearer to Johnson and the rest of his cabinet before Dallas," said Hal. "I'm not sure he was a hundred percent convinced in November of 1963 that we shouldn't be in Vietnam. But by 1967, he had convinced himself that there was more he should have done and he took the deaths of those thousands of soldiers very personally."

"It sounds as though he carried the weight of the world on his shoulders even four years after he left Washington," said Mahoney.

Hal thought about that statement for a moment before saying, "It's easy to focus on our failures in life and completely forget our successes. Jack was very much like the rest of us in that sense."

RYBACHIY NAVAL BASE, RUSSIA
February 24, 1968

It was impossible for Captain First Rank Vladimir Kobzar not to feel the same anger as his men displayed at the news that they were being deployed again so soon after their last mission. While it was impossible not to feel the anger, it was his duty not to show it. He was a Soviet submarine Captain, a product of the greatest navy in the world, and he would follow the orders that came down from command without question. Kobzar expected his men to do the same but it was difficult to explain to his crew why they were going back out on patrol while other boats sat idle at the docks and their crews enjoyed the relative comfort of the base housing.

As the tug boat eased his aged relic of a submarine away from the dock, a cold wind caught him squarely in the jaw. He pulled the collar of his jacket tight around his neck. There was something, maybe it was a premonition or maybe it was just his imagination but Captain Kobzar felt something. This deployment was different.

The tug gave two short blasts from its air horn as it backed away from the boat's bow. Captain Kobzar gave her a weak salute and then ordered "ahead slow". The vibration from the deck below him and a slight bow wake told him the propeller was turning and within a moment, it was clear to him that his boat was underway. With the forward momentum of his submarine, Kobzar felt he had control, he wasn't drifting with the winds and currents any longer. He chose the path of his boat and was responsible for her safety. The further away from Rybachiy they sailed, the more he felt empowered. On base he was compelled by his rank to submit to the orders his superior officers but once his propeller started turning, he was in control, he answered to nobody, he knew it and his men knew it. The cold ominous feeling from moments before faded away and his confidence was restored.

As *K-129* slipped out into the choppy bay, her First Officer, Captain Third Rank Alexander Zhuravin, climbed up the ladder to the bridge and after buttoning his wool coat to fend off the brutal wind, asked, "What is this all about, Captain?"

At 39 years of age, Captain Kobzar was an experienced veteran of the Soviet Navy. He had served proudly since he was a teenager and was fairly certain that this deployment would be his last. Young Zhuravin, while still wet behind the ears, was now experienced enough to take *K-129* and her crew out to sea. He deserved the opportunity and as much as Kobzar loved the freedom and power he felt while in control of his own vessel, he was ready to turn command of the boats over to the capable young men coming up the ranks below him.

"I don't know, Alexander," he answered the First Officer after a few moments. "Did you check to see that our guests are comfortable and do you have a schedule for their safety training?"

The 'guests' he referred to were seven men who had reported to *K-129* just before she left the dock. They arrived dressed in brand new uniforms, packing sea bags that obviously had just been requisitioned from the base supply officer. It was clear that these men hadn't served on a submarine before but it also was apparent that they weren't new to the military.

The orders the Captain had received directed him to take *K-129* back to its regular patrol area, just south of the 180th meridian, and to conduct a normal patrol with a return date of May 5th. The orders also included a personal note from the base commander, Vice Admiral Prjevalski, that read:

"Welcome and make comfortable seven men under my command who will observe your operations. Once at sea, obey any orders they present that have both my signature and seal."

"They have been issued bunks and Chief Manakov will see that they receive the usual safety training this afternoon," reported Zhuravin. "Who are these men, Captain?"

Kobzar shrugged his shoulders, "I don't know. I received a note from Prjevalski saying they were aboard to observe our operations but it is clear that they are not navy."

"Perhaps they are with the Army or the KGB?" theorized Zhuravin.

"My guess is that we will know much more soon," said Kobzar. He looked down at the large chunks of ice that bounced off his bow and slid along the hull of the boat as the cold wind burned his cheeks, "I hope they have orders for us to take them to someplace warm, somewhere near the equator, perhaps Tonga or Fiji. Then, while they sneak around the jungle, we will wait for them and swim in the warm waters and lie on the sunny beaches. That's my hope."

"Are there really such places, Captain?" asked Zhuravin, "where a man can swim where the ocean waters are warm?

Kobzar looked over at his First Officer and realized how young he truly was. "There really are such places, Alexander. One day you will take this boat and these men to such a place and you will see for yourself."

BOCA RATON, FLORIDA
Present Day

Nurse Charlene came in again, took Hal's blood pressure, looked at his red arm, and adjusted the rate of the IV drip. Mahoney was surprised when Hal continued talking before the nurse had left.

"In 1966 we started seeing some real pushback from the students and the hippies in the States. They started marching in the streets, they took over college campus buildings, and burned their draft cards. The popular musicians of the era started writing anti-war songs and guys like Kerouac and Keasey started writing books that helped incite the young masses." Hal grinned, "I would have loved to have been in the middle of some of that. When I was in college, we were pretty apathetic. There was nothing in the late 1950s to protest and very little to argue about. Our war was taking place in Korea but nobody seemed to care or even take notice of it. I think I really missed out on the passion and camaraderie created by protesting a great cause together; and along with great passion comes great sex," Hal chuckled. The nurse shot him a smile as she left the room.

"That's funny," said Mahoney. "My dad once told me that college peace protests were a great place to pick up chicks. I never understood why until now."

Hal smiled but his smile quickly faded, "In January of 1967 the shit really hit the fan in Vietnam when they organized the Tet Offensive. Until then, the war had been seen as a series of small battles with disorganized guerrillas who operated with hit-and-run tactics. The Tet Offensive was clearly organized and orchestrated, hitting multiple targets across the country at the same time. It was a real eye opener for our military brass as well as for Johnson and Jack Kennedy."

"How did that change things on Skorpios?" asked Mahoney.

"The night of the Tet Offensive, Jack, Stennfeld, Boulos, and I pulled an all-nighter listening to any news that came across the BBC on the shortwave and what little we were getting off our new TACSAT satellite radio. As it became apparent over the next several days that the North Vietnamese were bound and determined to kick our butts at any cost, we started white-walling our options."

"White-walling?" asked Mahoney.

"Oh, yeah, that was an island term," said Hal. "Remember, we wrote on the white walls of the radio room with black markers because we didn't have a chalkboard?"

Mahoney raised his head, "Is there a way to carefully remove those layers of paint and read the writing under each layer?"

Hal was a little dismayed, he was trying to tell an important part of history and Mahoney was still focusing on how to prove that his story was true. "That part of the guest house was torn down years ago to make a larger common room."

"Sorry," said Mahoney, "it was just a thought. You were talking about the days after Tet."

Hal dismissed his anger and said, "We started listing options to get us out of the quagmire of Vietnam. The easiest was to simply load everybody onto ships and go home but we knew that would never happen. It probably couldn't or shouldn't have happened at that time either."

"Why not?" asked Mahoney.

Hal looked to the ceiling while trying to find a way to explain the issue. "Think back to your elementary school days. If the big tough guy in your class was punched in the gut by the littlest kid on the playground, he had two choices. One, he could wallop the little kid, or two, he could walk away. If he walked away, he no longer would be seen as the toughest kid in school, he had to punch the little kid back. In the late sixties, the world was still maturing, we were at the elementary playground stage. We couldn't walk away from Vietnam without losing face and expecting the rest of the world to start picking on us."

"You're shittin' me," said Mahoney. "You're comparing the world political stage to an elementary school playground?"

"That was Jack's way of explaining it to me," said Hal. "Think about it, we had only been a player on the world playground for about fifty or sixty years. In World War One, we were in kindergarten and we sort of acted like it. In World War Two, we had probably progressed to the third or fourth grade and we reacted accordingly. By Vietnam, we let the emotions of a sixth grade bully get the better of us, but we were dealing with Russians, Chinese and others who were acting like sixth graders also."

"So what was the solution?" asked Mahoney after taking some notes.

"As with just about everything we dealt with during my years on the island, there was no clear solution," said Hal with a grimace. "President Johnson had positioned himself as pro-Vietnam war so backing away would be seen as backing down. He was clearly the wrong guy to get us out of the war. But if Johnson chose not to run for office in 1968, it appeared that the strong contender would be Richard Nixon. Jack was pretty convinced that Nixon would only escalate the war further in order to try to win it but the intel we had made it pretty clear that winning wasn't possible because of the support pouring in from the USSR. But we came up with an idea that should have worked."

"And what was that solution?" asked Mahoney

"Bobby and Jackie came over in late February that year and we had several days to engage in some real serious discussions. Bobby felt that Johnson was tired. He had been dealing with a lot since he suddenly became President. Bobby felt that he could politely ask Johnson not to run for President in '68 and to endorse his own bid for the office. He felt that if he handled it properly, Johnson would probably do just that."

Hal rubbed his neck for a moment before continuing, "A large part of Bobby's campaign would be run on the platform of the 'New America', a country dedicated to peace and understanding. Once in office, Bobby was certain he could change the tenor of the rhetoric coming out of the White House and under his new peace initiatives, he would be able to pull us out of Vietnam without it looking as if we were running away from a lost war."

Mahoney looked at the frail old man in the recliner. He wondered how much he could endure in his state of mind and physical condition. "That plan obviously didn't work," he said with a tone of caution.

"No," said Hal, his eyes glazed slightly. "No, it didn't."

ABOARD *K-129*, NORTH PACIFIC OCEAN
March 2, 1968

Captain Kobzar pulled his covers up around his neck, opened his eyes and listened. From the warmth of his bunk he could hear the sounds, feel the vibrations and the motion of his boat and get a good feel for the status of his vessel. *K-129* was running on the surface in moderate seas. Her diesel was pushing them along at about fifteen knots and the voices of men walking in the corridor outside his cabin were calm. In the dim light he could see the clock on the cabin wall adjacent to his bunk, it was 05:47.

Kobzar swung his legs out of the bunk and stood on the small, non-regulation wool rug his wife had made for him many years earlier. He looked in the mirror at his thick curly hair while he rubbed the whiskers on his face and decided he would shave later in the day, something he would never do on land. But on this boat, nobody would question a few indiscretions from the Commanding Officer.

After dressing and washing his face in the small sink in his cabin, Kobzar stepped out into the passageway and took four steps aft to the control room where the Officer of the Deck said loudly enough for everybody in the space to hear, "Captain's in control." Then he offered a quieter, "Good morning, sir."

"Good morning," said Kobzar. "Status, please."

"Sir, all systems are functioning properly, weapons are stable. We arc making 14 knots on a course of 097 degrees. We should be entering our patrol area in about two hours. May we get you a cup of tea?"

"Thank you, I'll go down and get a cup myself," he said wondering if any of the tasty black bread from the meal the night before had survived midnight rations.

Climbing down a ladder rather than going forward and using the stairs probably saved the captain only ten to fifteen seconds but wasting even a small amount of time went against every grain in his body.

As Kobzar entered the galley, the cook looked up saying, "Good morning, Captain," and automatically reached for a cup and the pot of hot water on the stove. Kobzar mumbled a response; his thoughts were deeply focused on the tasks that needed to be accomplished during the next twelve hours.

Life aboard a submarine at sea was incredibly busy. For eight hours a day, each man on the boat had a job that they were expected to perform to a very high level of efficiency. In their off-duty time, the crew was expected to study and train to rise to the next level of proficiency in their particular field. Actual downtime, time to sit and read a book, write a letter, or even visit with a fellow sailor, was very limited unless they were willing to give up the one great luxury on board, six to eight hours of sleep out of every twenty-four.

As the Captain left the galley, he glanced to his left and into the mess, the only real gathering area on the sub. A few men had their noses stuck in books; one looked as though he was writing a letter, another leaned back against a bulkhead, asleep. In the aft corner of the mess sat two of his mystery sailors. Kobzar decided it was time to have a little visit with these men.

"Good morning, may I join you?" he asked. The question was more of a statement since he was already preparing to sit when he asked.

"Yes, good morning, Captain," responded the older of the two men.

"I am sorry we haven't had time to talk, it has been a very busy deployment so far. I trust that you have been made comfortable in our cozy little boat?" asked Kobzar.

"Everybody has been very accommodating," answered the sailor. The older man was probably only in his early thirties but was already losing much of his hair. He was a large man, more muscular than fat but it was hard to tell in the ill-fitting uniform he wore. Based on the way he man carried himself, Kobzar was certain he had been in the military for many years, not the Navy but perhaps the Army. At his age and obvious level of experience he looked ridiculous to the Captain in the seaman's uniform he wore. The younger man was in his mid-twenties. He wasn't as big as the other man but his eyes held a steely look that spoke volumes to Kobzar. He looked like the type of man who would accomplish whatever task was before him and he would do so without concern for his own well-being or that of any innocent people around him. To the best of his knowledge, the Captain had met only one KGB agent in his life but he suspected he had just met a second.

Captain Kobzar suddenly lost interest in visiting with the two men, "I'm sorry, I just remembered an important detail I must attend to. We look forward to helping you with your mission when it is time."

The older man looked at the Kobzar with a slightly furrowed brow, "Captain, we are not on a mission. We are only here to observe your operations."

There it was; later, Kobzar would ask himself exactly what "it" had been, an eye movement, the man's tone of voice, or perhaps the Captain's own premonition. Whatever it was, a cold shiver shot up Kobzar's spine; he had the unmistakable feeling that his boat and his crew were in danger. He stood up quickly saying, "Then let me know how we might be of assistance with your 'observations'." His tone reflected his disbelief in their purpose.

In his years as commander of *K-129*, Vladimir Kobzar had never felt even once that his men and his boat were in imminent danger. They certainly had put themselves in dangerous positions but the feeling he had now was different; something was amiss. He walked quickly forward to his cabin. In the narrow corridor he passed several men who probably said, "Good morning, Captain," as they brushed past him but his mind was elsewhere.

Once in his cabin with the door shut, Kobzar wiped his sweaty hands on his shirt and carefully dialed the combination to his small safe, opened it, removed his service revolver, then carefully shut the safe again. He checked to see that the gun was fully loaded and placed the revolver under the pillow on his bunk.

"Think Vladimir, think," he said to himself while trying to calm down and put his fears in perspective. If these men were up to something, what would it be and what tools would they need to accomplish their task? There were three assets at his control that they may want and he couldn't lose control of any of them. There were his men, who might become hostages and therefore pawns in some larger scheme, there was *K-129* itself, a boat with the ability to take the men nearly anywhere on the globe, and there were the three thermonuclear missiles standing at the ready in the middle of *K-129*. Kobzar shivered.

BOCA RATON, FLORIDA
Present Day

Mahoney sat quietly as Hal composed himself. The look of sorrow on Hal's face changed back to one of resolve as the reporter took a new tack. "Hal, you mentioned that something happened in 1968 that allowed Brezhnev to gain real control within the Soviet hierarchy. What was it?"

"That," said Hal while pointing his finger at Mahoney, "is a very bizarre piece of history."

Mahoney laughed, "Which fits in with the rest of this story, right?"

"That's right," said Hal. "In the late fifties and early sixties, we became engaged in what would become known as the Cold War. As you recall, it really wasn't a war in any terms we had known in the past but people were dying and countries were falling. There were no battle lines and it was sometimes impossible to tell who were your enemies or even your allies. The two big players were Russia and the U.S. but people tend to forget about all the other players, China, most of Southeast Asia, and virtually all of Europe.

By the mid-sixties Russia had a lot to worry about. They were spending every penny they had trying to keep up with us in missile and submarine production while at the same time firmly engaging us in the space race. They couldn't sell enough oil to other countries to keep up with their expenditures. By the way, Ari was making fortunes shipping Russian oil, thanks to Boulos and Jack. So by 1966 or '67, the USSR was effectively broke. The Chinese recognized this opportunity and decided it was time to grab some more land along their southern border."

"Why would China need more land?" asked Mahoney.

"China needed more natural resources," answered Hal. "They knew the regions around Chita and Amur were very rich in both untapped oil and gold.

Mahoney stared at Hal for a moment, "And the Chinese thought they could just take that from the Russians?"

"They didn't know what was available for the taking. So they started some border skirmishes and made some incursions across the border to take the Russians temperature. They were trying to find out how ardently the Russians would try to protect those regions."

"Wouldn't the Russians simply stop any attack with a tactical nuclear weapon?" asked Mahoney.

"No, Mike. I don't think they would have," said Hal. "Imagine if a million Canadian soldiers suddenly poured across our border and tried to take the Alaskan North Slope. We could drop a small nuke in there and solve the problem quickly enough but then we would have screwed up our own oil fields for about two hundred years. If we couldn't defend the oil with conventional warfare we'd be much better off to let them have the fields and buy our oil from them than to shut down that much supply for that long."

"Were the Russian's willing to let the Chinese have those regions?"

"No," said Hal with his familiar grin. "A few of the top men in the Politburo and the Central Committee came up with another plan. What do you do when the playground bully is picking on you?"

Mahoney was amused that Hal continued to reduce world politics to the elementary school yard but played along, "You either fight or you run and hide until he finds somebody else to pick on."

"And when you are a big country like the USSR, there's no place to hide so you hope the bully finds another fight. Maybe you even try to start another fight by messing up his desk and putting the blame on somebody else."

"Like the United States?" asked Mahoney.

"Like the United States," answered Hal.

SKORPIOS ISLAND
March 1, 1968

The weather had turned pleasantly warm as the couple walked along the path holding hands.

"Where are we going?" asked Jackie.

"I want to show you something we've been working on," answered Jack with a smile. "Be patient."

The trail dropped down onto the beach and followed the crescent-shaped shore around to a rock outcrop at the north end. The light winds off the sea drifted through the black pine trees, providing enough of a breeze to lightly blow Jackie's hair off her shoulders. Jack looked at his wife, her hair softly blowing in the breeze and her beautiful face framed by the blue Ionian Sea in the background, and said, "I don't believe you have ever looked as gorgeous as you do right now." She smiled back at him with her famous shy smile and squeezed his hand harder.

As the trail reached north end of the beach, a structure up on the hill above the rocky bluff came into view. As the trail became steep, Jack helped Jackie to scramble up the rock-strewn hill. She waited for Jack to jump up onto a boulder then gave him her hand when he reached back down. With a quick tug, she was up on the boulder next to her husband.

She had been to the island only a few times during the last several years because the press had continued to hound her and she felt that her real obligation was to her children, but she was always amazed at the transformation taking place with Jack. His shoulders had broadened, his chest and arms had become muscular and defined and he walked without the back pain that had plagued him for years. Jack's face had also changed, it had softened and she wondered if this was from the lack of stress that had accompanied his former position.

His persona seemed to be changing as well. She thought that he had slowed down, and he seemed to think more, he seemed more analytical than he had before. When he smiled now, it wasn't to appease the cameras, he smiled only when he was truly happy which seemed to be most of the time when she was around him.

Reaching the top of the bluff, Jackie exclaimed, "Oh, Jack, it's beautiful."

Before them stood a small chapel that even wrapped in scaffolding and surrounded by construction materials showed its splendor. "It was here on the island when we arrived. Some of the locals think that it was built by the people who lived here well before the turn of the century, but nobody's sure," Jack said as he led her inside.

The interior was more impressive than the quaint exterior of the tiny building. Frescoes covered the ceiling, each depicting a biblical or a mythological scene including the betrayal of Christ and the last judgment as well as those of Zeus, Artemis, and Ares. The few remaining wooden pews were in poor shape and had been pushed to the side but the original marble altar still held its magnificence. Statues, now wrapped in tarps to protect them, guarded the altar which was backed by a large framed fresco, a local artist's reproduction of Michelangelo's *The Last Supper*.

"We've been walking past this old building for a few years," said Jack as his wife gazed up in amazement at the beautiful artwork. "We finally cut away enough brush to allow us to poke our heads inside and this is pretty much what we found."

"My God, Jack, this is amazing," said Jackie.

"We've been working our tails off to get it completed. When we're finished, we plan to surprise Ari with it," he said with a warm smile.

"Can we renew our wedding vows here?" Jackie asked.

"If we can find a priest who will cooperate, you bet we can," said Jack enthusiastically. Over the years of Jack's seclusion, the distance between them had been difficult. Jack had begun to feel as though Jackie was slowly slipping away from him. They had less to talk about when they were together because they lived in such different worlds and they had so few chances to spend any length of time together. Jack loved his wife but he was fairly certain he would never be able move back to her world and without finding a way to move her to his, he feared they would continue to slowly slide apart.

"Is this a private tour or may we join in?" asked a familiar voice from behind them.

Jack turned to find Bobby and Boulos standing in the doorway. "Jesus, there's a pair to draw to," he said with a laugh. "Come on in. I was just showing Jackie our latest project."

Bobby walked into the chapel and gazed at the artwork on the ceiling with the same awe that Jackie had expressed only moments before. "Mister Boulos was just telling me about the old chapel you guys were restoring. I had no idea it was so amazing. You guys have done a remarkable job."

"The builders deserve the credit for the restoration," said Jack. "I just do the grunt work."

"Doesn't this island become more fascinating each time you visit?" Jackie asked Bobby.

"It certainly does," said Bobby.

"We are about to have more visitors," said Boulos who was standing near a window looking out towards the sea. The *Christina* was steaming around the northern point of the island and turning towards the anchorage.

"It appears we will be having even more guests for dinner," said Jack with a smile.

ABOARD *K-129*, NORTH PACIFIC OCEAN
March 2, 1968

There had been so many changes during the past ten years, both in the Russian Navy and in the Soviet Union in general that Kobzar regularly questioned who might be his allies and who his enemies. He suspected that several of the men under his command might be or recently had become party spies. It wasn't hard to bribe a man with money, promises of money, or threats against his family to get even the most devoted and loyal crew member to start telling the party what they wanted to know. But despite the spies in his midst, Kobzar was certain that he could trust Alex Zhuravin. He had known his First Officer for many years and together they had built a strong and efficient crew. Zhuravin wouldn't compromise himself without at least giving the Captain some indication that something was amiss, "I'm spying on you and reporting your actions to the party, I just thought you might want to know." He, of course, wouldn't be so blunt but his message certainly would be clear.

Kobzar signaled Zhuravin into his cabin and with the door closed asked, "What do you know of the new men?"

"I haven't heard anything except speculation from the crew that we are taking them to someplace warm," said Zhuravin.

Kobzar rolled his eyes; obviously, a crew member had overheard them talking about Tonga or Fiji. Rumors spread faster on a boat of grown seamen than they did among a group of school children. "I don't trust them, Alex," he said.

"They seem very interested in the crew and the knowledge that each man has about certain systems," said Zhuravin. "If we were simply taking them somewhere for some mission, why would they want to know who can navigate, who can run the diesel engine and who manages the batteries?" he asked.

"I have a suspicion that they are going to try to take over *K-129*," said Kobzar quietly.

Zhuravin shifted uncomfortably in his chair, "For what purpose, Captain?"

"Maybe it is just a drill," said the Captain. "Perhaps our illustrious navy is simply checking to see if they can place a team on board and take over our boat," answered Kobzar. "In any case, we must make certain that we do not lose control of *K-129* to these men. I want you to make your revolver ready as I have done and keep a close eye on these new men. Just as a precaution I want you to instruct the navigator to start tapping us to the north as soon as possible."

A 'tap' was an anti-mutiny tactic that went back as far as celestial navigation itself. To throw off the mutineers at least for a short time, a navigator loyal to the captain would show the ship's position on the chart as though they were in a slightly different position than they actually were. In a relatively short amount of time, the vessel could be hundreds of miles off course while at the same time, the navigator could keep track of the ship's real position. In the case of a submarine, a 'tap' worked very well since there was no immediate feedback from the sun and the stars. On a submarine, the navigator would take an initial shot of the stars and then when his boat was submerged, he might work sometimes for days tracking only speed and distance to determine position. With a 'tap' change in place, those on board might assume they were sailing to an island, for example, but in reality they could miss their destination by hundreds of miles.

"Captain," said Zhuravin, "shall we also disable the fail-safe device?"

Kobzar thought for a moment, "This is easy?" he asked.

"As easy as disconnecting one wire from the electrical panel on each missile. I helped the technicians install the fail-safe when they put the system onboard last year. I think I can do it without anybody seeing me and once they are disconnected there is no way for anybody to know but you and me," said Zhuravin.

"And it is just as easy to make functional again?"

"Just as easy, Captain," answered Zhuravin.

"Yes, Alex. Make it so."

SKORPIOS ISLAND
March 1, 1968

It was unusual and nearly impossible for Ari Onassis to suddenly show up anywhere and even more unusual for the

Christina, his 325-foot luxury yacht to appear off Skorpios without his staff knowing. Even as a multi-billionaire, Ari Onassis was star-struck by celebrity and even more so by beautiful women. After hearing that Jackie Kennedy was going to be on Skorpios, he rearranged some meetings, postponed others, and canceled a trip to the States in order to 'suddenly' show up at his island.

The *Christina,* the pride and joy of his entire fleet was much harder to hide than Onassis himself. At 325 feet she was the longest private yacht in the world. She was originally a Canadian frigate launched in 1943 and christened as the HMCS *Stromont.* She had served as a convoy escort and was present at the D-Day landings. At the end of the war she was one of the many surplus vessels purchased by Ari, he paid just $34,000 for her. After spending more than $4 million dollars to convert her into his private yacht, he renamed her *Christina* after his daughter. The *Christina* had established a very impressive guest list over the years including Eva Peron, Frank Sinatra, Marilyn Monroe, and of course, Ari's mistress, Maria Callas. The *Christina* was one of the most celebrated social venues of the time; in 1957, Winston Churchill had first met the young Senator John F. Kennedy and his wife aboard her.

When Jack, Jackie, Bobby and Boulos arrived back at the main house it appeared that Demetrius might spontaneously explode from stress. He first had heard that the *Christina* had sailed into sight only half an hour earlier which usually meant that a visit from his boss was imminent. Just moments before the other four had made their way back to the house, Demetrius received word that Onassis was indeed aboard the yacht.

Over the years, Jack had found Demetrius to be a good friend. He was the perfect employee to run the day-to-day operations of any property or estate. He demanded perfection not only from every gardener, maid, and cook on his staff but he insisted on even more from himself. Never once had he heard Onassis offer anything other than compliments regarding the condition of the island and the quality of the service from the staff yet Demetrius constantly fretted over every little detail. As he nervously flitted about the island, it wasn't unusual to see him stop and pick up a fallen leaf that had dropped on the walk. If he found a chip in a cup or a plate, the item was discarded and the employee most likely to have caused the damage could expect to receive a verbal lashing.

As he scurried around the house yelling at this staff member or that in preparation for the boss' visit, Demetrius also talked to himself, or 'thought out loud'. This habit caused problems between him and his staff because they often didn't know if he was directing them to move the chairs from here to there or just 'thinking out loud' about moving the chairs. If an eager staff member moved the chairs while Demetrius was only thinking about moving them, that person could expect a stern verbal berating. Despite it all, each of the employees of the quirky little Greek enjoyed working for the man who also had a warm and generous heart and was quick to dispense compliments when they were warranted.

"How can we help you, Demetrius?" asked Jackie as the little man scurried past.

The words came almost as a slap in the face. A guest had just offered to help. "Oh, Mrs.Kennedy, thank you for asking but we have everything under control," he answered as he scurried off talking to himself.

"Let's grab a drink and sit down by the hammock," said Jack. "We'll be out of the way and we can talk more about your campaign," he said to Bobby. "Boulos, can I fix you a drink?" he asked. It was as much a question as a message, "My brother and my wife and I are going to go talk and you're not invited to listen."

"No, thank you, Mister Kennedy," replied Boulos. "With Mister Onassis' arrival, I have many details to which I must attend."

"Do you mind popping your head into the guest house and asking Hal to come join us?" Jack asked.

"I would be happy to do so," replied Boulos with a slight bow.

'Down by the hammock' was a reference to an area below the main house that the construction crew, with Jack and his men's help, had cleared away the brush and some small trees. Jack had asked the crew to spare two of the larger trees because they were tall, healthy and provided a perfect venue for the authentic Pawley's Island rope hammock his brother Teddy had given him for his birthday. Once the hammock was hung, the Americans found that the location often provided not only shade thanks to the leafy canopies of the trees but there was often a nice breeze blowing through the spot that didn't reach the house just a two hundred feet up the hill. They moved some chairs down by the hammock and Ari had his crew level the area and install a small brick patio. Jack's hammock still hung between the two trees but the solitude was occasionally breeched as it became the nicest place in the compound to gather on a warm afternoon.

Bobby, Jackie, and Jack sat in the comfortable deck chairs enjoying shade and the breeze. "I know it's a lot to ask but I'm not sure I see a better way out of Vietnam," said Jack.

"I know," said Bobby with a sigh of resignation, "and you know I'd do this in a heartbeat but I'm damn concerned about dragging Ethel and the children through it."

"I'm wide open to other suggestions," said Jack.

"There are no other suggestions," said Jackie. "If not Johnson or you," she said looking directly at Bobby, "then it's fairly clear that Nixon will win. And we know Nixon is convinced that the quickest way out of Southeast Asia is to escalate the number of troops and try to win the war."

Jack smiled. He loved it when Jackie engaged in these types of discussions. She was much more brilliant than the world would ever know. Her ability to think through complex issues and make decisions based on fact rather than emotion had served Jack well over the years. If he had listened to her, it would have saved him from several of the failures of his career including the Bay of Pigs. She had been adamantly opposed to the plan from the beginning. History wouldn't give her proper credit for counseling Jack on how to recover politically from the debacle but the post-disaster clean-up plan had been largely Jackie's.

"Are you plotting to take over the *Christina* or something less formidable like the free world?" asked Hal Rumsey with a big smile as he approached the group.

"Have a seat, Hal," said Jack. "Want a cold beer?" he asked pointing to a small cooler.

Bobby wasn't yet convinced that the young Secret Service agent was the great sounding board and advisor that Jack had pumped him up to be but he didn't argue his presence.

Jackie turned to Hal as he plopped himself into the deck chair beside her. "Hal, we were talking about Bobby running for President. He is still not convinced he wants to run but we're not sure we have a better solution. In my mind, it's either going to be Johnson, Nixon, or a new candidate and I only know of one other man who can win the election."

Hal pulled a beer out of the cooler next to his chair and popped it open with a church key hanging from a string tied to the handle of the cooler. "Okay, as I see it, Johnson can't back out of Vietnam. The only way out of that damn mess at this point is to evacuate all the troops at once and a sudden retreat would be seen on the world stage as a loss. Nobody wants to admit defeat, right?"

He took a big gulp of his beer and let that thought sink in, "Nixon clearly thinks an escalation policy is the key, he wants to win the war and we pretty much know from our sources that that will only lead to continued intervention from the Russians, so that won't work but Nixon doesn't appear to be listening to those who have tried to explain it to him." Hal clearly had the attention of the three Kennedys seated around him. "So the only clear alternative is to run a candidate against Nixon who will campaign on a platform of peace. If a new President who has preached a peace initiative from the beginning enters the White House, then pulling us out of Vietnam could be done without losing face around the world. It would just be a change in policy by a new administration. What does everybody think?"

Nobody answered for a moment. Bobby leaned forward in a newfound respect, "Well if nothing else, Hal, that's the clearest and most succinct explanation of the situation I have heard." He set his drink down on the small table beside him, rubbed his eyes and ran his hands through his thick hair as he thought about it. "I don't know, he said finally. Let me talk with Ethel about it before we make too many decisions."

Hal took another drink of his beer, "If we can talk Bob into it, we have our candidate. Now all we need is a bucket of money. Any ideas how we can come up with a bunch of money quick?" he asked.

"If we can win the Democratic bid," said Jackie, "we will have all the funding we need."

"But we need enough to get to that point," said Bobby.

Jack smiled and pointed through the trees at the magnificent yacht anchored just off the island. "Don't think of it as a bucket of money, think of it as a boatload of money."

ABOARD *K-129*, NORTH PACIFIC OCEAN
March 4, 1968

Captain First Rank Vladimir Kobzar by all standards of the Russian Navy was a top-rated commander with an excellent record and an outstanding career. He was well-respected by the men who served under him, by his peers, and by his commanders. But sitting alone in the wardroom with his cup of tea, the Captain now questioned his ability to lead his men and command his boat.

He was concerned but not yet convinced that the new men aboard his vessel were up to something. He saw them having their little whispered meetings, telling their little secrets and stopping suddenly when he approached. He saw their eyes as they watched his every movement and the movements of his crew. They observed shift changes and seemed to make mental notes of how many men were in different areas of the boat at different times of the day.

Kobzar figured he had just two options; do nothing and wait for something to happen and then react as needed or simply arrest the seven men and thwart their plans. Both ideas held within them the possibility of saving his boat and potentially ending his career. If the men were simply here to observe or to test him in some way, arresting them could end his career. If they were truly up to no good, doing nothing could be the end of his career and possibly his boat.

Kobzar continued to sit and slowly stir his tea in silence, trying to determine if his fears arose from appropriate caution or from paranoia. The mysterious men had presented him a handwritten note from Vice Admiral Prjevalski. He could break radio silence and send a message to Prjevalski to verify the note but if there was truly a mutiny in the works, the Vice Admiral might be in on the whole thing. If his boat was just being used for a drill or a test, then sending such a message questioning a personal note from the

Admiral would be detrimental to his career. Kobzar suddenly hated his job.

Fortunately, his disdain for his assignment would be short-lived. He turned at the sound of a knock at the door to find the older mystery sailor who said, "Excuse me Captain, may I have a moment of your time?"

"Of course," said Kobzar. "Please come in, sit," said Kobzar in a friendly tone, while wishing he had his revolver close at hand.

The man entered and took a seat on the bench opposite the Captain. "We have not been formally introduced. My name is Major Rostov with Army Intelligence.

Kobzar half-stood and reached across the table to shake the man's hand, "It is a pleasure to meet you, Major Rostov."

"As you probably have guessed," said Rostov, "we are not here to observe your operations. I have orders from Vice Admiral Prjevalski to share the details of our mission with you," he said as he passed a thin envelope across the table to the Captain.

Kobzar left the envelope sitting untouched in front of him. "What do the orders say, Major?"

Rostov smiled at Kobzar's little power play, "You are to take us to a location south of our present position, near the Hawaiian Islands, where we will probe the American defenses and map landing sites on the more remote islands."

"A rather simple mission," said Kobzar confidently, "something we might call a fishing trip." He tried to maintain casual attitude about the mission but he found himself breathing a tremendous sigh of relief. He had been worried that these men were up to no good but Army Intelligence simply wanted to send some guys out to play around in the tropics, make a few maps, and gain confidence that the Russian Navy could go anywhere they wanted to at any time.

"You will find that one other piece of the mission might not be as easy as fishing," said Major Rostov.

"What is that?"

"When our mission is complete, and a hundred percent at your discretion with regards to the safety of this vessel, of course," said Rostov, "we are to allow ourselves to be detected and identified as a Soviet submarine before affecting our escape. Vice Admiral Prjevalski and his colleagues would like us to strike some fear into the hearts of the arrogant Americans. We will show them that we can come right up to their doorstep and strike them at any time."

Kobzar smiled. The mission had just become a wonderful and dangerous adventure. Only a few minutes earlier he had been frightened that his last deployment might end in mutiny and now with a clear understanding of the mission, the Captain had a great feeling of pride and patriotism. The fears he had held only moments before had disappeared and he was proud that his boat and his men had been chosen to take part in this extraordinary assignment.

ABOARD THE *CHRISTINA*, OFF SKORPIOS ISLAND
March 4, 1968

It was one of those if-my-friends-could-see-me-now moments. The moon was only a sliver and had just risen above the horizon. The stars were bright and fabulous and a soft cool breeze blew across the water. Hal stood on the fantail of the massive yacht near its incredible mosaic-tiled swimming pool with a glass of what he was sure was very expensive scotch in a Baccarat crystal tumbler, smoking a Cuban cigar. Dinner had been completely over the top; in fact, Hal wasn't exactly sure what he had just eaten but every bite was extraordinary.

A few years earlier Hal couldn't afford to go out for a burger with his co-workers and now he dined on the finest foods and sipped best wines available with Aristotle Onassis, the President and Mrs. Kennedy, Bobby, and Ari's two children, Alexander, who was almost sixteen and Christina, who was fourteen.

Hal tried to drink in every moment, he wanted to remember the scenes, the smells, and the feelings of it all in case he ever had the opportunity to describe it to somebody.

His solitude was shattered as the party spilled out onto the deck. Jack, Bobby, Jackie and Ari walked out laughing and a little giddy from the alcohol.

"Here's Hal," said Jack. "We thought maybe you were chasing after that pretty little dining room attendant."

Hal certainly had been eyeing that beautiful young woman in the dining room and a time or two he thought she had been playing eye games with him as well. Nobody seemed to mind that he might have been off trying to woo a member of Ari's crew. He stored that little piece of information away. "No, I'm just out here enjoying the fine scotch and the superb cigars of our amazing host."

"Come join us, Hal" Jack said as they walked past him to the plush seating area aft of the pool.

An crew member followed with soft blankets to help guard Ari and his guests against the freshening breeze. The area was illuminated with soft candle lanterns that provided enough light to see each other's faces but not enough to block out the stars or shine to brightly in anyone's eyes. When Jackie commented on the wonderful crystal lanterns Ari explained that he preferred candlelight to electric lighting because of its romantic glow.

"It is so beautiful here," said Jackie. "Thank you so much, Ari, for being such a magnificent host to us on your island and aboard your wonderful *Christina*," she said with her famous graciousness.

"What is mine is yours," said Ari. "It is a pleasure to have such distinguished guests aboard."

"I must find a way to spend more time on the island and we have to find a way to bring the children out," said Jackie. "It has been ten years since I have felt the security, the peace, and the serenity that I find on Skorpios."

"You, of course, are welcome anytime, and for as long as you please," answered Ari.

Jackie's smile slipped from her face, "Unfortunately, I live my life in a fish bowl. It's nearly impossible to escape the eyes and ears of the press."

"There is a fairly simple solution," said Hal.

Jack smiled, "Here it comes. My young friend, Hal, here has the unique talent of taking just about any complex issue and simplifying it to something a third grader could understand. I swear to God you must have been raised on a farm in Kansas."

Jackie popped her husband on the knee, "Be quiet, Jack. I want to hear Hal's idea."

Hal realized that he was in way over his head socially but he pressed forward, "I'm sitting here with the world's most beautiful widow . . . ."

"Yes, keep going," Jackie interrupted, flashing Hal a wink.

". . . and the richest bachelor in the world," Hal continued. "It seems to me that if you two were married, Jackie could spend all the time she wanted to on Skorpios."

The group sat held in a charged silence for a few moments before Jack laughed saying, "I know the Mormons have multiple wives but which religion has multiple husbands?"

"Of course, you would only be married in the eyes of the press," said Hal to make certain that everybody understood his idea clearly.

"It's not a bad idea," said Bobby. "What do you think of it Ari?"

Ari chuckled, "It might upset Maria enough that she finally goes away," he said referring to the famed opera singer Maria Callis with whom he has shared a tumultuous ten-year relationship. "And it certainly wouldn't hurt my business to be photographed with Jackie Kennedy on my arm."

Jackie smiled nervously, "It is a rather creative solution to the problem, Hal. Let's think about it for a little while."

Jack sensed her resistance to the idea and changed the subject quickly, "Ari, your children are sure growing up fast. How are they getting along in school?"

BOCA RATON, FLORIDA
Present Day

"About another five minutes and you'll be finished, Hal," said Nurse Charlene, adjusting the IV bag hanging above him. "Let's take a look at that arm again."

"It's not so bad anymore," said Hal, "but my stomach is sure upset all of a sudden."

The nurse checked his chart, "I don't see any history of you having nausea or other reactions to the treatment. Why are you being so difficult this time?" she said with a grin.

"It's not the drugs, it's obviously Mahoney here," teased Hal. "The guy just makes me sick."

Mahoney smiled, "I usually only have that affect on ex-wives and girlfriends."

"I'll get a doctor in here to take a quick look if I have to drag one in by their ear," said the nurse in a firm tone. She flashed him another smile and left the room.

Mahoney glanced at his notes again and said, "You said the Chinese were probing the Russian boarder defenses to see how they might respond to a ground invasion."

"Right," said Hal, "they would send a group of twenty men over the border to attack a small Russian Army unit, or they would sneak in and blow something up, just to see what the reaction would be. It's an old tactic that is probably still in use today."

"And how did the Russians respond?" asked Mahoney.

ABOARD *K-129*, PACIFIC OCEAN
March 7, 1968

Captain Kobzar was sitting at his small desk finishing a report when again there was a knock at his cabin door, "Come in," he said without looking up.

The door opened and a voice said, "I am sorry, Captain, but we must now take control of your boat."

Kobzar looked up to find Major Rostov standing in the door with a standard Army Issue Makarov sidearm pointed at him. He was about to ask if this was a joke but there was enough conviction in Rostov's voice to convince him otherwise. "Please don't point that damn thing at me," said the Captain. "It could go off."

"If you will please come with me, Captain," said Rostov without moving his pistol an inch.

Kobzar stood, "I'll be right with you, Major," he said, glancing at the pillow on his bunk.

"I need you to come with me right now, Captain," responded the Major.

Kobzar was two feet from his bunk but he knew he would be dead before he could get his hand on the weapon under his pillow. He chose instead to follow instructions and live to fight for his boat another time. Rostov stepped into the passageway to allow Kobzar to pass and motioned him into the control room. The scene in control looked normal if unusually quiet, each crew member had a questioned look on his face as Kobzar entered the small space.

They appeared to be doing their respective duties but nobody spoke. The only thing out of place was one of Rostov's men standing towards the back of the control room holding a sawed-off shotgun.

Kobzar turned to Rostov, his irritation becoming anger. "I demand an explanation."

"Captain," Rostov said calmly, "we need your boat for a few hours. If you and your crew do as we instruct, we will complete our mission and return control to you. If you and your men do not obey us, we will do whatever is necessary."

A sweeping glance of his men in the control room exposed the glaring absence of Zhuravin. Perhaps his First Officer had been able to secure the engine room. The Navy manual specifically spelled out anti-mutiny instructions. "If unable to secure the control room, secure the engine room at once." Without control of the engine room, mutineers would be unable to move the boat or operate its heating or cooling systems. A few days bobbing in the middle of the ocean in the sweltering heat or frigid cold would take the enthusiasm out of any mob.

Kobzar glanced at the helm panel. They were making twelve knots on a southwesterly heading of 225 degrees. The tachometer indicated the propeller shaft was spinning and the vibrations he felt through the deck panels below his feet confirmed *K-129* was operating normally.

"We have asked most of your men to join my colleagues in the mess," said Rostov. "We have taken control of the engine, torpedo, and missile compartments, and we have secured the weapons in your armory. There is no need for heroics, Captain. We are all fighting for the same cause and working for the same Party."

"If we are all working together," asked Kobzar, "then why do you find it necessary to take control of my men and my boat? I have specific orders from Admiral Prjevalski to give you our full cooperation."

"Our mission is critical to the survival of the Soviet Union. We do not have the luxury of time to argue with you or your crew over our mission. Our orders are to take control of your boat, complete our mission, and then return control of *K-129* back to you. When you sail back into Rybachiy, you and your crew will be greeted as great heroes of the State. They will probably build statues to honor you, Captain."

Kobzar didn't believe a single word of it but he smiled a thin smile trying to cover his distrust of the man standing before him.

"Now, if you will please, Captain," said Rostov in a firm voice of command, "order your men to direct the boat to these coordinates."

He handed a slip of paper to Kobzar, written on it was, *"24°N 160°W"*

Kobzar looked at the paper for a moment then turned and walked five steps back to the navigator's table where a detailed map of their current position lay open. The navigator, a junior officer, who was fairly new to *K-129*'s crew, glanced at the coordinates and then removed the chart from his table. He quickly retrieved a new chart from the cubbies below the table and carefully unfolded it. With his right hand he found the north coordinates on the top of the map and with his other he found the west on the left side of the map. He brought his fingers together down their respective lines to where they met, about fifty miles off a tiny speck of land in the Hawaiian chain identified as Necker Island.

Kobzar, with his back turned to Rostov said to the navigator, "You will chart a direct course to this position," while purposely tapping his fingers on the slip of paper and raising his eye brows slightly.

The young officer nodded ever so slightly saying, "Immediately, Captain." He used three fingers to slide the small piece of paper towards the top of the chart indicating to the Captain that they were indeed off course to the north, three degrees, three minutes, or three measures of some kind. It didn't matter to the Captain how far they were off course, just that they were.

The Captain gave the officer a quick smile and turned back to Rostov. "We are about four hours from your coordinates. How else might we assist you?"

Rostov smiled, "Thank you, Captain. You have been most accommodating, your actions will be included in my final report," he lied. "Perhaps one more task."

"Yes, Major. Anything," said Kobzar.

"Will you be so kind as to make an announcement to your men to cooperate with us?" asked Rostov. "We certainly would not want any of your men to try something heroic and become unnecessarily injured in the process."

"An excellent idea, Major," said Kobzar. He stepped over to the Chief's panel, picked up the intercom's microphone, and selected the 'All' position. He cleared his throat before saying, "Comrades, the men who are currently controlling our boat are doing so under the orders of Vice Admiral Prjevalski. Before we sailed, the Admiral sent me a personal message asking me to cooperate in every way with these men. I am asking you to do the same. Unless you are asked to do something that would compromise the safety of our boat, do exactly as you are instructed. I have been assured that this drill will be over in a few hours. That is all."

Rostov smiled, "Thank you, Captain. We wouldn't want any of your men to be needlessly hurt."

"No, we would not," said Kobzar with a menacing look that silently added, "and they damn well better not be hurt." The Captain made a mental note of the time before saying, "If you will excuse me for a moment, Major." He put his hand over his lower stomach, "Either the excitement or the damn chicken has caused me a bit of distress. I need to spend a few minutes in my cabin alone."

"By all means, Captain," said Rostov politely. "By the way, for the safety of your crew I have removed your service revolver from under your pillow."

BOCA RATON, FLORIDA
Present Day

"The response of the Soviets to the Chinese probe attacks was, even in today's point of view, appalling. But you've got to take into consideration the time and the era," said Hal. "The Kremlin was backed into a corner. The Americans were building and deploying missiles as quickly as they could while at the same time the Chinese were threatening to take over the Soviet gold mines and oil fields. Remember that Brezhnev wasn't really in command because he had too many people pulling his strings. With no clear leader and threats increasing from all sides, it was only a matter of time before some group of dumb asses would hatch a really idiotic plan."

"And what did they come up with?" asked Mahoney. "Who were these dumb asses?"

"Some of Brezhnev's oldest friends, some of his allies against Khrushchev, came up with a plan to get the United States and China to engage each other in a nuclear war. If their plan was successful, all they would have to do was sit back and pick up the spoils of war, the USSR would emerge as the world's lone superpower.

Mahoney changed positions in his chair, "And how did they think they were going to accomplish that?"

"The men who designed this plan had at their disposal all the weapons, the ships, the troops, and the intel to put such a plot together. And they probably came closer than the world will ever know," said Hal.

ABOARD *K-129*, PACIFIC OCEAN
March 7, 1968

"Captain," said the young officer at the navigator's station. "Twenty-four degrees north, one-sixty west," indicating they had reached the requested coordinates.

Kobzar twisted to look at the lieutenant who had dropped his head back down to study the chart in front of him. The young man's hands rested on the table, three of the fingers on his right hand rapidly tapped the chart under it. "Thank you, Mister Goblinski."

Kobzar turned back to Rostov, "We have arrived at your requested position, Major Rostov. How may we further assist you?"

Rostov reached into his breast pocket and pulled out another slip of paper. In a very calm and matter of fact voice Rostov replied, "I need you to launch your number-one missile at these coordinates."

Kobzar laughed, "I'm sorry, Major. We have no orders to launch a missile this evening, perhaps another time."

Slowly and smoothly Rostov reached for his sidearm which was tucked in his waistband. He pointed the gun at Kobzar's head with his arm fully out stretched. "I am ordering you to launch your missile," he said.

The smile on Kobzar's face faded. "Major, even if we wanted to launch a missile without a launch authorization message, we still need the fail-safe code."

"I will provide the fail-safe code to you, and I am ordering you to launch your number-one missile. Or," he said while his thumb pulled back the trigger of his pistol, "I will find a crew member who will help me."

Both men suddenly turned at the sound of the loud thump from the back of the control room. As they turned, Kobzar's man with the shotgun fell to the deck unconscious, his weapon clattered on the floor.

Standing where Rostov's man had been only a second before was First Officer Zhuravin with his service revolver pointed directly at the Major. "You have two seconds to drop your weapon, Major." Rostov didn't move a muscle, his pistol still pointed at the Captain's head while Zhuravin counted, "One, two," and then fired.

From a distance of fifteen feet Zhuravin shouldn't have missed but he was a naval officer, not a marksman. His shot whizzed a half of an inch past Rostov's right ear and smashed into a panel behind him. Rostov turned and fired two quick shots from his semi-automatic pistol into Zhuravin's chest before Kobzar could react.

Kobzar grabbed the gun in Rostov's outstretched arm with his left hand as he charged, throwing his right shoulder into the Major's chest. They both tumbled to ground in the small space behind the helmsmen. The young helmsman seated at the right station controlling the diving planes twisted and grabbed for Rostov's gun as it fired again. The bullet smashed into his lower jaw obliterating his face.

Rostov rolled to the left and behind the Captain with his gun free. He put the muzzle to Kobzar's temple and said, "The next person who tries to be a hero will be responsible for your Captain's death." The startled men in the control room froze.

"Major?" a voice yelled from the ladder below the control room.

"I am fine," replied Rostov. As Rostov rose from the deck with his weapon still pointed at the Captain's head, one of his men rushed up the ladder to see the bloody scene. Zhuravin lay motionless against the radio panel, blood poured from his chest. His eyes were open and responsive but he didn't make a sound. The helmsman had fallen to the ground and writhed on the bloody deck, moaning painfully.

"Heroes," said Rostov in a breathless frustration. "We train our men to be good soldiers but they still want to be heroes." The Major looked at the scene and then pointed to the Chief of the Boat. "Get these brave men out of here and find somebody to attend to them," he said. He then turned to the Kobzar and calmly said, "Captain, please order your men to stop the boat."

Kobzar looked at the Officer of the Deck, a young officer whose eyes were wide with shock and his face white with fear, "All stop."

The young officer repeated the words, "All stop," which a chief then relayed to the engine room. A moment later the vibration of the deck ceased.

Kobzar looked at the young helmsman below him, his face was shattered and broken and a piece of his jaw was missing. He would live but he would never forget the last two minutes. He patted the man on the back and then moved past Rostov to check on Zhuravin. It only took a glance to see that his First Officer was dying. Alexander Zhuravin knew it and all the men in the control room knew it. Kobzar kneeled next to him, "Alex, is there anything I can do to make you more comfortable?"

Zhuravin tried to speak, his mouth opened slightly but no words came. He looked at his Captain, a man for whom he had held great respect for many years, and attempted to smile. His face showed neither pain, nor fear, nor despair, but reflected his calm resolve. He knew he would die from trying to save his boat, his men, and his Captain's life and for Zhuravin, that was an honorable reason. His eyes left the Captain's face for a moment and seemed to stare across the control room, locking on the missile console for a few seconds. He turned his eyes back to Kobzar and when he saw that his Captain understood, Zhuravin managed a thin smile.

"Excuse us, Captain," said a voice from behind him. "Please let us take the First Officer below so we may attend to him."

Kobzar leaned close to Zhuravin's ear and said, "Thank you, Alex. I'll talk with your wife and your daughters. I'll tell them you were a hero and they should be proud. And I promise you that I will get these bastards."

Kobzar stood as his men carried Zhuravin away. He turned back towards Rostov, his face filled with anger. Rostov was calm and composed, his weapon was still pointed towards the Captain but now held at his hip. "Captain Kobzar, please begin the process to launch your number-one missile to these coordinates."

"You bastard," said Kobzar in an unusual fit of anger. "I do not have authority to launch a missile."

"Vice Admiral Prjevalski asked that you cooperate with our mission . . . and I have a gun which you now know I will use," said Rostov. "I would think that is authority enough." His voice was cold and quiet and his eyes were steely and determined. "Please launch your number-one missile to these coordinates, now," he said holding the slip of paper out to Kobzar.

The Captain reached for the paper which held the coordinates, "21.21°N 157.56°W". Kobzar didn't need to look at the chart to know the general area Major Rostov planned to attack with the one-megaton warhead that sat atop *K-129*'s Serb missile.

Kobzar guessed they were at least 200 nautical miles north of the position Rostov had requested. Given the correct launch position, the rudimentary navigation systems aboard the Serb missile could hit any coordinates programmed into it. With incorrect launch position data, however, the warhead would likely drop into the sea short of its intended target, but Kobzar held his resolve. "Admiral Prjevalski has no authority to order a missile launch and," his voice cracked slightly with fear, "you and your gun have no authority to order a missile launch. If it is your intention to start a war with the Americans from this boat, you will have to kill me first."

Major Rostov, without emotion or even a word, raised his weapon to Captain First Rank Vladimir Kobzar's head . . . and did just that.

Thirty-seven minutes later, three Navy sonar technicians sitting at separate consoles thousands of miles apart in Adak, Alaska; Coos Bay, Oregon; and Barber's Point, Hawaii, asked at almost the same moment, "What in the hell was that?"

SKORPIOS ISLAND
March 16, 1968

"Hal," yelled Kennedy from the window. "Here it comes!"

Hal dropped what he was doing and ran to the open window of the room they called the radio room in the guest house. A familiar British voice of a BBC commentator was blasting across the speaker that sat atop the radio set.

"From Washington, D.C., just a few hours ago," said the voice over the radio, "Robert Kennedy, brother of the late President John F. Kennedy, has announced his intent to seek the office of President of the United States," he paused.

The next voice was a scratchy recording but it was classic Bobby:

"I am today announcing my candidacy for the presidency of the United States.

I do not run for the presidency merely to oppose any man but to propose new policies. I run because I am convinced that this country is on a perilous course and because I have such strong feelings about what must be done, and I feel that I'm obliged to do all that I can.

I run to seek new policies, policies to end the bloodshed in Vietnam and in our cities, policies to close the gaps that now exist between black and white, between rich and poor, between young and old, in this country and around the rest of the world.

I run for the presidency because I want the Democratic Party and the United States of America to stand for hope instead of despair, for reconciliation of men instead of the growing risk of world war . . .."

Jack was beaming ear to ear, "Grab your balls, Hal. This is going to be one hell of a ride!"

BOCA RATON, FLORIDA
Present Day

"The bastards running the USSR were so desperate to end the Cold War and stop the growing conflict with China that they tried to launch a nuclear missile at Pearl Harbor," said Hal quietly.

"What? Are you serious?" asked Mahoney.

"Yeah, a group of the Kremlin's best and brightest," Hal said sarcastically, "came up with their own little plan. They sent a submarine out to simulate a Chinese missile launch on Hawaii. The group figured that if the Americans thought that China had attacked Honolulu and killed half a million people or so, the U.S. would respond with an immediate counter-attack. The Chinese would react to an unprovoked attack by launching everything they had and in a matter of a few hours the Soviet Union would be the only man standing."

"Are you serious?" asked Mahoney. "Did they really think they could get away with something like that?

"They obviously thought they could and they almost did but something went wrong and the submarine blew up during the launch."

"Okay, this is crazy," said Mahoney with a look of disbelief in his eyes. "Take me through this slowly."

"All right," said Hal. "By 1968 the Soviets had sold most of their old Golf-One submarines to other countries, mainly to China. The Golf-One was an old diesel sub that could only launch missiles from the surface and only from a specific longitude and latitude. The guidance system had to know exactly where it was in order to launch a missile.

The submarine that blew up off Hawaii was a Golf-Two sub with improved targeting systems that could launch a missile while submerged from any location to anywhere they chose. And the sub that blew up was on the surface and at a specific longitude and latitude, a location that only the Golf-Ones would have required."

"How do you know the sub was Russian and what makes you think that it was trying to launch a missile?" asked Mahoney.

"We saw it and we heard it blow up. By '68, we had filled both the North Pacific and Atlantic with hydrophones, something called SOSUS or the Sound Surveillance System. We heard the explosion in Hawaii, in Alaska, and on the west coast. And we lucked out and caught it on a passing satellite. NORAD actually caught a thermal image of the sub as it blew up and burned."

"So we had a pretty good idea where it went down?" asked Mahoney.

"Between the satellite and the triangulation of the listening stations we had its location down to a gnat's ass. Close enough that we were able to get one of our subs to photograph the hell out of the wreckage."

"And obviously the photos were conclusive enough to show that the submarine tried to launch a missile?" asked Mahoney.

"They were pretty conclusive. The explosion on the sub was caused by an explosion from the number-one missile while it was still aboard the boat. There are a number of theories as to why the missile might have blown up. It may have malfunctioned, shorted out or something, and caught fire. They may have tried to launch it and it malfunctioned and blew up before it left the boat, or they may have not deactivated the fail-safe device.

"If there was some sort of fail-safe device, wouldn't those trying to launch a missile know that and have the information to defeat it?" asked Mahoney.

"Probably," answered Hal. "In the mid-sixties we gave the Russians our fail-safe technology just for this purpose, to keep a rogue captain or crew from launching a missile. It was a pretty crude system. A small explosive device was attached to each missile near the engine. If not deactivated it would explode. The idea was to damage the missile's engine enough to stop a launch. The problem was that the system hadn't been tested on a real submarine with a real missile; the explosive device might have caught the missile fuel on fire rather than just disabling the motor. If the bad guys on that sub didn't have the right fail-safe code or if the crew had disabled the fail-safe system, which I guess was possible, then boom!"

Mahoney shifted uncomfortably in the hard chair. "So we had the location of the submarine, the photos, and some pretty strong evidence that somebody had tried to launch a missile at Hawaii. What did you guys do with this information?"

"Once we received a copy of the photographs the Navy had taken, Jack sent a note to Brezhnev telling him they needed to meet. That meeting took place around June of 1968 in a little village near the Yugoslavian border with Greece. Brezhnev convinced Jack that he didn't know anything about the launch attempt."

"What do you think?" asked Mahoney.

"I was leery of Brezhnev's role in the whole thing at first. And not being in the meeting I don't know exactly what was said but Jack was convinced and that was good enough for me. The events that occurred in the Soviet Union over the next several months seemed to add up. Brezhnev cleaned house as only somebody who was innocent could have."

"What do you mean when you say he 'cleaned house'?" asked Mahoney.

"By late '68, Brezhnev had a pretty good idea who the top conspirators were in the submarine fiasco. The first 'cleaning' we heard of was the Admiral who made it possible for some men, probably KGB, to go to sea on the sub. I don't remember the Admiral's name but he died in a somewhat suspicious car accident."

Hal leaned out of his chair to look out to the hall to see if anybody was listening. "The guy who led the plot was Mikhal Suslov, one of the guys who helped put Brezhnev in power. He retired suddenly due to health reasons. Nikolay Podgorny and our old KGB buddy, Alex Shelepin, both disappeared from the public scene right about then along with Alexsey Kosygin. As I recall, they all seemed to have health issues that cropped up in the late sixties. Pretty much all of the serious hardliners in the Politburo and Central Committee died, retired, or simply faded away within a period of about six months at the end of '68. By the time it was all over, Brezhnev was the top man in the Soviet Union. Nobody questioned his authority or told him what to do."

"And you think that was because of the information that Kennedy gave him regarding the submarine incident?" asked Mahoney while jotting down a note to check the names.

Hal smiled, "I know it was. Jack took the photos and other evidence to Brezhnev and then politely but firmly told him that he had to clean house and take control of his country or we were going to take the photos to the Chinese and then to the world."

"I've never heard this story before, a rogue Soviet submarine sinking while trying to launch a missile at Hawaii," said Mahoney. "How would such a big story be kept secret?"

"I've only told you the first part of the story, it gets even crazier after Nixon found out about it and became obsessed with recovering the sub. I didn't get into the Howard Hughes connection or the *Glomar Explorer*, the ship the CIA contracted Hughes to build to recover the submarine," he said with a grin. "Go look up *K-129* and the *Glomar Explorer* on your computer there. I'm not making any of it up," said Hal with a slight chuckle.

SKORPIOS ISLAND
April 5, 1968

Hal was enjoying a cup of coffee in the radio room; he sat in his favorite position, a chair pulled over to the window and his feet on the sill. A warm breeze blew in from the sea below bringing with it a light scent of something in bloom. On the radio, a BBC reporter was talking about the previous day's student uprising in Paris as Hal tried to concentrate on Hemingway's, *The Old Man and the Sea.*

"From Memphis, Tennessee, in the United States, the Reverend Martin Luther King, Jr., has died as results of wounds from an assassin's bullet. No arrests have been and authorities have not released the names of any suspects. Rioting has been reported in New York City, Chicago, Washington, D.C., and other cities around the United States . . .."

"Damn it," said Hal as he set down his book and rose to deliver the news. He walked out onto the small patio where Jack was lightly sanding the laminated rudder he had been re-building for a small sailboat they had acquired.

"Hal, I think this repair is going to hold just fine," said Jack looking up. "We won't have to replace the rudder after all," his voice trailed off when he saw the look on Hal's face.

"Jack, the BBC is reporting that somebody shot and killed Martin Luther King," said Hal.

"Son of a bitch," said Kennedy. "Are they certain?" he asked while knowing the BBC didn't report speculation or conjecture.

"Yeah," said Hal. "He died in Memphis, no arrests, no suspects."

Jack set down his sandpaper and leaned back in his chair, his hands covered his face while he tried to comprehend the implications of King's death. "Oh, shit, Hal. This is not good."

"The BBC is also reporting rioting in New York, Chicago, Washington and other cities," said Hal.

"Son of a bitch," Jack said again. He stood and started walking towards the main house but then stopped and turned, "I'm going to walk down to the chapel and say a prayer," he said softly.

"May I join you?" asked Hal.

BOCA RATON, FLORIDA
Present Day

"I hear you don't care for the drugs we're giving you, Mister Rumsey," said the young doctor as he walked into the room.

"I think I'm paying you a hell of a lot of money for something that lights my arm on fire and turns my stomach inside out," said Hal. "Are you sure you gave me the right medicine?"

The doctor looked at Hal's arm and then at his chart. "You haven't had a reaction like this to Camptosar before, have you?"

"How the hell would I know?" asked Hal. "I've never had a reaction to the stuff you gave me in the past."

"This is the same medication as before, so I don't know why you're having a reaction to it now," said the doctor. "The rash should go away in a few hours. Call us if it doesn't. As for feeling sick, I can prescribe an anti-nausea medication if you would like."

"I've had about all the drugs I want from you people today," said Hal. "Just let me the hell out of here and I'll be fine."

The doctor laughed and turned to Mahoney, "Crusty old fart isn't he."

Mahoney didn't care one bit for either the young doctor's comment or his tone. He stood and stepped towards him saying,

"You will treat that old man with the respect he deserves. You are here making obscene amounts of money because you live in the country that this man helped save more than once. Don't you ever speak to him, or about him, that way again. DO you understand?"

Without a word the doctor turned and left the room. "Thank you, Mike," said Hal with a chuckle. "I appreciate that."

Out in the parking lot, Hal stopped and turned to Mahoney, "Mike, do you mind taking me home and catching a cab from my house to the airport? I just don't feel good."

"Do you want to go back in and see the doctor again?" asked Mahoney.

"That Doogie Houser S.O.B.?" Hal asked. "No, I'll be fine if I can just lie down and sleep for a bit."

Mahoney opened Hal's door for him and helped him into the seat as he had done many times for his aging mother. Hal didn't argue which worried Mahoney. Hal wasn't the type of guy to allow somebody to help him unless he really wasn't feeling well.

"Where were we?" asked Hal as they pulled out of the parking lot and back onto the street.

"We can talk more when you're feeling better," answered Mahoney.

"Talking will take my mind off the fact that I'm about to toss my cookies all over my nice clean car," Hal said managing a thin smile.

"Do you feel up to telling me about June of 1968?" asked Mahoney cautiously.

"Jesus, you really do want me to throw up," said Hal.

"We don't need to talk about that, we can talk about something else," said Mahoney quickly.

"No," answered Hal. "Give me a moment." Then he closed his eyes.

SKORPIOS ISLAND
June 4, 1968

It had been a great day on the Ionian Sea. The second launch of the *Honey Fitz Two* had gone much smoother than the initial launch a few days earlier. Hal had arranged the purchase of the tiny old sailboat after Jack had spied her sitting high and dry near the ferry dock in Nydri. After towing her to Skorpios, Jack and Hal had fashioned a cradle and using a pulley system and the island's only motor vehicle, a rusted and aging truck, they pulled the boat from the water and into the cradle where they could work on it.

As with many projects, what appeared to be a just a need for some cleaning and paint turned into a major project to replace dry rot and broken ribs. After several months of hard work by her new owners, the *Honey Fitz Two*, named after both Jack's grandfather and his own boat back in Martha's Vineyard, was ready. Her maiden voyage was delayed by an impromptu christening ceremony in which Jack couldn't help but make a speech.

"Once a politician, always a politician," joked Hal as Kennedy stood atop his new vessel and presented a grand oration to the resident pelicans and egrets. When they finally cast off and raised the sail, one of the main stays snapped with the first breath of wind, causing the mast to tumble into the sea only fifty feet from the dock.

A week later, with the damage to the mast repaired and reinforced with new stays and hardware, they re-launched the *Honey Fitz Two* and enjoyed a wonderful day of sailing.

By late afternoon, Jack became anxious and eager to get back to the island to hear the results of the California primary on the BBC. A win by Bobby in California would give him the momentum he needed to secure the nomination at the Democratic National Convention in August.

Jack and Hal secured the little boat at the dock and walked briskly up to the main house for a drink and what they hoped would be some good news. As they approached, they could see Demetrius sitting in a chair on the small porch of the guest house, his forehead on his knees and his hands covering the back of his head, his fingers laced together as though he was trying to protect himself from some unseen attack.

"What's the matter Demetrius?" asked Jack.

The little Greek sat up, his eyes were red and hollow and his face was white. "Mister Kennedy, it is your brother, the Senator Bobby."

BOCA RATON, FLORIDA
Present Day

Mahoney drove cautiously to make the ride as smooth as possible for his ailing passenger. Hal was slumped in the seat next to him with his head back against the headrest and his eyes closed.

"I think it's important to understand that after King's death, Bobby was seen as the great white hope to the nation's young people," Hal said suddenly after several minutes of silence. "Neither Jack nor Bobby would have tried to take political advantage of King's death but they were both smart enough to ride the tide. They had changed tactics slightly in April and made an effort to speak directly to the younger voters about racial equality and civil rights and it had worked. Bobby won the California Primary which put him on course to win the nomination at the Democratic National Convention and probably the election."

Hal grew silent again and Mahoney glanced over again at him. He was sitting in the same position, eyes closed and head back.

"Hal, are you okay?"

"I'm fine, Mike," he answered but remained quiet and motionless for several more minutes as Mahoney drove towards his home.

"We heard about Bobby's shooting and I've never felt so remote and so helpless in my entire life," said Hal suddenly. "There were confusing reports, even from the BBC who usually wouldn't report something until they were sure it was true. We used to laugh that the BBC hated to report news until it was printed in history books and gathering dust on library shelves," Hal said with a chuckle.

"We sat there on that damn island listening to the radio trying to understand how serious Bobby's condition was. Then, after a sleepless night, I took the launch to Nydri where I was able to get a telegraph to Ted Sorensen's office. A few hours later I got a sort of cryptic reply saying something along the lines of 'Situation is not good and more likely to worsen than improve, sincere condolences to J'."

Hal became silent again. Mahoney was uncertain if his silence was a symptom of the nausea or the emotion associated with the subject at hand.

"I remember sitting there on that bench in front of the telegraph office with that piece of paper in my hand. I kept thinking maybe Sorenson was wrong. Maybe one of the telegraph operators got it backwards and Bobby's condition was more likely to improve than worsen. Maybe Sorenson was talking about something else," said Hal. "But I knew it was probably all true. Jack was waiting at the dock when I got back but I didn't need to say anything. He could tell by my face that the news wasn't good."

"As I recall, Bobby lived for a day or so after he was shot," said Mahoney. "Do you recall how you heard that he had died?"

"We heard it on the BBC," said Hal quietly.

"What was Kennedy's reaction?"

"He walked down to the chapel, sat in the front pew, and cried," said Hal. "Jack placed a lot of blame on himself for the murders of both Martin Luther King and Bobby."

"Mahoney looked over at Hal with a surprised look, "How the hell could Kennedy blame himself for those two deaths?"

Hal opened his eyes for the first time in several blocks and looked out the passenger window. "Mike, there is a drug store a few blocks up on your right. I think some Pepto might make me feel better."

"Okay," said Mahoney glancing at his watch. "How could Kennedy assume any blame for those assassinations?" he asked again.

Hal let out a big sigh, "Jack felt that by faking his own assassination, he had in some way opened the door to others who thought that assassinations were the way to correct or prevent things politically in the States. Jack had been the one who pushed Bobby to run for the presidency in the first place and he couldn't get over the fact that his brother might still be alive if he had been left to enjoy the lower-profile life as a Senator from Massachusetts rather than running for president in an effort to save the country."

"But weren't the two guys who killed King and Bobby just a couple of wackos?" asked Mahoney. "How do you defend yourself from nut cases with guns?"

"Were they just wackos?" asked Hal with a glance out of the corner of his eye.

"Weren't they?" asked Mahoney with a surprised look.

"Here's the drug store," said Hal pointing to a chain store on the corner.

Mahoney turned into the parking lot and found a spot partially shaded by a small tree. He turned off the ignition and turned to Hal. "Are you saying that the deaths of Bobby Kennedy and Martin Luther King were part of larger conspiracies?"

"I don't want to mislead you. I have no knowledge that either of those assassinations were more than what has been reported. King's was certainly a conspiracy, though. James Earl Ray was supported by others, probably a faction of the KKK. Bobby was killed by Sirhan Sirhan, a pissed-off Palestinian who thought that his country had been wronged by Bobby's lack of support in the Six-Day War that had occurred a year earlier over on the Gaza Strip. But it was too cut and dried, too neat and tidy."

"What do you mean?" asked Mahoney as they got out of the car. He noticed that Hal seemed to have a bit more energy than he had shown even ten minutes earlier as he got out of the car unaided.

"Maybe," said Hal, "I'm jaded by Jack's 'assassination' or maybe I heard and saw too much over the years. Maybe Bobby's murder was that simple but it has always smelled bad to me."

"What did Kennedy think?" asked Mahoney as they walked through the automatic doors and into the refreshing cool of the air-conditioned store.

"We didn't talk much about Bobby's death. He would make a comment now and then alluding to his own guilt, and he made it clear that he thought he should have 'played the game differently' but we never had a real discussion about it. I talked privately with Jackie many times regarding Bobby's death and she suspected a larger conspiracy but I can't recall the particulars."

They walked to the back of the store where Hal picked up two bottles of Pepto-Bismol. "Since I was diagnosed with this shit, I've had hair loss, fatigue, nosebleeds, aches and pains you wouldn't believe, but I have never really felt sick to my stomach," he commented. "Why do I always feel worse after seeing a doctor than I did before?"

Mahoney laughed, "My grandfather was a stubborn old man. He claimed that he had never been to see a doctor until they carried him out of his house after he fell and broke his hip when he was eighty-seven. When I visited, he told me that hospitals and doctors would be the death of him. He contracted pneumonia and died in that same hospital bed."

Hal chuckled. "Think about it, Mike. More people die in hospitals every year than in bars or brothels. Hospitals are dangerous places."

As they walked to the checkout, Mahoney said, "I'll be right back, I have an idea," and darted away.

Hal paid for his purchase and stepped outside the store to wait. He scanned the parking lot and the surrounding area but didn't see anything that led him to believe they were being watched. He felt sure somebody was keeping an eye on them but he didn't see anything suspicious.

"Ready?" asked Mahoney as he exited the store with a bag in his hand. Hal nodded and started across the parking lot to his car.

Mahoney held the door as Hal managed his way into the passenger seat. Once they were seated Mahoney started the car and asked, "When did Jackie marry Onassis?"

"They were married in October of sixty-eight," said Hal. "A couple of things came into play that changed Jackie's mind about getting married to Ari. After Bobby's death, the press renewed its constant hounding of Jackie. She also grew fearful that Bobby's murder was bigger than just a single gunman and she feared for her children's lives. At the same time, Jack and Jackie both felt the kids were probably old enough to know the truth about their father. It was time for them to come to the island."

"Do you remember when that occurred?" asked Mahoney pulling back out onto the street.

"Yeah, they first came out in July of that year, probably a month or so after Bobby died," said Hal.

"And how did that first meeting go?" asked Mahoney.

"Hell, they were just kids. Caroline was ten, John John was seven or eight at the time. Jack had hoped that when they first saw him, they would run up and give him a big old hug but Jackie was much more realistic and cautioned him not to be discouraged when they met."

"Where did they first see each other again?" asked Mahoney.

"On the island," said Hal. "Jackie wanted it to be somewhat controlled. Jack, of course, wanted to meet them at the dock but Jackie insisted on meeting in the main house. I brought them from Nydri on the launch and walked them up to the house. I remember the poor kids being really tired from the long trip. We walked into the main house where Jack was standing and Jackie said to them something very simple to them like, "John, Caroline, this is your father.""

"Jesus, how did that go over?"

"Well, I think it went over as well as could have been expected. Jackie had prepared them for the meeting but I think Caroline still remembered the pain from the days back in '63. She clung to her mother and didn't let go for several hours. John on the other hand had been too young to remember the assassination. When his mother said the man before him was his father . . . that was good enough for John John. He walked over to Jack with a book he was carrying and asked him if he could read it to him. In all the years I was with Jack, I saw him cry three times. He cried the night Bobby died, he cried when John Junior was killed in the plane crash, and he cried on the day that same tired little boy crawled into his lap with his favorite book."

SKORPIOS ISLAND
November 5, 1968

"It's been one hell of a year, Hal," said Jack. They sat in the radio room and listened to the scattered reports of the election results from the United States. The best anybody could tell, it was a tight race on the east coast between Richard Nixon and Hubert Humphrey and there probably wouldn't be a clear winner until more of the western states started reporting results.

Since Bobby's death, Jack and his small band of contacts had gotten behind Hubert Humphrey in an effort to keep Richard Nixon out of the White House. The longstanding feud between Nixon and the Kennedys was well known. Jack had often said of Nixon, "I don't think he's a bad guy. I just don't like him or trust him." With a little help, Jack had been able to funnel nearly a million dollars to Humphrey's campaign from various sources that all had traces back to Skorpios.

Now the man who had been at odds with all three of the Kennedy brothers was knocking at the door of the Oval Office and stood a good chance of getting in. Jack's stomach turned every time he considered the possibility.

Hal stared intently at the radio as if willing the reporter to give an update. He turned to Jack saying, "You're right, it has been one hell of a year, Jack. And I'm afraid it's not over yet."

As soon as he said it, Hal immediately regretted his comment but he couldn't remember such a tumultuous period of time in American history. In January, there had been a faint glimmer of the hope of a pullout in Vietnam but the Tet Offensive changed the entire outlook of the war. Within days of each other in March, Bobby had announced his candidacy and a Soviet submarine had tried to level the Hawaiian Islands. Brezhnev had started cleaning house with the information that Jack had provided to him but as he gained power he also seemed to become more distant in his communications with Skorpios.

In April, Martin Luther King had been killed, which was like a dagger in the heart of the movement toward peace and equality, at the same time that the U.S. military was announcing the largest build-up of troops in Vietnam yet. Peace talks had started in May but later that month the *USS Scorpion* went missing near the Azores while investigating an unusual assembly of Soviet warships. That development worried Jack.

In June, Bobby was killed. In July, Jack finally got to see his children for the first time in years and in October, Jackie stunned the world by becoming the bride of Ari Onassis. While Jack thought it was a good idea for the two to wed, at least in the eyes of the press, it had a demoralizing impact on his ego. Jackie had to spend a lot of time in public on Ari's arm and while he didn't really think there could be anything going on, it was hard to live with the idea that the world thought that that crusty old Greek was sleeping with his wife.

Now it was November and Nixon could quite possibly win the election. Hal wondered if Nixon's win would be the icing on the cake of a very rough year or if the 'other shoe' would drop before 1969 began.

"I don't think I can take any more big events this year," said Jack. I was afraid life out on this rock would be boring and now I find myself praying for boredom."

Hal laughed in an attempt to add some levity to the conversation, "Jack, has there ever been a day in your life that you would consider boring? I'm not sure you even have a clear understanding of boredom."

"Well, I'm ready to give it a try," he said with a thin smile. "After the election results are final, how about we turn off these damn radios and start planning for a big old Christmas, something huge, over the top, that the kids won't ever forget?"

Hal smiled, "Well that's hardly boredom, but I'm happy to help you in any way I can."

Hal worried that 'the other shoe' falling for Jack might be Christmas itself. Since Jackie's pseudo-wedding, she had been busy convincing the world that she was now Ari's wife. Accompanied by huge bodyguards, she had been seen in the clubs and social scenes from Paris to Monaco. She had promised Jack the family would spend Christmas with him on the island "if she could work it out" and that concerned Hal.

Jack was busy writing plans, "Hal, I may need you to fly back to civilization, London or New York, to pick up some decorations. We'll do a Greek-American Christmas. I wonder if we can find a real pine tree on the mainland. Lights!" he said while jotting down a note. "We'll need lots of Christmas lights for the tree and the house."

Jack was clearly growing excited about the first Christmas with his family in six years. Hal made a mental note to contact Jackie and do his best to convince her to bring the kids to Skorpios for the holidays because he wasn't sure Jack could handle another disappointment.

"From the United States, in the presidential election," said the commentator on the radio, "Former Vice President Richard Nixon is gaining ground in the central section of the country while Hubert Humphrey clearly controls the northeastern United States and the controversial former Alabama State Governor George Wallace controls much of the southeast. The leaders appear to be Nixon and Humphrey with two key states, Texas and California still undecided."

"It's going to be a tight son of a bitch, Hal," said Kennedy.

Hal wanted to change the subject, to take Jack's mind off the election, "Why don't you go with me?"

"What?" said Jack looking up from the radio.

"Let's go to London together for a few days," said Hal. "Except for the trip to that little village in Yugoslavia, you haven't been more than a couple of miles from this rock in almost five years. Let's go to London and just relax. You can pay for a couple of expensive rooms at the Ritz and we'll do a little Christmas shopping, maybe take in a play, sit in a bar like grown-ups and watch pretty girls walk by."

Jack laughed, "I can't go to London, I'm dead."

"Bullshit," said Hal. "We'll let your beard grow out for a few days, put you in a pair of glasses, slick back your hair, and only speak Greek in public. Nobody will ever suspect a thing."

"I can't take the risk of being seen," said Jack.

"There won't be any risk, Jack, because by the time I'm through, you won't recognize yourself in the mirror."

"There's no way . . . is there?" said Jack, changing his tone in mid-sentence. "The Secret Service would have an absolute fit if they knew I left the island."

"Unless I report you left the island, they'll never know," reasoned Hal.

"Let's figure out who's going to win this election first and then we'll start planning vacations," said Jack.

Hal smiled, "I'm already planning. We'll go in a week; you quit shaving and I'll work up the rest of your disguise."

"Just me and you?" asked Jack.

"Just two Greek businessmen traveling to London," said Hal.

Jack turned and smiled, "I believe I could use a distraction right about now."

BOCA RATON, FLORIDA
Present Day

Hal had been quiet for several minutes, his eyes were closed and his head lay back against the head rest. As Mahoney pulled off the main road and into the subdivision, Hal suddenly started talking, "There were definitely two Jack Kennedys, one before 1968 and one after. I think the roller coaster year with Bobby's death and the guilt he suffered from that, the hits he took with Jackie and Ari's wedding, getting to re-connect with his children, Nixon's election, and all the other events of the year tossed him for a loop."

"How did he change?" asked Mahoney.

Hal opened his eyes but stared ahead out the windshield. "He became more fatalistic, if that's the right word. He felt that when his time was up, it was up and there was little he could do about it. With that in mind, he became less concerned about doing the right thing all the time. He seemed to become more impulsive and spontaneous. Everything in his life had been planned and calculated for years, after '68 he flew more by the seat of his pants."

"Interesting," said Mahoney while taking a slow, wide, right hand turn around an elderly man driving his golf cart down the street. "That must have made your job much harder."

"You mean the job of guarding John F. Kennedy? It was actually pretty damn easy. By the end of '68, I was the only man from the Service left on the island. There was no guarding to be done because nobody was looking for the man," said Hal. "And I had become more his friend than his security guard."

"What type of spontaneous or impulsive things did he do?" asked Mahoney.

"The first thing we did was take a trip to London to do some Christmas shopping before the kids and Jackie arrived on the island."

"You're kidding," said Mahoney. "President Kennedy went shopping in London in 1968? How did you pull that off?"

"Well, there again," said Hal, "nobody was looking for Jack Kennedy. He dressed in what would then be considered Greek business casual and greased his hair back. He had about a ten-day growth of a beard, and he wore glasses. We flew coach and made sure we spoke only Greek when we were in public. We kept a low profile, nobody was the wiser."

"And just what did you do while you were in London?" asked Mahoney.

"We got a couple of rooms at a fancy hotel in the heart of Mayfair. We ordered room service, smoked cigars in the hotel bar, took in a couple of plays, and did a lot of Christmas shopping. It was fantastic. For three and a half days, Jack was neither a high profile politician nor a criminal on the lam, he was just another anonymous tourist walking the streets and enjoying the sights of London."

Mahoney turned onto Hal's street. "And was there any backlash from the Secret Service for that trip?"

Hal laughed, "If my car is bugged, this is probably the first time they knew of it."

"How often did you travel off the island?" asked Mahoney.

"After that trip," said Hal, "increasingly more."

"Tell me about Christmas of '68."

SKORPIOS ISLAND
December, 1968

By the time young Caroline left the island at the end of her first trip in the summer of 1968, she had decided that the familiar-looking man living there was not a ghost and she had warmed up to her father. When the kids arrived on Skorpios a few days before Christmas, it was impossible to tell who was more excited, Caroline and John, or Jack.

Several changes had taken place since their last visit. With Jackie's marriage to Onassis, the press swarmed to get any picture they could of the famous newlyweds either together or individually. When the *Christina* sailed into the tiny anchorage off Skorpios, photographers surrounded the island; some actually camped out on small boats hoping to get a lucky photo and when Jackie and the children arrived, it was bedlam. The Phantom Force had their work cut out for them; they caught several photographers and even a few 'sightseers' trying to sneak onto the island to catch a glimpse of its famous inhabitants.

With the help of Demetrius, Hal, and several members of the staff, Jack had transformed the main house into a Norman Rockwell Christmas scene. With guidance from a simple photograph in a magazine, Boulos had successfully scoured the countryside near Nydri in an area dominated by scraggly black pines to find the perfect Christmas tree. Demetrius had run himself and his staff ragged to make the house look perfect with the boxes of decorations Jack had had shipped back from London. He even ordered his staff to remain on the island over the Christmas break but Jack wouldn't hear of it. When word came that Ari and his new wife would be on the island for Christmas, however, the staff canceled their plans and remained at their posts.

All their efforts seemed to be repaid when young Caroline and John walked into the big room of the main house and both said the same thing, "Wow!"

A ten-foot tree stood in the middle of the room complete with a thousand lights, a hundred yards of garland, and so many ornaments that the tree could hardly be seen. An electric train ran around the base of the tree past large piles of presents. Above the fireplace was a huge wreath built by the groundskeeper and decorated by the maid and below the mantle hung hastily made stockings, a detail that had nearly been forgotten. Large plates of cookies and fudge were placed around the house that now smelled of cinnamon and cloves. Other wonderful aromas came from the kitchen where pies and breads were baking. Even Jackie was stunned when she saw the effort that had been made for the kids first Christmas on the island.

BOCA RATON, FLORIDA
Present Day

"Christmas of '68 was a wonderful ending to one hell of a year," said Hal. "Jack had gone a little wild in London. He bought boxes and boxes of ornaments and decorations. He bought presents for the kids, for Jackie, for the staff, for the Phantoms, and even one for me," he said as he pulled up his sleeve showing Mahoney his vintage Breitling Navitimer Cosmonaute watch.

"Wow," said Mahoney leaning over to look at the watch. "So Jackie and the kids did make it out to the island for Christmas that year?"

"Yeah, and according to Jack they had a great time. Ari was there but stayed out on the yacht most of the time. Almost the entire staff was there but everybody, including myself, recognized the family's need for privacy and kept their distance. Jack invited Ari, his children, Alex and Christina, and me to Christmas dinner which was, of course, over the top. It was all about Jack's family and I was happy that I was able to help make it happen." Hal smiled and laughed to himself.

"What's so funny?" asked Mahoney.

"I was just remembering that Christmas dinner," he said with a smile. "Jackie looked incredible, absolutely stunning. Jack sat next to her, he was thrilled to have her there and be able to spend time with her. They had been growing distant but that night he had a smile on his face that told it all. Ari, who had always been and was still struck by Jackie's beauty and class, sat on the other side of the table. He loved the fact that the world thought he was married to her. Sitting next to him was his son, Alex, who must have been about twenty. He was clearly infatuated with Jackie even though she was almost twice his age."

Mahoney pulled the car into Hal's driveway and pressed the button on the remote control for the garage door. "And then there was you," he said with a grin.

A warm smile filled Hal's face as Mahoney pulled into the garage, slipped the car into 'park' and turned off the ignition. Hal stared at the back wall of his garage which for a few moments he didn't see, lost as he was in another time and place. "And then there was me," he said without looking towards Mahoney. Without another word, Hal opened his door and got out of the car.

Mahoney followed him into the house and to the kitchen where Hal looked at the clock before saying, "We need to get you to the airport. I have a phone book around here somewhere so we can call you a cab."

"No need," said Mahoney while pressing buttons on his smart phone, "I have a phone book right here."

Hal shook his head knowing that technology had passed him by sometime in the early seventies. "I'm sure sorry I can't take you to the airport myself, Mike. But I really don't feel very well."

"I feel bad leaving you when you aren't feeling well," said Mahoney. "Maybe I should stay and catch a later flight."

Hal walked over to his recliner and sat slowly, "No, don't worry about me. If I need anything I can call the old gal around the corner. Doris has been chasing me for years and would be over here in a heartbeat if I called. She thinks I'm a pretty hot ticket," he said with a laugh.

"You're sure?" asked Mahoney before the cab company dispatcher answered the call.

"I'm sure," said Hal.

Mahoney gave the dispatcher Hal's address and punched a button ending the call. "They said ten or fifteen minutes. Can I make you something to eat?"

Hal rolled his eyes, "I'm fine, Mike. Come have a seat."

Mahoney picked the bag from the drug store up off the counter and sat in the chair next to Hal. From the bag he pulled out a common plastic clamshell package containing a cell phone. "Hal, I know you're worried about your phone being tapped so I got you one of these pre-paid cell phones which I hear are almost untraceable. If I can get it out of this damn packaging I'll show you how to use it and we'll be able to talk without you having to worry about anybody listening in," said Mahoney struggling with the plastic packaging containing the phone.

"I'm dying and you people are still trying to drag me into the technological nightmare you've created for yourselves," said Hal with a tight smile.

"Whether we keep talking is entirely up to you, Hal," said Mahoney.

"I'm just kidding you, Mike. This is an important story and if you're not tired of listening I'm certainly not tired of talking about Jack."

"I'd like to call you tomorrow to see how you're feeling. If you're up to it, I'd love to hear more because I believe you have a lot more to tell me," said Mahoney.

"That I do," answered Hal.

WASHINGTON, D.C.
Present Day

Robert McQuade was finishing a BLT on rye as he read a *Wall Street Journal* article that discussed the traits of managers and executives who die prematurely from heart disease and stress-related illnesses. One of these common traits was the habit of eating lunch at their desks while they continued to work.

"McQuade," he said, answering the phone on his desk.

"Deputy McQuade, this is Lori Harris at the NSA, DMS section. Sir, we have a new development in your Boca Raton op."

"Son of a bitch," McQuade said to himself. This was not how this phase of the Skorpios project was supposed to have ended. The project, officially known as XA-413, should have simply faded away after Kennedy's death but it seemed to be growing a new life of its own since the helicopter accident. The project code designation of "X" or x-ray signified that the project was top secret. The "A" designated it as active, or in this case, alive. Since nobody could seem to remember the numbers associated with the project, internally it was simply referred to as 'Skorpios.' It certainly was not a designation that would help maintain its secrecy but it spoke to the lack of importance the project had retained over the years.

McQuade had only known about the existence of Skorpios, the truth about Dallas, and hence the continuing life of JFK, for eighteen months before his promotion to Deputy Director of Special Projects. While the Secret Service maintained many "X" projects that contained high levels of embarrassment for past and sometimes current Presidents, none held the toxicity level of Skorpios.

McQuade thought that perhaps it had simply been too easy. In 1963 the Service had faked the assassination of the President and then whisked him off to a little island half a world away where he lived a nice quiet life requiring only one agent to guard him and a small line item on the annual budget to support him.

Had there been reporters, congressmen, authors, or anybody else looking for the truth or searching for the former president, the project would have gained more attention from the Service but Kennedy had been very effectively swept under the rug and forgotten. There had been a plan in place to 'sanitize' the island and clean up any loose ends when he died. At that time the project would lose its "A" designation and become just another secret in the vault, not unlike those from the Truman era, Carter's administration, or even Obama's little skeleton in the closet that the Service guarded in their fight to preserve the public's respect for the Presidency.

"What's the development?" McQuade asked, setting down his sandwich.

"Sir, the new listening device installed this morning in Boca Raton is working correctly but in testing it we just overheard that your suspect has been provided with a pre-paid cell phone," said Harris.

"So?" asked McQuade.

"Sir," said Harris, she knew before she picked up the phone that she was going to have to explain this to him, "pre-paid cell phone conversations are almost untraceable. Each cell phone has an electronic serial number, a unique 32-bit number programmed into the phone when it is manufactured. There is also a mobile identification number derived from each phone's number and a system ID code that is assigned to each carrier by the FCC. While the ESN is permanent, the MIN and SID codes are programmed into the phone when it is activated."

That 'simple' explanation made McQuade's head swim. "So, if I understand you correctly, he can now talk on the phone without us being able to hear what he is saying or who he is saying it to?"

"If your suspect leaves his home, that is correct, sir," said Harris.

"Well, son of a bitch," said McQuade, this time out loud. "Thanks for the information. I can't believe we can watch two flies having sex in Afghanistan but we can't listen to an unsecured radio conversation in our own damn country. Can't we set up a scanner or something?"

"Not without a huge amount of luck," said Harris. "There are over 800 phones on a single frequency. If you multiply that by the number of frequencies per cell tower, and the 100 to 200 hundred cell towers in his area, we would be trying to find one conversation out of about a million."

"Well, that's just fucking great," said McQuade.

"Sir, if you get me the identification number off of that phone and figure out which carrier he is with, I'll have you listening to any conversation in less than an hour," said Harris. She was trying to at least offer some help.

"Thanks for nothing," said McQuade before he slammed the receiver down.

Robert McQuade had learned from the very best that he could get away with anything in his line of business, including murder, as long as he had some evidence to back it up, no matter how insignificant or circumstantial. If he had the evidence to support an action, he would be seen as a hero doing a job; if he didn't, he was simply a criminal. McQuade had the evidence he needed to support the actions he had already put in place, he just didn't know it. An email from Lori Harris sat unopened in his inbox with two attachments, Mahoney's notes and a large file that contained several hours of the digital audio interview.

McQuade dialed a series of numbers and waited impatiently, tapping his pen on the yellow pad on his desk.

"Telleria," came the voice on the phone.

"This is McQuade. We need to speed up the schedule on the project."

Telleria shook his head, "I can't speed up the process. It takes time if you want it to appear as part of the normal progression of the disease."

"He's talking and we need to silence him sooner than later," said McQuade. "DMS verified the bug is working but they said he now has a pre-paid cell phone. Apparently, we can't listen to those conversations because we're not as smart as a twelve dollar phone."

"Well I could simply walk in and put a bullet in his head if you think that would help," said Telleria cynically.

McQuade completely missed the cynicism, "The last thing we need right now is a suspicious death," he barked. "Did you find any information in the house we could use?"

"The only thing I could find was a sealed box addressed to the Kennedy Library, it contained a large paperweight with a handwritten note on the bottom indicating that Kennedy gave it to him for his retirement. An unsigned letter said he was returning it to the library. I replaced the paperweight with a rock, removed the note and the letter and resealed the box. Other than that, I found nothing of use."

"Damn it, Jose," said McQuade. "We need to find something concrete showing they are talking about Kennedy or our asses are on the line."

Jose Telleria felt a wave of panic sweep through his body. "You don't have anything solid indicating these two are talking about Skorpios?"

"What the hell else would they be talking about?" answered McQuade defensively.

"Robby," said Telleria, purposely using McQuade's first name to drive home his point, "I am too damn old to go to prison. If I go to prison, you are going with me and, trust me, you do not want to be locked in the same prison as me."

"You are threatening the wrong man, Agent Telleria," said McQuade. His voice cracked just enough to tell Telleria the warning was well received. "I'll find the evidence and shut down the story before it goes public and when the loose ends are tied up, you and I are going to have a little private time together," he said more convincingly.

"I'm looking forward to it," said Telleria, confident that one way or another, that meeting would never happen.

BOCA RATON, FLORIDA
Present Day

"You look like hell, Hal. Why don't you go lie down?" said Mahoney. He wasn't being mean, Hal truly looked tired and pale.

The real testament to how he felt came a moment later when Hal stood slowly and started walking towards his bedroom. "Okay," he said, weakly.

Mahoney followed him into the bedroom where Hal turned on a window unit air conditioner before sitting on the bed and slipping off his shoes. "Can you believe the crooks that built these places didn't insulate them well enough to keep the southern exposed bedrooms cool in the middle of the day?" He lay down on the bed, "Of course I didn't know that because I bought this place in the winter like everybody else around here."

"Well, other than that, it appears to be well constructed," said Mahoney trying to be positive.

"It's a piece of shit, Mike," Hal said as he lay down on top of the perfectly made bed. "We have a few minutes before your cab arrives, where were we?"

Mahoney laughed then looked at his notes for a moment, "I was going to ask another question about that Christmas. How long were Jackie and the kids there that year?"

"I don't recall exactly but at least a week or ten days. Jack wanted to take the kids sailing and fishing but it was chaos with all the photographers surrounding the island. Jack couldn't go anywhere he might be seen so they did some exploring around the island, built forts out of bed sheets, and played lots of board games. They were there long enough that Jack was able to spend a lot of time with them, together as a family and with each of them individually."

Hal stared up at the ceiling for a moment, "It was a good ending to a pretty shit-filled year," he said quietly.

SKORPIOS ISLAND
December 26, 1968

"I think he's finally asleep," said Jackie as she quietly walked into the radio room. She was dressed in one of Jack's old Harvard sweatshirts and a pair of tight shorts, a look that he found sort of sexy but one in which Jackie would have died if she had been photographed.

"He should have fallen asleep out of pure exhaustion," said Jack.

"Gee, I wonder why he was so excited?" said Jackie with a frown. John John and Jack had traded reading books before bedtime for roughhousing. After Jackie caught them and softly scolded Jack, she took on the task of getting their boy quieted down and asleep.

"Sorry, dear, we were having fun," said Jack.

She walked up behind Jack who was sitting at a small desk in the radio room writing in a notebook as the BBC reporter chattered away about some developing story in Iran. "If we were a normal family, if anything about this situation was normal, I'd be angry with you for winding him up before bedtime," said Jackie, "but it's important that he have fun with his father. Perhaps tomorrow you can have fun earlier in the day and read books in the evening," she said with a firm squeeze of his shoulder. "What are you writing?"

Jack placed his pen on the desk and closed the notebook, "Just some ramblings. It helps me keep things in order in my head."

"Are things messed up in your head?" she asked as she placed her hands on the back of his head and playfully gave it a shake.

"No, not really, but writing it all down seems to solidify it for me. Everything becomes much clearer if I put it into words on paper. Relationships between this country and that, between this world leader and another, and even my own situation here is easier to understand once I have explained it to myself with a pen."

"Interesting," said Jackie. "Maybe I should give it a try because I certainly don't understand anything about our world or my role in it anymore." She walked around him and sat on the edge of the desk with a pained look on her face. "I was sitting on the *Christina* in Monaco a few weeks ago, actually intentionally sitting where the photographers could get some shots of me on Ari's boat while reading a damn book. The whole time I kept wondering to myself, how did I go from being a simple Senator's wife and a mother of young children in Massachusetts to a woman enmeshed in a growing lie who actually felt the need to be photographed to help prove it all? Does your writing make it easy to understand what in the hell we are doing and how it will end?"

Jack took her hand and looked into her eyes for several moments before responding, "Jackie, I'm not sure what we're doing, or when it might all end, or for that matter if any of this will ever come to an end. But I am confident that regardless of anything else, we saved the lives of our children and probably the lives of another million or more children."

Jackie slid off the desk and into his lap where she buried her face in his chest, "What in the hell is going on in the world, Jack?" she asked quietly as her eyes welled up with tears.

"I don't know," he said holding her tight. "But I swear to you that I am going to figure it out and do my best to fix it."

WASHINGTON, D.C.
Present Day

"Lori Harris," said the security specialist when she picked up her phone.

"This is Deputy McQuade again, are you currently monitoring the Boca Raton bug?"

"It's recording constantly but no, sir, I am not currently listening to it," she said truthfully. "Would you like me to see if there is any activity on that link?"

"Please," said McQuade trying his best not to sound like a pissed-off asshole.

Harris opened up a new screen on her computer and selected the correct link from the menu then waited while the streaming audio loaded. The green sound bar indicated the sounds currently being picked up from the listening device were fairly loud and constant.

"Sir, we are picking up something currently but it sounds like a fan or an air conditioner." She turned up the sound and listened carefully. "I might be hearing voices but there is too much background noise to determine if anybody is in the home and talking at this moment."

"Can you screen out the background noise?" he asked.

Geez, she thought to herself, this guy was a fairly high-ranking Deputy in the Secret Service. "No, sir, that only happens on TV and in the movies. The sound we can capture comes as a single piece of information, a block of noise, not a collection of noises that we can sort and choose from."

"Well, I need to know what's being said in that room right now!" said McQuade with an edge to his voice.

"If you can ask them to turn off the background noise, I can probably record what they are saying," said Harris calmly.

McQuade slammed the handset onto his phone, "Damn it!"

BOCA RATON, FLORIDA
Present Day

Mahoney flipped though his notes, "In November of 1968, Nixon narrowly beat Humphrey in the Presidential election. Kennedy clearly didn't like Nixon, what was his reaction to the election results?"

"The one thing that Kennedy always believed, and if you look at history it has been proven over and over, is that the country and the Constitution would be strong enough to survive any prick we the people elect to office," said Hal. "He was rightfully concerned that Nixon would take us down the wrong path for the wrong reasons but, in the end, he felt that the overall damage Nixon could do to the country, in the big scheme of things, was pretty slight."

"Interesting," said Mahoney.

"Think about it," added Hal. "We've had some real bozos in office, James Buchanan and Ulysses Grant back in the 1800s, Calvin Coolidge, in the early 1900s, and more recently Carter and Clinton."

"Don't forget Ford and George Bush, Junior," said Mahoney.

"George W. Bush certainly had his challenges, but I'll tell you about Gerald Ford when we have a little more time to talk. That man was a bloody genius and despite being a Republican, he was a great friend to Jack in a number of ways."

"Ford knew Kennedy was alive?" asked Mahoney with a surprised look on his face.

"You have a cab coming, let's focus on Nixon for a moment and we'll get back to Ford and some of the others when we have a little more time," said Hal.

"Right," said Mahoney as he jotted down a note. "So Kennedy felt the nation was resilient enough to survive any harm Nixon could do, but it sounds like he also felt that Nixon had the ability to do quite a lot of damage to the country."

"Jack felt a pretty strong sense of gloom and doom for a few weeks after the election and a completely renewed dislike for the man after he took office," said Hal.

"Why?" asked Mahoney.

"There were many reasons. Nixon always 'wanted' to be president. He was in it for the power and the prestige, or at least that's how Jack saw it. Many of our best presidents ran for the office because they felt that they were the right person to get the job done. Truman, for instance, never wanted to be president or even vice president. He did it because he felt that we needed somebody to guide our country through the war and the post-war years. Jack sought the presidency far more out of a sense of duty, a sense that he could do it better than his opponents. Bobby seriously didn't want to be president, he only ran because there was nobody else. Hubert Humphrey ran for the same reason. But not Nixon, Nixon wanted the job; he salivated over the Oval Office and probably got a big woody every time he thought about riding around in that big jet with people waiting on him."

"That's pretty harsh on ol' Tricky Dick," said Mahoney with half of a chuckle. "Was any of that fact or just political hatred for Kennedy's opponent?"

Hal felt the hair on the back of his neck rising at the reporter's question but calmed immediately as he realized that it had been not only a good question but a fair one as well. "That is fact, that is researchable truth and there is more. Nixon immediately started taking credit for things that he had nothing to do with. If you're interested, go find copies of the numerous speeches he gave throughout the sixties denouncing NASA, calling the moon shot 'JFK's folly', then contrast them with the speeches he gave during and right after the moon landing where he took credit for the whole damn thing. And that was just the beginning."

"It seems that would be enough to piss off Kennedy, there was more?" asked Mahoney.

Hal frowned and shook his head, "As it turned out, the moon landing was just the tip of the iceberg. What really fried Jack's ass was Nixon's complete disregard for anything that got in the way of making him look good. He destroyed years of hard work and shattered many relationships in a matter of months. We are a resilient nation but it took twenty years to undo some of the shit he pulled in his political grandstanding."

"Do you have specifics?" asked Mahoney.

"Sure, we can start with the *K-129* submarine incident. Kennedy had been able, under the Johnson administration, to use that information to help Brezhnev become the undisputed leader of the USSR. Johnson thought the CIA was controlling and using the information, the CIA thought Johnson was calling the shots, but in the end it was Jack who was talking directly to Brezhnev."

Hal reached over and pulled a blanket over himself. "The understanding between Jack and Brezhnev was that as long as Brezhnev kept a clean house politically and helped get us out of Vietnam, the *K-129* incident would remain swept under the rug and forgotten. The two of them were smart enough to build a plan in which Brezhnev started pushing his idea of 'détente', a new era of reduced tensions and peace between the U.S and the Soviet Union. Neither of them felt that the Soviets could suddenly change years of posturing and rhetoric without raising suspicions around the world. At the same time, it was very important to stop the conflict in Vietnam and by early 1969 there was a six-month plan in place for the complete withdrawal of troops."

Hal breathed softly for a moment and said, "Nixon took office and immediately escalated Vietnam. He sent more troops over and pressed Congress for more funds. The asshole actually thought we could end the war by winning it."

"Did Nixon know of the photographs of the Soviet sub?" asked Mahoney.

"He found out about them right after he took office. That's what killed the relationship between Jack and Brezhnev. Nixon took the photos and other evidence right to the damn Chinese."

Mahoney looked out the window to make sure his cab wasn't waiting then turned back to Hal. "You're pretty hard on Nixon but in reality, he couldn't have had any idea that there was an agreement in place between Brezhnev and Kennedy, right?"

"You're right, it was the classic case of the right hand not knowing the left hand even existed but Nixon didn't stop and consider what the consequences might be to the relationship between the U.S. and the Soviets. He saw the *K-129* incident as a way to instantly become friends with Mao Zedong in China while at the same time, an opportunity to blackmail the Soviets into signing his strategic arms treaty. Both of these ploys worked; Nixon was the first U.S. President to visit China and was greeted as a welcomed dignitary and later he went to Moscow where Brezhnev signed the SALT One agreement."

"So," said Mahoney, "it sounds to me like Nixon solved a bunch of issues even if he did force the Soviets into the SALT agreement."

"Nixon's approach," said Hal with all the patience he could muster, "was like putting a band-aid on skin cancer. The problem was covered up and nobody had to see it but the wound was still festering and growing. By the end of 1968 Jack and Brezhnev had drafted an agreement that would end the Cold War, foster a lasting détente between the two countries, improve relations with China, end the Vietnam War, and reduce nuclear weapon inventories around the world to practically zero. After Nixon's stunt, Brezhnev became angry that the U.S. had betrayed the agreements he and Jack had made. So much damage had been done that Brezhnev broke off his relationship with Jack and the Cold War dragged on for another twenty years."

"Do you really think we were that close to the end of the Cold War?" asked Mahoney. "And do you really think Nixon screwed it up that much?"

Hal managed a smile, "We were that close to the end of the Cold War and a new era of peace, similar to what we now have. I know this because I was part of it. And don't get me wrong, Nixon didn't do anything that any other politician in his position wouldn't have done. He just had more tools than the presidents before or after him and he was very good at using those tools in a way that made him look good regardless of the costs."

Mahoney looked at Hal for a long time before asking his next question, "Did Kennedy have anything to do with Watergate?"

Mahoney was surprised to see that Hal looked somewhat troubled, "No, Nixon fell on his own sword with the Watergate scandal. He got caught doing what he shouldn't have been doing and, in the end, nobody won."

"Didn't Nixon and Henry Kissinger still negotiate our way out of Vietnam?" asked Mahoney."

"Nixon, like Jack Kennedy and Lyndon Johnson before him, quickly realized that Vietnam was a no-win situation. He ordered Kissinger to negotiate the Paris Peace Accords which turned out to be only a briefly held agreement between the U.S., the North Vietnamese, the South Vietnamese, and the Provisional Revolutionary Government, a fancy name for the Viet Cong. Under the agreement, everybody was to stop fighting and the Americans would go home. The reunification of Vietnam was to be carried out peacefully.

Kissinger was able to get everybody to consent to the terms of the Accords but the real goal of the three Vietnamese governments was to agree to something that would get the U.S. out of their sandbox so they could go back to fighting the way they wanted to fight. So, yes, he got us out of Vietnam but all of our efforts and all of the deaths of our soldiers were in vain. The North Vietnamese rolled into Saigon as we flew our diplomats out, and the reunification of Vietnam took place under communist rule.

Jack and Brezhnev's plan, on the other hand, had been to set our two superpowers on either edge of that sandbox and tell the Vietnamese solve their problems once and for all or we would do it for them."

"Wait a moment," said Mahoney. "North Vietnam was a communist country and the main reason for our involvement was to stop the domino effect and prevent communism from swallowing up other Asian countries."

"Right, but the understanding between Brezhnev and Jack was that the Soviet's new policy of détente would halt the communist progression that the U.S. feared," said Hal.

A honk from the driveway indicated that Mahoney's cab had arrived. "Shit," he said. He had more questions rolling around in his mind. He stepped to the front door and signaled to the cab driver that he would be out in one moment. "One last question before I go, Hal?" he said walking back into the bedroom.

"Sure Mike," said Hal.

"Why you?"

"Why me, what? asked Hal.

Mahoney rubbed the back of his neck, "Hal, by my rough guesstimate, at least a couple of hundred people knew that Kennedy was alive. Why are you the only one to come forward? Why are you the only one to tell the story?"

From his bed, Hal stared out the window, his eyes seeming to focus on nothing, as the question hung in the silence of the room. "There have been others who have tried to tell the story. They either ended up dead or were branded as lunatics. Those of us in the Secret Service who knew Jack was alive knew it was our job, it was our sworn duty to take the secrets of the Office of the President to our graves."

Hal's eyes misted slightly, "Hell, I swore the same oath as the others . . . I pledged to protect the President with my own life, if need be, to uphold the Constitution and all that other bullshit. But when I made that promise, 52 years ago, I was a pimple-faced kid who had no idea what the words loyalty and allegiance truly meant. And I never imagined that I would find myself having to make a choice between an oath I made when I was in my twenties and the responsibility of correcting history by revealing the legacy of a great American."

"Why me?" asked Hal, turning his head to look directly at Mahoney, a steely resolve now evident in his face. "Because Jack Kennedy deserves to be recognized in history for the invaluable contributions he made to the free world and the great sacrifices he endured. The man gave up everything and asked for nothing in return. The very least I can do is tell the world about the greatest man I ever knew and the truth about what he did for the world."

Mahoney looked at the frail man lying on the bed and wished he had known him twenty years earlier. "Hal, are you going to be okay?"

"I'm fine, Mike. Thanks for coming down," he said quietly.

"You take care, Hal. I'll call you tomorrow," said Mahoney before he walked out the door.

Climbing into the cab, Mike Mahoney felt just about as guilty as he ever had. There was a sick old man lying in that home with nobody to care for him. Mahoney briefly considered getting back out of the cab but before he could do so the vehicle was moving down the street. He quieted his guilt by promising himself he would call Hal in the morning.

SKORPIOS ISLAND
July 20, 1969

The radio room was full; Jack, Hal, Captain Papadopoulos, Boulos, Demetrius and several of his staff had crowded in to listen to the BBC broadcast. The room was stifling hot and even the slight breeze blowing in through the open windows didn't provide any discernible relief but nobody was about to move away from the radio.

Apollo 11, launched four days earlier, was now orbiting the moon with Mike Collins at the helm while Buzz Aldrin and Neil Armstrong descended to the moon's surface aboard *Eagle*, the lunar landing craft.

The mission, if successful, would fulfill Jack's goal of reaching the moon by the end of the 1960s. As the tumultuous decade rolled on, it became clearer to Jack with every passing event that the nation needed the boost in spirit that this incredibly expensive program would give them. It also became clear that the entire program might have been scrapped if he had not 'died' in 1963. In the minds of the American public, it had become President John F. Kennedy's legacy.

Captain Papadopoulos had surprised everybody with his appearance in the radio room that evening. He acted nonchalant but the truth was that he wouldn't have missed the event for any reason. He was amazed at the technology before him. On a little island in the middle of nowhere he was listening to a live broadcast that had originated just above the surface of the moon. The voices of the astronauts were coming from the moon, back to the United States, then across to England where the BBC was broadcasting them all around Europe. Kennedy told him the time delay between Armstrong speaking and them hearing him was probably a matter of seconds. The Captain could still clearly remember the first time he saw a car as a child and an airplane as a teen. Now there was a spaceship going to the moon and he was listening to the brave men aboard her.

With the NASA jargon and the speed and altitude data that was going back and forth it was difficult for the novice listener to understand much of what was actually happening during the landing but they knew from the tones of the voices that they were close to the surface of the moon

"Contact light!"said Aldrin.

"Are they down?" asked Boulos. Nobody responded. The room was silent as was the rest of the world. Five hundred million people around the globe were gathered around televisions and radios as the two astronauts completed the descent. For several seconds, those five hundred million people held their collective breath and remained silent.

"Shutdown" said Armstrong.

Aldrin immediately said, "Okay, engine stop. ACA out of detent…Mode control, both auto. Descent engine command override off. Engine arm off. 413 is in."

Charles Duke from Houston spoke a moment later, "We copy you down, Eagle."

Finally, several seconds later came Armstrong's voice, "Houston, Tranquility Base here. The *Eagle* has landed."

The level of carbon dioxide in the room and probably around the world must have slightly spiked as five hundred million people collectively let out a sigh of relief. On Skorpios, a cheer went up in the radio room as people patted Jack on the back.

"Don't congratulate me," he said with an ear-to-ear smile. "I just suggested this crazy mission," he pointed towards the sky, "they were the ones who pulled it off!" But even as he shrugged off the credit for the moon landing, inside he felt as though he might leap out of his own skin. America needed a big boost and through a series of events that he never could have dreamed of when he made his speech before Congress on May 25, 1961, two Americans were now sitting on the moon.

Demetrius appeared a few minutes later with three bottles of Champagne and a tray of glasses. Hal suggested they step outside where they might be able to see the moon so they could toast the astronauts; in reality, he simply wanted out of that little oven that the radio room had become. They stepped outside but the moon had not yet risen over the horizon on an otherwise clear and beautiful night. Unconcerned, they raised their glasses to the starlit sky and toasted the brave men far above them and the thousands of brilliant men and women across the globe who had made it all possible.

It was a wonderful celebration of human ingenuity. Jack refused to take any credit and also continued to deny that it was solely an American mission. He reminded the small group that it was the Germans who invented the rocket technology that NASA employed; it was the Portuguese who taught us how to navigate; the Chinese had invented metal fabrication; and it was the Greeks who had first studied the moon and the stars. While that statement may not have been exactly correct, everybody felt a part of the excitement of the moon landing. They toasted each other, raised their glasses to the unseen moon and talked about exploring other planets.

After a few hours, after the party had died down, it was just Hal and Jack sitting outside the window of the radio room listening to the BBC. A bright half-moon slowly rose over the horizon as a warm July breeze blew through the trees, keeping the temperature pleasant and the mosquitoes at bay.

"Can you see the Lunar Lander?" asked Hal as they both stared at the rising moon.

"I believe that's it right there," said Jack as he jokingly pointed, "just above that dark spot about a third of the way up from the bottom."

Hal smiled, "You're Jack Kennedy, why don't you simply ask them to turn on a bright red light so we can spot them from here?"

"I'll tell NASA to have them press the brake pedal a few times so my buddy Hal can see the glow from the taillights" said Jack.

"Thanks, that would be great," Hal said with a laugh. "Can you also ask them if they'll drop a pretty blonde and a case of Falstaff beer down here on the beach?"

Jack didn't laugh. He was serious as he sat forward and said, "When are you going to rotate back to the States and find yourself a pretty blonde?"

"What are you talking about?" Hal asked.

"You've been out on this island babysitting me for five and a half years," said Jack. "Don't you think it's time for you to go home, find a pretty woman to marry, buy a house you can't afford and make a couple of babies?"

"And miss all this?" answered Hal with a laugh.

"I'm serious, Hal," said Jack.

Hal turned towards him, "I am too. If I go back to the States, I'm probably going to end up sitting at a desk with a pile of paperwork to protect every day. If I'm lucky, I'll get to change my surroundings by hanging a new picture on my office wall. Out here, I'm protecting the damn President of the United States and I'm changing the world by helping to put new leaders and new policies in place. Hell, Jack, I have done more in the last five and a half years than I could possibly do the rest of my life if I go back now."

"Well, as far as changing the world, I don't know that we're getting all that much done out here. And I don't know if I even need protecting," said Jack. "The world has pretty much forgotten about Jack Kennedy."

"If you don't think you're changing the world, you haven't stopped to consider what the newspaper headlines would be reading today if you had been doing nothing; and if you think the world has forgotten about Jack Kennedy, you haven't been looking at the moon tonight," said Hal with an edge to his voice.

"Go home, Hal," said Jack. "They'll find some other putz to watch after me."

"Go to hell . . . sir," said Hal with a smile. They both turned back to watch the moon silently rise above the trees.

After several minutes Jack said quietly, "I'm glad you're here, Hal."

BOCA RATON, FLORIDA
Present Day

"Click, click, click."

Hal stirred in a half sleep, he was cold and he had to pee but his body wanted more sleep. He pulled the blanket up to his chin and told himself to ignore his bladder and go back to sleep.

"Click, click, click." A soft clicking or tapping noise emanated from somewhere, Hal's semi-conscious mind chose to ignore that as well. "Sleep," he told himself.

"Click, click, click." It wasn't a sound he was accustom to hearing, his mind started to waken. "Click, click, click." Hal opened one eye and could just make out the dimming light of dusk. He still had to pee and the tapping sound was still there, not constant or rhythmic but still there. He opened his other eye and listened, it was coming from his living room.

Hal looked towards the bedroom door. It was closed almost all the way but a crack of light spilled in from the living room. His mind started processing, a light and a sound in the living room, somebody was in his house. "Son of a bitch," he said to himself. He quietly rolled over and reached under the bed where his Glock 9mm pistol lay and retrieved the weapon. He considered jacking a shell into the chamber but was certain that whoever was in the other room would hear it, no matter how slowly and carefully he tried to work the action. Hal slipped his feet out from under the blanket and onto the floor, the bedsprings creaked just a bit as he stood but the clicking continued. He tiptoed to the doorway and tried to peek out but the door swung to the left and the living room and kitchen were both to the right.

His breath was coming fast, his heart was pumping, and every hair on his body seemed to tingle. "Do the hinges on this door squeak?" he asked himself. He waited a moment and listened, the clicking sound continued. Hal decided it was time. He pulled the door handle with his left hand and stepped quickly around it with the weapon level at his waist. A man sat in the far chair across the room with a laptop computer on his knees, his head and face hidden by the lampshade.

The man heard the noise from the bedroom and said in a familiar voice, "Evening, Hal," as he leaned forward to peer around the lampshade towards the bedroom door.

"Jesus Christ!" said Mahoney in a surprised voice when he saw Hal standing there with a pistol that looked more like a cannon to him.

"What in the hell are you doing here?" asked Hal as he lowered his weapon. His heart was pounding, "I could have blown your damn head off, Mike."

"I didn't know you were hiding a howitzer back there!" said Mahoney as he stood up.

"What in the hell are you doing here?" asked Hal again.

"I was worried about you. I wanted to make sure you were okay so I decided I'd spend one more night but I didn't think I'd get shot for it," said Mahoney.

Hal leaned against the wall, his pistol hung in his right hand. "Jesus, Mike, you scared the hell out of me."

"You just took a few years off my life coming out of that bedroom like John Wayne," said Mahoney.

"Well what in the hell are you doing here?" asked Hal. "I thought you'd be back in Washington by now."

"Sorry," said Mahoney. "You looked so sick earlier that I felt bad leaving. Then I realized when we were about a mile away that I forgot to lock your front door on the way out so I had the cabbie bring me back. You didn't wake up when I came back in so I decided to stay."

"Well, now that you're here, why don't you make some coffee while I try to take a piss," said Hal. "Jesus Christ," he said turning back to his bedroom.

Mahoney set his computer on the chair and walked towards the kitchen yelling after Hal, "I'll make some coffee if you promise not to shoot."

"Go screw yourself," came Hal's reply from the bedroom.

With the coffee brewing, Mahoney returned to his chair and saved the story outline he had been working on before Hal woke.

Hal shuffled out of the bedroom and sat down in his chair opposite Mahoney. "I should shoot you just for scaring the crap out of me."

"How are you feeling?" asked Mahoney.

"Better, I guess," he answered.

Mahoney looked towards the kitchen, "Coffee's on, can I make you something to eat?"

"I'm not hungry, Mike, but thanks," said Hal.

Mahoney looked at Hal who seemed to be looking blindly out the half-pulled shades into the growing darkness. The coffee maker puffed and chugged in the kitchen but other than that there was no noise in the house.

"Where were we?" asked Hal.

"Hal, we don't need to talk about any of that this evening," said Mahoney. "That's not why I came back."

Hal turned to look at him, "Humor an old man, Mike. Consider it therapy."

Mahoney shrugged his shoulders, "Okay," he said while fishing his digital recorder out of his briefcase, "I think we had finished up talking about 1968 and started talking about Nixon."

Hal struggled to his feet. "I need to move, let's get a cup of coffee and go for a little walk."

Mahoney followed Hal to the kitchen then out into the evening air. The temperature had dropped considerably and a fair breeze was blowing in from the distant ocean.

"As long as we keep moving, the mosquitoes shouldn't carry us away," said Hal with a laugh. At the end of the walk that led from his front door to the street, Hal motioned to the right. "Let's go this way, that old broad who wants a piece of this, lives down that other way."

"You're kind of a big deal around here, aren't you!" said Mahoney with a grin.

"All these old birds think I'm healthy and wealthy. I'll show em'. I'll just up and die one day."

"You haven't told any of your neighbors you're sick?" asked Mahoney.

Hal shot him a quick look and changed the subject. "After 1968 we sort of figured we could ride out '69 without too many bumps. The moon landing was a good boost to Jack's mood but Nixon kept us guessing at every corner. Then there was Joe's death."

"You're talking about Joe Kennedy?" asked Mahoney.

"Yeah, he had been a tough old dog, he survived a massive stroke and then spent six or seven years as a wheelchair-bound vegetable. It was hard on Jack to know his dad, a man who had been so strong and full of life, was living like that. He once told me that he wished his father had died of the stroke rather than having the world see him like that."

"Did Joe Kennedy know that is son was alive?

Hal stopped at the street corner, "I think they told him, that was my understanding."

"Did Kennedy see his father after the 'assassination?'" asked Mahoney.

"No," said Hal. "He never had the chance to make it back. It really hurt him that when Bobby was killed and when his father was dying he was unable to be there for the family or even to attend the funerals."

"What about his mother?"

"Rose?" said Mahoney. "Rose made it out to the island a few times before her health faded.

"What was your take on Rose Kennedy?" Mahoney asked.

"She was a wonderful lady who was bright, compassionate, and sharp as a tack in her old age. And she and absolutely fascinating to visit with . . . as long as you didn't disagree with her."

Mahoney laughed, "What happened if you didn't see things her way?"

"Then she quickly became the opposite of the description I just gave you," said Hal with a chuckle. "Jack gave me the heads up so I never disagreed with her and we always got along just fine. The only time I ever thought I was in trouble is when she asked in what religion I was raised. I made the mistake of telling her the truth . . . that my parents didn't really believe in attending church."

"And how did she react to that?"

"I saw a brief glimpse of her other side so I quickly said something like, 'Jack has been telling me all about the Catholic Church and I am very interested in learning more about your intriguing religion,'" said Hal. "Later Jack presented me with a ribbon for being the best side-stepper he had ever seen in his mother's presence."

"Tell me about John and Caroline," said Mahoney. "What did you think of the two of them as they matured?"

Hal glanced over his shoulder, almost as if he expected somebody to be following them, trying to listen to their conversation. "They were two fine children and I was proud to know them. They were the product of a caring and strong mother who kept them in line despite their fame and money."

"What do you mean?" asked Mahoney.

"Remember, both of those kids became teens in the seventies. A lot of kids in their social arena and in similar situations became freaks. They did drugs, joined cults, or ran off to India to find the true meaning of life. Not John and Caroline, those two were well-grounded, smart, good kids and Jack was a proud, proud father because of them."

Mahoney flipped through his notes for a few minutes, "Before I left this morning, we were talking about Nixon and it seemed that he was unknowingly but pretty effectively working against Kennedy. What became of that?"

Hal continued to shuffle down the street, "Nixon and his administration pretty much took the political winds out of Jack's sails. They started taking credit for everything good that was going on in the U.S., including NASA and relations with China. And they actually thought they could improve relations with Russia by using the information from the *K-129* incident and strong-arm techniques. The reality was that Nixon had pissed off Brezhnev who unfortunately couldn't see the distinction between Kennedy and Nixon. Brezhnev felt that he had made an agreement with the United States and that agreement was broken shortly after he shook hands with a former U.S. President."

"How did Kennedy respond to that?" asked Mahoney.

"Jack decided that he had done all he could for his country at that point in time and he turned his energies elsewhere," answered Hal. "I remember the evening we were sitting in Ari's bar on the *Christina*, it must have been late '69 or early 1970 when Jack was telling Ari about his frustrations with Nixon. Ari looked at him and in that deep voice of his said something like, 'Jack, you've done enough for your country. Come work with me and let's really build an empire.' So that's what he did."

"How did that change things?" asked Mahoney.

"Well, first of all, we started spending a lot more time off the island, which made my life a juggling act," laughed Hal, pointing to his right indicating they were to turn the corner.

"How so?"

"The Secret Service didn't want Jack out flitting around the world. They liked the idea that he was sitting on Skorpios behind a wall of Onassis-paid security. To be in business with Ari, Jack had to be close to him so Ari made the *Christina* his headquarters and turned one of the staterooms into Jack's office. My superiors would have flipped if they had known Jack was traveling around the globe on yachts and jets. I spent most of my time covering for our travels, but it wasn't as if the Service was monitoring us all that closely."

"So Kennedy and Onassis were partners?" asked Mahoney.

"Oh, no, it was very clear that Ari was Jack's boss but Jack brought a new level of professionalism to Ari's business. Ari was very much a 'my way or the highway' sort of businessman who got deals done in very one-sided transactions, an 'I win, you lose' sort of fashion. Jack had that way of looking at a deal like it was a political transaction. He liked to think, how can we cut a deal with British Petroleum that makes it almost impossible for Shell not to ship with us also? He showed Ari how giving away shipping for almost free to Syria could triple the business from the Netherlands, or how cutting ties with the Brazilian government could dramatically increase his revenues from the Israelis."

"Interesting," said Mahoney. "Did Onassis start seeing his business grow?"

"Oh, yeah, those were good years," said Hal. "Jack was having a lot of fun helping Ari. Jackie and the kids were spending as much time as they could with Jack, and I was courting a cute little French gal who worked aboard the *Christina*," said Hal with a smile.

Mahoney looked at the warm smile that had appeared on Hal's face, "So what became of her?"

"She moved back to France in 1975. I heard she married a rich guy from Reims and had a bunch of kids and got fat."

Mahoney laughed, "That sounds like some of my ex-wives. Heck, I moved to the city and got fat myself," he chuckled.

Mahoney recomposed himself and asked, "How long did the working relationship with Onassis last?"

"As far as I know it lasted, at least in some respect, until Jack died last week. I know he was still functioning as a conservator for part of Ari's estate when I retired."

"Kennedy was in charge of Ari's estate?" asked Mahoney in a surprised tone.

"Part of it, but let's get back to that," said Hal. "First, I think we need to talk about the events of 1973."

"Okay, what happened in '73?" asked Mahoney.

Hal stopped at a stand of mailboxes and put his hand on them, not really leaning on them but certainly using them for balance.

"Are you okay, Hal?" asked Mahoney.

"Just taking a breather," said Hal. "It's pretty pathetic that I can't make it more than two blocks without a rest."

"You've been through a lot, especially today" said Mahoney.

"Hal stared at the ground for a few moments before looking up. "In 1973 we started hearing about connections between Nixon and the men who broke into the DNC headquarters at the Watergate complex in mid-1972. I remember Jack laughing and wondering if Nixon was actually that dumb.

The first thing that started pulling Jack back towards his country was the Watergate scandal. Then in January of '73, Alex Onassis died, which was a massive blow to Ari. It affected his business, his relationships with his friends, his health . . . everything. And the third big blow-up of the year was the October Yom Kippur war between Israel, Egypt, and Syria which brought us incredibly close to the brink of nuclear war."

Mahoney stood there listening, he thought Hal didn't look good. "Are you sure you don't want me to go get the car?" he asked

"I'm fine," said Hal gruffly.

"Okay, okay," said Mahoney. "Help me understand these three events one at a time. Why was Kennedy concerned about Watergate?"

"Watergate hit at a time when the American public was already uncertain about their trust in government. Vietnam was pulling the country in two, students were taking over their colleges, and people were protesting in the streets. The country wasn't stable and now we couldn't trust our leadership," said Hal. "Watergate couldn't have come at a worse time."

Hal pushed himself away from the mailboxes and started walking. "Next came the plane crash that killed Alexander Onassis. Ari and Alex hadn't been very close when he was a child but they certainly made up for it in his late teens and early twenties. They bonded, became interested in what each other enjoyed and started spending a lot of time together. Alex loved anything motorized or mechanical and Ari loved business. Once the two realized how close Ari's business was to the mechanics that Alex loved, they found a bond that they could both rely on."

Hal seemed to be struggling to walk but continued to talk, "When Alex died, a part of Ari died. I don't know how to explain it but the life, the sparkle in Ari's eyes went away after Alex died. He no longer cared about himself, his business, or those around him. Jack felt it was a good time to give the man some distance so we decided to move his office off the *Christina* and back to Skorpios to give Ari some space and some time. But we didn't understand the depth of the depression that Ari would fall into," said Hal with a pause. "In hindsight, it might have been better if we had stayed close and forced Ari to work rather than allow him to be overcome by his grief."

The two walked half a block in silence before Mahoney asked, "And the Yom Kippur War?"

"What a damn mess," said Hal. "That was in October of 1973. The Syrians and the Egyptians decided to attack Israel after a six-year-long cease-fire to take back the land they had lost in the Six-Day war of 1967. The Egyptians attacked across the Suez Canal and the Syrians came across the Golan Heights at the same time, catching the Israelis and the rest of the world by surprise. The Israelis held their own and launched a series of counterattacks which drove the Arabs back out but after a week of defeats; the Arabs decided to step it up a notch and go nuclear. We probably came even closer to a nuclear exchange there than we had during the Cuban Missile Crisis."

"I know about the war but I had never heard that there was a nuclear threat between those countries," said Mahoney.

"The threat," said Hal, "reached all the way from the Gaza Strip to the plains of Kansas."

"What?" asked Mahoney.

SKORPIOS ISLAND
October 9, 1973

"Jack . . .," Hal said standing at the door of the dark bedroom.

"What is it?" answered Jack.

"Sorry to wake you but Boulos is here," said Hal. "We need to talk."

"Okay, give me a minute," said Jack. He rolled over and stared at the ceiling wondering, "What now?"

After splashing some water on his face and examining the four-day growth of his beard, Jack slipped into a pair of shorts and a sweat shirt and walked out into the main room where Hal and Boulos sat at the dining table. Every light, every lamp in the room was on and the table was scattered with papers and maps.

"What's going on?" he asked, wondering if he really wanted to know.

Boulos jumped up from his chair and shook Jack's hand, "Good evening, Mister President, I am sorry to disturb you."

"It's good to see you Boulos, but call me Jack." Boulos and Jack had known each other for almost ten years and Boulos still called him by his formal name. It had become a running joke between the two of them that Boulos refused to call his friend by any other name.

"Mister President, I have just returned from Egypt, you have heard they just attacked Israel," said Boulos with a concerned look.

Jack smiled, "You know, Boulos, it occurs to me that everywhere you go, there seems to be a war that follows. I'm beginning to wonder if you are more the cause rather than the observer."

Boulos, not smiling at the joke, continued, "As you know, the Egyptians have been purchasing weapons from the Soviets for years."

Jack became serious, "Yes, you have made us aware of that many times."

"The country now looks like more of a Russian stockpile than a casual purchaser of weapons," said Boulos. "They have MiG-21 fighters, T-55 and T-62 tanks numbering in the hundreds, and a huge number of SA-6 and SA-7 anti-aircraft missiles along with the new AT-3 Sagger anti-tank guided missile. Recently, we have also noticed a large number of Russian military advisors in the area."

"We've been expecting this Anwar Sadat character to attack Israel," said Jack. "Hell, he told *Newsweek* earlier this year he was going to attack to take back some of the land they lost in '67."

"It appears to be a little more sinister than that, Jack," said Hal.

"Oh, how so?" asked Jack.

Boulos lit a cigarette as he considered how best to describe the situation. "Algeria is sending a squadron of MiG-21s and a squadron of Su-7s to Egypt along with 200 more tanks. Libya has sent two squadrons of Mirage V fighters and the Saudis, the Palestinians, Pakistan and Kuwait have sent financial aid," he said as he pacing back and forth.

"But far more troubling is that the Soviets have started shipping military supplies to Egypt and Syria by both air and sea. To counter that, the Americans have moved the USS Roosevelt close to the situation and have promised to begin re-supplying Israel with materials to replace those lost in battle."

Jack smacked the table with his fist, "What in the hell is wrong with Nixon? Isn't he smart enough to know when it's time to back somebody in that region and when it's time to back away and let them slug it out on their own?"

"You're preaching to the choir, Jack," said Hal.

"If we let Brezhnev and his buddies continue to dive into these situations, they'll eventually get their heads handed to them," said Jack to the two men in the room. "We're so damn concerned about stopping the Red Tide that we allow ourselves to get sucked into every border skirmish, feud, or barroom brawl that occurs in the world."

"This isn't just a barroom brawl, Mister President," said Boulos. "I was contacted this morning, in the strictest of confidence, by Moshe Dayan, the Chief of Staff of the Israeli Defense Force. Apparently, Israeli Prime Minister Meir has ordered the assembly of thirteen twenty-kiloton nuclear warheads. With their Jericho missiles they could take action against the Syrians and the Egyptians if they are otherwise unable to turn the tide of the attack."

Jack sat down at the table, closed his eyes and tilted his head back. "And a nuclear attack against Egypt by the American-sponsored Israelis would be seen as an attack against the Soviets which would cause them to counterattack which would be seen by the Americans as a direct attack against us so we would have to launch . . .," his voice trailed off. "Son of a bitch, here we go again."

"Boulos," said Hal, "how confident are you that Dayan has accurate information concerning the nukes?"

"One hundred percent," answered Boulos. "He would not have contacted me directly if he was not greatly concerned."

"We need as much information as we can get," said Jack. "Boulos, how close to Dayan are you?"

"We have only started talking recently but he believes I have the ear of some high-level American insiders. I believe he will talk to me at anytime in light of the current situation."

Jack laughed, "You have the ear of some low-level American outsiders, but don't tell him that. Who do we know in the White House that we can trust?"

"Larry Wood," said Hal.

"Who's Larry Wood?" asked Jack.

"An old academy buddy and my new boss," said Hal, pushing a telegram across the table towards Jack. "I've just been asked to report to Washington in the next few days to meet with Larry. He was just promoted to Deputy Director of Special Projects to replace David Snyder."

"What does the Deputy Director of Special Projects do?" asked Jack.

"Apparently, the position was created last year by Nixon to protect the 'Secrets of the Presidency'. My guess is that Snyder got canned because, despite his best efforts, the Watergate break-in was still tied to Nixon," said Hal.

"And now you," Jack paused, "or I guess I should say we, fall under this new Director?"

"That's how I understand it," answered Hal.

"The Secret Service hasn't bothered you once in ten years and now this new guy wants you to come to Washington?" asked Jack. "What does he want to discuss?"

"I'm not sure what his agenda is, Jack," said Hal. "He's a good guy and I think there's a reasonable chance he can help us out by keeping us up to speed regarding the general tone and tenor of the White House."

Jack looked out the window at the light of a single boat moving slowly across the water a few miles out. "We have got to get to somebody who has Nixon's ear." He stood and walked to the window staring out towards the light on the distant boat but not really seeing it.

"Boulos, I need you to get a message to Brezhnev," said Jack suddenly. "Tell him the fall of the third temple is imminent and Pig needs to talk. Then get back with Dayan and assure him that we are working on a backdoor solution. See how much information you can pump out of him regarding Meir's temperament and do anything you can to calm the Israelis down."

He turned and said, "Hal, get to Washington, meet with your new boss, see what the temperature is in the Oval Office and find us a workable link to Nixon. Then get with my brother, Teddy, tell him everything you know. I'll contact Ted Sorensen to set up a meeting with you, Bob McNamara and Averell Harriman. We need to get our arms around this thing before it goes nuclear."

Hal smiled as a familiar and warm feeling welled up inside him. Jack was back.

BOCA RATON, FLORIDA
Present Day

"Why do you think some events, like the Cuban Missile Crisis are so well known and other events like the Yom Kippur War are not?" asked Mahoney.

"The press has a lot to do with it. The Yom Kippur War was happening 'over there' while the Cuban Crisis was perceived as a direct threat to the U.S.," said Hal.

"How did that war resolve itself and what was your involvement," asked Mahoney as they walked towards Hal's home.

"For several years, our friend Boulos had been snuggling up to both the Arabs and the Israelis purely for monetary gain," said Hal. "Boulos knew they had lots of oil that needed to be shipped and Ari had lots of ships. Boulos figured that if he could get to the top people in those governments, he could get to the oil and, in the end, cut a nice deal for himself. Despite his greed, he built some solid relationships with both sides and probably could have been shot for being a double-or even a triple-agent if anybody but Jack and I had of known."

"That sounds like a ballsy position to put oneself in," said Mahoney.

"Boulos had about the biggest balls of any man I knew," said Hal with a laugh. "He was a smart guy and if his brains had been half as big as his balls, he would have figured out a way to become supreme commander of the world."

Hal continued to shuffled down the street saying, "The same day we heard about the potential nuclear threat, I was called to Washington to meet with my new boss," said Hal, "The timing of the meeting was purely coincidental but I was able to gain insight to what was going on in the White House and open a new source of information for us."

"And who was your new source of information?" asked Mahoney.

"Henry Kissinger," said Hal with a glance towards Mahoney.

WASHINGTON, D.C.
October 12, 1973

Hal was tired. He had been up most of the night talking and strategizing with Jack and Boulos. After Jack and Boulos had gone to bed, Hal found the one suit he had on the island, dusted it off, and quickly packed.

In the morning Jack had taken him to Nydri on the launch where Hal made a taxi driver very happy by negotiating a generous fare all the way to the airport at Prevezai. The driver was careful to ask for half the fare upfront which Hal paid him, allowing him enough money to fill the petrol tank of the old Mercedes. From Prevezai, he caught the morning flight to Athens and then the afternoon flight to London before continuing on to New York in time to catch an early shuttle to Washington. His new boss, Larry Wood was waiting at the gate when he stepped off the plane at Washington National Airport.

"My god, Hal, you look good," said Larry with a big smile and a firm handshake.

"I can see the years haven't been very good to you, Larry" Hal joked.

Larry caught on, "Have you been working out, Hal? Because it's not doing you any good," he said with a laugh.

"What's new in Washington in the last ten years?" asked Hal.

"Jesus, has it been that long?" answered Larry. "Let's see, we have a new boss in the White House, the Redskins still couldn't win a championship game if they had to, and the manicotti over at Gino's has gone to hell since he sold the place. How are things in Greece?"

"I've got great food, fabulous working conditions, and a soft bed. I'm hoping this trip isn't about a new assignment; you're not going to tell me I can't go back are you?" asked Hal. He wanted to get that off the table right up front.

"I wouldn't dream of it," said Larry as he pointed the way towards baggage claim. "In my new position, I'm just trying to get a handle on what you need from us to continue your job in the same efficient manner that you've demonstrated so far. How was your flight?" asked Larry. The airport wasn't the appropriate venue to continue the current conversation.

"It was pretty amazing. I flew first class on Pan Am from London to New York on that new 747. That son of a bitch sure makes the trip easy once you get it in the air but nothing that big with that many people aboard should be able to get off the ground," said Hal.

"First class?" asked Larry with a raised eyebrow.

"Don't worry, boss, I paid for it myself. I really don't have much to spend my money on over there," said Hal.

They retrieved Hal's bag and headed to the curb where a government sedan and driver was waiting for them. They talked about the weather and sports during the quick drive from the airport to the nearby Holiday Inn.

"Can we talk for a few minutes now, Hal?" asked Larry.

"Sure, as long as you don't need me to answer any difficult questions. I'm a little out of it from the trip," said Hal.

"Give me fifteen or twenty minutes," Larry said to the driver as he retrieved Hal's bag from the trunk.

Hal checked in and they walked to his room. Larry threw Hal's bag on the bed and plopped down in one of the two chairs in the corner of the generic-looking motel room. "So, how are things going in Greece?" asked Larry.

"Just fine," answered Hal. "No complaints, I can't really think of anything we need.

"And your principal is fine, no complaints there?" asked Larry.

Hal smiled, "When were you promoted to this position, Larry?"

"Three weeks ago, why?"

Hal sat down in the chair next to him. Between them there was a small table with a simple lamp. Hal reached over and slid the lamp out of the way so he could see his new boss's face. "You don't have a clue what I'm doing over there, do you?" asked Hal.

Larry smiled, "Of course I do, you have the key player from the Kennedy assassination on ice in Greece." Hal stared silently at his boss until Larry confessed, "Okay, I was hoping I could fake it until you told me. Look, I'm currently in charge of more than fifty projects. Special projects were placed into one of three categories and your mission is a Category One, which means there is no documentation anywhere and information is on a need-to-know basis only."

"And the Service doesn't think that as Director of Special Projects, you need to know?"

"You've been out there long enough that the few people here in Washington who did know, like Director Rowley and Special Agents Walker and Thornton, have either retired or died. I'm in an awkward situation because I'm not even sure who I can ask about you without tipping my hand to the fact that you and your project even exist," admitted Larry. "When I asked Director Knight about Project XA-413, he told me to ask you."

Hal smiled, "You honestly have no idea what I'm doing out there?"

"I know you have a key element of the Kennedy assassination on ice," said Larry as he reached inside his jacket and pulled out an envelope addressed to Hal, "and I believe I know who it is."

Hal opened the envelope and removed a letter from Director Stuart Knight that authorized him to give Deputy Director Wood all pertinent information relating to Project XA-413. It was signed and embossed with the Director's seal.

"How many Category One projects are you in charge of, out of curiosity?" asked Hal.

"Larry smiled, "The actual number is classified, but just a few, thank god."

"You must know some pretty interesting shit about the past presidents," said Hal with a soft chuckle. "Today, you get to learn about a very big one."

"The question is . . . do I want to know?" said Larry with a pained look on his face. "Some of the projects we are in charge of, I wish I had never learned about."

"I'll tell you a fascinating story," said Hal, "but in exchange, I need some inside information and some introductions to a few key people."

Larry frowned, "You've been ordered to give me the information about your project and now you're trying to negotiate?"

"This letter authorizes me to relate the information to you, it doesn't order me to do anything," said Hal with a smile.

Larry's face twisted into a quizzical look, "Okay, tell me who you are protecting and I'll share what information I can, but you know I can't give you much."

"Fair enough," said Hal. "I'm hiding Lady Bird Johnson's lesbian lover."

"Are you serious?" asked Larry. His face held no surprise which made Hal wonder about the other secrets the Deputy Director might have learned recently.

"No, I'm pulling your chain," admitted Hal. "I'm protecting John F. Kennedy," he said bluntly.

Since his promotion, Deputy Director Larry Wood had learned many secrets about the current and past Presidents; some were personal indiscretions, others involved political foreign policy maneuvers and strategies, and a few were just simply weird. After a month in his new position, very little surprised him but his old buddy Hal had just fired a stunning salvo. Larry looked for something in Hal's expression, a twinkle in his eye, the slightest smirk, something to indicate he was joking he saw no smile nor any hint of mockery. Larry chose to play along for a moment while secretly hoping Hal wasn't telling the truth and would soon smile, "President Kennedy survived the assassination?"

"There was no assassination," said Hal without emotion. "Kennedy and a group close to him planned the entire incident; Oswald was firing blanks from the sixth floor window."

"Why?" asked Larry.

Forty-five minutes later, Deputy Director Wood walked in a daze to the Chevy where he found the driver standing next to the car over a pile of fresh cigarette butts. "Let's go back to the office," he said, trying his best to process the story he had just heard. In Room 221 of the Washington Airport Holiday Inn, Hal laid his head on a stack of pillows and closed his eyes. He was asleep before his buddy's car had left the parking lot.

BOCA RATON, FLORIDA
Present Day

Mahoney became nervous; for the first time since their initial conversation, he realized that if Hal was telling the truth, his own life might be at risk.

Hal shuffled on at the same pace and Mahoney grudgingly stayed at his side wishing they could move faster. "How did you connect with Kissinger?" he finally asked.

"I was asked to report to Washington to meet with my new boss in October of '73. He was an old buddy of mine from my early days in the Service and I was able to con him out of some inside information about what was really going on in the White House. If you want to know what's really going on in and around the Oval Office and the White House, you ask the Secret Service. They stand around acting like they don't hear or see anything but they hear and see it all."

"And what *was* really going on?" asked Mahoney.

"Nixon had pretty much checked out. He was so concerned about Watergate that he couldn't focus on anything else. The world was falling apart around him but his main concern was keeping his butt out of jail. Kissinger was making nearly all the foreign policy decisions for the country and often he wasn't even consulting with Nixon," said Hal.

"How did you actually connect with Kissinger?"

"I believe," said Hal, pausing to recall, "I sent a message through my boss to Kissinger's Secret Service detail." Hal struggled to remember, "It was something like, 'the third temple is about to fail.' It had a real super-spy sound to it."

"Do you recall the meaning of the message?" asked Mahoney.

"It meant, Israel was in big trouble," said Hal. "The word 'temple' was also a code word for 'nuclear'. The elapsed time from when I asked my boss to pass the message to Kissinger to when I was shaking his hand couldn't have been more than a few hours."

"What happened in that meeting?" asked Mahoney.

"Kissinger wanted to know if I understood the meaning of the message and, of course, he wanted to know where I got my information," said Hal. "I told him I was in contact with people who were very close to Egypt's President Sadat and Israel's Defense Minister, Moshe Dayan. I let him know that our people understood that Nixon was not in any frame of mind to be making weighty decisions. I told Kissinger that we also knew that he was, at that time, the person in Washington that we needed to be in contact with to help avoid a nuclear confrontation that would likely spread globally." Hal laughed, "I remember him looking at me over the top of those big thick glasses he wore and asking in his heavy Bavarian accent, 'And who in the hell are you?'"

"Did he believe you?" asked Mahoney.

"He did, especially after he received calls from both Ted Sorensen and Bob McNamara," said Hal with a grin. "Then I told him that if he wanted to meet my people he would have to do so in Geneva. I completely pulled Geneva out of a hat because one, it was easy for Jack to get there, and two, I'd always wanted to see Switzerland."

"Did Kissinger agree to the meeting?" asked Mahoney.

"He and I were on an Air Force jet flying to Geneva that night," said Hal.

"And did Kissinger meet with Kennedy in Geneva?" asked Mahoney.

"He did."

ABOARD *SAM 25183*, OVER THE ATLANTIC OCEAN
October 12, 1973

It was obvious to Hal that the hastily planned trip was nothing new to Kissinger and his small staff. Apparently, it was pretty easy for the Secretary of State to acquire the use of an Air Force VC-137, the military version of the Boeing 707. The aircraft they were on was an exact copy of Air Force One used by the President except for the exterior paint scheme. *SAM 25183* was nick-named *Vanilla One* because it was painted plain white and displayed nothing to designate it as an official United States aircraft. The plane was used when a senior official needed to go somewhere but didn't necessarily want or need the public and the press to know about it.

Hal received details about the meeting arrangement only after they were airborne. He assumed accommodations and ground transportation were being arranged as they were in flight.

A young, pretty, but very efficient-looking lady appeared at Hal's seat about two hours after take-off. "Hello, Mister Rumsey," she said. "My name is Shannon Moore. I do most of the travel arrangements for the Secretary. I have arranged a large house outside of Geneva that should have plenty of room for your group and ours. If you will let me know when your group is scheduled to arrive and how many there will be, I will make sure they are met at the airport and brought to the house."

Hal realized he was flying by the seat of his pants, "I believe there will be two but I don't yet know when they will be arriving. I was able to send a telex to them but didn't receive a reply before we took off."

Shannon gave a thoughtful look for a moment, "This aircraft is equipped with just about every means of communication known to man," she said with a smile. "If you would like to try to contact your group again, I am sure the communications officer would be happy to help you."

"Yeah," said Hal as he unbuckled his seatbelt. "We better make sure they received the message."

Just forward of the small section of seats that Hal had been sitting in alone was a bulkhead and just beyond that was a small communications area crammed with more electronics than Hal had ever seen in one place.

"Lieutenant Stallings, this is Hal Rumsey with the Secret Service," said Shannon to the man seated at the console. "Can you assist him in sending a message to Europe?"

Stallings spun his chair a quarter-turn and shook Hal's hand, "Of course. Telephone, telegraph, telex, radio, smoke signals, drums, we got it all. Whom do you want to talk to and what do you want to say?" he asked.

Shannon politely excused herself and stepped aft of the bulkhead to allow Hal his privacy. "Can you send a message over the TACSAT to one-twenty-one point zero-four-seven-six?" Hal asked.

Stallings flipped a switch, turned one dial and then another while the red display changed to the numbers 121.0476. "And the message is?"

"To Stranger from Slot Car," said Hal as Stallings started typing on the keyboard in front of him. Hal smiled because he and Jack hadn't thought of codenames before he left the island. He picked 'Stranger' for Jack because Hal often told Jack he was 'being strange' when he was depressed or moody. He picked 'Slot Car' off the cuff for himself because more than once he and Jack had raced John John's electric slot car set in heated contests over cocktails. "Verify receipt of earlier message and send approximate time you will rendezvous," Hal continued. "Our arrival at final destination approximately eight hundred zulu today."

Lieutenant Stallings looked up from his console, "Is that it?"

"That should do it," replied Hal.

"I'll bring the reply back to you as soon as I get it," said Stallings.

Sixty seconds later, the teletype in the radio room on Skorpios started chattering away. The man sitting at the machine in the little room read the message and typed a short reply.

A few moments later the teletype aboard *SAM 25183* typed out a reply which read, "Innkeeper to Slot Car, previous message received. Stranger and Hermes en route to rendezvous, expect they will arrive ahead of you. Contact at Swissôtel on your arrival."

Hal was surprised when Lieutenant Stallings arrived at his seat with a reply before he had even gotten settled. "What an amazing world we live in," Hal said to Stallings before he read the message. 'Innkeeper' was obviously Demetrius but he laughed at Demetrius' choice of 'Hermes,' the Greek God of flight, thieves, mischief, commerce, and travelers, as a codename for Boulos. "Perfect," Hal said to himself.

"Is there any reply you would like me to send?" asked Stallings.

Hal thought for a moment before saying, "Send the message, 'Thank you and good night.'" He knew if he didn't notify the Demetrius that his message had been received, he would sit in that little room all night long worrying that it hadn't been. Now they could both relax, Hal thought with a smile.

Hal laid his wide and comfortable seat back, adjusted his pillow, and pulled up his blanket. He could get used to traveling like this, he thought to himself, but before he could get too settled, Shannon Moore reappeared at his side.

"I am sorry to disturb you, Mister Rumsey, but the Secretary would like a few minutes of your time," she said with an apologetic tone.

"No problem," said Hal as he tossed the blanket aside and followed her towards the rear of the aircraft.

Henry Kissinger sat in front of a pile of papers at the end of a conference table with seating for eight, the largest meeting area that Hal had seen on the plane. Kissinger stood and offered a handshake to Hal before asking him to sit at the seat to his left.

Secretary Kissinger looked at Hal for a moment before saying, "I am flying across the world to meet with a mystery man at the request of Ted Sorensen and Robert McNamara. Do you mind telling me who this man is before I get to Geneva?"

"I'm sorry, Mister Secretary," said Hal with a wince. "I have not been authorized to reveal the identity of my boss. If he chooses to meet directly with you, that's up to him. I will tell you, however, that his identity is very top-secret, take-to-your-grave top-secret."

Kissinger started to assure Hal that he was trusted almost daily with top-secret information when two and two suddenly added up for him. "So it is true?" he asked, his eyes wide.

"What's true?" asked Hal.

Kissinger thought it through for a moment. He was seated with a Secret Service Agent and flying to Europe to meet with a man, recommended by Sorensen and McNamara, who had the inside track on both Egypt and Israel. That combined with some ambiguous rumors and speculation started to add up. "You work for President Kennedy," he said as a statement rather than a question.

Hal's expression gave away the secret even as he blurted out the words, "I cannot reveal the identity of my boss."

GENEVA SWITZERLAND
October 13, 1973

Hal stepped from the stuffy interior of the aircraft into a reasonably warm October morning and took just a moment to marvel at the distant mountains and breathe the fresh air before descending the stairs to the tarmac below. With all the legendary efficiency of the Swiss, two large grey Mercedes sedans pulled up near the aircraft and began loading both Kissinger's staff and their luggage. Hal and Shannon Moore were directed to the back seat of the lead car, Kissinger and two other staff members were in the second car, a Service Agent sat in the front seat of each car. A third Mercedes had been waiting at the gate and fell in behind them as they left the airport. Within a few minutes, they were traveling through the Swiss countryside.

"I need to contact my group at someplace called the Swissôtel," said Hal.

"That would be the Swissôtel Metropole Hotel near the river," said Shannon. "After we get to the Balmer House we can send a car for your party."

Ten minutes later they turned off the road into a small lane and drove through a large gate where two uniformed guards saluted as they passed. The single lane weaved through the woods for nearly a mile before entering a large clearing and revealing a huge old house sitting atop a rise. Three men and two maids stood in a line waiting as the cars drove up and stopped in front of the large front doors. One of the men opened Hal's door and in perfect English but with a heavy Swiss accent said, "Welcome to the Balmer House."

Hal watched as Kissinger and his staff walked purposcfully into the house; they had obviously been here before and looked as if they were heading to an important meeting. The staff from the house started unloading luggage and Shannon waited next to Hal.

"The Balmer House was built in the 1890s by a wealthy Swiss family who had businesses throughout Europe," said Shannon. "They lived in the house until World War II when they lost everything because of financial interests they had in Germany, Belgium, and Poland. The home was then converted to a guest house and in the last twenty years or so, it has become a high-security accommodation for visiting dignitaries." She started walking slowly towards the front door, "I am told that the home has accommodated Khrushchev, Brezhnev, Presidents Truman, Kennedy, and Johnson, and many other world leaders."

"With so many different leaders and their staffs, along with the security and intelligence people they bring along, does anybody worry about somebody bugging the place while they are here?" Hal asked as Shannon started slowly towards the door.

"That," said Shannon with a pause "is the beauty of the Swiss. They work so hard to be a neutral country that they wouldn't allow a bug to be placed in a home like this. They sweep the estate every day. If a bug were found and traced to the Americans, we'd never be allowed to come back here. We'd be back staying in hotels and having conversations in the bathroom with the shower running."

The interior of the home was exactly what Hal expected, marble floors, high ceilings and a massive winding staircase to the second floor. A huge vase of fresh flowers sat on top of a table in the middle of the entryway, the vase so large that a small child could have easily fit inside, but it was dwarfed by the immense size of its surroundings.

"This is Mister Rumsey," said Shannon to a waiting maid. "Will you please show him to his room?" She turned to Hal, "Why don't you freshen up a bit and then I'll have one of the drivers take you to the Swissôtel to retrieve the others in your party."

"That will be fine," he said with a smile while trying to be the suave and debonair international man of mystery that he hoped she thought him to be.

Shannon giggled at his obvious attempt to be polished and sophisticated. She was flattered by his interest in her but knew that this wasn't the time or the place to pursue romance. "I'll see you back down here in fifteen or twenty minutes," she said in a tone that had just a hint of mockery.

"Strike one," Hal said to himself as he followed the maid up the stairs.

BOCA RATON, FLORIDA
Present Day

"The son of a bitch guessed it," said Hal, following a few minutes of silence as they continued their walk.

"Who guessed what?" Mahoney asked.

"On the flight from Washington to Geneva," said Hal, "Kissinger guessed that Kennedy was alive."

"How did he figure it out?" asked Mahoney.

"I guess when the calls started coming from former Kennedy cabinet members and staffers asking him to meet with a certain Secret Service Agent, along with his awareness of some rumors that had been floating around the White House, he made a wild but correct guess," answered Hal. "But until we walked into that meeting, he didn't know for sure. Kissinger was quite surprised to see Jack alive and well."

"What was Kissinger's reaction when Kennedy entered the room?" asked Mahoney.

"He was visibly shocked," answered Hal.

"Did it take him long to get over the shock?" asked Mahoney.

"Kissinger was an incredibly bright man," said Hal. "When he guessed that we were going to see Jack, he did a little quick research. He knew that the head of his own security detail had been on the presidential detail in '62 and '63. He had a conversation with that agent before we landed in Geneva and pumped him for some information."

"So he found something he could use to verify that the man he was about to meet was really Kennedy?" asked Mahoney.

"Yeah, as he shook Jack's hand he said something like, 'You are looking well, Mister President. Have you spoken with Devon Clancy lately?' to which Jack answered, 'The Irish boy who busted up the Russian hit squad in Duganstown?' With that, Kissinger knew he was talking to Jack and not some look-a-like."

"Okay, but how did Kissinger move from the shock of seeing Kennedy alive in front of him to sitting down and having a real conversation?" asked Mahoney.

"Most of it was the gravity of the situation," said Hal. "Kissinger, Jack, Boulos, and myself sat down at a small table and in about twenty minutes we laid out everything we knew about the Arab/Israeli situation. Then Kissinger then took over and, based on the knowledge and the resources he had sitting around the table, proposing a plan. I've never had much of anything nice to say about Nixon but I'll tell you what, Kissinger was a bright S.O.B."

"And what plan did he propose to solve the situation?" asked Mahoney.

"Goal number one was to keep the war conventional. We had to find a way to keep Israel's nukes from being used. Kissinger contacted Israel's Prime Minister Golda Meir and their Defense Secretary Moshe Dayan and told them we would offer all of the aircraft, tanks, and ammunition they needed to defend their positions as long as they kept the nukes out of the war."

"That was a good idea," said Mahoney. "Did they buy it?"

"The Israelis agreed to it for a five-day period but as Jack suspected would happen, as soon as we started moving equipment into Israel, the Soviets started their own air and sea lifts into Egypt and Syria," said Hal.

"If the two superpowers were supplying all the weapons," asked Mahoney, "what kept the war from growing outside the region?"

"The Soviet resupply of the Arabs was exactly the chess move Jack was expecting. He told us at the initial meeting that if Kissinger offered weapons to the Israelis, the Soviets would do the same for the Arabs and that played right into his hand," said Hal with a smile.

"How so?" asked Mahoney.

"Anwar Sadat was another smart guy," said Hal. "He saw the writing on the wall years ahead of most of the world. He knew the fall of the Soviet Union was only a matter of time and that his country had hitched its horse to the wrong wagon. He desperately wanted to build relations with the U.S. but we had repeatedly thrown the Egyptians to the carpet because of their relationship with Moscow and their continued aggressive stance within the region. We had known that they were buying weapons from the Soviets but once we had hard evidence that the Russians were *giving* them weapons, we had the card we needed to make some real changes."

"How did you use that information?" asked Mahoney.

"Over the years Boulos had built a business relationship with a close friend of Sadat," explained Hal. "That connection gave him the ability to communicate almost directly with Sadat so when Boulos sent a message through his associate that the Americans wanted to talk, Sadat jumped at the chance. Kissinger couldn't be seen anywhere near Sadat because of his relationship with the Israelis, we didn't dare trust Sadat with the knowledge that Jack was alive, and it was imperative that we acted quickly so I became the odd man out. Boulos and I flew to Cairo to meet with Sadat."

Mahoney laughed, "You met with Sadat to negotiate the end to the Yom Kippur War?"

"Yeah, somebody had to do it," said Hal with a smile. "I walked into that meeting with my twelve-year-old, thirty-nine dollar, off-the-rack suit, my six dollar shoes from Sears, and my Timex watch. I was so scared that I thought I was going to puke my guts out but I did what Jack had told me to do, I acted like I owned the damn country. I pointed my finger in the face of the most powerful man on the African continent and told him just what was what."

"How did Sadat respond to that?" asked Mahoney.

"He actually responded quite well. I, on the other hand, was convinced there was no chance in hell that neither Boulos or I were going to make it out of the country alive," said Hal.

"What did you tell him?" asked Mahoney.

"I told him that we knew the Russians were supplying them with weapons and ammo," said Hal. "He looked at me with this sort of smug look and said that he knew we were supplying the Israelis with the same type of equipment. Then I leaned across the table just like Jack had told me to and I told him that the only reason we were supplying the Israelis with conventional weapons was because that was the only way we could keep them from launching their nuclear missiles at Cairo." Hal paused for a second, "Sadat's face went sort of white and the tone of the meeting changed right then and there. After that I really started having fun."

Mahoney looked at Hal with a an expression of shocked disbelief, "What was the outcome of the meeting?"

"I kept it within the lines that Kissinger and Jack had laid out. I told him that he would agree to a meeting in Geneva to negotiate a cease-fire and then he would start working with us to help bring peace to the region. He would participate in the peace accords that Kissinger had outlined and that Egypt would become a friend and an ally to the U.S."

"How did he respond to that?" asked Mahoney.

"Nobody likes it when the big bully comes into your yard and starts telling you what to do," said Hal sympathetically. "When Sadat refused the terms I laid out, I told him that if he didn't cooperate, the Americans were going to take their promise to supply conventional weapons to Israel and go home. I told him the Arabs and the Israelis then could play with their nuclear weapons in their own sandbox but we weren't going to be involved. We couldn't be involved because if we and the Russians were, it was going to go global very, very quickly. He hadn't realized how close the Israelis were to launching a tactical nuclear attack. Once he did, and understood that we were willing to pull out of the conflict altogether, he became very interested in what I had to say."

Mahoney glanced at Hal, "And you were . . .?"

"Scared shitless," interrupted Hal. "Even after Sadat agreed to meet in Geneva, I still felt as if Boulos and I had less than a fifty/fifty chance of getting out of Egypt and back to Greece alive."

"But you obviously made it out just fine," said Mahoney.

"Oh, just fine," said Hal. "Sadat couldn't kill the Americans messengers and expect the U.S. to live up to their end of the bargain. I probably knew that but that wasn't uppermost in my mind at the moment. This little ol' no-account, small-town boy from Illinois had just poked his finger in the face of one of the world's most powerful men and told him how it was going to be," laughed Hal. "If Sadat had found out that I was a $600-a-month employee with the Secret Service, he probably would have done us in right then and there. And because I was young and cocky, that wasn't the end of it."

"There was more?" asked Mahoney.

"Yeah, the meeting went faster than expected and we had several hours before our flight out of Cairo so before we left Sadat's office I told him that I had never been to Egypt before and I wanted to see a pyramid."

Mahoney laughed, "What did Sadat say?"

"He turned to his aide and said in Egyptian Arabic, which I didn't speak but Boulos did, 'Take these two out to the pyramids' and then after a long pause, he said, 'and bring them back'. So we were assigned a guide and a car and we drove out and saw the Giza Pyramids and the Sphinx."

As they approached an intersection, Hal pointed to a bus bench and said, "Let's sit down for a moment, Mike." He winced in pain as he slowly sat. "We flew to Athens that evening and met Jack there. After we gave him our report, he called Kissinger who had set up a meeting for us with Israel's Prime Minister Golda Meir in Tel Aviv. So the next morning Boulos and I were on the early flight over to Israel.

"Didn't Golda Meir have pretty strong ties to the U.S.?" asked Mahoney.

"Very strong," said Hal. "She was born in Russia but grew up and went to high school in Wisconsin."

"And you actually met with her?" asked Mahoney. "If Kissinger already had ties with her, why didn't he take that meeting?"

"She was in the middle of a huge attack, she wasn't able to leave her country and Kissinger didn't feel he was the right person to deliver the message, especially after he heard about our success in Cairo."

"What message were you delivering to Prime Minister Meir?" asked Mahoney as he sat down on the bench next to Hal.

"Essentially the same as we had given to Sadat, that she needed to agree to a cease-fire or we were going to pull out and leave Israel to the Arabs and the Soviets."

"What was her response?" asked Mahoney.

"Golda Meir," said Hal as a warm smile came to his face, "reminded me of my best friend's grandmother when I was growing up. She was warm and loving yet sharp as a tack and tough as nails. When we met with Mrs. Meir, there was no table between us, we sat in chairs facing each other. When I told her we were pulling out if she didn't agree to peace, she leaned forward and placed her hand on mine and said, 'You and I both know the Americans cannot and will not let Israel fall to the Soviet Union.' When I tried to get tough and tell her we would rather Israel fall to the Soviets than engage them in a global nuclear war, she smiled and asked me where I was raised, if I was married and if I had any children."

Mahoney laughed, remembering his own grandmother. "What was the outcome?"

"When she was done playing me for the fool that I was, she patted me on the arm and told me she thought I was a good man with good intentions. She knew I was way out of my league. Then, as she led me out the door, she said something like, 'You tell Henry that I will come to his little meeting in Geneva and I will help him with his so-called peace plan. But you make sure he understands that his plan had better have some real teeth to it.' The way she said it left me far more frightened of her than I was of Sadat."

"As I recall," said Mahoney, "that war only lasted a few weeks so your efforts must have paid off."

"We, I mean Jack, Kissinger, Boulos and I, thought that we had once again saved the world," Hal said while looking up towards the stars. "We felt pretty confident that if we could get everybody together we could initiate a cease-fire and a peace plan that would work."

"Didn't it?" asked Mahoney.

"The cease-fire that was negotiated in Geneva lasted almost twenty-four hours and when it blew up, it blew up big. The Israelis were probably the first to violate the cease-fire, but we'll never know for sure. When the fighting resumed, Brezhnev sent a letter to Nixon telling him that both the Soviets and the Americans should step in and force the observance of the cease-fire and if we would not do that, the Soviets would be compelled to back up the Egyptians. Then, to make his point clear, they started moving airborne divisions, troops, and ships into the area. Nixon responded with the same, we moved to Defcon Three. By the 25th of October of 1973, the world was at the brink of a world war again between us and the Soviets."

"How close did we come to that?" asked Mahoney.

"We were much closer to a nuclear confrontation in October of '73 than we were during the Cuban crisis." Hal put his index finger and his thumb close together, "Just that far away from the big boom."

"How did it get resolved?" asked Mahoney.

"The gutsiest move I ever saw," said Hal with a shake of his head. "Jack and I flew to Cairo on one of Ari's big jets. I requested five minutes with Anwar Sadat which, after a few hours, he grudgingly gave us. When he and one of his aides walked into the room, Jack took off his hat and glasses and said, 'Mister Sadat, I'm Jack Kennedy. I'm here to stop this war and I need your help.' Sadat nearly fainted," laughed Hal.

"Geez," said Mahoney. "Are you serious?"

"Dead serious," said Hal. "The war had reached a critical point. The Israelis had a huge division of the Egyptian Army trapped and were poised to annihilate them. The Soviets were planning a rescue mission at Sadat's request, and the Americans were ready to back up the Israelis if they were attacked by the Soviets. On top of all that, Israel still had its trigger finger on the button of their missiles if things didn't go their way. Jack knew we were heading down the wrong road fast he decided that the process had to be stopped, even if it meant exposing himself to Sadat and the rest of the world."

"But didn't you tell Sadat in the earlier meeting that he needed to comply with the U.S. or we would back out of the region all together?" asked Mahoney.

"I did," said Hal. "But that was before the Russians came boiling over the hill with all their support. If we would have backed out at that point, you'd be buying your gas from Kominski Oil rather than Texaco, they'd have taken over the entire region and two-thirds of the world's oil reserves."

"So what was Kennedy's solution?" asked Mahoney.

"Kennedy saw an opportunity. He told Sadat that he would save his army, which at that point was out of food, water, and gasoline, if Sadat would break all ties with the Soviets and help him restore peace to the Suez Canal region."

"And Sadat agreed?"

Hal struggled to his feet, "Let's start back, these damn mosquitoes are chewing me to pieces. Yeah, he agreed, he really had no choice. His army was trapped and about to be obliterated." Hal glanced at Mahoney, "There was that, and the fact that Sadat was a fairly superstitious man who had just talked with the ghost of an American President."

"Sadat didn't really believe Jack was a ghost, did he?" asked Mahoney.

"I don't think so but the drama seemed to influence his decision making," laughed Hal. "Once Sadat agreed, I borrowed a phone and called Kissinger who, in turn, called Golda Meir and convinced her to allow non-military supplies to reach the Egyptian Army while he negotiated a real, sustainable cease-fire. She agreed and the crisis was effectively over. Egypt sent the Soviets packing and convinced Syria, the last big Soviet foothold in the area, to do the same."

Mahoney reflected for a few moments before asking, "After the Yom Kippur conflict ended, what was the backlash from your end?"

"Well, let's see," said Hal. "I guess I'd have to say that we pretty effectively cut the Soviets out of the Middle East and really pissed off Brezhnev . . . again."

"Was there any communication between Kennedy and Brezhnev during that conflict?" asked Mahoney.

"None, we reached out to him, sent a few messages asking for his advice, his opinion and his cooperation but he never responded."

Mahoney turned with a quizzical look, "That seems odd, any idea why not?"

"I have to believe he was still angry with us over the fact that Nixon gave the *K-129* submarine photos to the Chinese," said Hal bluntly. "When he didn't respond to Jack's requests to talk about the situation in Gaza, we responded by cutting them out of the region."

"Wasn't Kennedy worried that he might need a working relationship with them in the future?" asked Mahoney.

"Concerned, yes. Worried, no," said Hal.

The two men walked for a block and a half, each deep in his own thoughts, Hal thinking about the past and Mahoney thinking about the future and how best to structure this amazing story.

"I haven't told you much about Jerry Ford," said Hal suddenly.

"You mentioned earlier a link between Ford and Kennedy," said Mahoney.

"Yeah, Ford was a good guy, a good American, and a pretty smart bastard as well," said Hal. He stopped again to catch his breath.

"Most historians wouldn't classify Ford as a 'smart guy'," said Mahoney.

Hal smiled, "Most historians wouldn't classify Jack as alive after November, 1963. Ford was a master at playing the bumbling country farm boy from Michigan. He loved to say things like, 'Well I don't know how you all do it in Washington but back in Grand Rapids we look at things a little more simple.' He played that every day of his public life as a way to throw his opponents off track. The truth was that Ford was a brilliant tactician and a really bright politician who got more accomplished than history has given him credit for."

"Did he know that Kennedy was alive?" asked Mahoney.

"Yeah, he was in the original group that Jack brought together to help plan the assassination. Ford was brought in originally as the liaison for the House of Representatives. Later he convinced Johnson to appoint him to the Warren Commission."

"You mentioned earlier that the Warren Commission was set up to stop people from chasing rabbits down conspiracy-theory holes," said Mahoney. "Didn't President Johnson set it up?"

"Yeah, the commission was a special task force set up by Johnson to investigate the assassination. But Jack always knew it would be set up and who many of the players would be because while Johnson set it up and made the appointments, he was doing so under the advice of the Secretary of Defense, the Attorney General, and other 'advisors' who were steering him in the wake of Kennedy's death. The Warren Commission was set up by Johnson but almost all the appointees were chosen months before Dallas."

"Jesus," said Mahoney as they slowly walked down the street. "I'm starting to get a completely different view of how Washington really works."

Hal smiled, "It's all about steering others to do what you want them to do."

"I'm beginning to see that," said Mahoney. "So Ford's task, along with others was to steer the Warren Commission to a set of findings that would help dispel all the conspiracy theories that kept cropping up, right?"

"Right," answered Hal. "And as I said before, they didn't end up doing a very effective job; but keep in mind, they didn't have a lot to work with."

"What do you mean?" asked Mahoney.

"Well, remember that the dead president wasn't really dead, the fake assassin who was supposed to confess that he was the lone killer *was* dead, and the chairman of the commission, Chief Justice Earl Warren, wasn't in the loop, he never knew Jack was alive. Then the CIA got involved when somebody discovered a link between Oswald and the agency. They panicked and destroyed all the records pertaining to Oswald's recruitment and his training.

That move was misinterpreted as possible collusion between the agency and the assassination. What was supposed to be a fairly open-and-shut case turned into a worldwide controversy that continues to this day."

"Did Kennedy and Ford communicate with each other?" asked Mahoney.

"Not in what you might call, direct terms," answered Hal.

WASHINGTON D.C.
June 12, 1976

At forty-three years of age, Donald Henry Rumsfeld was the youngest Secretary of Defense in the nation's history. The Eagle Scout from Winnetka, Illinois, had quickly ascended from a stint as a naval aviator to an administrative assistant for Ohio Congressman Dennison and from there to his own seat in the U.S. House of Representatives. He served under Nixon as an economic advisor and as Ambassador to NATO and was called back to the White House by President Ford to serve as his Chief of Staff. In October of 1975, Rumsfeld became the Secretary of Defense and he was now seated in front of Ford's desk in his personal office waiting for the president to get off the phone.

Gerald Ford hung up the phone then half stood and reached across his desk to shake Rumsfeld's hand. "Don, thanks for coming over on such short notice."

"You said you had a special project you needed to run past me, what's up?" asked Rumsfeld

"I need to send a special message to somebody, a show of force, I guess. I need it to remain strictly off the record and top secret."

"What message would you like to send and to whom?" asked Rumsfeld.

"The 'who' is the secret part," said Ford. "The message would be something short and simple."

"What exactly do you have in mind, sir?"

Ford stood and walked around his desk, "How do I go about ordering a flight of four fighter jets to fly a secret mission over an island in the Mediterranean?"

"As long as you don't plan on actually attacking an island flying a foreign flag, you would just need to let me know what you have in mind. I'll do a risk scenario for you to let you know what the ramifications of buzzing another country might be and then we'll get it up to SECNAV to put it together," said Rumsfeld.

Ford reached for a yellow legal pad on his desk and tore out the third page. "Here are the coordinates and the date. I don't need a risk scenario, I don't need SECNAV involved, or any other hoopla. Just find a squadron to fly the mission and never speak of it again.

Rumsfeld took the paper from the President and looked at it. In the President's handwriting were the instructions:

Noon local time, 4 July, 1976
38°41'35.00"N 20°44'54.00E

"Where is this, sir?" asked Rumsfeld.

BOCA RATON, FLORIDA
Present Day

"When you say they didn't communicate in direct terms," asked Mahoney, "you mean to say that they did communicate, right?"

"I spoke with President Ford a few times and through my contact with the Secret Service I spoke with his people when necessary. I don't know that Ford and Kennedy ever spoke a word to each other after November of '63. I think Ford wanted to maintain a distance from Jack because he understood the repercussions if Jack was ever discovered. But at the same time, Ford had very clear knowledge of many of the projects we were working on around the world and the relationships that we were trying to establish. He received reports, written by Kennedy, detailing the relationship with the Russians before and after Khrushchev's plot and also before and after the *K-129* incident. And he knew how Nixon's involvement had changed that relationship." Hal looked at Mahoney, "I know he had that report because I personally handed it to him and then I spend two hours the following day talking it over with him and answering his questions."

"Were you the go-between for other presidents?" asked Mahoney.

"No, just Jerry Ford," answered Hal. "Contact with others were much more direct."

Mahoney smiled, "Which others?"

ABOARD *USS AMERICA,* AEGEAN SEA
4 July 1976, 0600z

"What in the hell are we doing up so early, Rob?" asked Lieutenant Jerry Van Engen as he stumbled into the ready room.

"We're doing what we do best," said Robert Johnson, Commander of VFA-143, the *Pukin' Dogs.* "We're making noise and going fast." Van Engen was the last of the eight airmen to arrive in the squadron's ready room. "Glad you could join us, Jerry."

"Can't we make noise after ten-hundred hours?" asked Van Engen as he fell into a seat in the third row.

Johnson walked over to the door and closed it. "Gentlemen, this is a highly classified mission that comes from the top," he said. "Somebody in Washington wants us to show off our muscles to somebody in Greece. Our orders are to fly in undetected, under the radar, then pop up and show somebody that we can easily get to them if we need to. We'll begin launching at 0800. Once in the air, we'll fly a course of three-four-zero until we rendezvous with a tanker out of Aviano that will be towing a flight of F-4's tucked up close enough to her so that she shows-up on radar as only one aircraft. After we refuel, we'll dive for the deck, one at a time; as we do the F-4's will come off the wing and replace us making it look like we are remaining with the tanker. We'll fly due east under the radar and hope nobody is paying too close attention.

"Ground or air threats?" asked Lieutenant Commander Mike Giltzow.

"We don't believe there are any defensive sites near our objective either air or ground. It's a pretty worthless piece of earth from a strategic point of view. I hear the fishing's pretty good but let's not find out today," said Johnson with a smile.

"And that's all we know at this point?" asked Giltzow. "We're going in just to show somebody we can?"

"Mike, you're new to the squadron. *The Dogs* are called on occasionally to fly these missions. We go in, we intimidate or piss somebody off, and we never speak of it again. This is one of those missions. I doubt we'll ever know what the message is that we are sending or who it is being sent to, but it is not our question to ask. Today, we are just our nation's mailmen."

"Fair enough," said Gitzow.

WASHINGTON, D.C.
Present Day

Purely out of curiosity, Lori Harris clicked on the link that coupled her computer to the listening device in Hal Rumsey's home in Boca Raton. When the link became active, she was surprised to hear two men talking. Their voices were clear and easily understood.

"Care for another cup of coffee?" asked a voice.

"I don't want to overstay my welcome. Are you feeling up to chatting a bit more?" said the other.

"I'll let you know when I've had enough."

"Then I'll take another cup. Here, let me help."

"Sit your ass down, I'm still able to get coffee for my guests," said the older sounding voice.

"Okay, okay, just trying to help," said the other man. "What about Jimmy Carter?"

"We didn't have any communication with Carter," answered the older man. "But we did bail his butt out of the Iranian Hostage Crisis."

Lori Harris picked up the phone and dialed the number for McQuade.

"McQuade," he answered gruffly on the second ring.

"Deputy McQuade, this is Lori Harris over at the NSA again. Your link in Boca Raton is active."

"What the hell does that mean?" he asked in an irritated voice.

"If you will go to the link I emailed you, you can listen to what is being said in the home right now, sir," said Harris with all the patience and kindness she could muster.

"Are they talking?" barked McQuade.

"Yes, sir, the link is active," repeated Harris. She heard a click and the line went dead.

McQuade searched for the email from Lori Harris and quickly found it. He opened it, clicked on the link embedded in the email and was amazed when, within just a few seconds, a digital audio meter appeared. He was even more amazed when two seconds after that, he heard the voices of two men. This type of technology never seemed to work for him.

". . . and then Ari died," said one of the voices.

"From what?" asked another voice.

"Complications from surgery was the official reason. But he had been so depressed after Alex's death that his health had simply gone to hell. We tried to get him to get some help and Christina tried to spend more time with him but he just wasn't able to be happy again after his son's death."

"So you think depression was a contributing factor in his death?"

"It was a huge factor."

"How did things change for you guys after that?" asked the younger sounding voice.

"After his death, Jackie couldn't get out to the island to see Jack as easily or as often as before. Their relationship had been strained for years but at that point, it really started to fade. The two of them got along just fine but they were living such different lives and they were drifting apart. Both of them knew it. I don't think either of them wanted it but those were simply the cards life had handed them," said the first voice, seeming to reflect a note of sorrow.

"You said a few minutes ago that Kennedy bailed Carter's butt out during the Iran Hostage Crisis. How did he do that?"

McQuade sat up in his chair, he hoped this was being recorded.

"It was simple maneuvering. All sorts of diplomatic negotiations had been unsuccessful and there was the disastrous rescue attempt by the military. Finally, after those poor hostages had been held for more than a year, we came up with a plan. We threatened the Ayatollah Khomeini, without any authority to do so. We told him that if they didn't release the hostages, Reagan would fully support an attack from Iraq by Saddam Hussein. The Iranians refused to have it appear as if they were surrendering to Carter after the failed rescue attempts and all the threats so we agreed to allow them to release the hostages after Reagan was sworn in as President.

"Did Kennedy deal directly on that one as well?" asked the second voice.

"No, it was Boulos and me again. We were getting pretty good at allowing people to believe that they were dealing with somebody from high inside the White House but Jack wasn't even talking with Washington at the time. We were acting completely on our own and we should have known that would eventually backfire on us."

McQuade leaned back in his chair and smiled. "I got you, you bastard," he said out loud. Hal had used the name that proved he had violated his oath of secrecy.

OVER THE ADRIATIC SEA
4 July, 1976 10:00z

"Pacer flight, your tanker is three-five-zero at two hundred miles," the radio crackled interrupting the conversation Commander Johnson was having with Van Engen, his Radar Intercept Officer.

"You got him, Big Guy?" Johnson asked his RIO, using his "call sign".

"I've got our tanker at three-four-nine degrees, a hundred and ninety-seven miles, closing at a bit over six hundred," said Big Guy.

RJ keyed his radio microphone, "RJ has the tanker."

The controller in the E-3 Sentry, a Boeing EC-137 that was essentially a flying control tower, answered back, "RJ, contact Mobil One-Five at two-thirty-five point one."

"Two-thirty-five point one, roger," said RJ.

The flight of four F-14's continued north on an absolutely beautiful morning. Below them the Adriatic Sea was an incredible shade of ultramarine blue, the skies were clear and at 21,000 feet there was nearly zero turbulence. At a hundred miles, Big Guy watched on his AWG-9 radar as the big tanker started a lumbering 180-degree turn to take up a northerly course ahead of and just below them. Five minutes later they could see the odd-looking KC-135, its normal silhouette disfigured by the four F-4 Phantoms that were tucked in close behind her wings.

"Mobil One-Five," said RJ, hailing the tanker. "Navy Pacer flight has four thirsty Tomcats coming up on your six."

"Pacer flight of four, you are go to refuel," came the reply from the tanker.

"I'd never admit it to their face," said Big Guy, "but those Air Force jocks can sure fly formation."

RJ maneuvered his Tomcat up to the refueling boom and connected on the first attempt. After topping off his tanks, he slowly backed off on the throttle and allowed his aircraft to drop 50 feet in altitude and drift just to the left of the formation. The F-4 pilot flying on the outboard side of the left wing gave him the thumbs up then dropped back towards him. RJ pushed his stick forward, putting his F-14 into a 65-degree dive towards the sea. Forty-five seconds later, he pulled back on the stick and leveled the big jet at 40 feet above the ocean heading due east at 250 miles per hour. Eight minutes later, the three other Tomcats had joined him. They accelerated to 500 miles an hour and headed for Greece.

SKORPIOS ISLAND
July 4, 1976

It was the noise that first caught his attention. Hal looked up from his five-month-old issue of *Life* Magazine and squinted against the sun to see what could be making such a sound, like a rolling thunder but steady and growing. As the noise continued and grew, he stood and walked to the rail of the balcony where his view to the north and the west was unencumbered. The island's largest mountain blocked his view to the east. Hal looked down to where

Jack was repairing a torn sail off the *Honey Fitz Two* and saw that he had also stopped what he was doing and was standing and gazing out across the sea.

They appeared to the north, flying low out beyond Skorpidi Island, the smaller island that lay off the bay of Skorpios. Four fighter jets in a tight V-shaped formation were banking around from the east and lining up on Skorpios. As their wings leveled, Hal guessed that they were no more than a hundred feet off the water and approaching at a fair speed. He quickly looked back at Jack who stood watching their approach over the trees and he realized there was nothing he could do to protect himself or his friend. The fighters burnt up the three-mile distance from their turn to the island in just over a half a minute.

Hal could easily see the missiles hanging below their wings but he couldn't tell if the aircraft were friend or foe. The fighters were strange-looking with twin tails and angular intakes, unlike any of the American fighters he had seen. The sun glistened off the canopies and the shimmer of the super-heated exhaust they left in their path made the jets seem to move slower, yet there was no time to run, no time to hide, or even to duck. Hal stood frozen, expecting the missiles to launch towards them at any second. This wasn't how he had expected to die.

As the aircraft crossed the beach, one of the middle two pulled up abruptly flying almost straight up while the other three fighters continued straight and steady across the island. The noise from the single ascending jet's afterburners vibrated through Hal's body. It was the loudest sound he had ever heard. Then, as quickly as they had appeared, they were gone.

"What the hell was that?" Hal yelled at Jack who was standing with his mouth open staring up at the sky.

"Those were the new Navy F-14s," Jack yelled back.

"Ours? What in the hell were they doing?" asked Hal. He was holding onto the railing to keep his hands from shaking. It was the first time he had ever really felt true fear for his life.

"I think somebody, somewhere just wished us a happy Fourth of July, the Bicentennial" said Jack with a catch in his voice. "That was called the missing man formation. I think Jerry Ford may have just sent us a little salute, a message acknowledging that we are the missing man."

Hal calmed himself a bit, "They were Americans?" he asked.

"They were Americans," said Jack. "Damn right, they were Americans," he said in a breaking voice.

RJ broke radio silence as he climbed through twenty thousand feet, "Nice job, Dogs. Turn right to two-six-five, form up on me and let's get the hell out of here."

BOCA RATON, FLORIDA
Present Day

Hal handed Mahoney a cup of coffee and motioned for him to sit at the small table just off the kitchen.

"What backfired on you after the Iran Hostage Crisis?" asked Mahoney.

"'Backfire' might not be the correct word to use. After the release of the hostages there were rumors floating around about the secret negotiations that ended the crisis. President Reagan wanted to know who was responsible so when he reached the usual dead ends, he asked the CIA to look into it. They were able to find out that the negotiations had taken place between representatives of the Ayatollah Khomeini and an American and a Greek," said Hal. "All roads led back to Greece but they then ended there."

"Did they ever figure it out?" asked Mahoney.

"Eventually," answered Hal. "Remember, George H.W. Bush, Reagan's Vice President, had been the director of the CIA under Ford. Bush knew that somebody had an operation in Greece but he wasn't sure which faction of the government was running it."

"So how did it all end up?" asked Mahoney.

"I got a phone call one day, shortly after Reagan took office in the spring of 1981, from my old buddy Larry Wood. He said very bluntly, 'Reagan wants to talk with your principal'. I asked him how Reagan knew who my principal was. He said he didn't know how Reagan had found out but that he had identified him specifically by name and asked Larry to set up a meeting between the two of them."

Mahoney jotted down a note, "Did Kennedy really meet with Reagan?"

OTTAWA, CANADA
March 10, 1981

It seemed perfectly natural at the time, two grown men sitting in an upscale hotel room munching on cheeseburgers and french fries, slurping milkshakes and watching American television stations. It had been years since Jack had been this close to the U.S. He had dreamed of getting a good burger in Ottawa but was sadly disappointed. At the concierge's recommendation, Hal had walked three blocks to a burger joint aptly named, "American Burgers," and ordered two of their best deluxe burgers. It was a letdown.

Before the two men had finished eating, the phone rang, "Good afternoon, Hal, it's Larry. Rawhide is on his way down."

They scrambled to clean up the refuse of their meal but Hal had barely set down the phone when there was a knock at the door. He opened the door to see a fellow Secret Service agent who quickly and silently scanned the room then stepped aside. The man behind him stepped forward and thrust out his hand, "Hello, I'm Ron Reagan."

Hal shook the man's hand saying, "It's a pleasure to meet you, sir. I'm Agent Hal Rumsey with the Secret Service." He stepped aside and motioned for Reagan to enter the room and said, "Mister President, I'd like you to meet John Kennedy."

Ronald Reagan would later admit that in spite of the information he had received prior to the meeting, he hadn't really expected John F. Kennedy to be in that hotel room. It was just too much of a stretch to assume that Kennedy was still alive. Neither did he expect the former president, who was six years younger than himself, to look so fit and robust.

Reagan strode across the room, "President Kennedy, it is a pleasure to finally meet you, sir."

"The pleasure is mine, President Reagan. Please call me Jack. I'm a big fan."

"A fan of my political career or my acting career?" asked Reagan with a smile.

"I didn't know there was a difference," laughed Jack.

Reagan leaned forward and put his hand up to the side of his face as though he were sharing a secret, "I didn't get elected until I figured out that there wasn't a difference." Reagan laughed heartily and slapped Jack on the shoulder. "Call me Ron," said Reagan. "I've got to tell you, Jack, never in a million years did I ever believe I would be standing here talking to you. I'm a huge fan of yours as well."

"A fan of my politics or my acting?" asked Jack with a smile as he motioned Reagan to sit down.

"I heard you talk at Berkeley in the spring of '62. You said something that changed my life."

"Oh, what was that? asked Jack with a smile.

Reagan sat in the wing chair opposite Kennedy. "I was at a point in my life where I was frustrated by the status quo and the lack of change that was taking place in America. You were voted into office with such hope and promise but after a year, I couldn't see any real change taking place so I joined those who were openly speaking out against you and your liberal ideas."

"There were plenty of you," smiled Jack. "But the freedom to disagree is what makes our country work."

"I'm just now starting to understand that," said Reagan. "That day at Berkeley you told the story of the great French Marshal Lyautey who once asked his gardener to plant a certain type of tree on his property. The gardener objected, saying that the tree was slow growing and it would take a hundred years to mature at which Lyautey replied, 'In that case, there is no time to lose, plant it this afternoon.' You closed by saying something like, 'a just and lasting peace may be years away, but we have no time to lose. Let's plant our seeds of peace this afternoon.' That idea . . . that we may not be able to change the world today but we need to start now changed how I viewed politics. Probably more than any other single point, it inspired me to begin to think about how I could start changing the world."

"Well, thank you for sharing that with me," said Jack with great sincerity.

"Five minutes, sir," said one of the Secret Service agents stationed near the door.

"I'm sorry I don't have more time, Jack," said Reagan. "I promise I will find some time in the very near future when we can sit down and talk some more but as you know, time is precious in this job."

"How can I help you in the next few minutes, Ron?" asked Jack.

"I know you were somehow involved in the Iran Hostage negotiations and I believe you may have directly or indirectly had influence on several other events in that part of the world during the last several years," said Reagan.

"Those accusations might have merit," answered Jack.

"If thanks is due, then thank you for your help with the hostages and your service to the country," said Reagan. "The CIA believes there is a rogue element of the U.S. operating out of Greece that has been directly involved in several major events in the past ten years. They haven't yet identified who is involved in this group but they are looking and, if need be, I will be happy to urge them to redirect their efforts. I want to make certain that as we are moving forward, we keep communications open so we can work together rather than separately."

Jack grinned, "Ron, I have no knowledge of a rogue element operating out of Greece but I do sometimes hear things from sources that you and the CIA probably don't have access to, so I would be glad to pass along information to you through the Secret Service from time to time."

Reagan smiled back, "And how can I help you, Jack?"

Jack reached into his briefcase beside his chair and removed a white envelope with a single word printed in black ink on its front, "Cyclone". "If you would take a look at this, Ron, I think you will see that we have a rare opportunity before us. This outlines that opportunity and also presents what I feel is the best option to take advantage of the rare occasion we have to grow a tree of peace very quickly."

Reagan held the envelope in both hands as though it was a fragile object. "I will take a look at this after I meet with Prime Minister Trudeau. Will you be here this evening to visit a little more?"

"I have a dinner date with my daughter tonight," said Jack, "but I'd be happy to meet with you as early as you would like tomorrow morning."

"Great," said Reagan. "I'm much more of an early bird than a night owl. How about breakfast in my suite at five a.m.?"

Jack laughed, "That will work just fine. With the time change that's just about my bedtime."

"Then I'll have coffee and you can have a snifter of brandy," smiled Reagan as he stood to leave.

"That's a deal," said Jack as the two men shook hands.

Reagan stepped into the hallway and when the door to Kennedy's suite closed, he turned to the Service agent next to him and said, "Son of a bitch, I just shook hands with Jack Kennedy!"

BOCA RATON, FLORIDA
Present Day

"You were involved in Afghanistan, too?" asked Mahoney.

"Hal stared at the wall on the other side of the room. "Yeah, we were in the middle of the Soviet/Afghan war before the first shot was fired. We didn't really intend to be involved but found ourselves up to our necks in it. Then we found a unique opportunity within the war."

"How did the war come about?" asked Mahoney. "I don't really remember the details."

"The USSR had been providing support and aid to Afghans since the 1920s. At some point in the late-seventies they found their relationship with Afghanistan was weakening. The Soviets snuggled up closer to them and signed an agreement that promised military support if needed. Shortly after that agreement was signed a civil rebellion rose up against the reigning Afghan government. By the end of 1979, the Afghan leaders were in trouble, more than half of their army had either been killed or gone AWOL. They called on the Soviets for help. The Soviets figured they could run in there, kick the rebels butts, and be back home in a few months."

"And what opportunity did you guys see there?" asked Mahoney.

"We knew the USSR was broke. They couldn't afford to fight a sustained war but the Afghan rebels didn't have the money or weapons to survive very long either. Jack believed that if we could do something that would prolong the war and cause it to be very expensive, it could bankrupt and cause a break-up of the USSR."

"That actually happened," said Mahoney.

"Yes, that happened, but not all by itself."

"Okay," smiled Mahoney, "how did it happen?"

"We secretly funneled billions of dollars in aid and weapons into Afghanistan."

"*Charlie Wilson's War*," said Mahoney, referring to the book and subsequent movie about the Texas congressman.

"Charlie Wilson was the go-between who got all the credit for the Afghanistan effort, and we were fine with that," said Hal with a thin smile. "But make no mistake, it was Jack Kennedy's War."

"Were there discrepancies between Charlie Wilson's story and reality?" asked Mahoney.

"For the most part they were pretty close," said Hal. "In the early '80s, Charlie Wilson was a member of the House Appropriations Subcommittee on Defense which was responsible for funding CIA operations. He effectively lobbied congress for billions of dollars which were funneled into Afghanistan and used to kill Russians. That ultimately led to the victory there and became a major contributing factor in the fall of the Soviet Union."

"But he wasn't the brains behind the operation, is that what you're saying?" asked Mahoney.

"Charlie Wilson was being played like a fiddle but he stepped up and had the impact of a full orchestra," said Hal.

"And how exactly was he being played?" asked Mahoney.

"You gotta understand Charlie Wilson," said Hal. "This guy had an ego bigger than life itself and a heart the size of Texas coupled with a pea-sized brain. The guy would go to any lengths to help a child in trouble then leap into a hot tub full of hookers and cocaine. Then he would brag to the press about the hookers and cocaine and completely leave out the fact that because of his actions, two hundred kids in Nicaragua have a place to go to school."

"Interesting guy," observed Mahoney.

"A very interesting guy," said Hal. "But exactly the type of guy we needed in Washington."

"How did everything come together?" asked Mahoney.

"By the late seventies, Jack was more than fed up with Brezhnev. The relationship between the two of them had great possibilities early on but after the submarine incident with Nixon and the Chinese, their relationship cooled. Brezhnev may have even gone out of his way to seek revenge. It was about then that I was introduced to Gust Avrakotos, a CIA case officer, an American-born Greek who hated the Russians."

"Where did you meet?" asked Mahoney.

"It was in Athens. Gust recognized my American accent when I ordered a drink at a hotel bar and he struck up a conversation with me." Hal chuckled, "I had arranged a meeting in that bar with Boulos and when he walked in and saw me sitting with Gust Avrakotos, he absolutely froze. Boulos and Avrakotos had been exchanging information for several years and had a good working relationship.

Over the next few weeks, Gust, Boulos, and Jack built a plan. We identified Congressman Wilson as a possible ally in Washington and all we needed to do was to convince him to lay his career on the line in order to get the funding we needed."

"How did you manage that?" asked Mahoney.

"Part of it was Charlie Wilson's love of hookers and cocaine. Part of it was a rich Texas gal, Joanne Herring or Herrington or something like that who was a CIA operative of sorts.

"How did hookers and cocaine play into it?"

"Charlie loved to party; in fact, his nickname was 'Good Time Charlie,'" said Hal. "His opposition in Texas got word that he had been snorting coke in a Las Vegas hotel suite and they were trying to get him convicted on narcotics charges and thrown out of Congress. Jack had his brother, Teddy, make a few calls to some of the right connections and the case against Wilson melted away. Good Time Charlie knew he was beholden to somebody but we let him squirm around a bit and didn't tell him who was looking out for him."

"And the Joanne woman you mentioned?" asked Mahoney.

"Joanne was another interesting character," said Hal. "She was a wealthy Texas socialite who loved to throw over-the-top parties in Houston. Joanne had been introduced to and become close friends with the dictator of Pakistan, Zia ul-Haq, and had become sympathetic to the plight of the people of that region. Joanne knew the way to help the people of the Pakistan and Afghanistan region was to make their troubles better known in the U.S. They needed aid, military support, and money and she knew America had it all. As she started making noise to the wealthy people and prominent politicians she knew, she came up on the CIA's radar."

"But, her interests seemed to be based on humanitarian aid" said Mahoney while standing up, "the CIA just wanted to kick the Soviets in the balls. Why was the CIA interested in her?"

"There really wasn't much of a difference in the methods they would have to use to reach to their separate goals. To improve the plight of the people of a war-torn region, you had to stop the war. To stop the war, you needed a friend who was willing to give you lots of money and lots of big guns. I think Joanne understood that pretty clearly," said Hal.

Mahoney stretched his back, "And how did this Joanne woman get Charlie Wilson to step up to the plate?"

"They had known each other for years. She simply turned on her charm and either slept with him or assured him that this would be his road to the fame that he wanted so badly. If somebody had told Charlie that jumping off a cliff would get him a bestselling book and a hit movie starring Tom Hanks, he probably would have jumped before asking for any details. Once Joanne had him in her grasp romantically, she probably said something like, 'Charlie dear, you really need to come over to Pakistan with me to see what the bad Russians are doing to the poor little children over there.' They flew to Pakistan and toured an Afghan refugee camp full of people who had been injured by the Soviets, children with hands and feet blown off, men and women who had been tortured and disfigured by Russian soldiers. It was pretty gruesome. Before they left the country, Charlie met with the Pakistani leaders including Zia ul-Haq and promised them U.S. aid."

Mahoney stretched his back then sat back down at the table.

Hal continued, "When Charlie returned to the States, Gust Avrakotos approached him and told him that he was his guardian angels from the Las Vegas debacle and if he could help him obtain funding from Congress for the weapons needed, he could make sure that a lot of Soviet helicopters would get shot down and a lot of Russians would die."

"And he was obviously receptive to the partnership," said Mahoney.

"He was so excited about it that he went out, got drunk, and was involved in a hit-and-run accident in Washington that we had to clean up," laughed Hal.

"This guy was a real Boy Scout," said Mahoney.

"He was exactly the person we needed at the time."

WASHINGTON, D.C.
March 14, 1981

Ronald Reagan sat alone on a couch in the living room of the White House residence reading through the file that Kennedy had given him. It was still surreal to him that a few days earlier he had been speaking face to face with John Fitzgerald Kennedy. Now he sat reading a comprehensive plan, contrived by that same man, that meticulously sketched the fall of the USSR.

After the November election but before he took office, Reagan was briefed by then CIA Director Stan Turner. During their meeting, Turner had told him about the growing problems in Afghanistan and had also disclosed the possible existence of a faction, apparently directed by some U.S. agency other than the CIA, which was operating out of Greece or Turkey. A few days later, Reagan mentioned the unknown group to Vice President Elect George H.W. Bush who responded with a blank stare. When Reagan pressed former CIA Director Bush for more information, Bush commented, "I have nothing concrete to substantiate what I am about to tell you but I believe the group operating out of Greece may be led by . . . JFK."

Even after shaking the man's hand and talking with him face to face, Reagan still was having a hard time believing what his eyes and ears had told him.

Kennedy's plan was brilliantly simple. Start sneaking Stinger missiles into Afghanistan and train a few soldiers how to use them. The Stinger anti-aircraft missiles would give the Afghans their first real defense against the armored Soviet Hind MI-24 helicopters that had been killing the mujahedeen resistance fighters without opposition. Once the threat from the Hinds was neutralized, the plan called for supplying the Afghans with better arms than the World War II surplus rifles most of the mujahedeen carried. The resistance could then move men and materials through the mountains and build a real force to launch counterattacks against the Soviet.

Reagan frowned as he turned the page and found Kennedy's cast of players for the plan. The first person mentioned was Joanne Herring, the Houston socialite. Everybody who had campaigned in Texas knew Joanne, wife of oilman Robert Herring. Joanne was such an institution in the high society world of Texas that ignoring her during any campaign would spell certain defeat in that important state. Reagan had pegged her years earlier as a wealthy woman who had become bored with the country club scene and had embarked upon a mission to change the world. She supported whatever cause interested her, from saving the whales, to building a camp for foster children, to raising funds for single mothers. Her latest interest was helping the Afghan war refugees living in the squalid camps of Pakistan. Reagan was surprised, however, to read in the report that she was an operative for the CIA.

Herring's case officer was another 'character' according to his bio in the report. Gust Avrakotos didn't seem to fit the 'mold' of the typical CIA recruit. He was born in the small steel mill town of Aliquippa, Pennsylvania, the son of a soft drink manufacturer. The small photo stapled to his bio pictured a short, stout, serious man with a bushy mustache and wavy hair receding up his forehead. He looked more like a street smart Greek thug than the Princeton-polished and educated young men the CIA typically recruited.

The next major player in Kennedy's plan caused Reagan to pause. He couldn't say if he had ever actually met Good Time Charlie Wilson before but he certainly knew him by reputation. Charlie was a man known for his love of booze and women. His reputation made it hard to take him seriously but a note after his brief bio laid out the reason he was chosen. "Wilson is a viable choice because of his position on the House Appropriations Subcommittee on Defense, his existing relationship with Joanne Herring, his unmitigated desire to leave a positive legacy, and a need for intervention into his various legal matters ranging from suspicion of narcotics use to felony hit-and-run." It was clear that Kennedy saw him as a well connected Congressman who would be easily manipulated. Reagan smiled and nodded. In that light, Good Time Charlie probably made as much sense as anybody else.

The final major player to be identified was President Ronald Reagan. The bio in the file for Reagan was short, "President of the United States, January 1981 – ". The role of the President was almost equally as short, "Provide cover and distraction, remain informed but officially unaware". Reagan read this to mean, stay up-to-date on the operation while denying publicly that the U.S. was involved in Afghanistan at all. Interestingly, Reagan noticed that after the report's summary, there was neither a call for or even a request for Presidential approval of the plan. He picked up the phone on the table next to him and dialed the White House operator. "Will you connect me with Larry Wood over at the Secret Service?" he asked.

"Of course, sir, one moment please," answered the operator.

The phone rang twice. Reagan cleared his throat, certain that a receptionist at the building on Murray Drive would answer within seconds.

"Larry Wood," a voice came on the phone.

Reagan glanced at his watch, it was after 9:00 p.m. "Good evening, Mister Wood, I didn't expect you to be in your office at this hour."

Wood was shocked to hear the familiar voice on the other end of the line. "Good evening, Mister President. How may I help you?"

"I'd like you to pass on a message to our friends in Greece," said Reagan. "Tell them I approve of Cyclone."

"Yes, sir," said Wood. "I'll pass that on right away."

"Tell them I am here to help in any way I can," added the president.

"Yes sir, I will," answered Wood. "Have a good evening, Mister President."

"Good night, Mister Wood," said the president before the line went dead.

OKAP KHANA PASS, AFGHANISTAN
March 24, 1985

Daylight, thought Mushkai with dread. The snow had slowed their progress through the pass, they were still at least a mile from cover, and the entire group was completely exposed on the barren mountainside. Nobody spoke of the dangers the light of day brought with it. They all knew being caught out there by the helicopters spelled certain death. Mushkai urged his mules on faster and prayed that maybe on this day the helicopters wouldn't come.

The group of seventeen men each leading a string of at least three supply laden mules had started the fifty-mile trip out of Dowshi two days earlier. They could usually make the trip in two and a half days but the snow had slowed their progress. The Okap Khana Pass, with its narrow trails and steep drops was the most treacherous section of the trip. More than once, a string of mules had plunged to their deaths and taken vital supplies with them, but Mushkai wasn't worried about the steep embankments or the slick trail. He was much more afraid of getting caught in the open by the Soviets.

They plodded along in the cold, happy the sun hadn't yet reached them. There was still some protection in the shadows. Each man hoped the next turn in the trail would expose the summit of the canyon ascent where they knew they could rest in the security of the field of large boulders. There they could eat and even sleep for a few hours. The man leading the string in front of Mushkai slipped and fell to his knees again, it was clear by his constant stumbling that he was incredibly tired. There was nothing anybody could do for the man but encourage him along.

As Mushkai stopped and waited for the man to get back on his feet, he thought he heard something. "Move," yelled his friend Urat who was leading the string behind him.

Mushkai raised his hand to silence his friend as he looked up and down the canyon nervously. There it was again, the deep sound of an approaching helicopter, its engine and rotor noise bouncing off the canyon walls as it flew slowly, looking for targets on the trail below.

"*Shaitan-Arba*," or Satan's Chariot yelled Urat in a panicked voice when he heard the noise.

Mushkai moved quickly to the side of his first mule where he tugged at the straps holding the Silver Bullet, a new weapon that he had just been trained to use. Called a "Stinger" by the American who had trained him to use it, the new weapon was supposed to easily knock down the Hind-24 helicopters. Once the weapon was free from its straps, Mushkai stepped between the mules and hoisted the long tube onto his shoulder just as he had been instructed. He reached into a pouch hanging around his neck and pulled out the BCU, or battery unit, which he inserted into the hand guard. With the BCU inserted, the missile came to life and started emitting a low humming noise. Mushkai waited as he had been taught. "A good hunter is a patient hunter," the American had told them.

Lieutenant Vasya Drubich flew his big Hind helicopter down what had become known among the pilots in his squadron as 'Slaughter Alley'. Just ahead of and slightly below him he could see the helmet of Gunnery Sergeant Andrey Bondar who was searching from side to side looking for movement on the canyon walls. Almost every morning for the past several months, a Hind-24 from Drubich's squadron was sent down the Alley to find stragglers from the movement of the night before. Hunting had been good for the first few weeks when they found large groups out in the open in the daylight but the Afghans had changed their tactics and now moved along the trails of Slaughter Alley at night.

As Drubich swung his chopper around a bend in the canyon, he and Bondar saw the large group of Afghans at the same time. At least fifteen men and as many as fifty mules were stopped on the wall of the canyon only a mile from them. They were completely trapped, exposed out in the open with nowhere to run and nowhere to hide.

"Vashi, do you see the poor bastards?" asked Andrey.

"We'll swing around and come at them from the other side, it's a better angle," said Vasya. "They have nowhere to go."

"It's a gold mine, Vashi, make sure you turn on the camera," said Andrey in an excited voice. The squadron gunners had an unofficial pool going on based on the number of kills for the month. Getting even half of these men would put Andrey in the lead and he was sure they could kill them all.

Vasya swung in close to the group. He was not worried about the effect of the small rifles the Afghans might be carrying; the armor on his aircraft couldn't be penetrated by the toy guns of the mujahedeen.

Mushkai could see that the Hind wasn't going to strafe them on the first pass. They had come around the corner of the canyon below them at a bad angle, the pilot would fly by and attack on the next pass. Mushkai pointed the Silver Bullet at the passing helicopter and found it in the sight. Immediately, the missile let out a tone acknowledging that it had picked up the heat signature from the helicopter's exhaust. He took a deep breath as the Hind flew away from them, widened his stance, and pulled the trigger. The small launch rocket fired, carrying the Stinger missile out of the tube with a firm jolt that surprised Mushkai. Fifty meters out of the tube, the Stinger's large engine fired and propelled the missile at a speed of almost 1500 miles an hour. From the launch of the missile to impact with the left Klimov turboshaft engine took only seconds.

Vasya Drubich had just begun his sweeping left turn to bring the helicopter around for their attack when he felt a lurch and heard a loud bang. A barrage of warning lights lit up on the panel in front of him and the warning horns sounded in his headphones as the nose of the Hind dropped towards the ground. Vasya pulled the stick back to correct the attitude of his aircraft but the more he pulled back, the more the bird wanted to nose towards the ground. He jammed the left rudder pedal to the floor while slamming the stick full left in hopes of bringing the big Hind back into his control. Despite the pilot's best efforts, nothing worked. Vasya's beautiful aircraft continued to plummet toward the bottom of the cold and miserable canyon.

The men with Mushkai cheered as they watched the *Shaitan-Arba* fall to its death and burn 500 feet below them. "Keep moving to the top, there could be another," Mushkai warned.

Unknown to Mushkai, he was the first Afghan to shoot down a Hind-24 with an American-supplied Stinger missile. He was completely unaware that he had just fired the first shot in a war that was to become far, far bigger than he could have ever imagined.

BOCA RATON, FLORIDA
Present Day

Mahoney wrote feverishly in his notebook while the digital recorder on the table continued to pick up every sound. "Once you had all the players in place, did everything go as planned?"

Hal took another sip of his coffee before answering, "Nothing of the size and magnitude of Operation Cyclone could go exactly as planned. But with Jack at the helm, Reagan secretly greasing the skids behind the scene, Charlie Wilson aggressively campaigning for and successfully getting more funds, and Gust Avrakotos working with the mujahedeen, it came pretty close to Jack's plan for the first year or two."

"You called it 'Operation Cyclone'?" asked Mahoney while writing. "What happened after the first year or two?"

"Operation Cyclone became the largest and most expensive covert operation the CIA has ever undertaken," said Hal. "We got it started but as soon as the operation began showing success, everybody wanted to jump on the bandwagon. Top officials in the CIA jumped in to help. Other Congressmen and Senators wanted their names attached to it, even other countries wanted to contribute funds to support Cyclone. It became so successful and popular that Jack decided to completely back out of our end of the operation because one, we weren't needed any more and two, continuing to be involved might blow our cover."

"Did this Operation Cyclone really lead to the eventual fall of the USSR?" asked Mahoney.

"It was a major contributing factor. The Afghan war did indeed bankrupt them, it caused all sorts of political dissent within the

Politburo, and the deaths and other losses in the war killed what little morale the citizens of the USSR had left. Unfortunately, the operation did more than its share of damage in the U.S. as well."

Mahoney looked up from his notes, "What do you mean?"

"Cyclone was so successful that when the National Security Council approached Reagan a few years after the start of our operation with a scheme to sell weapons to Iran in order to get Iran to convince Lebanon to release six U.S. hostages, Reagan bought into it. After all, what could possibly go wrong?" said Hal with a grimace.

"Was that the Iran-Contra scandal?" asked Mahoney.

"Exactly, the idea was to ship weapons to Israel who, in turn, would sell them to Iran," said Hal. "Iran would then pay the Israelis who would send the money back to us and then we could divert those funds to help support the Contras, the anti-communist faction in Nicaragua.

"But something did go wrong?" said Mahoney.

"Yeah, the press found out that the White House was selling weapons to Iran, which was subject to a U.S. arms embargo. The public didn't care that the weapons were being sold to help secure the release of hostages or that the funds were being used to fight communism in Central America. All they wanted to know was who was going down for the crimes being committed by those at the very top of the house."

Mahoney stopped writing and looked up at Hal, "Did the crimes go all the way to the top?"

"I'm sure they did," said Hal. "The intent was good but a crime based on good intentions is still a crime."

"And you guys didn't have anything to do with the Iran-Contra affair?" asked Mahoney.

"We weren't involved or even consulted as far as I know," said Hal. "But we had sure made it look easy to pull off a big operation. I'm sure Cyclone had its share of influence on that 'arms for hostages' mess."

"Didn't a bunch of high-ranking people go to prison for the affair?"

Hal laughed, "Not even one. As I recall, ten or eleven were convicted of crimes but most of their convictions were overturned on appeal or on technicalities, and the other were pardoned by President Bush while he was in office. Hell, George Bush, Junior, selected a few of them, including Admiral Poindexter who was right there in the mix, as some of his top cabinet members. The good ol' boys club was and is alive and well. Washington, in an odd way, works because of that club."

Mahoney noticed that Hal's voice was trailing off, "I should probably get out of here and let you get some rest."

Hal smiled, "I hate to end this party so soon but I *have* been awake for more than an hour."

"I'll call a cab and get out of your hair," said Mahoney.

"I've got a spare room, you're welcome to it," said Hal

"Thanks, Hal, replied Mahoney. "I don't want to be a bother. And I've got the early flight out of here in the morning, seven a.m. I don't want to wake you in the morning."

"Hell, Mike, I'll be awake most of the night anyway. Go use the spare bedroom, it will be the second time it's been used since I moved in here."

"If you're sure I'm not imposing," said Mahoney with a serious look.

"Not at all," replied Hal with wave of his hand. "Everything you need should be in that bathroom, yell if you need anything at all."

WASHINGTON, D.C.
Present Day

McQuade picked up his phone and dialed Telleria who answered on the third ring but it didn't connect until Jose entered his security code. "Telleria."

"It's McQuade. We've got Hal and the reporter on tape talking about the Skorpios project."

"You damn well better have," said Telleria.

McQuade ignored the insubordination, "There's more. Both Hal and the *Post* reporter are staying at Hal's home tonight."

"So what in the hell do you want me to do?" asked Telleria in an irritated voice. "Go in there like John Wayne and start blasting?"

"I'm just passing on the information to you," said McQuade.

"Stick to the original plan, Deputy Director McQuade," said Telleria, his voice full of contempt.

"You're the pro," said McQuade, his tone implying that Telleria was simply a filthy killer.

"And don't you forget it for a second," said Telleria in a threatening tone. The phone went dead.

"Prick," said McQuade after hanging up the phone.

"Asshole," said Telleria.

SKORPIOS ISLAND
March 26, 1985

Jack sat at his desk in the main house struggling to understand the piles of paperwork associated with Christina's fortune. Ari had personally asked Jack to keep an eye on his only daughter and especially on the billions of dollars that would be trusted to a conservatorship after his death. Rumors had been flying around for years about Christina's drug use but they seemed to have escalated in the past several months. While Ari had asked him to keep an eye on his daughter should he die, he had given Jack no real power or authority to actually do anything.

Christina had recently given birth to a child with her fourth husband, Thierry Roussel, but according to Jack's sources, that marriage was on the rocks due to Roussel's affair with another woman. Even more disturbing, Christina had completely abandoned her duties with Onassis Shipping and was now asking for more money from the trust. Jack felt that he hadn't done justice to his friend's request so he was now dedicating himself to understanding more about Christina and her financial position before he met with her in person.

Jack had always liked Christina and had a warm relationship with her. Ari and Alex had been serious Greeks, competitive and driven while Christina had always been the comedian. She loved practical jokes and lively entertainment. Christina would have been just fine letting her brother run the serious shipping business while she had fun in the clubs and beach resorts of the world but life had come crashing down on her while she was in her early twenties. Her brother, Alex, was killed in a plane crash in 1973, her mother took her own life a few months later, and her father died in 1975. In a period of only 24 months, Christina had lost her entire immediate family and in her grief had been called upon to run the Onassis empire.

For several years Christina had done an excellent job at the helm of Ari's many companies. Jack had been impressed with her devotion to the business despite the constant turmoil of her personal life. He had helped where he could but it wasn't easy for him to work with her because of his need for secrecy and her need to be surrounded by good advisors.

Something had changed; Christina hadn't returned the messages he had sent to her. She had broken promises to visit him on the island and had become distant since the birth of her daughter, Athina. Jack wanted to believe that it was because she was a busy mother with a newborn baby but he was aware of the publicity generated by the media who followed her out to the clubs and photographed her with other men, obviously very drunk or stoned.

In the stacks of documents before Jack was a copy of Ari's 200 page will. Jack shook his head remembering the media frenzy. Word had spread from an 'unknown source', probably a person associated with Ari's company, that after Ari's death a feud had started between Christina and Jackie. As it turned out, Jackie was not even mentioned in the will nor was she paid a penny out of the estate because she was never actually married to Ari.

"Nothing?" The press couldn't accept that America's favorite daughter was getting nothing from the wealthiest man in the world. Finally, to placate the world, Christina agreed to disperse to Jackie $26 million of company shares, that Jack had rightfully earned while working for Ari, and call it a settlement from the estate. Jackie and Christina had never enjoyed the same close relationship that Jack and Christina had, but there was never a feud, not even a cross word between them.

Jack picked up Ari's will, opened it for the first time and thumbed through it. The first several pages discussed his leaving all his worldly possessions, with a few noted exceptions, to Christina. His personal money was to be put into a trust.

"They did it Jack!" yelled Hal as he ran into the house startling Jack.

"Jesus Hal. Who did what?"

"The mujahedeen, they shot down a Hind gunship with one of your Stingers!" said Hal in a victorious voice.

"I didn't know we had delivered any yet," said Jack as he closed the will and stood.

"Gust called, he said we have about twenty Singers in the country right now, actually nineteen now that one of our mule tenders has shot down a Hind," said Hal. "Imagine the surprise on that pilot's face when he saw that missile coming at him," Hal laughed.

"Don't laugh, Hal," admonished Jack. "Remember that somebody's son died because of our little plan."

"And don't forget that twenty or thirty brave Afghans made it home because of us," replied Hal.

"That's true. How about I buy you a vodka tonic?" asked Jack.

"You're on."

BOCA RATON, FLORIDA
Present Day

The alarm clock in Mahoney's room went off at 5:00 a.m. He rolled over and fumbled to turn off the alarm then lay quietly on his back, trying to force his eyes to stay open. There was a noise coming from somewhere in the house, it sounded like running water and he thought he could smell coffee and sausage. He threw off his covers and pulled on his pants before taking the four steps to the door and quietly opening it. In the kitchen, the lights were blazing, Hal was humming a song and flipping sausages in a large frying pan.

"What in the heck are you doing?" asked Mahoney as he emerged from the spare bedroom.

"Just what my mother taught me," smiled Hal. "I'm sending my guest off with a full stomach. You've got time to catch a quick shower if you want, then I'll drive you to the airport."

Mahoney scowled, "I'll call a cab, there's no need for you to go out at this hour."

"I've got a few errands to run," argued Hal. "I feel good so I'm going to get a few things done this morning and I may as well take

322

you to the airport on my way. You have ten minutes to shower," he commanded.

Mahoney shook his head, "Okay, Chief, "I'll be right back."

Hal was sitting at the small table just off the kitchen with a cup of coffee reading the morning newspaper when Mahoney emerged, showered and shaved, from the spare bedroom.

"You almost look respectable enough to be a *Washington Post* reporter," said Hal with a smile as he jumped up and headed into the kitchen. "Come sit down, I have eggs, sausage, toast, and coffee."

"Just a piece of toast and a cup of coffee would be great," said Mahoney as he sat at the table.

Hal stirred in the kitchen for a moment then brought a plate with the biggest breakfast Mahoney had seen before him in years. "I can't eat all of this," he protested.

"You've got about fifteen minutes before we have to go," said Hal ignoring the protest. "Traffic can get bad even at this time of morning."

Mahoney shrugged his shoulders and dug into the large plate of food. If the old man was going to cook it, the least he could do was try to eat as much as he could.

"I've been thinking, Mike," said Hal. "There's so much that we haven't talked about yet so I started making a list, an outline of sorts so we can get through it on the phone."

"Great, that will help keep us on task," said Mahoney between swallowing a mouthful of food and taking a big swig of his hot coffee.

"I wanted to ask you," said Mahoney, "in your opinion, how much did you guys influence the outcome of the Soviet-Afghan war?"

Hal sat down beside his guest with a fresh cup of coffee. "There are always hundreds of different factors to something like a war. I know that without our initial support, the Afghans would have fallen pretty quickly. We forced both sides into a long and costly war and a lot of brave Afghans lost their lives where they might not have if we had kept our noses out of it."

"But wasn't it for the greater good? Kennedy's plan kept the Soviets from gaining a foothold in that region and possibly using it as a stepping stone to the entire middle east, right?" asked Mahoney.

"That's the way it worked out. What I want to know is what the world would look like today if we had just sat on the beach and done nothing?" asked Hal.

Mahoney took a big sip of coffee, "The world is what it is today, for better or worse, because a lot of people didn't just sit around. Did you guys bankrupt the USSR and cause the breakup?"

"That's a question for the historians," said Hal, "but I believe we helped the process along."

SKORPIOS ISLAND
March 26, 1985

Jack opened his eyes and stared at the old clock beside his bed, it was still a half hour before daylight but he was wide awake. He swung his legs out of bed, pulled on a pair of sweatpants and a hooded sweatshirt and walked out into the main room where he was startled to find Nik Contos sitting at the dining table next to two large boxes. Contos had replaced Captain Papadopoulos as head of island security a few years earlier and had succeeded in making Papadopoulos look like a saint in comparison.

"What can I do for you on this fine morning, Niki?" asked Jack in Greek.

"I would like you to explain this to me?" he said, pointing to the boxes on the table.

"That looks like two boxes I have never seen before sitting on a very expensive table. If you scratched that table, I'll sand out the scratches with the skin off your ass," said Jack.

Contos ignored the threat, "An hour ago my men found these boxes at the dock, perhaps you know who delivered them?"

"What's in the boxes?" asked Jack.

"Beer," answered Contos with a tone of contempt.

"Beer?" asked Jack as he walked to the table with a look of surprise.

"Beer and this note," said Contos as he handed the piece of paper to Jack. Jack looked in the boxes to find about fifty bottles of Heineken Beer, his favorite.

The note simply said, "Happy Cyclone Season - Ron."

Jack smiled then turned to Contos, "I helped arm a group of Afghan rebels with Stinger missiles so they could shoot down Russian helicopters. The President of the United States sent me a couple of cases of my favorite beer to thank me."

Contos glared into Kennedy's eyes. He didn't believe the wild fabrication he had just been told. "No unauthorized deliveries to the island. The next time your friends from Nydri deliver beer, I will personally smash it."

"If you smash a single bottle of Heineken, there will be hell to pay," said Jack in a faked angry tone.

Contos stomped out of the room as Jack broke into a wide smile.

BOCA RATON, FLORIDA
Present Day

"We better get going," said Hal as he finished his coffee.

"I sure do appreciate all your hospitality, Hal," said Mahoney.

"I'm a little rusty at entertaining guests but you're welcome to come back again, I'll do better next time."

Mahoney retrieved his bags from the guestroom while Hal backed the car out of the garage and lowered the top. Mahoney carefully put his bags in the back seat and settled into the front passenger side.

"Where were we?" asked Hal in a chipper voice. He was feeling well considering a short night's sleep and the reaction he had had the day before.

Mahoney reached for his digital recorder, "I believe you had just dismantled the Soviet Union."

"They did it to themselves," said Hal as he backed out of the driveway. "We would have loved to have taken credit for their fall but in the end, it was economic failure combined with runaway corruption and general discontent among their people. The system was broken and nobody could fix it so in 1991, the whole thing collapsed. The separatists won out and there was a rush by the individual republics to become countries."

"The USSR as we knew it was gone, right?" asked Mahoney.

"Yeah, but as wonderful as that sounded at the time there were details of the breakup that nobody, including Jack, had thought through," said Hal as he swung onto the main road through the subdivision.

"Such as?" asked Mahoney.

"Like who was then in control of the Navy and their nuclear subs, the Army and their ballistic missiles? Who was making sure that a leader of a small, newly established country wasn't going to take the weapons stored in his country and try to take over the country next door?"

"And, as I recall, there was some fighting in Soviet Georgia," said Mahoney.

"Some of the civil wars in the new countries and fighting between some of the new countries still goes on today. Luckily, Russia was able to recapture most of the nukes and the U.S. was smart enough to stay out of it," said Hal. "Massive change doesn't come about without encountering some bumps in the road."

"But overall," asked Mahoney, "we are far better off with without the USSR, aren't we?"

"We questioned that for several years but things are improving there. Most of those former Soviet Republics have been countries only for twenty years now; the U.S. is almost 250 years old and we are still trying to figure it out," said Hal with a smile. "But to answer your question, yes. For fifty or sixty years, the USSR had a goal of expansionism that, if we hadn't of resisted them in Greece, in Korea, in Egypt, Turkey, East Germany, and Vietnam, they might have taken us down too."

Traffic was light as Hal turned onto Yamato Road. The sun was just starting to rise in the east and while it was going to be a hot and humid day, it was warm and pleasant at that moment. Mahoney closed his eyes, leaned his head back and let the wind blow through what little hair he had left as the big convertible accelerated down the road with a satisfyingly deep roar.

"What year did Christina die?" Mahoney asked after a few minutes.

"I believe it was 1988," said Hal.

"And that was due to a drug overdose?"

Hal rubbed the whiskers on his face, "I don't know for sure. She died in Buenos Aries. The official report listed the death as pulmonary edema which I think is water in the lungs. That may or may not have been due to a drug overdose. She was taking pills to lose weight, to sleep, to stay awake, and every other thing you can imagine."

Hal was quiet for a moment and then said, "She had spent a little time on the island in her last few years and had brought her baby, Athina, with her. Jack and I loved that little girl. We fought over who got to hold her when she was a baby and even when she grew into a toddler, we fought over who got to play with her. She had the cutest little laugh and loved to play hide and seek."

Hal shook his head saying, "It was pretty hard on both of us when Christina died. Jack tried to get her to clean up her life and get some help to straighten out her head but she had too many demons floating around up there. We rarely got to see Athina after her mother's death and when we did, she didn't remember us."

"It seems that Athina has grown up to be pretty level-headed," observed Mahoney.

"Yes," agreed Hal. "She seems to have generally shrugged off the money and fame and enjoys living a quiet life in Brazil."

Mahoney watched the city go by for a few minutes. He casually observed the people of Boca going about their early morning business as they passed grocery stores, used car lots, bus stops, and jewelry stores. Except for the palm trees, they could have been in any sprawling suburb in the country.

"Can you tell me about Jackie's death?" asked Mahoney quietly.

For a few moments Hal appeared not to have heard the question. Mahoney considered whether he dare ask the question again or change the subject.

"We had known for months that Jackie was pretty sick," said Hal. "I still remember the day we got the call from John Junior. Jack spoke with him for a few minutes then hung up the phone and told me he needed to go to New York. I arranged a helicopter to pick us up and a private jet to meet us at the airport."

"You went to see her before she died?" asked Mahoney.

Hal stopped at a red light. A young woman pushed a baby stroller past them in the crosswalk. She had one arm full of groceries and a three or four year old lagging behind her.

"Yeah," he said finally. "We went to see her before her final trip to the hospital. She asked to see us individually. Jack was in with her for almost two hours. He came out of the room and I remember him quietly saying that Jackie wanted to see me."

"And you got to visit with her?" asked Mahoney.

"I did," answered Hal. "She was sitting in a chair in the corner of her bedroom near the window. She was fully dressed, her hair was done and she was wearing makeup but she looked awfully thin and frail. I hadn't seen her in quite a few years and I was shocked by how much she had aged. Don't get me wrong, at 64 and dying from cancer, she was still stunning but she certainly had changed."

"May I ask what you talked about," asked Mahoney in a respectful voice.

"Jackie did most of the talking. She thanked me for my service to our country and to her husband. I thought it was noteworthy that she still referred to Jack, at least in my presence, as 'my husband'. She told me she had the years of wonderful memories of us together on the *Christina* and on Skorpios. Then she took my hand and said, 'Hal, I'm a better person for knowing you.' I suspected that might be the last time I would ever see her . . . she knew it was."

"How long was that before she died?" asked Mahoney.

"Less than a month," Hal answered with a catch in his voice. "She asked to come home from the hospital one day in the middle of May and she died the next day in her sleep. She died in her own way and in a place of her own choosing."

"Did you or Kennedy attend the funeral?" Mahoney asked.

"No, it was a media circus. There was no way Jack could have been there, even in disguise," answered Hal as the light turned green. "After she died, I remember Jack saying of his marriage to her, 'We had a one hell of a run, we just didn't make it to the finish line.'"

Mahoney made a brief note of the quote before saying, "Rose Kennedy died just a few months later, didn't she?"

"Yeah, Jackie died in May of 1994, Rose died in January of the next year," said Hal.

"And were you two able to make that funeral?" asked Mahoney.

"No, that again was a media blitz," said Hal. "Jack got a chance to spend a few days with her when we were in the States before Jackie died and then we spent Christmas in Hyannis Port the month before she died. Teddy called a few weeks before Christmas that year and told Jack that it was time to come home to see his mother."

"She was getting up there in years at that point, wasn't she?" asked Mahoney.

Hal smiled, "Rose was 104 when she died. She had a stroke about ten years before she died which left her wheelchair-bound and, at times, it was difficult to understand her. But at 104 she was still sharp as a tack and witty as ever."

"Was it difficult on Kennedy not to attend those funerals?" asked Mahoney.

Hal thought for a moment as he turned onto the freeway on-ramp. "Sure, it was. Jack was Catholic, they believe funerals are as important as baptisms and weddings, but he missed most of those as well. The one he couldn't miss was John Junior's."

As Hal accelerated up the on-ramp to the freeway, the noise increased and Mahoney feared that his digital recorder wouldn't pick up Hal's comments. He thought about holding it closer to Hal but worried that it might distract him and he really didn't want Hal to skip over this particular death."

"John Junior was killed in 1999 if I remember right," said Mahoney. "And you said Jack attended that funeral?"

"Yeah, Jesus, what a messed-up deal that was," said Hal in a heavy voice. "I remember getting out of bed that morning and getting the phone call from Teddy before my first cup of coffee. I assumed he wanted to talk to Jack but he said, 'No, I need you to break some bad news to him for me.' It was important to Ted that somebody close to Jack give him the news in person rather than him hearing it over the phone."

"And that task obviously fell to you," said Mahoney.

Hal responded somberly, "That task fell to me."

SKORPIOS ISLAND
July 17, 1999

Hal hung up the phone on Jack's desk then fell into the chair. He buried his face in his hands and wondered if somehow Teddy was wrong or if the authorities had been mistaken and had reported the wrong plane down. But hope as he might, he knew in the back of his mind that John Junior and his wife Carolyn were gone. His mind was in turmoil, should he wake up Jack or let him sleep? Should he arrange for a private jet for later that day or wait to see when Jack wanted to go back to the States? Should he make coffee or just go throw up?

He stood and walked blindly and thoughtlessly out to the veranda where he grasped the rail and, in his anger tried as hard as he could to shake it loose. "No, damn it, no!" he screamed under his breath.

"What's going on?" came Jack's voice from behind him.

Hal turned around, his face was white, the veins in his forehead and neck bulged and his eyes were swollen and teary. He tried to speak but the only sound that came out was a labored sigh of frustration.

"Hal, what the hell is going on?" asked Jack again, a concern in his voice.

"It's John and Carolyn" Hal forced out. "Their plane is down and presumed lost off Martha's Vineyard." Hal realized he hadn't delivered the message in the tone that Ted had hoped he would. He slumped down into the deck chair beside him.

Without a word, Jack walked back into the house and turned on the television. The first image he saw on CNN was that of a Coast Guard commander being interviewed and then the screen flashed to a file picture of John, Carolyn, and her sister Lauren Bessette above the word, "MISSING".

Jack turned back to Hal, "Who called and what exactly did they say?"

Hal took a moment to compose himself. "It was Teddy. He said that John's plane had crashed off Martha's Vineyard a few hours ago. A search was underway but they weren't expecting to find survivors."

Jack listened to the reporters for a few minutes. It was apparent they didn't know any more than he did. "Did Teddy say where he was?"

"Yeah, he was at Hyannis Port," answered Hal.

Jack started towards his desk then stopped and turned. "Hal, I'm going to call Ted. Can you make some coffee and then put the fastest jet you can find on standby?"

"Yes, sir," replied Hal as he started for the kitchen.

Hal put the coffee on to brew then decided to make some scrambled eggs and toast. From the other room he could hear the muffled sounds of Jack talking to his brother but he couldn't hear well enough to catch any of the conversation nor did he want to hear it. He still held hope that this was all a big mistake, that at any moment CNN would report that John, Jr., and his wife had decided not to fly out to the island until the following morning and had been found sleeping soundly in their New York apartment.

That hope was lost when Hal glimpsed Jack outside the kitchen window. He walked out towards the guest house then turned as though to walk down towards the water. He stopped and just stood still looking out towards the sea for a full minute. Then, Jack Kennedy, the greatest man Hal Rumsey had ever known, dropped to his knees and cried.

BOCA RATON, FLORIDA
Present Day

Mahoney was impressed by the ride of the nearly 50-year-old car on the freeway at 65 miles an hour. The morning wind blew his hair around but even with the wind, the roar of the engine, and the noise from the surrounding traffic, he and Hal could still hear each other.

"There were three services," said Hal. "There was a very private Catholic funeral mass in Hyannis Port; then, a public memorial service at the St. Thomas More church in New York. I went to that one but obviously Jack couldn't."

Mahoney looked over at Hal, "I was there, too. I'll never forget Ted Kennedy's eulogy. He said something like, 'we dared to think that this John Kennedy would live to comb gray hair but, like his father, he had every gift but length of years.' Did you sit with the family?"

"No," said Hal. I was just one of the hundreds who crowded in to pay my respects."

"We might have sat next to each other," said Mahoney.

Hal drove for a few minutes without speaking and then finally said, "A private ceremony was held aboard the navy destroyer *USS Briscoe* where they spread the ashes of the three kids at sea near the crash site. The navy did a great job of keeping everybody miles away so the family could mourn privately. The media never knew that the reason for the no-fly zone and the five-mile restriction around the *Briscoe* was because a father wanted to pay his last respects to his son."

"Did you go out aboard the *Briscoe* with the family?" asked Mahoney.

"No, I wasn't invited and I didn't ask," said Hal.

"How did Kennedy keep his presence aboard the ship a secret?" asked Mahoney. "There would have been sailors, members of the Bessette family and others. Wouldn't somebody have noticed him and said something?"

"I wondered that for a while too," said Hal. "The navy does a lot of things that never make the press. I'm sure they had it all figured out. Who would notice an old navy captain standing in the background?"

The two drove to the airport without further comment. Mahoney made some notes, he had some more questions he wanted to ask but he felt that for now, after talking about the deaths of Christina, Jackie, Rose, and John, Jr., he had harassed this sick old man enough. If Hal wasn't going to offer more information, Mahoney wasn't going to pry it out of him. There would be other days.

Hal smiled as he pulled to the curb, "Mike, you're always welcome in my home. But I'll shoot you if you scare me again like you did last night."

"Sorry about that, Hal," said Mahoney with a laugh. "I was worried about you."

"Well it wasn't necessary," offered Hal, "but I'm glad you stayed another night."

"You watch out for that crap they are putting in your veins. When's your next appointment?" asked Mahoney.

Hal frowned, "Tomorrow morning. Maybe I'll have that old hen from around the corner go with me. She'd like that," he said with a grin.

Mahoney opened his door and then reached across and shook Hal's hand. "I'm going to go back to Washington and start doing some research. I want to roll this story out in such a way that it is both believable and respectful to you and President Kennedy. I'm sure I'll have many more questions."

"Well, you call me anytime on that fancy new cell phone you gave me and if I can remember how to answer it, I'll tell you almost anything you want to know," said Hal.

"Almost?" asked Mahoney as he got out of the car and retrieved his bags from the back seat. With a laugh he said, "You aren't holding back information on me, are you Hal?"

"There will always be a few things the public doesn't need to know," said Hal in a serious tone.

Mahoney stood frozen in shock for a moment, "You have just told me the most fantastic story of the last hundred years and now you're telling me there is more?"

"Yeah, Mike, there is always more," said Hal.

"Can you give me a hint?" asked Mahoney.

"I shouldn't have said that much," laughed Hal. "And to a reporter! What the hell was I thinking?"

"You can't leave me hanging," said Mahoney in a begging tone.

Hal took his foot off the brake and started to idle away, saying over his shoulder, "Have a nice flight. I'll talk with you soon."

Mahoney stood watching Hal drive off in his classic convertible. "That son of a bitch," he said out loud. He turned to walk into the terminal when his cell phone rang, "Mahoney," he answered.

"Hi, Mike, its Bob. Where are you?" asked his editor Bob Blurton.

"I'm at the airport getting ready to catch my flight," he answered. "Did you get my message that I was delayed coming back?"

"I did," said Blurton. "Listen, there have been some new developments on your story. I need you to come straight to my office when you land, and don't talk to anybody about what you're working on."

"That sounds intriguing," said Mahoney as he approached an automated kiosk to get his boarding pass. "What's going on?"

"I don't want to talk about it over the phone," said Blurton. "Just get to my office as quickly as you can and keep your mouth shut."

Mahoney was curious. He and his longtime editor had never had this type of conversation about any story before. "Okay, I'll see you in a few hours."

Mahoney hung up the phone and started poking at the touch screen on the kiosk before him. Something big was going on and it felt as if he, Mike Mahoney, might be riding the top of the wave. He felt some of the excitement return that his years on the job had taken from him.

SKORPIOS ISLAND
May 29, 2006

It was the time of day on the island when the sun dropped just below the trees, the shadows were long and the entire earth seemed to let out a collective sigh of relief as the afternoon's heat was pushed out to sea by the cool evening winds. It was time to sit in the big comfy chairs on the veranda and watch the sea turn from an austere blue of the day to a bluish gray of evening and eventually to the black of night.

This particular evening was even more special. Jack watched the ocean change colors while he enjoyed a vodka tonic with a fresh lime, sitting in his favorite chair next to his daughter Caroline. After a long day of fun, sailing and swimming, Ed, Caroline's husband, and their children, Rose, Tatiana, and Jack, were relaxing in the guest house while Caroline and Jack enjoyed a drink on the veranda. It was Jack's 89th birthday.

"I have always loved these islands," said Caroline, resting her head back against the soft cushion of the chair.

"Yeah," said Jack. "One of these days I might move out here permanently."

Caroline laughed, "And the last forty-some years have been just temporary?"

"Has it been forty-some years already?" asked Jack. "I promised Ari that I'd only stay for a little while," he said. "Maybe I should think about kicking in to help pay the power bill or something."

Caroline grinned at her father's humor. "I should seriously consider moving out here full time. The thought of being insulated from everything that is going on back in the States is tempting."

"Things aren't as easy out here as they look," said Jack. "Just the other day I saw a boat going that way while another was trying to go that way," he said, pointing out beyond the anchorage. "It was like a damn New York traffic jam."

Caroline smiled. "At least you don't have 'W' in the White House creating wars, telling lies, and raising taxes."

"He's not all bad," said Jack. "If he would think a little more and talk a little less, he'd be fine.

"Sometimes I wonder if he thinks at all before talking or taking action," said Caroline.

"You know what I've always told you," replied Jack.

"I know, if you don't like the way the bus is being driven, drive it yourself," she said.

Jack smiled at the thought, "You would make a great president."

"I don't want to be president," said Caroline. "But we have got to find some way to change the course we are on. The Republican status quo has got to change."

Jack sat forward, "What's the inside line? Who are they going to run?" he asked.

"At this point, either Mit Romney or McCain depending on who catches the public eye."

"And the Democrats have Hillary?" asked Jack with a raised eyebrow.

"That's who they seem to be currently dancing around as their savior," Caroline answered.

"Jesus, where has the party gone?" he said, staring into his drink.

"We need Jack Kennedy," said Caroline in a very upbeat tone.

"I'm retired," said Jack wryly, "and dead."

"Yeah, I didn't really mean you," said Caroline with a wink. "What we need is a young, ambitious, and enthusiastic candidate who could run on the platform of renewed hope and change. We need the promise of a new Camelot and a new direction for the country."

"Okay," said Jack. "You go find the candidate, somebody with a fresh face, a squeaky clean reputation, and a pretty spouse and I'll help you put him in the White House."

"You know," said Caroline while standing up, "there is a junior senator out of Illinois who has been making some noise about running."

"What's his name?" asked Jack.

"Barack Obama," she said.

"Excuse me?"

"Barack Obama," she repeated.

"Is he Muslim? There's no way in hell that the American public is going to vote a Muslim into the White House right now."

"Dad," said Caroline with an eye roll, "He's black and I believe he's a Christian."

"Hmm," said Jack, rolling the ice around in his glass. "A black candidate might play well into the 'change the status quo' idea that you want to promote."

Caroline looked at her father for a moment, considering the possibility of helping to promote the next great president, an idea she found quite intriguing. "I'll do some research into his background and, assuming we don't find any major skeletons in his closet, I'll set up a meeting with him when I get back."

Jack laughed, "I can't believe you're ready to back a guy who has the most unfortunate name in the history of American politics."

"Dad!" said Caroline as she threw the ice from her empty drink at his feet. "You're horrible. Want another?"

SPRINGFIELD, ILLINOIS
June 12, 2006

Even at 46 years old, Senator Barack Obama didn't feel a day over eighteen. This had its advantages but he was occasionally shocked into reality when he thought about the big decisions he had made. He and Michelle had a home with a mortgage, just like grown-ups. He was regularly interviewed by the media and asked his opinion on important topics, just like grown-ups. And he had somehow convinced the Illinois voters that he was the best choice to represent them in the Senate.

He knew, deep down inside, that he was a responsible grown-up who made responsible decisions but he couldn't get over the fact that he still felt young and immature, a feeling that was becoming even more troublesome as he seriously considered running for President of the United States.

The phone rang as he tapped away at his laptop trying to find the right words to express his feelings on an editorial he had been asked to write. "Yes?" he answered.

His assistant Ashley paused, "I think it's Caroline Kennedy on line two."

Obama sat up straight, "You think it's Caroline Kennedy?" he asked.

"The woman said she was Caroline Kennedy. It sounds like her," said the young assistant.

"Okay," said Obama. He cleared his throat and punched the blinking line on the aging phone system. "This is Barack."

"Mister Obama, this is Caroline Kennedy," came a vaguely familiar voice.

Obama swallowed, "Well good afternoon, Miss Kennedy, it's a pleasure to speak with you."

"And you as well, Senator," said Caroline.

"What can I do for you, Miss Kennedy?"

"I have heard that you may be considering running for President in 2008," she said.

Still concerned about the true identity of the caller, Obama replied coolly, "I haven't made any final decisions, but why do you ask?"

Caroline smiled, she knew the game. Keep them guessing until you make your official announcement. "I represent a small but powerful contingent that is searching for a new, fresh face to back in the next election. If you're interested, I'd like to meet with you when I'm in Springfield next week."

"I'd be honored to meet with you," said Obama.

"Great, I'll firm up my plans and call you back to set something up. Is there somebody in your office who handles the scheduling?" she asked.

"If you would like to contact me directly, I'll get my assistant Ashley to move the sun and the stars to make something work out," he said in an enthusiastic tone.

"Great, I'll be in touch in the next day or two," said Caroline. "Have a nice day."

"You as well," replied Obama before returning the receiver to the phone.

Ashley rushed to his door when the light on line two went out. "Was that really Caroline Kennedy?" she asked.

"I . . . I think it really was," he said.

SKORPIOS ISLAND
August 13, 2006

Hal woke and rolled over to look at the clock beside his bed which showed 6:54 a.m. He debated whether to crawl out of bed or allow himself the luxury of slipping back to sleep for a bit longer. Before he could make the decision he remembered the significance of the day. He threw off the covers, swung his legs over the side of the bed, and sat there for a moment to allow his brain to catch up with his body.

"Seventy," he said to himself. "How in the hell did I get to be seventy?" Hal stood slowly, mentally scanning his body for the aches and pains a 70-year-old man should have but they weren't there. Forty years of working out every day, eating healthy food, and keeping up with Jack Kennedy had left him with the body of a much younger man. His vision wasn't as sharp as it used to be and sometimes his aging hearing missed a word or two of a conversation but his daily regimen of push-ups, sit-ups, and pull-ups, along with a brisk walk to the helipad at the top of the mountain combined with Jack's swimming and weightlifting program had worked wonders to ward off aging.

As he dressed he looked in the mirror; his hair had turned white, his face was thinner than it had been ten years earlier, but his looks and his age shouldn't matter. It was all about his ability to do his job, to protect the President of the United States which he had done faithfully and diligently for almost forty-three years on Skorpios . . . until today.

Secret Service agents were forced to retire at age 60 but Jack had raised such a ruckus when Hal's previous boss tried to retire him that they had granted a special exemption that allowed Hal to work until he was 70. The new Deputy Director in charge of the Skorpios project, McQuade, wasn't as easily persuaded as his predecessor had been and he demanded that Hal retire and be replaced with a younger man.

In Hal's mind, the solution was simple. Agree to retire, allow the Service to change his compensation from payroll to pension, and welcome a new guy to the island. Jack had other ideas. When Hal had presented his solution months earlier, Jack had frowned, saying, "Hal, you've done your duty. You have served me and your country in the finest tradition of the Service for damn near 43 years. Now go home and find yourself a 40-year-old divorced lady and try like hell to get back some of the years you sacrificed."

Hal ran a comb through his thin hair. It hadn't been the life he had envisioned when he graduated from college. He saw himself with a wife, two kids, a house, and weekends spent mowing grass and napping in a hammock under a tree in the back yard. Instead, he had lived single, been an honorary uncle to Jack's children, and spent his weekends flying to places like Oslo or Diego Garcia to meet with presidents, premiers and dictators. When he napped in a hammock under a tree, it was on a private island; when he mowed the grass . . . well, he smiled, he hadn't been behind a lawn mower since he was eighteen.

Over the last several days, Hal had gone through his belongings and reduced them to the few things he planned to take with him. He had a few favorite books, a few mementos of his travels, and his clothes. Everything he had collected in his life that had need or meaning fit into two suitcases and a medium-sized box. The keepsakes in Hal's life were stored in his memories and he hoped they would stay with him as long as his heart beat.

"Good morning, Hal," said Demetrius with a large smile as he entered the main room. "Mister Jack has been up making you a big birthday breakfast. Please sit and I'll get you coffee."

Demetrius had Hal beat by a few years and while Jack was never able to talk the little Greek into his exercise regimen, the man remained healthy, propelled through life by his nervous energy. Hal couldn't remember a single time when Demetrius hadn't been rushing here or there to take care of some detail or another. For his faithful duty to herself and her father, Christina, before her death had granted him "employment for life", the highest honor bestowed on an employee by an employer. The man would receive pay for the remainder of his life even if he chose to quit and move back to his native village.

Like Hal, there was no reason for Demetrius to retire. He enjoyed living on the island where his duties were light but still gave a sense of importance to his life. He had become good friends with both Jack and Hal and together the three of them felt as though they had changed the world, even if just a little, for the positive.

"Happy birthday, Hal!" said Jack as he walked into the room with a spatula in one hand. "The coffee's on and I just about have breakfast ready."

Hal glanced at Demetrius with a grimace. Demetrius smiled and whispered, "Don't worry, Mister Hal, I helped."

Breakfast was quite a spread. There were eggs, bacon, and hash brown potatoes along with fresh fruit and toast. Jack said that he wanted to acclimate Hal to the "American Breakfast" that he was certain he would be feasting on regularly at the Waffle House back home.

When breakfast was finished, Jack told Demetrius he would take care of the dishes and clean up the kitchen in a little bit then asked Hal to follow him out to the veranda. Demetrius ignored Jack, knowing that as good as his intentions were, the clean-up duty was going to fall to the cook anyway.

"I'm going to miss your company, Hal," said Jack as they stepped into the bright sunlight. "You've been a wonderful friend for more years than I care to count."

"I'm going to miss you too, Jack," said Hal. It wasn't like either of them to be so straightforward with their feelings.

"I have a going-away present for you," said Jack as he pointed to a small wrapped package on a nearby table.

Hal unwrapped the present and was stunned to find Jack's coconut paperweight inside. "Jack, there is no way I can accept this," said Hal.

"I'm not giving it to you," said Jack. "I'm lending it to you. You hang onto it and someday when you are done with it send it to the Kennedy Library."

"This should be in the museum right now," protested Hal.

Jack's expression changed to a solemn look, "Not everything of mine should be in a museum. I'm still alive and I still get to make choices. I choose for you to keep that as a reminder of the years we have spent out here and all that we accomplished. When you're done with it, then it can go to a museum."

Hal felt a tear welling up in the corner of his eye but he tried his best to quell it. "I'll take very good care of it, Mister President," he said out of respect.

Kennedy turned and looked him in the eye, "Call me Jack."

SPRINGFIELD, ILLINOIS
August 15, 2006

"Miss Kennedy, it's a pleasure to finally get a chance to meet with you," said Senator Obama.

"I'm glad we could make our schedules work out," said Caroline.

The Senator's Springfield office was small but well appointed. He led her past his assistant's desk into his office and motioned for her to take a seat. "Can I get you anything to drink?

"I'd take some water if you have it," she said with a smile.

"Ashley, would you please get us two bottles of water," he asked his assistant before sitting at his desk.

They chatted briefly about the weather until Ashley returned with the waters. She closed the door behind her as she left.

"So you think you want to be president?" asked Caroline directly.

"I'm not sure that's a correct statement," said Obama. "Somebody needs to step up right now and promote the values on which this country was built."

"You don't want to be president?" asked Caroline with a twisted expression. "I'm not sure I understand?"

"How can I put this," answered Obama thoughtfully. "Of course, I want to be president. I believe the course the country is currently on is both dangerous and misguided. We need leadership to guide us through the coming years that is young, insightful, energetic and resourceful. I believe we need a leader in the White House who offers a different look and feel from the last several leaders."

Obama paused to take a sip of water and said, "A good president is one who feels the need to be a leader, out of both duty and love of country. A bad president is one who wants to sit in the big chair behind the fancy desk and worry about how history will view him in the future."

Caroline smiled, "If elected, are you willing to make decisions and implement programs that are needed for the good of the country rather than the ones that are just popular with the public?"

"Any man who sits in that office and spends all his time worrying about winning the second term or looking good in the history books shouldn't be in that office," said Obama. "The same goes for any man who seeks the office just to boost his ego, and we have had a few of those recently."

"Like?" asked Caroline.

"Like the last Democrat we elected," he said, putting his index finger in front of his lips and blowing, "Shhh."

SKORPIOS ISLAND
August 16, 2006

Jack shook his head as he shared the morning paper from Athens on the veranda with Demetrius. A new Secret Service agent, Brian Avery, had been assigned to the island but they didn't think he was going to work out. For the last fifteen minutes, they had watched him darting across the clearing below them checking motion sensors and charting where additional ones needed to be installed. He looking at lines of sight for snipers and complained about how lax the security on the island had gotten.

He had already raised his concerns to Demetrius and Nik Contos. He had so upset Contos that, for a moment, Jack thought Contos was going to pull out his pistol and shoot the American dead. He tried to explain to the new guy that you never tell a retired Greek military officer how to do his job but Avery had stomped off.

The two men on the veranda watched Avery who was standing near the tree line below the main house pointing an imaginary rifle towards them. He shook his head and jogged up to the house. As he walked out on the veranda he said, "Sir, you cannot sit near the railing like that until we've installed either a solid railing or bullet-proof glass."

"Brian," said Jack in an irritated voice, "sit down."

"I'd prefer to stand if you don't mind, sir," said the agent.

"And I would prefer you sit down before I throw you over our non-bullet proof railing," answered Jack.

Brian almost laughed at the threat by the old man but he saw that neither the President nor the old caretaker was smiling. He pulled up a chair and sat.

"Brian, I can't help but notice that you're new around here," said Jack sarcastically. Before Avery could answer, Jack continued, "We have been living on this island since before you were born. For the first couple of years we were a little concerned about security. You see, the Russians, the Cubans, the mafia and a few others didn't like me very much."

Brian started to speak but Jack cut him off, "After the first twenty or thirty years, we realized that very few people were looking for me. To keep ourselves from going crazy we lightened up and learned to live in these peaceful surroundings . . . peacefully."

"Sir, my job is to protect you and the secret of this project with my life. I am trying to . . ."

"I don't want to hear your academy rhetoric, Brian," said Kennedy as he again cut him off. "If you feel the need to run around in the bushes and play secret agent man, you go for it but eventually, you're going to peek inside one of the wrong bushes and a Phantom is going to blow your head off."

"Sir, the local island security is a joke," said Brian. "They have too few men and the ones they do have are positioned incorrectly to stop an advance by any well-motivated force."

"Do you have knowledge of a well-motivated force planning to attack Skorpios?" asked Jack with an aggravated voice. The phone inside the house rang and Demetrius hurried to answer it.

"No sir but my job is to . . ."

"Look Brian," said Jack cutting him off once again in mid-sentence, "you've been given a sweetheart position here. I don't know if you got this assignment because you were a really good agent or at the bottom of the barrel but you're here and you are either going to get along with the staff and the island's security or you're going to go the hell away. Do you understand Agent Avery?"

Brian stood, "Perhaps I am the wrong agent for this assignment. I'll visit with Deputy Director McQuade and obtain his advice on my duties here."

"I think that's a grand idea," said Jack. "Tell Robby McQuade that I send my best."

Brian stood and started to walk towards the house when Jack had a change of heart. "Look Brain, nobody's lurking out there waiting to attack us, nobody knows we're here and even if they did, they probably wouldn't give a damn. In forty-three years we have been invaded once and that was by Navy Seals delivering a couple of cases of beer."

Jack spun his chair to face the agent, "I don't know what you were told your duties would be out here, but your job is to babysit an old man, to keep me from getting into trouble, and to make sure that when I die, there isn't a trace left to show I was ever here. We can get along or not but I'd just as soon we enjoy what time we both have left on this wonderful island."

Brian turned to look at the man, "I'll visit with McQuade and let you know what I decide."

Demetrius appeared in the door, "Mister Jack, it is Miss Caroline."

"I hope you make the right decision," said Jack as he stood. "Excuse me Brian, my daughter is on the phone."

Jack walked to his desk and waited for the new agent to leave the room before he picked up the phone. "Hi honey," he said in a cheerful voice. "You're up pretty late," he said while glancing at the clock on his desk.

"Hi, Dad," said Caroline. "We were at dinner with Senator Obama and his wife, Michelle. I wanted to call you before I went to bed."

"What do you think of this guy?" asked Jack.

"I like him," said Caroline. "His background checks out and I like the answers to the questions you wanted me to ask. Besides all that, he's really a nice guy and I like his wife, too."

"Do you think they can handle the ride?" asked Jack referring to the pressures of the campaign.

"We talked about that at length," answered Caroline. "I believe they both clearly understand the road before them. They brought up the subject of the stress a campaign would have on their marriage and their family and they talked about how they planned to mitigate those tensions as much as possible."

"Do they have any other concerns?" asked Jack.

"Senator Obama was very interested in knowing exactly who I represent," said Caroline. "He is concerned that the small and powerful group I represent may present issues down the road."

"What did you tell him?" asked Jack.

"I told him that I represent myself and my father," said Caroline bluntly.

Jack laughed, "How did he respond to that?"

"Of course, he thought I was representing you symbolically. He got a little misty-eyed and said something about how it was a tremendous honor to be sponsored by the family of a great man."

"Jesus, what a politician," chuckled Jack.

"Dad," said Caroline, her unseen eye roll reflected in her voice.

SPRINGFIELD, ILLINOIS
February 10, 2007

Barack Obama announced his candidacy for President of the United States in front of the Old State Capital building in Springfield not because it was a convenient location. The choice of that site was because of its symbolic significance; it was the same spot where Abraham Lincoln had delivered his 1858 speech, "House Divided".

Obama's speech, written by him and his team of speech writers, clearly contained overtones of speeches given four to five decades earlier by John F. Kennedy. Historians would pick up on the verbiage and wonder if Ted Sorensen, JFK's speech writer had lent a hand in the preparing the powerful message.

Thousands of miles away on a little island in the Ionian Sea, Jack Kennedy and Ted Sorensen listened to the speech live over something called a streaming audio made available by a high-speed internet connection that somehow linked Brian Avery's laptop computer directly to Springfield. Jack had quit trying to understand technology years before.

When the speech ended, Jack turned to his longtime friend, "Nice job, Ted."

"Thanks, Jack."

"Do you think it's time?" asked Jack.

"I think it's clearly time," said Ted.

"Then set it up," smiled Jack.

"What are you two talking about?" asked Avery.

NEW YORK CITY, NEW YORK
March 26, 2007

The $1000-dollar-a-plate fund raiser had gone exceedingly well. Every chair was full and the crowd listened intently to Obama's comments during his speech. They laughed at every joke and showed fire in their eyes when he spoke of the change and hope that he would bring to the White House. After stepping from behind the podium and shaking at least two hundred hands he was led to an elevator by Bob Gibbs, his spokesman.

"Geez, Bob," said Obama wearily, "how many more months of this until the election?"

"Nineteen and a half, we're on the downhill side," said Gibbs with a smirk.

"What now?" asked Obama.

"Now we make a quick stop to meet with Caroline Kennedy in her room, then we buzz upstairs to a $5000-dollar-per-person meet-and-greet hosted by the New York Democrats. After that, you can have a few hours of sleep before we head for Atlanta in the morning."

The two stepped off on the fourteenth floor and Obama followed Gibbs down the long hallway. At room 1465, Gibbs stopped, turned to check out his candidate and friend to make sure he looked properly presidential, then knocked on the door.

"Senator Obama?" asked the man who opened the door.

Obama stepped forward and thrust out his hand, "Barack Obama, it's nice to meet you."

The man shook his hand with a bit of a laugh, "I'm Agent Avery, United States Secret Service. Please come in."

The two men stepped inside the suite and followed the agent into the living room where Caroline Kennedy stood next to another man. "Thank you for taking the time to see us, Senator. I know your time is short and that you have another engagement upstairs but I wanted to introduce you to a couple of guys who have been key to your campaign so far." She turned to the man next to her, "Barack Obama, this is Ted Sorensen."

Sorensen stepped forward, "We met briefly at the DNC in 2004," he said.

"I remember," answered Obama. "You congratulated me on my keynote in the hallway just outside the Green Room."

Ted turned to Caroline with a smile, "He's good. He's very, very good."

"Have a seat," said Caroline, pointing the two men to the couch. "The identity of the other man I'd like to introduce you to must remain classified, it's a matter of national security. You have to agree right now that you will never, and I mean never, speak of this man's presence in this room or even the fact that you met him."

Obama glanced at Gibbs before saying, "I'm good with that."

Gibbs nodded his head in acknowledgement.

Agent Avery stepped forward, "Gentlemen, raise your right hands." Both complied and then Avery gave a fake oath he had made up only moments before. "Do you solemnly swear to uphold the secrets about to be revealed to you until death? And do you further understand that breaking this oath and revealing these secrets will be considered a capital offense against the United States?"

Both men answered, "I do." Caroline quickly turned towards the bedroom door to hide her laughter. She opened the door and said, "Come on out." Both Obama and Gibbs stood.

Jack Kennedy emerged from the room wearing a suit and tie and sporting a new haircut. Bob Gibbs was expecting somebody controversial but recognizable to materialize from the room and was surprised when an old man, somebody he wasn't familiar with, stepped forward.

Obama's reaction was entirely different. For the last several years, he had been studying films, videos, and audio tapes of history's great orators. The man's face was slimmer, his hair was white and thin and the wrinkles around his eyes spoke of his years, but his smile was unmistakable.

"Holy shit," said Obama out loud before he caught himself.

"Senator Obama, I'd like you to meet my father, John Kennedy."

Jack strode quickly across the room and thrust out his hand, "My friends call me Jack. You can call me Mister President or Mister Kennedy," he said with a laugh.

Bob Gibbs turned to Caroline, "Is this some sort of a bad joke?

"Yes, that was a bad joke," said Kennedy fully aware of what Gibbs really meant, "you can call me Jack."

Caroline laughed, "I assure you, Mister Gibbs, this is no joke. Have a seat and we'll give you the quick version of what really happened in Dallas and tell you why we are all here this evening."

The two men sat back down on the couch next to each other as instructed but neither of them took their eyes off Jack's face. Caroline stepped forward, "You are both aware of the history of the Cuban Missile Crisis in 1962, right?"

Both men nodded.

"After the Crisis, Nikita Khrushchev went . . . well, a little nuts and became hellbent on revenge for his loss of face over the outcome. He decided he was going to kill my father and he didn't seem to care if he did it with a single bullet or a bunch of missiles. After several attempts to assassinate my father, Dad and a group of insiders decided the best way to stop a major confrontation, should Khrushchev actually succeed, was to beat him to the punch. They faked the events in Dallas, Johnson took over as president, and JFK went into hiding."

After a few moments of silence Obama turned towards Caroline, "Why are you telling me this? Why me, why now?" he asked.

"We believe you have what it takes to win next year's election," said Jack. "But in order for you to win the election, I think you need to have a certain amount of confidence. I thought it was important that you know who is backing you and why. We believe the country needs a new direction and we are looking for a man who is willing to put aside his ego, roll up his shirt sleeves, and push through the necessary changes the country needs to insure its future. The question is, Senator, once you are elected, what are your plans?"

"I plan to end the war in Iraq, decrease our dependence on foreign oil, and provide universal health care," said Obama in a well-practiced elevator speech.

Gibbs just continued to stare at Jack with his mouth open.

"I know what you're spouting as your platform; what I'm asking is are you willing to make the hard decisions to help steer this country in a new direction or are you going to bow to the public sentiment and do what's popular?" asked Jack.

"I'm not sure I understand the question," said Obama.

Jack sat down in a chair across from the young man. "It's pretty simple. There arc two kinds of president. One is willing to make hard choices and push the country in the right direction even if it's not the popular thing to do. The other is worried about winning a second term and securing his legacy. Our current president is among the first group. He has become very unpopular because of decisions he had to make in Iraq and Afghanistan for reasons which will become clear to you after you are elected and receive your first security briefing. What we need right now is a president who will push hard for the right referendums. We need to make some serious changes in this country and we need a man who is more concerned about making those changes than winning a second term in office. We can put you in the White House next November but we need a man in the Oval Office who is willing to take one for the team, to push unpopular policies because they are the right thing for the country right now."

Obama sat up straight, "I appreciate the offer to help with the campaign but I will not be a puppet once I'm elected."

Jack leaned forward, "Good, because I won't back a puppet. What I am suggesting is that you push forward with Health Care Reform and you be prepared to make some hard economic decisions as this mess that Wall Street has gotten us into begins to unravel. You need to get us out of Iraq and then kick the hell out of some bad guys in Afghanistan. When your approval rating falls into the basement because the economy that you have inherited is in the toilet, because you are still pushing for Health Care reform when people simply need jobs, and because American soldiers are dying in Afghanistan, you will maintain your course and not bow to public pressure. That's the man we are looking to support."

Senator Obama sat quietly for a few moments, "My advisors tell me that it is a long shot to get past Hillary and then win the election."

"Horseshit," said Jack. "You need to tweak your branding a little, build your campaign coffers, and stay the course. We think you can win by using the subtle message of 'the new Camelot.' You will appeal to the younger voters because of your own youth. You'll offer young Americans a new sense of optimism in their leadership and they'll fall all over themselves to vote for you. To the older voters, we'll leak some well-timed messages about your similarities to myself. They will fondly remember a time when life seemed easier and the grass seemed greener and they'll long again for those times as they mark their ballot for you. The only demographic we don't have pegged is the 40-to-60-year-old group, but we'll find a way to get enough of them."

Jack paused for a moment and looked at the two men sitting on the couch, "If you're willing to help us, we'll get you elected next November."

Obama looked over at Gibbs who gave him a nod. "I'm your man, Mister Kennedy. What do we do first?"

"First, call me Jack." He turned towards Caroline, "Hand me the plan, please."

WASHINGTON, D.C.
Present Day

Deputy Director Robert McQuade looked at his yellow legal pad where he had drawn a series of circles connected by lines. The circle at the top contained the words "Chopper Crash". A solid line led to a circle containing the word, "Pilot". That circle had a diagonal line drawn through it. Another solid line led to a circle containing the names of the two fishermen who had witnessed and helped after the crash, "Kissos and Geordi". That circle still had a question mark next to it even though Telleria had told him there was no reason to worry about them. A third line dropped to circles containing the names of the Onassis employed 'Phantom' guards along with Demetrius and Brian Avery. The last line from the top circle ran to a circles holding Hal Rumsey's name which, in turn, had lines to more circle containing the names of Mike Mahoney and Bob Blurton.

McQuade hoped that in the next day or two, all the circles on his flowchart would have black diagonal lines drawn through them indicating that the persons named within the circles were no longer a threat to the secrecy of this project.

The 'projects' that McQuade protected were similar in his mind to artifacts in a museum. He was the curator and it was his job to make sure that the artifacts in his museum were never stolen and never damaged. The only difference was that nobody was ever allowed inside McQuade's museum nor were the artifacts ever to be viewed publicly.

Skorpios had been a big project with many moving parts but now that Kennedy was dead there would be a little clean-up, a little cover-up, and the project could be put to bed. It would lie there quietly until the next reporter started poking around McQuade's museum, at which time he would do whatever he had to do to protect his artifact.

Robert McQuade saw himself as a true American hero, sworn to protect the sanctity of the Office of the President of the United States of America. He was a soldier at war against those who would try to reveal facts that would discredit the office of the president. It was his duty to keep Skorpios a secret along with other projects, some as recent as the Obama administration and some as old as Lincoln's. Some of the secrets would have minor impact while others, like Skorpios or those involving Franklin Roosevelt, Lyndon Johnson, or Richard Nixon, could have major repercussions on the faith and trust the American people had in their government.

McQuade nervously tapped on his yellow pad. He looked at his phone and tried to will it to ring with news from Telleria and others that diagonal lines could be drawn through the last of the circles. He tapped and waited.

SKORPIOS ISLAND
January 27, 2008

As much as he cussed the computer on his desk, Jack loved the instantaneous news that the damned box brought to him. Before most of the East Coast of the United States had awoken, Jack was reading an op-ed piece penned by Caroline entitled, "A President Like My Father," in which she publicly endorsed Barack Obama in the coming election.

Her concluding lines were: "I have never had a president who inspired me the way people tell me that my father inspired them. But for the first time, I believe I have found the man who could be that president—not just for me, but for a new generation of Americans."

Jack leaned back and smiled; he hadn't given his daughter a single piece of advice on the piece, she had written every word herself. Caroline Kennedy had, very much on her own, taken her first step towards becoming instrumental in American politics. Jack was a very proud father.

He reached into his bottom desk drawer and retrieved his journal to make a note of the day his daughter became a driving force in the Democratic Party. She may choose never to hold an office but a new generation of young American voters would now look to her for advice and direction.

WASHINGTON, D.C.
Present Day

Mike Mahoney felt like the Red Skins must have felt returning from the Super Bowl as he swaggered back into the office. He had arrogantly envisioned being greeted with a huge round of applause but it was obvious that nobody was yet aware of the big 'win' he had pulled off. He had the biggest story of his career and probably the biggest story the *Post* would ever print.

Bob Blurton caught him in the hallway, "Drop your bags in your office then hightail it to mine. Don't talk to anybody and bring whatever you have from your interview."

"All right," said Mahoney. In Mahoney's mind, the emphasis on secrecy was further confirmation that Blurton had found something to authenticate Hal's story.

"What's up?" he asked as he walked into Blurton's office.

"Shut the door and have a seat, Mike," said Blurton.

Mahoney settled into one of the two chairs at his boss's desk with a self-assured look on his face.

"Your guy's a fraud," said Blurton.

Mahoney felt the air being sucked from his chest. "No, he's not" he said defensively. "I know fakes and this guy's not one."

"You may have just met the best con artist of your career, buddy," said Blurton. "He's been trying to sell this story for years."

"What in the hell are you talking about, Bob?" asked Mahoney.

"I had Botterbusch do some research on your guy yesterday. There has been only one Harold Rumsey who has ever worked for the Secret Service," said Blurton, opening the file on his desk. "He was there for about three years and was fired shortly after Kennedy's assassination for some undisclosed reason. After that, he got a job with the Social Security Administration where he worked as an underpaid cubicle dweller until he retired several years ago."

"Yep, that's pretty much the cover story he told me," said Mahoney.

Blurton continued, "He lived in the same apartment on Westover from 1961 to 1984 when he was forced to move because they were tearing the building down. Then he lived in an apartment in Alexandria until he retired and moved to Boca where he bought a home in a retirement village. The guy seldom took a vacation, didn't own a car, probably went home after working exactly eight hours a day and sat around his dismal little apartment cooking up the story he told you."

"That's all part of the cover story put together by the Secret Service," said Mahoney with newfound confidence.

"There's more," said Blurton while flipping the page in the file. "He tried to sell this same story to *Newsweek* a few years ago, he tried to sell it to Oprah before that, and two weeks ago was talking with a reporter at the *Miami Herald*."

"He's not trying to sell the story," said Mahoney. "Never once was there a mention of any sort of payment at all."

Blurton raised his finger indicating he still wasn't finished. "The guy's been trying to sell this story for fifteen years at least. Now he's dying, we were able to verify that. If he gets somebody to bite on it now then at least he is vindicated in death. It's no longer about money."

"No," said Mahoney. "I don't buy it. He knows too much, he knows too many details about history and about Kennedy himself."

"If all you did was sit around for 47 years after the Secret Service fired you and thought about the same story over and over again, you'd be pretty convincing too," said Blurton. "Look, Mike, the guy took you for a ride and you bought it. I don't want it to leak that we were even talking to this guy. Our reputation is on the line here and we're not going to damage it over some nut."

Mahoney leaned forward in the chair, "Bob, you need to meet this guy. Once you do you will see that . . ."

"No, Mike," interrupted Blurton. "I don't need to meet him, the guy is a fraud. Unless you have some solid piece of evidence that validates this guy's story even a smidgen, we're done talking about him."

Mahoney sat up straight, "He's got the original coconut that Kennedy carved his message in to save his crew in World War II. I held it in my hands."

"Oh, yeah, I forgot about that" said Blurton as he flipped through the file, "The original coconut paperweight disappeared off the Oval Office desk during the Kennedy-Johnson transition. It probably was stolen by a White House staffer. Jackie later had two replicas made; one which she kept in her home, the other went to Kennedy Library. Your guy was fired shortly after the assassination. Maybe he was the guy who stole the coconut."

"Look, Bob, this guy is legit. I'll get the proof. This is the biggest story of my career and probably the biggest story in the paper's history," said Mahoney.

Blurton shut the file, "Mike, go look at yourself in the mirror. You're searching for a pot of gold at the end of the rainbow but there's no gold and there's no rainbow. I'm not going to allow you to spend any more of my time on this searching for something that's not there. Let it go, Mike; if you don't, you'll ruin your reputation. My job here is to protect the reputation of the paper and I'll do what I need to in order to maintain the character and standing of the *Post*. Let it go."

Mahoney stood and started to say something but caught himself. He picked up his notebook from Blurton's desk and turned for the door. "I wish you could meet this guy, Bob."

Mahoney walked quietly back to his office. He stood in the doorway and looked at the numerous awards hanging on the wall that stood for excellence in reporting and writing. The awards reminded him that he was a good reporter, an honest judge of the facts, and a decent judge of character. He closed the door to his office and sat at his desk to try to clear his mind and to honestly judge the facts. "Caroline!" he said to himself. He punched at his cell phone until he found her number and hoped she would answer.

"Hello?" came a familiar voice after two rings

"Caroline, its Mike. Do you have a moment?"

"Mike Mahoney? Twice in the same week? What an honor," she said in an upbeat voice. "Sure, I have a moment for you, what's up?"

There was no need to beat around the bush, he dove right in, "I met Hal Rumsey a few days ago and I know the whole story."

There was a slight pause, "Who's Hal Rumsey, what story?" she said.

Mahoney smiled, "I believe you used to call him Uncle Hal? Look, Hal's dying so he broke the entire story to me. He wants the world to know that your father made the ultimate sacrifice, that he gave up everything and continued to serve the country until his death."

"You're losing me, Mike," said Caroline. "I don't know who this Hal guy is and I'm not sure what story you're talking about."

"Caroline, I know your father died last week in a helicopter accident in Greece. I'm going to break the story of his last forty years and put an end to all the secrecy. The world needs to know what a great man he was and all that he gave up to save the country."

For a few moments there was silence on the other end of the phone. "Oh, my god, Mike," said Caroline. She paused, "I don't know who you've been talking to but . . . Mike, you're heading down the wrong road here."

"I'm breaking the story," he said excitedly. "The country needs to know that your father gave up the presidency, went into hiding, and still continued to serve his country. History has got to be changed and by damn, I'm going to be the one to do it."

There was a pause on the other end of the line, "Mike, listen to me carefully. We've known each other for a very long time. This is your friend talking, Mike, drop this story."

"I can't drop it," said Mahoney. "This is huge."

"Mike!" said Caroline with a hint of anger in her voice. "STOP and listen to me. My father died in Dallas, Texas, in 1963. I read the CIA reports a few years ago, he was killed by a single gunman, a man who wanted to be famous, notorious at any cost. There was no conspiracy, no other gunman, and no magic bullets. And as much as I ache in my heart for it to be true, he didn't survive."

"Caroline," said Mahoney, "I know that he did. You know that he did, and now it's time the real story is told."

"Mike, this is a toxic story, this will ruin your career. Whatever you have been told isn't true and never happened. Listen to that little voice inside yourself, the one that is screaming at you right now to not believe the lies you've been told. Look at all the people who have killed their careers and in some cases even themselves trying to change the history of that event. There is no conspiracy; my father died in that car in 1963."

Mahoney felt that bad feeling again, the air being sucked out of him but he tried to push it aside, "Do you deny spending Christmas of 1968 on Skorpios?"

"I spent several holidays on Skorpios, but not with my father," she answered. "Mike, get your head together. Go see a counselor if you need to but get it together. You seem to be having trouble separating fact from fiction and that's just not like you. Nobody can see through bullshit better that Mike Mahoney."

"You're not going to help me out with this story?" Mahoney asked weakly.

"I hope that I just did," she said. "I hope I've kept you from becoming a fool by reporting what sounds like an amazing lie. Listen Mike, I'm just stepping into a meeting so I need to go. Somebody's messing with your mind and you are buying into it. You're better than that, Mike."

Mahoney set down is phone and leaned back in his chair. The room seemed to swirl around him in a confusing myriad of details, fact and fiction collided in front of him as he questioned what was real and what was not. He stood, steadied himself for a moment against his desk then walked out of his office. He needed some fresh air, a walk might help him clear his mind.

He walked down the hallway to the elevator and reached for the 'Lobby' button but suddenly changed his mind and pressed the button for the basement instead with a sense of newfound hope.

The basement of the *Washington Post* building held a massive collection of documents, old newspapers, court documents, research materials, and other items waiting to be digitized and stored on a computer. Mahoney stepped off the elevator and turned left, he knew exactly where he was going and what he was looking for; the old phone books.

On a shelf not far into the catacombs of disorder, exactly where he remembered them, was a large collection of phonebooks dating back to the 1930s. Mahoney scanned the Washington, D.C., phonebooks until he found the stack from the late seventies and reached for the book dated 1978. He flipped though it quickly until he found the right page then he ran his finger down it to where he hoped he would find nothing. His world seemed to close in on him when he read the name, "Rumsey, Harold – 3176 Westover Drive, Apt 12-B".

"A coincidence," he told himself as he returned the phone book to its place on the shelf. He continued to search the shelves until he located the phone books for Alexandria and found a tattered copy that covered the years 1995 to 1996. He opened the book and slowly turned the pages, looking for but hoping not to find the name, yet there it was, "Rumsey, Harold – 2500 N. Van Dorn St. #307".

BOCA RATON, FLORIDA
Present Day

Doris Mifflin was young for her age. At 74, she was spry and active. She played golf two days a week, she volunteered for Meals on Wheels one day a week, and taught water aerobics on Tuesdays and Thursdays. She had organized the local bridge club and was involved in two book clubs.

Doris had met the love of her life when she was 22 years old and working as an airline stewardess. Lee was a dashing pilot, a married man, seventeen years older than her but bold and confident. He had the commanding presence of a former Marine pilot, which he was, and a powerful charisma that had swept her off her feet. Lee divorced his wife, married Doris, raised two daughters, and had enjoyed a wonderful life with his family before his years caught up to him. He died, leaving behind a young widow with a fair amount of money in the bank, two married daughters, and several beautiful grandchildren.

Doris had met Hal Rumsey a few years earlier. He was a mysterious man who maintained that he had worked for the Social Security Administration in D.C. for most of his career but too often he revealed facts that just didn't add up. He didn't seem to know much about Social Security. In casual discussions at social gatherings, he seemed to know way too much about Idi Amin and his tumultuous rule of Uganda; he would occasionally mention that he had been to Moscow, to Cairo, or Johannesburg; he had opinions on past Presidents and other world leaders that seemed to be based on more information than the average person was likely to possess. Then, when he realized that his opinions on this or that were captivating the attention of the entire room, he would suddenly shut down or change the subject.

Hal and Doris had been keeping each other company, or what some people might call dating, for a little over a year and while she couldn't say she loved him, she certainly enjoyed his company. Hal downplayed their relationship to everybody in their social circle, referring to her as the 'old hen' who lived around the corner. It might be macho bravado but she suspected that it was more like adolescent embarrassment at having a girlfriend. She suspected that Hal, who said he had never been married, hadn't dated much in his life either.

Doris knew that Hal was suffering from cancer but he kept the details very close to his vest. He downplayed the seriousness of it telling her that it was a minor form of the disease that was easily curable.

She knew that Hal had had company during the last few days and she also knew he probably wouldn't provide her with any details about his mystery guest. The neighborhood gossip circle had already reported to her that he was a short, slightly pudgy man whom nobody had remembered seeing around before. He and Hal were seen coming and going in Hal's car and out walking after dark.

Now that the mystery guest had left, Hal was calling her again. He asked Doris to give him a ride down to a clinic, saying that his car wasn't running just right. Doris was thrilled to help and hoped she would find out more about both Hal's cancer and the details of his meetings during the last few days.

WASHINGTON, D.C.
Present Day

Mike Mahoney couldn't decide if he were more embarrassed or angry at being taken in by Hal. He didn't know if he was angry at Hal for deceiving him or angry at himself for falling for the old man's story.

He walked down the street towards the Post Pub where he planned to down a few stiff drinks but instead of turning left at L

Street, he continued south on 15th. He wasn't going anywhere in particular, rather just walking in a haze, not really seeing anybody or anything. He walked past McPherson Square then down Vermont Avenue to Lafayette Square and soon found himself on Pennsylvania Avenue among the ever-present crowd of tourists who were staring at the White House. The weather was hot and muggy but the tourists were still there, they were there in the rain, in the wind, and even in the snow. Mahoney walked blindly past them down Pennsylvania to 17th where he turned south and, a short while, later stood at Constitution Avenue on the north side of the Washington Mall.

Mahoney's day-to-day travels often took him past the Presidential and War Memorials but after nearly thirty years in D.C., he rarely noticed them. He hadn't actually stepped foot on the Washington Mall in years. The Vietnam Memorial was only a few blocks to his right. He remembered that it was there that his real career in writing had started.

Twenty-six years earlier, Mahoney had been working as a string reporter covering drive-by shootings, small fires, and city council meetings. His sister, a Junior High Social Studies teacher, had sent him a letter asking what her eighth graders should see when they visited Washington the following month. He typed a partial reply and inadvertently left it in his typewriter where a fellow reporter read it and showed it to his editor who, with Mike's permission, published the letter and provided the springboard that eventually got him out of the City Desk and into his own column. Mahoney remembered parts of the letter as he approached the Wall.

"What should you see in Washington?" he had written. "Any guidebook can tell you what to see, the better question is *why* your students should experience the amazing history here." He spoke of the artifacts in the Smithsonian and of standing before the massive figure of Lincoln, a statue so giant and yet so real that you began to understand what a huge figure Lincoln had become in our nation's history.

Of the Vietnam Memorial, Mahoney had written, "To get the full meaning of the wall, be certain to visit the wall at night. Prepare your students for the experience because if you do they will never forget their visit or the tremendous sacrifices the wall represents.

"Tell them to stand silently before the wall and look at the names until they start to move, and they will move. Slowly they will begin to realize that each unfamiliar name represents a father who never got to see his children grow up, a son who never again had the opportunity to hug his mother, or a husband whose last thought was for the grieving wife he would leave behind.

"When the names start to surround you, to encompass you, to move you, step forward and lightly touch them, because if you touch the wall at that moment, the wall will forever touch you."

Michael Mahoney sat on a bench and watched a steady stream of solemn tourists timidly and reverently approach the wall. Some were obviously touched and emotional while others seemed to stop just long enough to look, as if they were simply trying to check it off their "been there" list before they scurried off to see other sights.

He wondered when his life had stopped having a special meaning and when he went from being touched by events to simply checking them off some mental list. It probably happened about the same time that his love of journalism had gone from a consuming passion to just being a job.

Mike leaned forward and rested his head in his hands as he wondered where in the hell the years had gone.

BOCA RATON, FLORIDA
Present Day

"How was your visit?" asked Doris as she maneuvered her Toyota Camry through traffic.

Hal didn't feel much like talking, the pain pills he had taken the night before to insure a decent night's sleep hadn't completely worn off, he was still fairly groggy but tried his best to put up a good act. "It was fine. The guy was the son of an old friend who was looking for some background information on Social Security for a story he's writing for some magazine," lied Hal.

"He was at your home for a couple of days," said Doris as she slowed to a stop behind a short school bus. "How many questions could he ask about Social Security?" She knew she was prying but she suspected that Hal was probably making up the unlikely story anyway. It had become a game to her over the last year to see how far she could push him before he clamped down.

Hal knew he had to come up with something, "He was specifically looking for information on Social Security fraud. Past schemes, how we discovered them, and the processes we put into place to prevent them in the future." Hal felt pretty darn please with himself for coming up with that answer.

"How interesting," said Doris. "I didn't know you had worked in the fraud section."

The school bus started moving again. "Oh, yeah, I did for several years," he answered. "You know, this school bus is going to stop at least another fifteen times between here and the school up the road. Why don't you turn here and kick over to Freeman Street."

"Are you in a hurry?" Doris asked.

"At my age, I've got to do everything in a hurry," said Hal with a thin smile.

Doris laughed, "That explains a few things." She looked over at Hal who wasn't smiling. "Sorry, dear."

WASHINGTON, D.C.
Present Day

Perhaps Mahoney was just imagining it but there seemed to be a change in the air as he entered the *Post* building the following morning. People on the elevator and in the bullpen seemed to be as pleasant as normal but he sensed, or imagined, that they didn't seem to hold him in the same regard as before. Mahoney went out of his way to walk down the corridor near Bob Blurton's office. Bob was standing in the hall speaking with his assistant and not wanting to disturb their conversation, Mahoney simply said, "Good morning, Bob, Tina," as he walked past.

"Mister Mahoney," came the cold reply from Blurton. He couldn't ever remember his friend, Bob, calling him 'Mister' before. He felt like the walking dead.

In his office with a fresh cup of coffee, he decided there was only one thing to do. He would write a column like he hadn't written in years, something powerful, something so thought-provoking that Blurton would clearly see that Mike Mahoney still had it.

He opened his laptop and searched for his 'future story idea' folder, a spot where he kept all his great ideas for columns yet to be written. Finding the folder, he opened it to discover half a dozen mediocre ideas, he had already used all the good ones.

Mahoney sat back in his chair and closed his eyes. Was there something to be gleaned from his experience in Florida? Perhaps a story about an old man so desperate to become famous in death that he would tell one of the greatest lies ever told and the newspaper columnist who was so desperate for a story that he believed every word?

The idea suddenly hit him. Hal was the story, more or less. He turned to his computer and started tapping away. The title came to him immediately, "The Desperate Press." In recent years, people in the newspaper business had felt an increased pressure to rely on sensationalism to sell more papers which in turn would sell more advertising. The instant news available on the internet and TV was taking a major toll on the world's newspapers. Mike Mahoney had been a victim of it, he had bought into a fantastic tale, an unbelievable farce told by a dying man because he was desperate to get his column into the hands of more readers.

He began to write.

A half hour later, as Mahoney sat back to read the beginnings of his column his phone rang, "Mike Mahoney," he answered.

"Mister Mahoney, this is Doris Mifflin from Boca Raton, Florida. I am a friend of Hal Rumsey."

Mahoney cringed slightly at the mention of Hal's name. "Yes, Miss Mifflin, what can I do for you?"

"Hal gave me your phone number this morning and asked me to call you if anything ever happened to him. I don't think he thought it would be so soon, though," said the caller in a soft voice.

Mahoney sat up in his chair, "Has something happened, Miss Mifflin?"

"Yes," said Doris with a catch in her voice. "I went with him to get his treatment today. During his treatment he passed out. They rushed him to the hospital where his heart stopped but they revived him. The doctor says he isn't doing very well."

"I'm sorry to hear that, Miss Mifflin," said Mahoney in as sympathetic of a voice as he could muster. "Does the doctor know why Hal became so sick?"

"Apparently, Hal was much worse off than he let on, at least to me. His cancer has taken over much of his body. The doctor said that when the body can't fight any more, it starts shutting down."

In a much more compassionate voice Mahoney said, "I am sorry to hear that. Is there anything I can do?"

"Thank you, Mister Mahoney. I don't think there is anything anybody can do. Hal just wanted me to let you know if anything happened to him," said Doris.

Mahoney was angry with the old man but he couldn't help but like Hal. Despite his tall tales, he was a genuinely nice guy. "Is he conscious?" asked Mahoney.

"He comes and goes," Doris said sadly. "I'll sit with him as long as I can today, then I'll come back tomorrow."

"If you get the chance, please tell him that he is in my thoughts and my prayers," said Mahoney kindly.

"I will do that," said Doris. "Goodbye, Mister Mahoney," she said and hung up.

Mahoney stood and stared out his office window.

BOSTON, MASSACHUTESETTS
John F. Kennedy Presidential Library & Museum
Present Day

With the Curator out on maternity leave, all of her duties fell on Margaret Spencer. The day-to-day scheduling, the tasks of payroll, the employee performance reports weren't more than she could handle but it all certainly kept her hopping. She felt certain that if the double duties became too much for her to handle, Director Putnam would step in and help. She prided herself on not asking for his assistance, yet.

"Margaret Spencer," she said cheerfully when her phone rang.

"Hi, Miss Spencer, this is Chad Vanucci. DHL just delivered a large box addressed to the curator. Would you mind coming down to the loading dock for a moment?"

"Certainly, Chad, I'll be right there," she said. Margaret looked at her desk; she had at least ten hours of work to complete in the next six but she knew a break from the paperwork would do her good. On her way to the loading dock she passed a group of school children, fourth graders, who were running here and there while their teacher tried to corral them. Margaret smiled and remembered those days fondly.

"Good morning gentlemen," said Margaret to Chad and Bob Coles, her two maintenance men. They were standing next to a shipping crate just inside the rollup door that led to the loading dock. "Wow, you said it was a large box, you didn't say it was a good sized crate," she said. "Who sent it?"

"It doesn't say," said Coles as he leaned carefully over the crate.

Margaret gave him a quizzical look and walked over to the four-foot-long crate to inspect the shipping label. The crate was a standard four-foot by three-foot shipping crate. The label showed it had been sent from a DHL facility in Patra, Greece, but the shipper's name on the label had been damaged during transit and was unreadable. Out of curiosity, she nudged the crate with her foot to see if she could determine the weight of it. The crate didn't move but Bob Coles did.

"Jesus, don't kick it!" said Coles.

Margaret laughed, "This crate just came across the Atlantic Ocean, handled on both sides by workers who just wanted to get it out of their hair. I don't think a little kick is going to damage the contents."

Coles grimaced, "I'm more worried that the contents may damage us."

"Do you think somebody in Greece shipped us a bomb?" she asked.

"Maybe," answered Coles. "Chad and I think you should call the police to have them look it over before it's opened."

Margaret smiled, "Do you think we should dump it in the bay and let the saltwater soak the artifacts inside for a few days before we chance opening it?"

Chad stepped forward, "I'll open it," he said. "I just wanted your okay in case it did go boom. I wouldn't want to be the one responsible for blowing up the museum."

"I can't think of a single reason why a terrorist would want to blow up the Kennedy museum," said Margaret. "Let's open it," she said excitedly.

Chad took his Leatherman's tool out of the pouch that hung from his belt and used the knife to cut the plastic straps. Then he snipped the tamper-proof seal and cut the zip-ties before unsnapping the crate's two latches. Chad stepped back and motioned towards the crate, "It's all yours," he said to Margaret.

Margaret eagerly stepped forward and pulled upwards on the lid but it didn't budge. She got a better grip and tried again. One side of the lid started to give but the other held fast. Chad stepped forward to help while Coles moved slowly back towards the door.

With Chad's assistance, the lid gave and opened. The contents inside were protected against moisture and dirt by a thick plastic covering which Chad carefully cut with his knife. He stepped back as Margaret pulled the covering aside to reveal the contents, an old steamer trunk, in quite nice condition. She undid the latch on the trunk and opened it to reveal a single manila envelope sitting atop a trunk full of carefully packed, spiral-ringed notebooks.

Margaret lifted the envelope out of the crate and opened it. A bulky ring spilled out and she held it in her hand with a confused expression on her face. It was embossed with the words, *"Harvard University"* and *"Class of 1940"*. An inscription on the inside of the ring had been so worn down over the years that it was unreadable to her aging eyes but she was certain that a younger set of eyes would be able to decipher the inscription. She dropped the ring back into the envelope and set it aside for a moment while she turned her attention back to the crate full of notebooks. Randomly selecting one of the notebooks, she eased it out of the collection and carefully opened it to the first page. The handwriting was the shaky cursive of an older person.

April 19, 2009 – A quiet but productive day. With Brian's help finally finished sanding small cabinet, ready to start varnishing tomorrow if we don't go fishing, depends on winds. Finished

"Cannibal Queen" by Coonts, a great flying adventure. Sort of like "Travel's with Charley" with an airplane rather than a dog.

April 20, 2009 – Winds calm, took the launch out for about an hour before the winds kicked up. Missed a nice Bluefin, would have made a couple of nice dinners. Applied first coat to cabinet. Watching Fiji situation with great interest.

"What are they?" asked Chad, startling Margaret.

"Somebody's journals," she answered as her voice trailing off. She spent a minute flipping through the notebook in her hand before closing it and staring at the hundreds of notebooks in the crate. Then she reached over and closed and latched the trunk before turning back to the two men, "Will you please take this crate to my office, and make sure nobody opens it?"

Margaret left the mysterious box to the two men and walked back to the museum with the one journal and the manila envelope in her hand. She paused near the Oval Office display where a framed handwritten letter from President Kennedy to the Attorney General hung on the wall. She opened the journal and compared the handwriting. Perplexed, she walked quickly to Director Tom Putnam's office where she found him on the phone.

On seeing her outside his door, Putnam excitedly motioned her in and pointed to one of the two chairs in front of his desk. When he finished the call he said, "Hi, Margaret. That was the Director of the International Hemingway Conference. They are considering holding a future conference here!" The Kennedy Presidential Library and Museum also held the world's largest collection of Hemingway's work.

On any other day, this news would have excited Margaret Spencer, a huge Hemingway fan. She looked at the Director as if she hadn't heard what he had said, she had in fact heard it but it hadn't registered in her mind. "Tom, remember the old rumors about JFK living somewhere in the Mediterranean?"

"Oh, boy," he said, shaking his head, "are those surfacing again?"

"Maybe," said Margaret, "but with a new twist," she said, handing the journal to Putnam. "We just received a crate shipped from Greece containing a few hundred of these."

Tom Putnam opened it, read a few of the handwritten entries and then flipped through the pages randomly reading other entries. After a full minute, he looked up at the Assistant Curator and quite out of character said, "What in the hell is this?"

WASHINGTON, D.C.
Present Day

Secret Service Director Mike Sullivan had earlier in the day sent an instant message to Deputy Director McQuade saying, "I need to see you regarding disposition of XA-413." McQuade had answered that he would be in Sullivan's office in a few minutes. It was now four in the afternoon and Sullivan still had not seen sign of his D.D., nor was Robert McQuade answering his instant messages although his status showed him logged on to his computer.

Frustrated, Sullivan decided to walk down to McQuade's office to find out what was so damn important in his day that he couldn't respond to his superior. Sullivan, as usual opted for the stairs over the elevator. Three stories down, he opened the fire door and entered a long hallway. He turned to the right and started down the hallway nodding to a short stout man coming from the other direction.

"Director Sullivan," said Telleria with a nod of his head as they passed.

Sullivan recognized the man's face but couldn't put a name to him. "How are you," he said but neither expected or received a reply. Twenty-five steps further on, he entered McQuade's office. The outer office was empty but he no more than stepped in when McQuade's secretary, whose name he could never remember, rushed in behind him with a soda cup from the cafeteria in hand.

"Is D.D. McQuade in?" Sullivan asked her.

"No, sir," said the young, pretty secretary. "He received a call about two hours ago and left in a hurry. He said he'd be back in a few minutes. Would you like me to try him on his cell phone?"

"Yes, I'd appreciate that," said Sullivan. The door to McQuade's office had been left open and Sullivan decided to step in and wait there while the secretary tried to locate him. Director Sullivan hadn't been in McQuade's office in over a year. He had learned that when you are the director, your people come to your office for meetings.

McQuade's office was nicely appointed, the blinds were wide open and the window afforded the room a nice view of the Capitol building. On the wall opposite the windows was McQuade's 'wall of fame', something Sullivan personally found detestable. The wall seemingly held every plaque and honor the man had ever received along with photographs of McQuade standing with every dignitary and celebrity who was willing to stand next to him. It didn't look as though he had missed any opportunity to have his picture taken with everybody who came to the White House.

"Deputy McQuade isn't answering his cell phone, sir," said the secretary from her desk in the outer office. "I'll page him '911' which usually gets a call back right away."

"Thank you," replied Sullivan.

McQuade's desk was spotless with the exception of his laptop, a telephone, and a single yellow legal pad with a pen and his reading glasses sitting on top of it. Sullivan stepped behind the desk to get a better look. On the yellow pad was some sort of a flow chart.

On top was a circle containing the words, "Chopper Crash". From that circle were solid lines to other circles containing names, some of whom Sullivan recognized and some he didn't. Many of the circles had solid diagonal lines drawn through them. One of the circles contained the name "Hal Rumsey" with a dotted line drawn diagonally through it. From that circle there was a line drawn horizontally to another circle. Clearly written in a different handwriting was the name, "Robert McQuade." That circle also had a solid diagonal line drawn through it.

"Oh, my god," Sullivan heard the secretary say from the outer office. "When?"

Sullivan picked up the yellow legal pad. If it was what he thought it might be, it shouldn't be laying out in the open. That was one more thing he would discuss with McQuade.

"Is he okay?" Sullivan heard the secretary ask. He started towards her desk.

"Oh, my god, no," she said clearly upset.

As Sullivan neared her desk she turned to him and clutching her hand over the phone said, "Sir, there's been a horrible accident."

BOCA RATON, FLORIDA
Present Day

It was shortly after six in the evening. Doris Mifflin had been sitting by Hal's side since eight that morning. He had awoken a few times but he wasn't coherent enough to say much. A couple of her friends had come to sit with Doris for an hour or so but they could tell there wasn't much anybody could do. They visited with her and tried to keep her spirits up but they all knew, including Doris, that it was a hopeless situation.

When the shift nurse came in, Doris said, "I need to go, would it be all right if we left the television on for him. He never liked his home to be quiet."

The nurse feigned all the sympathy she could, "That's fine. You go home, get some rest and I'll check on him as much as I can, dear." The nurse knew that she was telling the woman what she wanted to hear and that no doubt some other nurse would turn the TV off as soon as the visitor was gone.

"Thank you," said Doris. "I'll be back in the morning."

A few hours later, Hal struggled to wake himself. His head hurt so bad he thought it would split open and his tongue felt as though it had swollen to twice its size, he was so thirsty. If he could just wake up enough to get somebody to give him three aspirin and a glass of water, he could go back to sleep. He opened his eyes; the room was dim but not dark. With great effort he rolled his head from side to side but he could see the room was empty. He was aware that he was in the hospital and he knew there must be a call button nearby but couldn't he seem to will his hands to move. He tried to speak but only managed a weak and hoarse noise from the back of his throat.

The television mounted on the wall opposite his bed was on. He thought that maybe if he could concentrate enough on the program, he would wake up enough to move.

The mindless sitcom was suddenly interrupted by an NBC Special Report. Hal forced his eyes open and blinked several times, trying to get his eyes to clear enough for him to see.

The television screen showed a tight shot of Brian Williams with a strained look on his face, he was pale, almost ashen. Williams obviously was in no hurry to start talking. He nervously shuffled the papers in his hands and starred at the camera for several seconds before saying, "Tonight, there is startling yet compelling evidence that John Fitzgerald Kennedy, the 35th President of the United States, may have not died in Dallas, Texas on November 22, 1963 . . . . .

. . . to be continued

About the Author:

Dan Sullivan was raised in the small town of La Grande, Oregon. He spent his youth enjoying great adventures exploring the endless roads, streams, and trails of the Blue Mountains. Soon after graduating from Oregon State University, however, he discovered the rest of the world. He has traveled extensively through Europe, Asia, Central America, Mexico, and the Caribbean.

Dan lives in Boise, Idaho with his wife Amy and their two children, Abigail and Kevin.

Other books by Dan Sullivan:

Travels with Amy

Downwind Run

www.thegreatestpatriot.com

Made in the USA
Charleston, SC
25 September 2011